Dancing with
the Dead

Dancing with the Dead

Deborah Gregory

Published by Solidus
www.soliduspress.com

For Josh and Zuleika
and all other members of my family,
past and present

I'd like to thank those who helped and encouraged me: Tessa Biddington, Frances Day, Elorin Grey, Tessa Hadley, Rosie Jackson, Elisabeth Lindsay, Maria McCann, Annie McKie, and Julie-Anne Rowell.

Also, Wally K. Daly, John Harvey and Carol-Ann Duffy, who were the tutors from the 1987 Arvon course on which I began to write this novel.

Deborah Gregory

1.

Late August. 1980.

'Houses, houses, we lodge in such husks!
inhabit such promises...'

Gill's fingers curled over the wooden handle of the old bell-pull, like four young animals snuggling into their burrow. Reaching for the handle was instinctive; it was proof that she had yet to accept change. There was nobody to hear the bell at the end of its wire, deep within Ramsons. From now on, no one would exclaim with delight at Gill's arrival, wipe flour from her hands, hurry down the stone passageway. Gill must let herself in. She unhooked her fingers and stretched the back pocket of her jeans to release the key, which was large enough to seem a pantomime prop and which had been branding her left buttock throughout the journey from Bristol to Lincolnshire.

Behind Gill an eager queue had formed. Helpers, family, friends, sheltered from bright sunlight by the arch of box hedging that lined the front path. Beyond them, in the top corner of the village square, was the convoy of vehicles that held everything the Murphy family possessed. Gill raised the key in the air, "I feel like Saint Peter," she said, but each member of the queue had his or her reasons not to respond. Seb, Gill's husband, who was carrying their daughter, Rosie, was telling an inattentive audience that there ought to be a blue plaque over the door. He had an actor's reverence for fame. "Gill's great-granddad was one of this country's most celebrated theatrical architects," he boasted on his wife's behalf. Bella, Gill's closest friend, was stroking her proudly pregnant belly. Others were gazing hopefully at the pub across the road, or taking in the impressive façade of Ramsons, a house that had previously been mere fable to them.

Gillian Murphy suspected their arrival was being noted; watched by overt and by hidden eyes. Not a decent set of wheels between this lot, that's what the locals would be thinking. An old Volkswagen camper, one dirty Transit van and a Morris Minor in need of renovation. Typical modern scruffs, that's how they'd seem to the inhabitants of Staunley. Women in tie-dyed cottons, sporting long skirts and loose morals. Men with no collars to their shirts. The Great Unwashed. Staunley was no place for their kind, Gill imagined them mumbling, no matter if some of them were related to the Durrys.

The ornate key had been sent to Gill's mother; posted special delivery by Great-Aunt Tilly's solicitor. A baffling note had been enclosed with the key, one that hinted at communications to follow - instructions, possibly, for whoever became resident at Ramsons? Although Gill was doing her mother a favour by moving in to the family home, the key had been handed over with poorly disguised reluctance and a list of 'don'ts' that had made Gill want to abandon the move and head, instead, for some seriously remote hills. Now, Gill felt unsteady as she slotted the key in the lock. Due to yesterday's rain, the box hedging smelt of cats' pee, as it habitually did when refreshed. Her audience unnerved her. And the future, beyond the solid door, couldn't have been more uncertain. Ten years ago, she'd have been welcomed by Great-Aunt Flora, stout and over-excited, bearing pots of China tea. Only last summer, Tilly had put on an old silk dress to greet her. Today there wouldn't be so much as a small dog to hurtle down the passage and nip at Gill's flip-flops.

Before she pushed the door open, Gill turned and gave Seb a smile. Holding a damp, sleeping Rosie in his arms, he met Gill's eyes over the top the child's head. His returning smile encompassed the house, the situation and their other child, little Adam, who was screwing up his nose at the smelly hedge.

As Gill stepped inside, one of the helpers leaned forward and tugged at the bell-pull. From a distance, came a faint ringing, eerie as the bell of a ship lost in fog. Gill spun round to glare at a man named Marty, whose face was only inches from her own. She could smell the spaces between his teeth, she could have counted his pale eyelashes. Marty was one of Seb's hangers-on, a man who'd invited himself to partake in Gill's immediate family: well, he wasn't having any of this branch, he wasn't insinuating himself into the ways of the Durrys. She said, "Don't," to him, a sulky command, straight from her childhood.

Once inside the cool hallway, Gill bent to gather post from the flagstone floor. Junk mail, mostly - an irritating new phenomenon that was no respecter of trees, or in this case, of death. The entrance hall to Ramsons was lined with glass cupboards in which the aunts had always kept their jams and pickles. Having fermented, these preserves now scented the air with strawberries, plums, vinegar and decay. "Welcome to the home that time forgot," Gill joked to those who had come to help: but the confrontation with Marty had given her voice an unwelcoming edge. Her companions blinked and sniffed, trying to adjust. A bluebottle wove through the invasion of people, escaping the house only to be imprisoned by the heavy hedging.

Seb moved down the passageway and lowered Rosie to the floor. The little girl groaned, snuggled against her father's legs. Gill noted that Seb was standing directly under Cedric, the plaster cherub who hung, in a cheery, eternal freeze-frame, over the wide front stairs. Cedric's plump right cheek was still tinged with pink where Gill, as a child perched on her older sister's shoulders, had once smeared him with redcurrants.

"It may seem sacrilegious," Seb whispered to his wife, "but we have to make room for our stuff, somehow." Gill nodded: of course. They must unload their tatty chairs, their stained sofa. The bunk beds must be installed in Aunty Flora's lilac bedroom. Their array of discoloured beach towels had to be stacked in the world's prettiest bathroom. They'd brought these possessions, paid good money to transport them across the country. Undoubtedly they must re-home them.

"Just give me half an hour," she begged. "Take the kids outside, show off the garden. You can pick up fallen fruit, or something. Would you?" Sure, Seb nodded; he seemed to understand. But could he? How could Seb, who'd seen Ramsons only once before, on a flying visit during which they scoffed cakes, their behinds barely touching chairs, how might he be expected to even guess the way Gill felt? Somewhere, probably, there'd be a place that was special to Seb. She couldn't remember having discussed this. It might be a field or a garden shed - but it must exist. How would Seb like it if he were asked to more than share his personal space? To unload on to his prime memories the junk that accompanies couples with young children?

In another life, before having babies, Gill had been a photographer. Instinctively, she headed for a photograph, knowing it would help to ground and reassure her. Suspended over the breakfast-room fireplace, she encountered the entire clan. The Durrys: a study in sepia. A family headed by Edward, the famous architect whose speciality was theatres and music halls. Having once posed for this portrait, Gill's ancestors existed forever in a Spalding photographer's version of Egypt. The adults perched on elaborate winged chairs. Their children gathered round them under potted palm trees. Jethro, son and heir, stood behind his father, while the daughters were positioned according to height. Behind this group, screens depicted the dessert of a Lincolnshire man's imagination, a landscape overrun with pyramids, where plagues of slaves crawled the earth, each with his burden of stone. Flora, the eldest but not the tallest daughter, appeared to bear the full weight of one pyramid on her shoulders. The point of this architectural marvel adorned the top of her head, a stone pixie hat above a plain, round face that, thanks to the click of a lens, smiled spryly across the years.

Having studied all the Durry girls, Gill ultimately singled out her grandmother, Evangelina. Although Evangelina's temperament had been far from heavenly, she had possessed a face to match her angelic name. Having heard repeatedly of her grandmother's crowning glory and having been obliged to feel dreary simply for not inheriting this resplendence, Gill couldn't help but colour in the red-gold hair of this favourite daughter. In fact, as she stared harder, Gill would have sworn Evangelina's tresses broke through the sepia tones, gilding the photograph with one brilliant spill of colour.

Gill hadn't touched a camera, professionally, for years: but in her allotted half an hour, as she wandered from room to room, she collected an album of images. This corner had to be fixed in memory, precisely as it was. That sideboard must be captured forever, with its dulled decanters full of ancient sherry, its sewing baskets, doilies, sticky biscuit tins. It's dust. A monument to those who defied change and worshipped thrift.

It was the purity of Ramsons that defeated Gill. Decades of progress passed this house by. There was no fridge, not a hint of stainless steel or chipboard anywhere. No storage heaters spoilt the lines of floral bedrooms. The bathroom, a converted back bedroom, had a temporary air. On the tops of old dressing tables china bowls and jugs still resided: Ramsons had no faith in the reliability of modern plumbing.

Yes, it was appealing. Beautiful. Mahogany, lace, damask and velvet. Delightful to behold and lovely to the touch. Old, dear, unsullied. And all of it, every last curtain, each fluffy feather pillow, on the point of collapse. Gill could see that; she smelt the impending decay, sensed that she stood in the exact moment when change, which had waited patiently, must come.

Even without their intrusion, had they stayed in Bristol and left Ramsons alone, this would have been the day when things here began to rot. Was it a force, or the lack of any energy whatsoever, that Gill experienced? It was the slowest, smallest of movements: a sigh. A beat in time. It was pods bursting, silently. Eggs hatching in dark corners.

In Tilly's bedroom, Gill cried quietly for loss in its many guises. She pulled one of Tilly's handkerchiefs from a lavender seeded drawer and blew her nose against the inevitability of change. "Sorry," she told her deceased Great Aunt. "I'll open a window, let the sun in." Talking to Tilly didn't seem the least eccentric; the old woman was there, in the cupboards and the papier-mâché boxes, in the almost imperceptible holes that worms were chewing throughout. On her way to the window, Gill bumped into a white enamel bucket resting at the foot of the bed. It was a lidded bucket with a thin blue rim and a wooden handle. The lid, jolted by Gill, slid off to expose the contents. A smell escaped. Gill's grief turned instantly to tears of mephitis. The overpowering stench filled the room, sent Gill stumbling to the window, gave her arms super strength with which to shove a pane upwards.

Fresh air cleared her head. It didn't take a genius to work out what was in the bucket. For as long as anybody could remember, Tilly suffered from what was euphemistically referred to as a bad tummy. She'd lived on saucerfuls of grated apple. Presumably, Tilly had been taken short on the night of her death; and the nearest receptacle had been that bucket. "No worries," Gill said aloud, as if the spirits of those who would have fretted over such things were close by, "I'll deal with it."

Not straight away, though. Some actions need to be taken under cover of darkness. Right then, Gill wanted to find something bright, comforting. A familiar object she could call her own. She wasn't materialistic, the prospect of ownership didn't much excite her. Ramsons had been left to Gill's mother, June; but the contents were to be divided between four women. Along with June and Gill, her sisters, Sarah and Kate, were to have their share of this not inconsiderable hoard of antiques. The arrangement was fine by Gill: she had only one claim to stake.

When other voices sounded nearby, Gill hid. Time enough to socialize later. She crept down the back stairs, heading for the drawing room where her treasure waited. The place was in darkness, the brocade curtains having been closed since Tilly died. Gill let in the light, shielded her eyes against the sun and the powder that danced free in its path. She could smell dog. Tilly's last hound, a hairy Pomeranian called Tricksey, must have used the Turkish rugs as toilets. A mystery surrounded Tricksey, who had been alive and well right up to Tilly's death but had disappeared by the time the family arrived for the funeral.

There was a damp feel to the room, as if the green wallpaper was actually moss and the floor was becoming compost. The impressive furniture was caked with thick dust. On the marble mantelpiece plants were so long dead that they resembled piles of tea-leaves. None of that bothered Gill unduly; she had her mind set on making music.

From faded photographs and paintings, her ancestors watched as Gill patted the stool and sat at the piano. It was an upright, wooden framed instrument, made of walnut, decorated by gilt candlesticks and an ornate trellis that covered a tapestry whose reds and blues had dimmed to mauves. Gill stroked the lid, coating her fingers with the time since the piano had last been played. When revealed, the keys were creamy: Gill's hands hovered over them, reverently. They were the essence of legend, the clue to her ideal of motherhood.

On summer nights, when Gill and her sisters had been staying at Ramsons, Great-Aunt Flora would tell the little girls stories of the hours spent in this room, around this piano. Tilly had played well, if a bit reservedly. But it had been Elizabeth Durry, a matriarch reportedly grim as any fairy-tale character, who'd played the Durry family into life. According to her surviving daughters, Elizabeth had been strict, demanding: a despot to her children at all times except when she sat here, on this stool. Then, apparently, she had been transformed; transported by sheer joy. And in the place she inhabited when she played, even her least favourite children had felt themselves accepted; almost loved.

Gill, who could hardly play, promised she would learn. She envisaged evenings to come: she would be the musician and Adam and Rosie the dancers. They'd polka up and down this grand room while

Gill did what mothers should - made music to feed their souls. There was a song about the moon, Tilly had taught it to Gill long ago. It had a light, lilting melody. With her right hand, Gill pressed middle C. Nothing happened. The next note was also mute. And the next. Gill explored further, a spider and an elephant, sometimes tripping over and sometimes thumping notes of cream, notes of black. Occasional keys made a sad sound, muffled as gagged singers; but most were horribly silent.

"Beautiful piano." It was Bella who spoke, silencing the thuds in Gill's head. Bella was pregnant for the first time. Her right hand, usually employed in fondling her bump, stroked the wooden fretwork. "Rosewood, isn't it?"

"Walnut, I think," Gill answered.

"Ah. Can you give me and my sprog a tune?"

"I can't," Gill stood, climbed up on the stool. "It's not working - probably busy digesting a dead mouse." She opened the piano's lid, peered inside. A hint of seasoning drifted from the piano's innards, making Gill think of the exotic, not always successful meals she and Seb had cooked for Bella and her partner, Jon - a man who liked his dinners spiced with ginger, cayenne, chilli.

Tentatively, Gill lowered an arm to reach the mechanism. As her fingers found the hammers, clouds of yellow powder rose into the atmosphere. "Happy worms," she said to Bella, "munching through a world of music."

"Coffee?" Seb suggested, appearing at the door. The women nodded, their throats feeling sandpapered.

There existed, Gill was certain, a kettle. Rather a special, copper affair; but, special or not, the thing had vanished. And the kettle they'd brought from Bristol wouldn't work because of Ramsons's primitive wiring. "Can't fit a square plug in a round hole," Gill observed, "so we'll have to light this thing." She gave the old Rayburn a friendly kick. There must be plenty of kindling outside, it couldn't take long to get the cream monster roaring.

It was still warm, but as she pulled an entire branch from a plum tree, Gill mumbled, "It's almost September." And the moment of change was with her again, pronounced in the garden as it had been in the house. Summer slipped away behind a cloud. Autumn fell as over-ripe fruit, around her feet.

"It's still August and I'm roasting," Bella told her. Every aspect of Bella was comforting, rounded. Her belly and her breasts. Her face, pink as a child's painting -with blue button eyes. Even her feet, in hand-made purple sandals, were oval.

They had to abandon all hope of coffee. The Rayburn hissed, spat at the apple and plum wood, blinded them with smoke - and remained decidedly cool.

"Anybody fancy rose-hip syrup?" Gill asked.

"Where there's smoke, there's hope," Jon noted and produced, as if by magic - since he was cloaked in thick smog - several cans of beer. The new occupants and their helpers carried kitchen chairs through the scullery to the garden. Quite apart from the fog, the house already looked like a heritage museum that was in the throes of holding a jumble sale. Although their chairs wobbled in the long grass, everybody preferred being outside. Once seated, they took long gulps of beer, clearing their throats, mussing their heads.

"You've made a fairy ring," Adam told them. It was true, the marks from the chairs would look like one of nature's circles.

"Ring-a-ring-a-Rosie!" Seb sang, watching Rosie totter around the adults, fall, be lifted, cry a little but laugh a lot. Gill smiled at her friends and noticed, mid-smile, that Marty, the lame duck who had so rudely pulled the bell, was now swinging something from his left hand. Waving whatever it was, like incense. An object fashioned from red glass; its arc seemed to scorch the grass as the sun caught it. The rise and fall of reflected colour was hypnotic. Marty winked at Gill. "Neat bottle," he told her, "what's it for? Perfume?"

"No. Actually it's not a bottle. Its use was medicinal - it's a phial." How could she sound so pompous? "It was Granddad's," with this statement, Gill turned nearly as red as the phial. All eyes were on her; she felt herself caught in a double betrayal. True, her step-grandfather had been a chemist, but he'd hardly have kept his pharmacopoeia at Ramsons. That phial must have belonged to Elizabeth Durry, who had no right to meddle, as meddle she did, in medicine and so-called homeopathy. As well as lying, Gill had denied her upbringing. Grandfather Tomas had been Dutch, straight-laced. His grandchildren never called him 'Granddad', never shortened Grandfather Tomas by a syllable. He would be positively rotating in his grave. The glare Gill gave Marty was enough to make him toss the phial at her with a grunt; "Here."

She caught it, just. Once she held it safe, Gill understood how Marty had been hoping she'd say 'keep it, if you want', which was all very well. Of course she'd like to give gifts to each of the helpers. A glass paperweight, a silver box, something small but precious. But nothing was hers to bestow. Her mother knew every item. One intricately patterned glass, missing from the sideboard, would be enough to send June stalking the house. Already there was the copper kettle to be accounted for.

There had been a time, Gill thought wistfully, when she was proud of owning nothing but her photographic equipment. This lack of possessions set her apart from her family, who were notorious hoarders. She had moved from flat to flat with carrier bags. Carrier bags! Now it took a camper, a Transit and a Morris Minor; next time, no doubt, it would require a fleet of pantechnicons. Because whatever might be her share of this bounty, Gill would be obliged to keep it safe for eternity. Bits and pieces must become her charges. Her family would expect to see those pretty, but mostly useless heirlooms when the mood took them. They'd want to know they could open a coronation cake tin and exclaim; 'Oooh, here's the belt from your Froggy-went-a-courting dress that you wore when you were six.'

Sarah and Kate, Gill's sisters, joined June in a vision. They had the eyes of a trio of bullfrogs as they ogled the red phial on Gill's knees. But in reality, where were these other beneficiaries now, when needed? Where were their helping hands now that there was sorting to be done and buckets to be dealt with?

Rosie climbed on Seb's knee, stuck her thumb in her mouth. "Oh no you don't," he warned gently, "sleep now and you'll be awake tonight." The toddler gazed adoringly into his eyes. Daddy's girl. She never gave Gill enchanted stares. Seb stroked curls from his daughter's forehead. When left alone, Gill's hair was mousy; Rosie had her mother's colouring but hair that twisted like her father's, while Adam had straight locks, like Gill's, but in a dark brown inherited from Seb. Gill thought again of Evangelina's tresses, realizing that her own brightly dyed spiky style might be the result of a life-time's longing for, and envy of, her grandmother's glorious head. Gill's lap felt suddenly empty; she was considering how to tempt Adam on to her knee when the party of beer drinkers began to disperse.

"Back to work," Jon announced, giving Bella a smile.

Unable to lift heavy furniture, Bella offered to help clear out a chest of drawers, to make space for her friends' clothes. Seb and Gill would use the master bedroom, as Tilly had done. In the room once occupied by her parents, Tilly had slept, and eventually she had died, in the big, brass bed, indenting the mattress on which she had been conceived. Gill hurried ahead, giving herself time to shove the enamel bucket out of sight. "In here," she called over her shoulder, and admitted, "I've always wanted to have this kind of treasure hunt through Tilly's things."

The friends sat together, sinking into the bedding. They grew childish with anticipation. Between them was the top drawer from the chest of drawers.

"You first."

"No, you."

"It's your stuff, you put your hand in first."

Gill hesitated. Those were somebody else's possessions, no matter if the somebody was six feet under. She took a brooch, pieces of felt shaped like flowers, bunched on to a circle of linen, shades of purples and pinks. An inventive use of leftovers, as women's magazines might say. Bella held up a string of paper-twist beads. Gill found a notebook bound with passe-partout.

"Where are we supposed to be putting this?" Bella asked as she explored deeper.

"In another drawer," Gill grinned. It was all they could do, squeeze one lot of Tilly's belongings in with another.

"Dance cards!" Bella cried, showing her friend a tiny card and its companion pencil. It was just possible to read the faded writing, to tell that the holder had been popular. Gill had never thought of Tilly out dancing, rarely pictured her as a young woman. But Tilly's youth was confirmed by the next discovery: a scratched photograph. A group of young women sprawled on a mound of grass, in a semi-circle. Most sported hats, all wore white blouses and dark skirts. What astonished Gill was the cigarette burning in Tilly's hand, that and the roguish grin on her tanned face. Surely Tilly had never been a smoker? Gill tried to pair the word 'fag' with the name 'Matilda'. "I'm just lighting up a fag, Dear," her great aunt announced in her soft, refined tones. No, Gill thought not. Turning the photo over, Gill read: *'Hampstead Heath, me and the Clan. (For Flora's eyes only!) Tilly xxx.'*

"Where was she when it was taken?" Bella wanted to know.

"Teachers' training college, for gentlewomen. Very exclusive. Only Tilly went. Her other sisters didn't make it, and because Flora was the eldest, she had to stay home and help her mother."

As Gill spoke, Bella was already studying the next find, a postcard showing embroidered flags. Gill knew it had to be from Jethro, Edward and Elizabeth Durry's only son, but she said nothing. As before, she found herself defeated. A lifetime in a drawer, it was too much for one sultry afternoon. It involved more sharing than she could cope with, at a single sitting.

Perhaps all families were as special, complicated, secret and sinister as Gill's. She included sinister in her list of adjectives because she'd grown up with half known facts, with hints of a lost room, and other such mysteries, here in Ramsons. Certainly there were dark corners to her history. As a child she'd occasionally rounded these corners, running smack into the unfinished sentences of furtive adults. With her sisters, she had stood on the tips of her toes to peep at the goings that went on behind the shy smiles of those who had, long ago, been different people, more mobile and perhaps less decent. Implications, tempting as lumps of sugar, had been passed across the tea table. Without a doubt, disasters had struck, once-upon-a-time. Sometimes, Gill now believed, she might have heard screams, or their echoes. There was supposed to be a lost room, here in Ramsons. And then, of course, there was the cellar.

Enough, enough, she told herself. Remember how you loved Aunty Tilly, how kind she was, how constant. "I feel her here," Gill said quietly.

"When my sister died," Bella whispered back, Gill had noticed before that Bella couldn't speak of this loss in anything other than a whisper, "I saw her in the most unlikely places. Shops, car parks, public toilets. I thought it sad we had no special meeting place; but then we didn't have that when she was alive. The dead do sometimes meet with us, Gill. Nobody dares to mention it but it's true."

Whenever Bella spoke of her dead sister, Gill would suffer a glow of guilt because Seb, ever the actor, had once asked Gill to see if she could 'get inside Bella's sorrow'. He'd wanted to know, never having lost anybody dear to himself, how long-term, heavy-duty grief *really* felt. Gill had treated this suggestion with the disdain it deserved. She'd actually hit Seb, she recalled, hard enough to make her point.

Without releasing it, Gill was replacing Tilly's treasure in the same drawer, laying each item down gently. She lifted her head to Bella and asked, "Have I disturbed a hornets' nest by coming here, do you think?"

Bella pursed her lips, thought this over. "If you have," she answered at last, "you needn't worry. They'll be your hornets; they'll have to accept you as their new queen."

"Somebody had to come here," Gill explained. "Mum's too settled, Kate's abroad, Sarah's got a nice home anyway…"

"*This* is a nice home," Bella reminded her, "big and quiet and almost sacred, to you. I worry about this one," she touched her bump, "starting out in a shared house full of scruffs like me and Jon, with nothing but sacks of wholefoods to play with. Can I be as good a mother as my mate Gill, I ask myself, when I have no ancestral home to share with my babe?" Gill smiled, having no need to answer. The idea of Bella being anything but the most delightful, joyous mum was too absurd. But, as if it did feel a call to respond, the lucky baby in Bella's womb gave a kick of appreciation that sent waves of pleasure through both the women on Tilly's bed.

2.

Things have their own lives here. The hall chairs
count me as I climb the steps...

Having said their goodbyes to friends and helpers, Seb and Gill
meandered through the house hand in hand. "We can never be the
owners here, you do understand that?" Gill asked. "Tenants yes,
owners never."

She considered the fresh owners of their Bristol home, a childless,
professional couple, spending their first night in Gill's place. They
would probably feel as if they were camping out, roughing it until they
could redecorate. Ultimately, they would paint over the mural of ships
at sea that Adam had chosen for his bedroom walls. Most likely they'd
hate all Gill's bright colour schemes and change the house throughout.
The grass-green walls of her Bristol kitchen faded as she moved around
Ramsons, one home dissolving while the other loomed, grubbier and
decaying faster than she had anticipated it could.

"If I became rich and famous," said Seb, employing his stock phrase,
"wouldn't your mum let us buy her out?"

"You don't buy people out of Ramsons, you carry them, feet first."

"My dearest and most jolly little thing," and he blew on her neck
until her fiercely cropped hair lifted half an inch. They would make
love later, this was understood by the grip of hands, the light in their
eyes, the sexy prospect of invading a maiden's bed.

In the bathroom, Seb threw the window open and leaned out to
check on the children. Rosie and Adam were playing with a plastic
motorboat, floating it in a stone birdbath that was too high off the
ground for Rosie who jumped up and down in frustration. Joining Seb,
Gill wondered what had become of Man, Tilly's gardener. It would
seem nobody had worked in this untidy garden for some time. Gill
tried to remember why she and her sisters had called the gardener
simply Man; presumably his real name had been too long for them
to pronounce. Now that she came to think of him, Gill was unable to

recall having spoken a single word to Man. He'd just been there, with his wheelbarrow and his spade, dressed in shades of brown, always down the next path, bending over the next flower bed. She watched her kids at play - and beyond them she caught a glimpse of herself, aged seven, with Sarah and Kate at her sides. The three sisters had boats of paper, the sails coloured in with crayon. Katie's sank and she pulled a face, lips beginning to quiver. Baby Kate, expecting one of her sisters to part with their boat now hers was soggy and would float no more.

Am I also to be haunted by the living, Gill wondered; as if the dead weren't invasive enough. She called so sharply to Adam that her cry made Seb wince; "Time for bed Adam, time to try out your new room."

"Look, Rosie," Gill attempted to keep her voice low, calm; it wasn't easy, "since this is a new room, let's make a fresh start, hmm?" Rosie sulked, she wanted her daddy to undress her but he was busy, swapping plugs.

"Your Great-Great Aunty Flora used to sleep in here, lilac was her favourite colour. See the pretty paper with the flowers?"

"I want ships again," Adam announced.

"This is more a 'secret garden' than a ships room, don't you think?"

"No."

"Just put on your pyjamas, please Adam. Rosie and I are tired of looking at your bare bottom, aren't we?" As if programmed, Adam chuckled at the word 'bottom'; and he reached for his pyjamas. But mere words wouldn't move Rosie. Gill forced those stubborn arms upwards and whipped off the child's dress as deftly as a magician might perform the tablecloth trick.

"Good. Now on with your nightie. There. Ready for bed. I suppose you want a drink?" Silence.

"She does want one," said Adam, always the mediator, "and I do."

"You have to talk to me, Rosie," Gill assured her daughter. "Apart from the vague possibility of it being fun, one day communication may be vital. It might even save your life."

"Like in a fire?" Adam enthused. He stuck his face very near his sister's and yelled, "Fire, Fire!" Instantly, Rosie howled.

From a distance Seb asked if everything was all right and Gill shouted that they were fine. "Thank you, Adam," she muttered, "for setting off the siren. Hush, hush. I'll get you both some milk, then to bed and no more messing."

"Drink it." Gill held the beaker to Rosie's lips. "You wanted it," she pointed out, although this may not have been strictly true, "I went all the way downstairs to get it, so now you can bloody well swallow it." The child's jaws clamped shut. Two baby blues gazed steadfastly at a point beyond Gill's head. "Once you've had this, Daddy will come and say goodnight." The lower jaw slackened, Gill tipped up the beaker hopefully but two gulps later Rosie snapped her mouth in crocodile fashion and Gill lost the desire to make a new start with her truculent toddler. With one chubby hand, the child shoved the beaker away. The drink took flight, spraying the room with milk. Gill's hand was also in the air, then it was hitting Rosie, once, twice, just above the elbow: slaps that stung both mother and daughter.

By the time Seb arrived, Rosie was screaming wildly and Gill was standing at the window, shaking as she glared into the darkening garden.

"I can't even give the poor kid a proper hug," Seb complained as he held Rosie and stroked her sore arm. "Look what you've done, Gill. Look! We agreed, we swore we'd never do this. It's archaic, and so cruel. You agreed, slapping, hitting, you said we'd never..."

"She hates me."

"Is that surprising? If it's true, which of course it's not. Come on, you two. Make it up. We're all shattered, worked up. Have a hug, please, for my sake." For Seb's sake then, they held each other, lightly. Rosie's cheek was hot and wet. Tiny shudders running through the child brought echoing trembles from her mother.

"Sorry," Gill whispered; and she was. But it wasn't over yet.

As soon as her parents tiptoed from the bedroom, Rosie gave a fresh, shattering cry.

"What is it now, Poppet?" Seb asked. His daughter's face was contorted with genuine despair; Adam, on the top bunk bed, was shaken by his sister's sobs. Even to her father, Rosie seldom spoke, a fact that would have bothered her parents had they not known she could speak well enough when she'd a mind to. This time she threw the name of her lost one directly into Seb's ear, "Mr. Tibbs, Mr. Tibbs, he gone."

"Oh God," Gill mumbled from the doorway.

"Oh God," Seb echoed. "Well, we shall find him, don't you fret. Find that old chap in no time, won't we Mummy?" Mummy nodded, of course they'd find Mr. Tibbs, he was Rosie's favourite, special, soft toy. Life for the four of them would be unbearable without that scruffy, stuffed cat.

"When did you last see him?" Seb whispered to Gill, "I suppose he did travel with us from Bristol?"

"You think she'd have slept on the journey without him?"

"Good point. You take the house and I'll search the garden."

Gill found the toy cat in the bathroom, dropped by the basin while Rosie had been given a flick with a flannel. Cat in hand, Gill stood at the window and watched Seb's shadowy form moving about, behind a beam of torchlight, through the undergrowth. At one stage, he passed directly beneath her, shuffling close to the house, below the decrepit balustrade. Gill felt removed from him, left out like a child with no playmate. Rosie was still crying, not desperately but with admirable persistence: yet her mother stood like stone. Why didn't she run to the lilac room with her prize? Here was an ideal opportunity to be a heroine in Rosie's eyes. She didn't believe it was a taste of power that kept her there, listening to Rosie's misery, observing Seb's distress. Not power but something equally disturbing. The air was growing cold; Gill shivered. She wouldn't name her reason, wouldn't let it rule her. Gently, still with slight reluctance, she pushed open the window. "Found him!" she called, finally.

"My great-grandmother had five children in this bed," Gill announced once she and Seb had settled between the worn, cotton sheets and in - rather than on - the old feather mattress of Tilly's bed.

"Not all at once, I hope," Seb murmured. He was nibbling his wife's neck, concentrating on a taut but unbearably soft patch of skin behind her left ear, just below her hairline. It smelt of baby soap and of smoke from the unobliging Rayburn.

"Jethro, Flora, Tilly, Evangelina and Agnes," Gill told him, although he hadn't asked. "And Tilly once hinted to me that there may have been more, miscarriages or stillbirths. Mishaps, she called them. 'Many a mishap,' she said, 'has taken place here, Gillian. Many a poor mite has floundered at Ramsons.' Bit of a poet, was Tilly, I suppose. Maybe

16

a bit of drama queen too. Seb?"

"Umm?" He closed his lips firmly around her ear lobe.

"How does it feel, really, to you, being in a house so essential to my family? You don't think it's possessed, do you?"

"Well, I am a bit itchy," he teased, "feather mattresses are notorious for that. They're also renown for being sexy, so they say..."

Their lovemaking was somehow infused with the down on which they lay. Gill became pliable in Seb's arms, while Seb was light with his touches, careful and caring. It seemed they fairly drifted together, sinking into the bed and into each other.

"Oh," Seb said afterwards, just 'Oh'; as if he'd discovered an altered state of being, all by himself. He fell straight to sleep then, his back curved where it should have been flat, his knees being eaten by the tiniest of insects.

Gill felt her muscles tense, one final time, a reflex action of love. She lay awake beside Seb, listening to Ramsons as it sighed and creaked. She thought of old bones, scrubbed, chewed clean of flesh, buried in churchyards or in gardens. White bones that no amount of earth could darken. And teeth; yes, it was as if Ramsons was grinding its teeth.

Please, please, she begged silently, don't let me be alone here. Not for one single night. How many nights must Tilly have spent on her own? Lying exactly here, in the dip in the bed to which a body had no choice but to roll, absorbing the sounds of Ramsons. Learning the language of the house.

It was easy for Seb, he had only to breathe, as he was doing, deeply and methodically, in his sleep. No worries for him; no midnight excursions. But Gill must leave the bed, like a lizard she had to slip from the sheets and touch the cool floor with one toe, one foot, then the other. So. She had work to do. Family affairs to deal with. A rite she alone could perform. Would there be a moon, she wondered, to light her through the shrubbery.

In her fanciful mood, Gill, who had been naked as she stepped out of bed, found an old white nightdress to wear. She thought of herself as inhabiting a layer of Tilly as she put on this garment; but the nightdress was one generation older than Tilly. Before being put away, its cotton had been severely stiffened with Robin's Starch. Gill's arms wriggled through the long sleeves, moles tunnelling parchment. Her head emerged above a neckline that was rigid and frilled. Her knees made crisp sounds as she walked.

The enamel bucket was waiting, its lid, thankfully, firmly in place.

Lined up by the back door were wellingtons and galoshes in many sizes; surely an optimistic array - Tilly had hardly been inundated with the kind of guests prepared to plod around in dead people's footwear. Gill slipped cold feet into even chillier wellingtons and opened the door. No moon, only a faint flicker from the children's room where a night-light burnt, and this light from the scullery, a beam that fell directly behind Gill casting her shadow ahead, obliging her to point her own way. She took a key from a hook by the door. For years Tilly had used the old wash-house as a garden shed. In there Gill would find the spade she needed.

A coat would have been more sensible than the nightdress. It was not a warm night. The garden was aromatic with scents belonging to dried herbs rather than fresh, green plants. Why hadn't she brought a torch? She must be treading on creatures that had stolen over the curled, Victorian edging stones. The bucket banged against Gill's leg as she pushed brambles and bushes aside in an attempt to follow these paths that crisscrossed the garden. Although she knew she was sharing the night with living things, she saw nothing definite. The sounds would be hedgehogs, she hoped: rats did dart across her imagination, greasy, pink-tailed - but she wouldn't allow them a grip on her fear. From time to time she squashed slugs, sliding on their crushed bodies, and once she heard the crack of a snail's shell underfoot. But when resolved to carry out a plan, Gill was a determined woman. This, her final tribute to Tilly, was a kindness long overdue.

The wash-house was outlined against a slightly lighter sky. Gill fumbled for the door, cobwebs lacing her fingers as she discovered the keyhole. And then, miraculously, as she turned the key, the moon shone. Having assumed there was no moon, its appearance made Gill fret at first. She turned, looked up and saw the moon through the leaves of the walnut tree. She sighed with relief. Now she could see the spade, leaning against the far wall, its blade glinting in anticipation. She thought, once again, of Man, who might have left this spade here for her, knowing the night would come when she'd have need of it. As well as garden implements, the building was full of sacks; Gill could only guess the contents - fertilizer, garden refuse somebody had once meant to burn, rags being saved for dusters. Dried dog food, perhaps.

They gave off a lethal combination of stenches and their bulky shapes filled her head with images of poachers, body-snatchers, murderers. Well, she was a match for anybody tonight, with her wellingtons and her spade. With her jaw set tight. Maybe she did look a comic ghost, but she fairly marched to the far end of the garden, the so-called orchard where plums and slugs and Lord-knows-what turned to slush under her tramping feet. The world would smell like summer pudding when she used the spade to bite the soil.

She chose a spot under an apple tree; it seemed appropriate since Tilly had lived on apples, more or less. As soon as she began to dig, Gill's back complained at the effort involved. But Gill relished the chance to suffer and strain; she almost hoped for bruises, blue and yellow emblems to show for her troubles. Obligingly, the spade pressed through the rubber sole of a wellington each time she encountered tree roots. There were stones of all sizes in this earth, from dismantled outhouses and fallen walls. Once the spade rang out as it hit one of these stones, a noise that jarred the still night. Gill stopped digging to listen for other sounds. She heard a plane in the sky, not close, probably over the Fens. Cars on the main road beyond the village were blissfully faint, after the constant traffic in Bristol. No owls; but those rustlings in the undergrowth were still audible. Then there was the stream on the far side of the boundary wall, not gushing tonight, just trickling with summer lethargy.

How would she sound, to a listener? The ring of the spade, the sighs of a woman working her entire body. The squelch of wellingtons on rotten fruit. What might a spy imagine Gill was up to in the garden in the deep of the night? There had been previous burials here, amongst the trees and flowers. Animals, of course, were put to rest in this garden; and Tilly had mentioned other rituals, hinted at expeditions not unlike this one, where flesh, cloth, bone and bits and pieces, the real and the imagined, had been consigned to the pungent, fruit flavoured earth.

The moon vanished and reappeared, playing peep-o with Gill's nerves. She dug deep. Her spine bent grudgingly lower, until she was obliged to climb into her hole, soiling the nightdress, cringing at the thought of what lived alongside her. But depth was required; she wouldn't flinch. Nobody should come across this accidentally, when playing; no dog should be able to unearth this in the course of an afternoon. Gill buried all - bucket, lid, contents. Then she covered the evidence and stamped down the earth. When she straightened up, her muscles delighted, reaching for the sky. She lifted tufts of grass back into place. Again she stamped; it was a dance this time, a celebration of completion. Finally, in her grubby, dampened nightdress, with her spade held out in front like the stick of a blind person, Gill turned back to the wash house and then the scullery.

Having laid to rest the very last remains of her Great Aunt Tilly, Gill had joined the ranks of women who belonged, who knew what had to be done in Ramsons, and did not shrink from their tasks. Kicking off the wellington boots, standing barefoot on the flagstones, Gill understood that she was accepted now: she was mistress here, like it or shudder at it. She shut out the night, the movements in the undergrowth, the fickle moon, the garden with its buried secrets. She stood looking inwards, through the scullery to the kitchen and beyond, to the back stairs: taking possession of Ramsons - allowing Ramsons to slide itself around her.

3.

We are always waking in bedrooms of the dead...

There were warm days at first. For hours at a time, Ramsons did seem to be paradise. Gill knew this couldn't last; the inevitable wind would blow from the North Sea, skimming the Fens, raising skirts, lowering spirits. But until then, while evenings were merely chilly rather than cold, Gill appreciated the rarity of Ramsons. The house, like the bulk of the village, was of stones not dissimilar to those in the Cotswolds. These absorbed sunshine, glowing yellow by day, reflecting soothing pinks at dusk. The back of Ramsons had the feel of a long cottage, being lower than the front that brazenly faced the street. Gill could lean out of back bedroom windows and be in the garden, inches from being able to pluck the withered, dusty grapes that persisted in clinging to the balustrade. Enjoyed from here, the world was fruity and floral, smelling perfect, looking as if Monet had designed it.

Downstairs, the French windows were thrown open and sunlight came to visit, never venturing far into the dark interior, brightening an oblong of moss coloured carpet, the fringe of a Turkish rug. Adam and Rosie ran in and out of this exit as if they'd never seen a door before. They played with the puddle in the birdbath in the manner of poor souls previously deprived of even the tiniest rainfall. Gill remembered finding these and other novelties enthralling when she'd been their age. To her, a clump of raspberry canes had been an unexplored jungle. A couple of stone steps had represented an enchanted staircase. The sun was a blessing Gill the adult seemed to have forfeited; if it had shone, in London and more recently in Bristol, on Gill's neck, on the row of washing decorating her six feet of garden, its magic had been depreciated by traffic, chimneys, other people's radios, cooking smells. Now here it was again, making everything shimmer, scenting a person's flesh, inciting insects to hum.

When the first clouds of autumn blocked the skies, the children discovered the Belfast sink in the scullery, carried their boats in there, sailed on contentedly. Gill donned an excess of clothes and considered the worse that was to come. Seb roamed the house with his arms full of treasures. He was constantly searching for Gill, to show her what he'd unearthed. As the days passed, the place grew more dishevelled, less habitable. Gill found herself keeping out of her husband's way. She appreciated it was necessary to make a mess here and there, in order to create storage space; but Seb never finished any task to the point of actual improvement. The house developed collections, Gill thought of them as warts, in every corner. Stacks of papers on the landings. Bottles glinting on windowsills. Piles of shoes climbing the stairs. Ramsons became an obstacle course; on finding an uncluttered chair, Gill felt like crying, 'I win'.

Possessiveness added to her irritation. Gill loved Seb and she was glad of his buoyant enthusiasm while hers was subdued but these weren't his papers or his bottles. That ledger he'd found, containing Edward Durry's expenses for the year nineteen fifteen, that had nothing to do with Seb, fascinated as he might be by the cost of rail travel and the price of brown shoe laces. Edward Durry belonged to Gill, to her sisters Sarah and Kate and to their mother, June. He was their relation, railway tickets, shoelaces, warty belongings and all. What right had Seb to go skipping about with his wife's heritage clutched to his chest?

There was always the likelihood that he'd discover answers to puzzles Gill longed to solve. The lost room, for instance: she had mentioned this to Seb and the last thing she wanted was for him to stumble on it accidentally yet, somehow, triumphantly. In her imagination, this room was set apart: sometimes she'd see it as perfect, spacious but snug, comfortably furnished, filled with pearls, at other times she believed it must be a cramped, windowless den in which beetles and spider did battle in stale and aged air. Still, she reasoned, in reality, how would anybody distinguish a lost room from all the other cluttered spaces? There may be a place the aunts had shunned, locked or hidden somewhere in the house, but to Seb it would be just another dusty, intriguing mess.

While Seb delved into the contents of the house, Gill wandered around the garden, feeling damp, sulky, childish. When called, she'd respond by saying she hadn't time to nose about in suitcases; somebody had to keep an eye on the children, *their* children, somebody had to coax the Rayburn to life so they could have warm, if not actually hot, water from time to time. Of course, while outside, Gill wasn't caring for Adam and Rosie or dealing with the Rayburn; neither was she doing constructive gardening. But she did keep fit, covering miles each day, circling the paths, pulling out what she thought might be weeds.

One afternoon she lit a bonfire in the area Tilly had described as 'the forbidden place'. Gill heaped greenery on top of old newspapers, where it burnt reluctantly, glowing, fading, threatening to extinguish itself at any hint of a breeze. Gill enjoyed the smoke. Her eyes had been asking for a reason to water. Her nasal passages had been blocked by self-pity, now they might ooze freely, allowing her to make trails of silver across her bare forearms. Sweat surfaced on her skin, a moustache of moisture, a narrow stream between her breasts. Gill welcomed this letting of liquids. Seep and weep, she told herself, sniffing, perspiring, crying tracks down her dirty cheeks.

There was something exotic in the air, amongst the swirls of smoke, under the more mundane garden refuse. Herbs perhaps, or the perfume of certain petals. Gill knew this area had been out of bounds to Elizabeth Durry's children and to her servants. Elizabeth had cultivated this place herself, not allowing the gardener of her time anywhere near. There had been a hedge of yew to hide secret blooms. Years after the death of their mother, Tilly and Flora paid a man to uproot that hedge with a motorised shovel. Gill could remember the scar of ripped roots and upturned soil where the yew had thrived. The garden had seemed twice its normal size for a while: barren as a desert. But Tilly and Flora had blossomed once the yew was pulled up.

Maybe this scent emanated from kindled remnants of the departed hedge. Maybe it was the roots of whatever had grown within the hedge's confines. It was sweet and suffocating, like incense in a warm church.

With a rake, Gill lifted burning branches, clumps of grass and weeds, airing the flames until they soared energetically. The smoke rose straight to the sky then, leaving Gill in a clearing; revealing her audience. Adam, Rosie and Seb were watching, from a safe distance, clustered together in a three-headed squat. The flakes of paper and ash dancing in the surrounding air gave them the look of figures captured in a snow-shaker.

"Grrrr," Gill cried, brandishing her hot rake at them. Rosie howled in fright. Adam leapt to his feet. Seb jumped up too, dropping a tin of bottle tops, instinctively putting both his arms round his frightened daughter.

"Sorry," Gill told them, tossing the rake aside. She knew she must have looked a classic devil, with her spiky, henna-red hair and her smeared face, with a rake of flames. "I didn't mean to scare you." Clearly, none of them believed this; but it was true. Gill was the most alarmed of all. She had only intended to make them move: to recover them.

Later, Gill hurried to see why her children were screaming. They had uncovered a toad as they poked about on the flagstones underneath the balustrade. With nothing more than a wink, the toad appropriated the role of ogre from Gill, leaving her free to be the one who does good deeds. She calmed her children. She made the poor disturbed creature a shelter of stones and sticks, by way of showing her gratitude. Although the toad had frightened her little ones, Gill was comforted to see him there, where she thought he had always been. It was soothing to think of something continuing, something other than the walnut or the fruit trees, alive here, as it had existed for years.

As if inspired to goodness, she cooked proper food that evening. A lentil and ham bake, with celery, onions and one limp leek. Achieving this treat took her the best part of three hours, since the Rayburn was as reticent as ever and she needed to scrub each utensil before daring to use it.

What had become of Babs, Gill wondered, unable to prevent a shiver from travelling the length of her spine. Gill had been expecting Babs to put in an appearance, waiting for her knock on the door, or the clattering of the ancient bell. Anticipating a visit from Babs with a dread she only now acknowledged. Babs had been Tilly's daily helper, the 'woman who did' - although she never had done quite what she was supposed to do. Clearly she hadn't cleaned a cooking pot in years. Grease was ingrained into every saucepan; when scoured from its resident surface, the fat of a thousand dinners stuck to Gill's fingers as if fearing the pull of the plug-hole. Precisely who had enjoyed these unctuous meals? It definitely hadn't been Aunt Tilly, her illness couldn't have coped with fat in any form. Also, tomato pips were embedded in the chopping board: tomatoes would have been lethal for somebody with Tilly's stomach. It was so ensconced, this muck, so at home here; it seemed immutable. But Gill persevered, banishing her fear of Babs by cursing as she scrubbed. She boiled kettles to ensure cleanliness and, to enhance the taste of the food, she stretched to the shelf above the stove for canisters that still housed Tilly's home grown herbs. A pinch of this, a suggestion of that. Umm. Good, it smelt positively professional.

They'd eat together, for once. A family of four. Two of each gender. Perfect; the standard, happy family. Nobody would arrive at the table late, having allowed the food to cool. There'd be no asking for chips instead. The daughter wasn't going to spit out the very first mouthful, sending the mother's blood in a furious gallop. Stir and sieve, chop and sprinkle. Bake - admittedly at too low a temperature. Inhale the aroma. See the anticipation on the face of the husband: desecrating somebody else's house was obviously hungry work. And, finally, behold - the meal. Hot, almost steaming. Smelling, perhaps, of a summer evening at a small but renowned country restaurant. Chez Something-on-the-Water.

"What is it?" Adam asked.

"Crispy hammy bake with herby topping," Gill responded. Having once cajoled her son into chewing his way through burnt toast by describing it as 'crunchy, twiggly bites', she appreciated the appeal of the 'y' sound.

Seb sniffed the meal with exaggerated approval. His nose wriggled like a rabbit's. "I once knew a man named Herby Topping," he told Adam and Rosie, "lived in a phone box on the edge of a golf course. Made a living retrieving and then unravelling lost golf balls. Later he'd join together short bits of their rubber innards to provide rubber bands for the local jam factory." He was spoon-feeding Rosie as he told his unlikely tale. It was working, her mouth opened with interest and shut when the food landed on her tongue. "Old Herby was often interrupted by people calling wrong numbers, so he took to leaving his receiver off the hook. He slept curled up with his head on the Yellow Pages." Seb juggled food from his plate to his mouth, from Rosie's plate to her mouth. "Plumbers and Pneumatic Drill Rentals were his preferred pillow, since their page allowed an equal division of information to both sides of his brain. And another thing about Herby, he was the world's best ever golfer. Yes, could have won cup after cup, old Herby. But the sad thing is, Mr. Herby Topping never played in a single competition. Never played with anybody else. You see, he was so shy he couldn't bring himself to utter a word about his skill to another living soul."

"Only at night," Adam took over, "Mr. Herby would stop work on the lost golf balls and sneak out to the pitch..."

"Course," Seb corrected. Adam misunderstood; "Yeh," he enthused, "so Herby went out in the dark..." He too was eating the bake, a meal he'd have spurned had his attention not been diverted. "...and he secretly played the best golf in the world." A stringy piece of celery hung from his lips. Adam loathed celery; he licked it upwards without noticing, he chewed, he swallowed. Gill ate stealthily, afraid they might spot her and look down at their food in disgust.

"Under the light of the moon," Seb continued, "Herby hit ball after ball. And although he was brilliant, because he could only play when it was dark, he often missed his mark and the balls he thwacked went flying into the undergrowth or splashed into one of the ponds. So, unbeknown to him, in daylight, when he retrieved lost balls, Herby was actually finding the very same golf balls he had hit during the night. He was not only the World's Greatest Golfer, he was Ace Recycler Of Balls. Absolutely, no question about it, top of the Toppings, World Number One." He popped the final spoonful of bake into Rosie's mouth. She smiled around the spoon, which was clamped in her baby teeth.

Gill and Seb grinned at each other: true victors. They'd done it, fed good sized helpings of wholesome food to both their children. The sense of achievement was awesome. In fact, everything seemed overwhelming to Gill. Her plate was suddenly enormous. And on this blue and white china landscape the smear of leftover sauce appeared a vast wasteland of pap from which she couldn't drag her eyes. A pair of clown's hands hung at the ends of her arms. In dismay, she flapped these white, floppy appendages. The kitchen felt close and hot. Close as in having the walls move towards one another. Hot as in ripe for making passionate love. Across the table, Seb seemed all smile. His mouth was his sole feature, wider than the Cheshire cat's. In the middle of the room, Adam was spinning. It took a moment for Gill to discern whether her son was actually on his feet, going round and round, or whether this twirling boy was an illusion. She studied him as a scientist watches life forms through a lens. Boy goes whirling round. Most interesting. Oh, whoops! Boy falls on flagstone floor. Fascinating. Is he hurt? Well, he laughs - he doesn't cry. Amazing. Seb was laughing too, schoolboy giggles, high and silly. Adam stood up, wobbled to the table, clasping

26

it for support. He cried, "Wow there," as if trying to steady a restless horse. Now the four of them were nothing but a chorus of mirth. Rosie was banging her fists on the table, swinging her legs against its underside, motivated, for once, by joy. She possessed a good sense of rhythm, Gill thought, clapping along: this was how families should be, weak with silliness, rocking and laughing to a shared beat. Rosie's cheeks were puffed and shining, little pink balloons full of laughing gas. "Let go of her hand, Seb," Gill suggested, "and see if she drifts away."

It felt so good; like having your feet massaged, your head rubbed. Like being tickled by somebody you had always really, secretly fancied. Gill stood, unsteady but determined, pushing her chair away with her backside. She had to have sex. Had the children not existed, she'd have humped Seb there and then, amongst the unwashed crockery. "Bed," she declared, aiming for a wink at Seb but in fact squinting like a mole surfacing. Adam's hand was in hers. He was drained now, an old bear minus its stuffing, being dragged by Gill up the back stairs. Rosie's balloon cheeks had burst; her head drooped over Seb's shoulder, her mouth was slack. And was that foam at the far corners of her lips? Seb sang as he staggered upstairs: Gill thought it was probably the dwarves song from 'Snow White' but at that moment she was unsure about everything - everything except the desire that was shooting through her torso. Between them, she and Seb threw their already sleeping children onto the bunk beds. They scrambled across the back landing to what was now their bedroom.

I remember, I remember, Gill thought as she tore Seb's clothes from his back. How long it was since she'd been this eager. Hello lust! Oh yes, here it was again, an exciting old acquaintance, welcome as a truck full of champagne. Energized to the very edge of pain, Gill undressed in a frenzy, gripped her lover's hips, dug nails into his flesh. She didn't need, she wasn't prepared to tolerate foreplay - Gill wanted him, as much of this hot, enthusiastic man as she could accommodate: Seb, Seb, she might have whispered, don't kiss, just get inside quickly - no - not quickly but instantly and all the bloody way.

He didn't need telling, though. As she arched her back and made her body pulse against Seb's, Gill was aware of rising hysteria, stemming from the emphasis this situation threw on opposites; soft and hard, phallus and hole, man and woman. There was fire in both lovers. It was exhilarating but also, as they grasped each other's bodies, frightening. White heat was drying them out, threatening to drain them before they were finished. They raced against the flames, hurting each other, lovingly.

They fell back on Tilly's crisp white linen and panted at the ceiling. It was only eight o'clock. There was dim daylight in the room; they might get up, put on the radio, make each other cups of tea. Gill felt her eyes close, like up-and-over garage doors dropping to a concrete floor. She was a saturated princess; one who'd had much more than her finger pricked. How very, very rude, she thought as she snuggled against Seb's chest. She was all set to sleep for at least one hundred years.

By ten o'clock, Seb and Gill were awake again, discussing what had happened in slightly embarrassed whispers. They told each other they ought to check on the children but their limbs were lumpen, their heads were fizzing. "Obviously there is somewhat more to Herby Topping than meets the eye," Seb muttered. After that, it was a restless night for both of them. Neither could sleep for another moment, nor could they bear to touch each other. There was no more laughter, either. They lay on their backs, in silence, overwhelmed. Overdosed.

*

The herby meal may in itself have marked a change in life at Ramsons, emotions were certainly dulled once the family had digested whatever was going through their systems. Seb continued to enthuse about the house and its contents but once he'd tasted danger, his enthusiasm was forced, if not feigned. Some of the doubts, which had always formed part of Gill's overall view of Ramsons, had taken root in Seb's mind; Gill could discern this uneasy growth by his ponderous footsteps, his caution when opening doors, the way he stopped prying. But then again, he was an actor. He knew how to put on a show of optimism as the hours of daylight shortened and mists crept right up to the windows. He had every reason to look on the bright side, anyway, since he anticipated being whisked away to work before the fogs settled or the rain became constant. Only weeks before leaving Bristol, Seb had been taken on by an agent who was new to him; a woman called Pamela, with a record of finding the best work for her actors. The likelihood of Seb's departure was now the main cause of tension between husband and wife, a thread on which only the high notes played.

And then the letter arrived, incongruously fresh in a manila envelope; and if the hazardous meal hadn't troubled Seb and Gill, this macabre piece of post was enough to ensure their being upset. The envelope contained two letters, in fact, one from the family solicitor explaining that the second letter was from Matilda Durry. Miss Durry had requested the enclosed be posted to the inhabitant of Ramsons once said inhabitant had resided there for a period of two weeks. Tilly's letter was written on faintly scented, lilac paper, as all her unofficial post had been throughout her later life. Holding it, with Seb looking over her shoulder, Gill experienced a gust of possessive nostalgia. She told her husband that she thought she'd like to read it by herself, first. Seb was hurt, he sloped off with shoulders hunched, but Gill remained resolute.

She took the letter to the widest of the front stairs, where the staircase curved and stained glass from an arched window threw blue and red shards over her shoulders.

'My Dearest Great Niece,' Tilly began, 'I am confident in this address because June has insisted *she* couldn't live at Ramsons and my will was designed, I'm sorry to say, to ensnare some other relative as occupant: since I have no relatives but you, my three girls, Ramsons must be home to one of you. I wonder who you are? Sarah, Gillian or Kate? I admit that I have, over the last few years, suggested to each of you how good a home Ramsons might be and how, by living there, you would give me peace of mind. I suspect you to be Gillian, as she showed the greatest interest, along with that handsome husband of hers! Oh I do hope you have settled in, Dear, and are coping. Beware of the scullery door, it sticks shut in wet weather and can leave you 'locked' out in the garden. There is a wedge nearby, best use it every time to be on the safe side.'

Gill lifted her head from the letter and squinted at the colourful window. Had Tilly written from beyond the grave merely to have a cosy chat? She tried to remember if her Great Aunt had shown signs of dementia, or even eccentricity, in life. No. Gill's recollections were of a woman whose body was wasting but whose mind was a prism, glinting with perception.

She read on: 'Silly me, drawing attention to a single fault when Ramsons is a mass of foibles and frictions. I am attempting to buy time, the asset I have least of. The truth is that I fear the telling of these tales, for this is more than a story, told in instalments. My letters will disclose entreaties and confessions, will expose secrets of the soul and will exhume, I am afraid to say, some terrible accusations.

'Please do not be put off by my early ramblings. Believe me, Dear, they are more than the whims of an old woman. Writing down the episodes has helped me to exorcize certain ghosts while allowing me to feel reunited with others. It has gone some considerable way to relieving my anxieties. It has given me hope at a time when I have hardly any future remaining.

'Maybe you will say, well, this nonsense has served its purpose, having kept old Tilly quiet and out of harm! There is more to this than pacifying me; it is essential that your generation understand certain facts. Is it essential in order to safeguard future generations of Durry women. Please give each letter your full attention. They should arrive at regular intervals over the next few weeks but I have tucked the second instalment behind the one-and-only family photograph, so you may decide for yourself when to read that.'

Gill told herself she had been wrong about Tilly. This must be the work of a disturbed, if not entirely mad, old woman. Driven to the edge by loneliness, for which Gill knew she was partly responsible. They had rarely visited Ramsons, Gillian and her 'handsome husband'. Yet, supposedly, she had, on one of these visits, implied that she was keen to live here. Probably Gill had nodded, absent-mindedly, at whatever Tilly suggested. A lack of concentration, while sipping tea, whilst chewing walnut and coffee cake, had lead to the supposition that Gill was ready to step inside Tilly's well-maintained shoes and to take on board whatever 'revelations' were to be found in these letters.

Seb called to her from the foot of the stairs. "Well?" he wondered. Gill glanced at the sheets of paper, noting how many pages she had yet to read. She folded them with what seemed guilty haste, tucked them in the pocket of her jeans, said it was just some nonsense. Seb remained hurt. He grew cunning in his questions. Of course, Gill would share with him sooner or later, they both appreciated this - but for a while the letter seemed to be her only true possession, the one item she could keep from him.

By the evening, having been stalked by Seb and followed from room to room by Adam, Gill was feeling homesick for Bristol and for Bella in particular. She reminded herself how she'd been persuaded to leave behind much of what she valued. Off to a better life together, that had been the theme. Away from traffic and litter. Free of noise and those annoying hangers-on who attached themselves to Seb in the city. No mention of leaving genuine friends, no talk of the lack of nightlife, of any life but that spent in a great, damp, cluttered house. A home in which she was now supposed to hear a dead person confess, to gather up accusations as if they were balls of fluff.

It had been Seb who had wanted to make this move. His plans weren't based on anything more solid than dreams: The Life Of Sebastion Murphy, Famous and Well Loved Actor, at home with his delightful family in their rambling, country house. The wife of this good-looking paragon flicked through the glossy magazines of Seb's imagination. See the Little Ones gathered round a roaring fire while a giant Christmas tree glitters, oh so charmingly out of focus, in the background. Look at the loving couple, relaxing in their gorgeous garden, under lilac trees, with their weekend guests, the artist, the director, the model recovering from her horrific car accident. Doubtless, in this, his own version, Seb's eyes are dark liquid pools, his smile quite irresistible. He will be besotted with his children in spite of, rather than because of, rarely being at home. And what of his wife, Gillian, who takes such super photographs? Well, she may be considered a tad eccentric in an endearing, colourful way. Like a parrot, she darts about, jolly and madcap, talking nonsense, drinking too much, ignoring her kids. Cooking fairly awful meals. But nobody minds because she makes guests laugh even as they surreptitiously spit quiche into their napkins.

Sadly, it seemed Gill couldn't picture herself an unqualified success, even when she took control of what went on in Seb's fantasies.

"Tell me how you feel about me," Gill ordered Seb that evening. They were side by side on an old chaise longue; if it had possessed a back, they might have cuddled up. As it was, they were required to sit bolt upright or risk falling backwards on to an assortment of hats Seb had gathered and abandoned. There was no sofa in Ramsons, no place below stairs designed for relaxation, or certainly no venue for the joint relaxation of two people at one time. Gill and Seb compromised by holding hands, like a couple that had only recently begun to date; as formal with each other as those with straight spines ought to be.

"I love you, of course," Seb began. He wasn't looking at his wife. He wasn't focusing on anything inside the dusky drawing room. His gaze went beyond the long windows, past the end of the village street, all the way back to a studio in Bristol where, while he was still a drama student, he'd been called to take part in a short film. It was to be his first role in front of a camera. He was nervous and yet confident. Only four lines, already learnt, practised before a mirror in the house he shared with several others. Seb would somehow shine with a brilliance that eclipsed his meagre part in this work. This, he'd been certain, was the break he needed.

There was only one person in the studio when Seb pushed the door open: a single figure kneeling over a case of equipment, absorbed in its contents. He couldn't see much of this person's face - a sheet of hair hid the features, but he knew she was female by the long, efficient fingers that were cleaning and setting up a camera and some lenses. Then she flicked her hair from her eyes and looked up, squinting a little because Seb stood in a lit doorway. She probably said "Hi," although Seb isn't sure, in retrospect. Despite her baggy clothing, it was obvious that this camera-woman was slim, perhaps a shade too thin for perfection. Her skin was clear, bordering on olive, her eyebrows high and arched, her eyes dark, round, questioning. Her hair was almost purple, with the sheen, Seb thought romantically, of the raven's wing. For some reason, she made Seb think of holidays, of bodies warmed by sunshine, of salt and sand between the toes. The link, he decided, was her fingernails, which were opalescent, pink as freshly washed shells.

"I'm Gill," she said, because he was silent, "here to do the stills." The rhyme jolted Seb to life. He muttered his name, his part in the day's work. He offered to make tea if only he could find a kettle. He parked his coat on a chair, was embarrassed when he realized he was messing up the set. Gill smiled, accepted the possibility of tea; her attention returned to her camera. It was the way she lost herself to this work that made Seb fall in love with her.

"When I first saw you," he told her in the drawing room of Ramsons, "I thought of hot evenings on exotic, holiday islands." Gill sighed. She had thought of London when she spied Seb; parks, pavements, red buses. The wide river, fogs during which it might be good to huddle inside another person's coat.

"I'd never seen a woman so secure in herself, so possessed by her craft," Seb continued. "I was jealous of your camera, of the way your fingers knew it so well." He had turned, once, from the mugs and kettle he'd found, to watch Gill's back, curved as gracefully as a piece by Rodin, leaning towards her cloths and brushes. At that time, Seb would happily have changed professions, becoming a film-maker in order to spend a day, a week, his working life, studying this woman, following her movements, getting her to look his way.

"And I still find that you are the most fascinating, beautiful woman I could hope to meet," he told her, squeezing her hand. Yet you will leave me, Gill thought, in the style of a Henry James character. Why, here was red plush, albeit faded to damask, and gilt trimmings. The setting cried out for heartache. The carpet expected to be paced by the lonely; the mantelpiece was built to support the clammy hands of those who'd recently received the worst of news. Only the distraught would stand before the windows of this room, slipping a finger between lace curtains, peeping at a world where luckier folk went about their business. Oh my Lord; how cruel of Gill's ancestors to have decorated for desertion.

"Tell me about the letter," Seb begged. "I saw the bit from the solicitor. Why is Tilly writing to you two weeks after we moved in? What message has she from 'beyond her grave'?"

"She tells me to beware of men who pry," Gill said. But her head was taken up with images of solitary women, aunts, grandmothers, even June, left alone by the time they reached middle age. And here was Seb, declaring his devotion: she should be grateful.

"I know, I've got it, " Seb said, eagerly ruining his chances. "Tilly writes to warn you of that cleaning woman, doesn't she? That person who wears high heels and serious suits and looks, frankly, quite the stranger to dusters and to all brooms but those that fly on dark and starless nights." His reference was to Babs as she had appeared at Tilly's funeral, Gill supposed, although Babs did in fact wear absurd heels on most occasions, including, presumably, when employed as a char lady. She also favoured black clothing, hence Seb's poke at witchery: and there was more than a hint of malice, if not downright evil, to Babs.

Seb was waiting. He was actually sitting on his hands, as if to stop himself from grabbing Tilly's letter, but it was safely wedged, Gill would have to stand to ease it from her pocket. She sat tight. Her thoughts returned to Babs, as she had presented herself during Tilly's funeral. A slim, dark woman, a person without curves. Her hair, her lips, even her relentlessly brown eyes were variations on the straight-line theme. She had made Gill uneasy, with those squared-off finger nails, with her rectangular handbag suspended from its golden links. Gill never dressed up - not even in the face of death - but June and Sarah had clearly minded being outsmarted by a cleaner. Not that Babs described herself as a cleaner; "I was Miss Durry's companion for many years," Gill had overheard her telling a young man, "we were devoted to one another." Well, Gill sighed, there was some question about that - companion, devoted. There had been what June described as hanky-panky, tricks had been played by both parties. The result hardly indicated devotion on either side.

Gill licked the patch of skin below Seb's left ear, thus persuading him to go directly to bed - and to put off his attempts to obtain Tilly's letter until the following morning. "You are such a push-over," she told him fondly, on the way up the stairs.

"I have to go to school on this day," Adam announced the next morning. 'This day' was ringed in red felt pen; it loomed large as his parents gawped at the calendar. 'This day' was a mere three days away. They knew nobody connected with the village school. Ought they to have registered their son? Or was that too Eton, too Harrow? So far they had made one phone call, months ago, from Bristol. The secretary had given them a date: 'this day'. It had seemed to belong to another lifetime. Throughout the summer it had been one-day-in-the-autumn. Now it was almost here. Uniforms and stationary hadn't been considered. Would Adam need a lunch-box, a satchel, a pair of little football boots? Was he prepared, mentally? Were his parents?

Frantic as this situation was, Gill welcomed the distraction. Somehow, she hadn't warmed to the prospect of handing Tilly's letter to Seb, especially since she'd yet to finish reading it herself. Thankfully, he was occupied in arranging to see the Head Teacher, busy talking to Adam about the importance of education, or calling his clan together so they might drive to Market Carney and shop for the forthcoming event.

It was as this flustered clutch of Murphys were scrambling for the front door, car and house keys in their hands, pushchair folded under an arm, bags full of drinks and face cloths hanging from their shoulders, it was then, a moment before their exit, that the phone shrilled its fateful call.

4.

Of course people
go off course sometimes, radio to the outside world...

Seb accepted Pamela's offer of a spell in Edinburgh without question, without asking his wife's opinion. Well, the chance to do some decent theatre for a change... Whatever Gill might have said, he'd have gone anyway. She did imagine an altered world in which it was possible to persuade him to stay; but even in this haven, bliss would inevitably sour. To keep Seb from the stage was to dry out the gills of a fish. He'd only feel sorry for himself and flap about under her feet. She may as well come to terms with the unavoidability of being left, alone and gently freezing, in Ramsons. Just as she'd suspected.

But she couldn't bear to see him pack. She tried to be upstairs when he was down, in the garden when he was in the drawing room, out of earshot when he wanted to know how many clean shirts he possessed. Once, she encountered him by accident, which was a constant risk in a house with two sets of stairs. During his brief period as lord of this manor, Seb had married his possessions to those of Gill's family. Now he needed to divorce them. Gill was climbing up the back stairs with her arms full of blankets her husband had, for reasons she couldn't fathom, transported to the dining room, when she encountered Seb, lost in his own, cluttered world. At his feet lay his collection of Penguin plays, bright paperbacks with striped spines. Gill spotted Wesker, Arthur Miller, Conrad and Coward; she hated them, every one. But Seb's attention was on flimsier things; he didn't notice her at first because he was studying an assortment of cardboard hands. From the frown on his face, it was clear Seb hadn't discerned the purpose of his latest find. He held several of these in each of his own hands, making many fingered fans. Gill coughed gently and Seb dropped his fans to his lap, where they pointed suggestively at his crouch. He smiled, picked up a single hand, waved it at her.

"Glove patterns," she informed him. He was blocking her way. Her arms ached, her chin was obliged to rest on the blankets, which were hairy and none too hygienic.

"They made their own gloves?" Seb queried.

"They made everything, my aunties," she told him. "They lived the life of postal orders and catalogues, sending away for endless samples, then weaving these into patchwork and stitching that into eiderdowns. They knitted not only hot water bottle covers but the hot water bottles themselves – well almost. Gloves were a sideline, as were purses and wallets. You don't know them," her voice had taken on a note of accusation, as if he ought to remain in the house long enough to become decently acquainted with the craftswomen of yesteryear, "they were never idle, never careless of resources. If it existed, it had a use. Excuse me but you're in my way." Looking duly chastened, Seb stood to let her pass. The glove patterns, which were designed for remarkably dainty hands, fell a little further, to his feet. Both he and Gill appreciated that these now represented an audience of ladies, applauding the actor as he shifted to one side for his wife.

It was the last evening, before Seb set off for Edinburgh and A Life, as Gill saw it. All day, she had been throwing 'what ifs' at his back. What if the Rayburn were to explode? What if one of the children were to get very ill, develop consumption say, and Gill could find no way of warming them? Cold and dark threatened to be Gill's most vicious enemies, the foes she feared. But there would be other horrors, of this she was certain. What if the cellar was full of rats? Ah-ha, Seb had forgotten the cellar, hadn't he? No, he didn't think he'd known of its existence, actually. Well, she would show him. Gill led him by the hand, along the stone passage lined with cupboards stacked with mouldering jams, out of the front door. "You can get to it through an inside door," she explained, "a door hidden behind a velvet curtain, then you go down some steps and there you are. But that entrance is too scary, believe me. This way we see the proof without having to fight cobwebs, without walking on beetles."

They were in the front garden. They looped around the box hedging to stand before the drawing room window, their feet planted in an overgrown flower bed that still boasted, amongst brambles and nettles, clumps of ice plant and one moth eaten yellow rose. Having cleared a space, Gill knelt on the soil and revealed a grill. Rather than looking through this, she watched as Seb did so. She nodded at his reaction. "We also used to think that they were shrunken heads," she confided in a whisper, "but they're only cooking apples, laid on racks, left to rot."

Kate had been remarkably frightened of this scene: no amount of reassurance would convince her that what she saw through the grill wasn't the work of an evil wizard or a psychopath. To Gill's knowledge, Kate had never once descended the stone steps, although the door had been opened for her, in games, or as a threat. Gill wondered what it was like, being the youngest child, having an excuse for cowardice always to hand. Perhaps Kate hadn't been born timid but life as the littlest had thrust timidity upon her. Gill and Sarah weren't unkind to their baby sister, not often, not drastically, but there had been times when they'd felt compelled to frighten Kate, in order to vent their frustration at her.

"All right," Seb owned, standing up, "there is a cellar full of nasties. The Rayburn may burst. The sky may fall, so what do you want me to do? Should I ring Pamela now and tell her I can't do the job on offer? I can't be an actor, it's too harrowing for my family. I shall have to be an office boy in nearby Market Carney instead. Home at five fifteen just in case a door should jam or a light bulb needs changing."

Gill had frequently suffered this 'I am but a poor actor who must follow my calling' speech. It left her unimpressed. Besides, it was unfair of Seb to suggest she was incapable of simple domestic chores; she'd dealt with hundreds of lights, kicked many a door. This was different; couldn't he see? Ramsons wasn't some terraced house in Bristol, it was a monumental disaster waiting to happen. Here, there were no pals down the road, no Bellas and Jons, no Petes and Julies only a local phone call away. Even Babs, the one person Gill did know in this village, was strangely absent.

"There is another option," she ventured. Seb frowned. Clearly he hadn't seen this possibility as just that - a possibility. Gill understood then that he had already departed. He was on his train, heading north, up the coast to Scotland. Alone with The Guardian and a bar of dark chocolate, his wife and kids having been kissed, hugged, and left behind. "We could come with you," Gill muttered, her eyes on the brown, imprisoned apples. "Or, if that's too much to organize, we might be able to follow later, once you've found some digs. How about that?" How about *them* apples? Gill aimed for flippancy, inside her head, because she foresaw rejection and was working up to a suitable shrug, an appropriate smile. For a while, Seb disembarked from his train to give the idea what seemed due consideration. "I suppose...," he muttered. "If I found a big enough place..." Gill had to give him credit, he played these lines to perfection. If only they might! Oh what fun they could have! Sharing the sights, the exhibitions, those nearby lochs and mountains. The couple were united, for a few moments in the evening sun: touring Scotland in their Morris Minor, their children on the back seat, eating dried fruits, gazing out of the window at deer and other wild life. Then the light in the sky over Staunley faded symbolically and Seb contemplated the cons of having his loved ones with him. He'd never be able to afford a family sized flat. Along with his living space, his style would be catastrophically cramped. Besides, Adam must go to school, was due to do so here, the very next day. Ramsons must be maintained, lived in, cared for.

Gill shivered and moved towards the front door. She had half a mind to make another hammy bake, with extra helpings of herby topping. At least then she would be able to abandon herself to the pleasures of the flesh for Seb's final night at home. But the way she felt, she wasn't sure she could recover from such a dish, nor was she convinced she would want to; a drugged state did have a certain appeal.

On her way down the passage, she paused and glanced up at Cedric the cherub. If only I was a believer, she thought, I might ask this little guy to intercede. An entire renaissance of heavenly bodies filled her head, fluttering, chubby and useless, in a sky whose blue was threatened by the dark clouds of thunder.

"Did you tell them?" Gill asked when Seb returned to the kitchen having soothed his restless children in their beds, for the third time that evening. "Do they know they have to spend the next six weeks or so with nobody but their unreliable mother for company?"

"You see yourself as unreliable, do you?" Seb countered. Gill studied an ink stain in the grain of the table. There were tears, more of anger than of sadness, welling up behind her eyeballs.

"Yes, I told them," he said, firmly. The trouble with actors was they always sounded rehearsed: Gill recognized every inflection in her husband's voice. She felt she'd been sitting on the same flip-up theatre seat, watching the same production, for many a long year.

"I made the future sound like the landscape of highs and lows that it will inevitably be. Gave them my homecoming to look forward to, promised postcards and telephone calls. Tried not to seem guilty at having been given work that will provide for their needs, you know?"

"What time tomorrow will you have to leave?" There was a limit to the number of words Gill might safely utter. She needed to know the hour of his departure; was she going to rise and dress in the dark? Would they be driving to the station with headlights on or not? This rehearsing of scenes was obviously catching.

"Well," Seb considered her question, "it is a long old drive…"

"To Peterborough? It's about twenty miles, that's all."

"Peterborough? Why would I go there? I'll be heading north, up the A1 until I join the M1, won't I?"

Gill saw what the problem was. Having assumed her husband could never be selfish enough to abandon his brood in a one-shop hole like Staunley without a car, she had supposed Seb would travel by train, while he had envisaged driving away in their only means of transport.

She called him mean.

He told her she was thoughtless.

She asked had he any idea how infrequent the local buses were? Had he in fact seen any sign of a bus during his sojourn in this backwater?

Seb thought there were buses, green ones, compact and comfortable, stopping outside the pub about three times a day.

"Three times a century, more like," Gill spat.

"Why do you always have to look on the worst side of things? You won't need to leave the village much anyway. There's a school, a shop, a pub. What do you want the damn car for?"

"Heaven forbid that I might go to a town, or even, Lord knows, a city while you're swanning about in Scotland. Oh no, it's the village or nothing for little old, unreliable me. Remember those apples?" Gill cried. "Well, before you go, Seb, why not take me down to the cellar and pop me on a rack, leave me *there*, why don't you, to shrivel up over the winter months."

"For God's sake, woman," Seb began; but Gill's apple imagery was too much for both of them. Anger seeped away; laughter took over. They caught each other's eyes and giggled. They hugged for the longest time, each feeling the bones of the other. Each sighing as they experienced the other's heartbeat.

"I'll come straight back," Seb promised, "if you need me to. Phone me, night or day, should you feel the beginnings of any shrivelling up. And I won't take the car, all right?" Gill nodded gratefully, her head against his sweater, her nostrils filling with woollen fibres.

"It does break my heart, you know," Seb assured her when they were in bed, "leaving you and the children. I do not go gently... but acting is what I do, it makes me who I am. Like any artist, I am driven..."

"Yes, but only as far as Peterborough," Gill reminded him. She felt his smile against her cheek. His breath tickled as he told her, "I think I only wanted the car because it would be part of us. Like having one room from our home with me at all times." Gill saw the truth in this, knowing that their car contained books, picnic cups, toys and rubbish that would remind Seb of his family and their outings. It smelt of Rosie and Adam, of small items of underwear, damp with urine, of dribble and vomit that had been wiped but never quite removed from the upholstery. There was a Fisher Price toy radio stuck under the passenger's seat: every time the Morris hit a bump, it played a couple of notes from 'Waltzing Matilda'. Gill imagined Scotland as a land of uneven roads. Seb would have no chance of forgetting them, if he had the car with him. And there was the effect his vehicle, with its smells and sounds, with its chocolate animal biscuit boxes and Smarties tubes, would have on any woman who might set her sights on Seb. Gill couldn't allow herself to think of Seb chasing other women, but she often suspected them of pursuing him. After a romantic dinner for two, a ride home in the Morris should be enough to put the hardest heart off a man who was clearly father to some sweet-toothed, musically-gifted little dears. But Gill couldn't let him have the car, she wouldn't survive the claustrophobia of being without it. She told Seb, "You'd be taking more than a piece of home. The Morris is almost all the home we have, right now." Her husband's sigh was all too familiar. Yet again, she had overplayed her part, trampling the moment.

They were up at six in the morning, shivering under the old yellow lights of Ramsons, dressing as if for a trip to the Arctic. Rosie whimpered without ceasing, as she was plucked from her bed, as she was twisted this way and that, into warm tights and a cosy, knitted dress. She moaned while Seb fed her fingers of toast; she whined as she was carried out to the car. Once Seb's cases were loaded in the boot, the

41

family sat inside the Morris watching their breath, waiting for the mist on the windscreen to clear.

"We never took a walk on the Up and Downs," Gill pointed out as they approached this landmark. The Ups and Downs were the overgrown remains of a stone quarry, a series of small hills and dips where wild flowers flourished in chalky soil. Having provided the stone for Staunley and other settlements the area was now a nature reserve, on the edge of the village. In Bristol, when planning the move, Gill had envisaged herself and Seb running down the hills, staggering up again, towing breathless children. Although Gill knew little about garden plants, she could have astounded Seb with her knowledge of wild flowers. On childhood walks, she had listened to Flora and Tilly as they named each bloom, catching their enthusiasm and maintaining this, like pressed petals, throughout her life. Squinting out of the window, she remembered Seb's phrase from the previous night, about the future being a landscape of highs and lows. In the morning's half light, the Ups and Downs were an amassment of shadows, the road through their centre a clearing across the surface of the moon.

"Don't talk as if walking here is something we'll never get to do," Seb warned her. "I'll be back before Christmas, we can march off our Christmas dinner here, how about that?"

"I want a fort," Adam announced, "for Christmas, with soldiers, of course."

"You only say that because I used the word 'march'," Seb pointed out. "You wanted a Scalectric track last week."

"You mean you did," Gill accused Seb. She turned to grin at Adam. He was studying the back of his father's head; perhaps, like his mother, he needed to commit it to memory in order to love or hate Seb sufficiently during his absence.

"Keep me up-to-date with your progress where Tilly's letters are concerned, won't you?" Seb asked. Gill nodded her lie; she intended to keep every word Tilly wrote entirely to herself.

On the drive back from Peterborough, the passenger seat was not so much empty as hollow. In the rear of the car, the children had fallen asleep, leaning one against the other, breathing in harmony. 'Ping-ping...' went the toy radio under the seat, 'Who'll come...' The car had developed a series of illnesses the moment Seb slammed the boot and turned on his heels. Minor illness, Gill teased herself. Each ailment was accompanied by a disturbing sound effect. Whistles, farts, the rattle of an engine in trouble. No doubt she would break down, on the quietest stretch of road, and be required to wait for hours, in freezing weather, for somebody to stop and help her.

When she reached Staunely without a mishap, Gill had to admit to being pleasantly surprised. The car had kept going, an old retainer, grumbling but faithful. With the wracking cough of the truly ancient, it stopped outside Ramsons. Gill didn't expect it to move again, ever.

There were children and parents hurrying by as Gill lifted Rosie and shook Adam awake. Kids on their way to school, as Adam should be. Some women said Good Morning to Gill, a greeting that unnerved rather than gladdened her. Both children were still exhausted, Gill half carried, half dragged them inside the house. It wouldn't have been fair to send Adam to school - to dump him in a room full of strangers when he'd just lost one of the people he knew best in the world. Gill got them back to their beds, tucked them in, gave them their soft toys to protect. Then she went to Tilly's bed, to rest. Her body ached as if it had been assaulted.

On the pillow next to hers she found one cardboard hand with the word 'Help' written across the palm. She turned it over and read Seb's message, which was arranged so that each digit had a word at its tip: 'Help is always on hand'. Her instinct was to tear the glove pattern to shreds, to rip off each finger in slow torture fashion, since the words were clearly lies. But, as a member of the Durry family, she was conditioned to keep messages, notes, letters - to treasure even false, stiff fingered missives. Thinking of letters, she took Tilly's lilac notepaper from her pocket and put it under her pillow.

As she fell asleep, Gill was conscious of the village outside coming to life. She heard delivery vans and beer lorries arrive at the pub. She knew Seb was right about the bus, because one drew, throbbing and purring, to a stop not far from Ramsons's front gate. People called to each other, Lincolnshire accents bouncing on the paving stones. Gill pulled a pile of blankets over her head but she couldn't block life out. There was a moment of panic during which she thought maybe she should get Adam up, rush him to school with a flurry of apologies. But she lay still, cold but not uncomfortable, and she relaxed into the knowledge that this was probably the form her life would take for the next few weeks.

She was still holding the cardboard hand, her fingers weaving through the upright pattern. Whether or not she cared to be reminded of her husband, there was something salacious in the ease with which the stiffened fingers slipped under her pillow.

5.

The piano
is playing at will from behind three potted plants,

Gill woke in the dark and wondered how she could have slept through a day and an evening. The covers were over her head, she was suffocating herself with her own perspiration, with the warmth of her breathing. Why, she wondered, did her sweat smell of tin? Once she emerged she found it wasn't night, only late afternoon. She lay still, stretched like a corpse. This time, along with voices on the street outside, she heard the songs of birds, water struggling through pipes clogged with lime scale and one car, not close by, being driven by a speed freak. She felt removed from all these noises, including the silence of her children. What was she doing there, in a place at once familiar and utterly strange? She was a hostage to this crumbling house, to a clan of dead relations and living, but unsympathetic, family members. Pinned, by old-fashioned duty, to a vast, sagging bed. Gill considered her future and found it damp, chill, remorseless.

But hey, she remembered once telling Bella, when Bella was deep in mourning for her sister, people have to invent fresh joys, to create moments that will later shimmer in memory. Here she was, Gill reminded herself, young, healthy, talented, with an amazing house to explore and a collection of stories to read. How Sarah and Kate would envy her, when she told them about Tilly's letters. They'd lean across the kitchen table, if they did finally get around to visiting and claiming their share of the furniture, shaking their heads.

Gill got out of bed and went to the chest of drawers she had begun to unpack on her first day in Ramsons. Now, along with Tilly and Flora, each object in the one drawer reminded her of Bella. The brooch of felt flowers was heavier than before, the dance card dustier, as if other layers, sticky as honey, were forming over each and every item she encountered.

Rediscovering the photograph of Tilly and her friends on Hampstead heath, Gill felt the hairs on her neck rise. She had previously found this image of her maiden aunt unsettling, a free spirit, a woman smoking, laughing, far from her restrictive home life: now there was the added frisson of being contacted by a woman who had been this alive, and who was no longer on this earth. Gill ran a finger over the picture, clearing a trail through grime. She propped it against the alarm clock, on the small bedside cupboard. If she hadn't needed to use the toilet, she would have read the remainder of Tilly's letter right then.

When she opened her bedroom door, she was confronted by Adam. How long had he been standing there? Framed in circles of taut, beige skin, his stare was hostile. Gill knelt so that she was on his level. "Hi there," she said. "Have you only just woken up?"

"They're going home," Adam whispered, "those children. Going home from school. I'll never make friends now." Gill smiled, hearing echoes of herself in this comment. "It's not funny," Adam cried, "I wanted to go, I've got a Snoopy pencil case."

"You can take it with you tomorrow," Gill explained. "And I'll look for something old and special to add to your crayons, if you like." Adam blinked slowly, a child's equivalent of rolling the eyes. "I can't take stuff tomorrow," he explained, now sounding all too like his father, "because *today* was the day I was supposed to go. *Today.*" He raised his left foot and thumped it on the landing. Suddenly Gill thought she understood. Did her son believe he'd missed his opportunity for education? Could it be that Adam thought he was intended to spend a single day in school – and that this essential date had passed him by? The poor kid. She reached for his shoulders and found he was gently quivering, presumably with self-pity. "Adam, do you think that the children you heard leaving school just now will be going back tomorrow?" Gill asked, needing to check.

"Of course not," his voice was sour with sarcasm, "they're today's lot, like I was."

"Oh, Sweetheart, you have got it wrong," Gill began. She explained his mistake to him several times, in various ways. But his frown remained, etched deep in disbelief; like a slice from a sculptor's blade.

Rosie had to be woken, which was a shame. In sleep the little girl was pink, pretty, silent and at peace. She was warm in her mother's arms, when lifted from the bed, and she snuggled Gill's neck for at least half of the journey down the back stairs. By the time they reached the kitchen, Rosie was groaning, cranking herself up, as Gill saw it, for a serious bout of complaining. Gill made sandwiches and milky drinks, ignoring Rosie's sound effects. Then she fed her daughter with regular jabs of food, in spite of the child's twisting head movements and clamped lips. Next, she unearthed an oil-filled radiator and plugged this in a socket in the school room, where the open fire had been boarded up. Gill hadn't known this room when it had been a tiny school but she had heard of the days when seven or eight children came here to learn the three Rs, before sitting entrance exams to public schools. Tilly had taught while Flora provided the meals. Cupboards on either side of the fireplace still housed games, puzzles, learning aids. Gill pulled a selection of cards and colouring books from the cupboards and told Adam to make sure neither he nor Rosie sat too near the radiator.

She noticed, in her search for a comfortable place in which to sit and read, that every chair in Ramsons was covered in papers. Tilly had been far from tidy, how could she have kept pace with the gatherings of a hundred years? But Seb's mark was now also on everything. He'd moved bits and pieces around the way some birds do, creating a network of disarray that he alone could comprehend or unravel.

Gill cleared herself a seat in the kitchen and unfolded the lilac letter.

'I shall begin to tell you about your family, the Durrys, as promised,' Tilly had written. 'Do bear with me if I relate facts already known to you, and forgive me if I surprise or frighten you with some information you undoubtedly have been saved from, until now. Your Great Grandfather, Edward, was, as you know, an architect, famous in his own lifetime for creating some of this country's finest theatres and entertainment halls. (Only last month I was contacted by a woman who is trying to arrange for Ramsons to boast one of those blue, ceramic plaques in my father's honour! Imagine that.) His work took him away from us, his children and, more injuriously, from Elizabeth, his wife. Why did she never travel with him, when they could easily afford servants and when she was truly devoted to him? Because Edward had 'married beneath himself', to coin a phrase. He was the son of Percy Durry, a man who owned a substantial portion of Southern Lincolnshire, complete with several rather fine houses, while Elizabeth was the daughter of a labourer, a man who dug ditches, in fact, as I recently discovered in my family-tree research! By the time I was grown enough to notice, my mother had rounded her vowels and forfeited her fen accent, except when she was more than usually riled. She did employ somewhat coarse expressions, mind you, throughout her entire life, but she minded her tongue in public. She learnt to be careful in front of others, not only with her choice of words but with her appearance and her attitudes. However, early in their marriage, when Edward was working his hardest, meeting wealthy men and their wives, his wife was far from groomed for society. Elizabeth used to insist she didn't care to travel, that she felt family duties required her to remain at home while her husband went about his business but the truth was, she might have embarrassed Edward, even to the extent of costing him work. I doubt if he ever actually invited her to accompany him; but he did love her. I see now that it was passion they felt for each other, an unlikely but entirely romantic love, in the manner of Eliza and her Professor Higgins.

'It wasn't only in terms of class that they were distinct. My father was a quiet but enthusiastic man, cheerful in most instances, sorry when he saw any creature in pain (if he only knew…) moved by almost every image from the natural world - emotion he reflected in the floral annulets of his theatres, in the flocks of birds traversing his domed ceilings. Mother was a harsh, undiminished soul, a woman enslaved by her emotions, with no interests beyond her immediate needs, no loves but her husband and her music. When she was pleased with life, when roused you might say, Elizabeth was a firework, captivating, exciting - yet always, potentially, dangerous. My father had not previously met anybody as volatile, as *alive*, as my mother. With her, he also came to life, I suppose, although we children would have loved him in his comfortable, sleepy state, I'm sure.

'I grew up not knowing how they might have met and, believe me, it wasn't easy to place them together anywhere other than Ramsons. I could imagine my father faint with admiration and my mother blind with hope but I cannot put this early couple in a landscape. They weren't given to talking about their relationship; their generation didn't consider the spreading of detail to be quite delicate. I assume, too, that they wanted to keep to themselves the time they had before their babies started to arrive. There was nothing wrong with that. What did seem to be amiss, or problematic at the least, was that Elizabeth continued to want Edward to herself long after she had produced his children.

'Of course, Dear, you are acquainted with us, his children, but humour me while I recount the order of our entrances. Jethro was their first-born, the only boy, or certainly the only boy to live more than a day or so. Then came Flora, my big sister (she was always big, I'm sad to say, always somewhat overweight, but she had a great heart, to match her size.) I was next, the third child to survive. From my beginnings, I idolised Jethro, a worship that made me a tomboy and distanced me from Flora. I expect you remember me and your Aunty Flora as the best of friends, living together in Ramsons when all the others had gone, running our school, sharing one dog after another. It took us years to achieve that harmony. Many years and more than our share of tragedies, I'm afraid.

'The child who followed me into the world was Evangelina, your grandmother. She was born to be Mother's favourite, no doubt about it. To begin with, Eva looked strikingly like Elizabeth, with reddish-gold hair and periwinkle eyes. She also shared many of Mother's characteristics, including a fearful temper. In one respect, they were not a matched pair, because Evangelina was a natural spy, whereas Mother had no interest in the activities of others. In fact, Mother shunned all company but that of her husband, an aversion that left her bored and out of sorts for the greater part of her life. Eva, of course, was never bored; how could she be, when the world contained keyholes and binoculars, when a glass against a wall or an ear pressed to a door could produce a harvest of information? A spy and a sneak, I'm sorry to say... but a beautiful child, pretty enough for any postcard, with her gold tresses, her little heart shaped lips. So charming, on the outside: she remained spotless, somehow, when the rest of us were in trouble for grass smears or ink blotches. I see sunlight on inconsequential clouds when I remember Evangelina: I see lace also, decorating a celestial creature, or one that has crept in, unbidden, amongst angels.

'Ultimately, there was Agnes, a late and not perhaps entirely wanted, addition. Lizzy, who was the family's maid for the greater part of our childhood, used to hint at Mother having attempted to *get rid of* the final fruit of her womb; and I believe Mother may have tried, with potions at least if not with other, more sinister methods, to end that pregnancy. Yet Agnes arrived unscathed, possibly to Elizabeth's surprise if not to her delight. Your Aunty Flora, then a girl of eleven, took one look at Agnes and found herself filled with love. She was to be Agnes's surrogate mother, in her way, when Mother was lost to us either in Father's company or in the act of awaiting his return, which is to say most of the time.

'I have leapt ahead of myself, an amateur story teller if ever there was one. I intended to travel back to the time before Agnes was born. (Now I come to think of it, the day I wish to recall may very well have been the day of Agnes's conception. How extraordinary to contemplate. I'm blushing, Dear, alone at my desk in the school room. Mother has never ceased to embarrass me, nor has she allowed me a night free from worry, not in all the years since she died.)'

At the mention of the school room, Gill thought perhaps she ought to look in on her children. She found they were both lying on the floor, on a blue patterned carpet that was so thin it was possible to see the lay of the flagstones beneath. Damp had merged the various blues of the carpet: Gill half expected to find her children's stomachs dyed in sky and sea tones when they rose. Adam was colouring on a piece of pink card, filling in what looked like a potato on toothpicks but which was, Gill appreciated, his version of a man. She assumed it was meant to be Seb; her heart went to her son in sympathy. When she studied Rosie closer, she seriously wondered if her daughter was alive. Rosie was pressed into the carpet, her face as immersed as possible in the worn wool. Gill tugged at the child and found, when Rosie's head was lifted, that she had been biting the carpet, inhaling it even. There were dog hairs stuck to the little girl's face, which was bathed in sweat. In a cartoon flash, Gill wondered what had become of Tricksey. The bloody dog might be alive and stalking them, secretly. The house certainly smelt as if he was ever present. Rosie now lay, face upwards, across Gill's lap, howling at having been disturbed. With a corner of her shirt, Gill wiped the child's face, removing not only dog hair but tears and a gathering of snot that might have suffocated Rosie had she been left a while longer. Gill considered telling her daughter off but what could she say? We don't eat carpets, lovey, they are bad for our tummies? The child's crying was aimed directly into Gill's face, a sound as devastating as an electric saw. Gill hauled Rosie up to her feet then lifted her on to a chair. "Stop that now," she said, ineffectually, "you're alright, you're lucky not to have died from swallowing dog hair and snot, but you didn't, so stop crying over nothing." Rosie drew breath and began a fresh round of grating noise; but then the phone rang, saving Gill from any obligation to stay in the same room as this onslaught.

The phone was in the passage, where those who used it were doomed to suffer from cold feet and crippling draughts. Maybe installing it there had been an act of economy. It was Seb phoning to let Gill know he'd arrived safely, that Edinburgh was still buzzing with the dregs of its festival. He hadn't been to his digs yet but they were walking distance from the theatre, and wasn't that lucky? She berated him for calling too soon. There would be a phone at his digs, most probably, she needed to know that number. It was essential for her to be able to contact him, at any time.

"Why?" Seb wanted to know. "Is anything wrong? Has something happened?"

Oh, what's the use, she thought. He was hardly in a position to help out in a crisis.

"Can I speak to the kids?" he asked, when she didn't respond.

"No," she told him, resenting his suspicion, "I chopped them into manageable pieces this afternoon and planted them amongst the fruit trees."

"Gill..."

"Adam!" she yelled. "Come here and convince your father that you haven't been propagated into next year's Orange Pippins." Adam hurried to the phone. By the time Gill set off to fetch Rosie, he was telling his dad how he'd missed school and would never make any friends now.

Rosie stopped crying when she heard Seb's voice. She didn't speak to him, as such, but she responded with endearingly emphatic nods of her head and even, at the end of her turn, with kisses into the mouthpiece.

"What was Adam on about?" Seb inquired when Gill reclaimed the phone. "He seems to think he won't be going to school after all. Has he been expelled already?"

"I didn't think it was fair to send him today," Gill explained. "He was shattered, so I let him go back to bed. Then I discovered that he believes each child in the land gets one day, and only one day, at school. He thinks he's missed his day. No education for Adam Murphy."

"So every time he saw a group of school children in Bristol, he believed they were having their day?" Seb marvelled. "I guess it makes sense, though, considering how many times we told him 'You'll be going to school one day soon.' He must imagine an endless flow of kids - some go to school when they are little, some when they're big…" Both parents would have enjoyed a longer conversation on this theme but Seb's supply of coins was running out. They each shouted "I love you'" as the line went dead and Gill added, too late, "Call me tomorrow."

Gill did try to make excuses for Rosie at bedtime. It was her first night without her daddy, she was bound to be upset. Also she'd been asleep for the best part of the day, perhaps she wasn't tired. Then, of course, the child had a throat full of carpet, but whose fault was that? Gill fed her, for God's sake, with perfectly nourishing meals. Throughout the evening she'd made a steady flow of drinks, most of which had been tipped, untouched, down the drain. And Rosie kept complaining. Nothing pleased this particular little girl; nothing but the undivided attention of her father. "I miss him too," Gill insisted, "as much as you, believe me. We'll have to work harder at being friends, won't we? Then when Daddy gets back, he'll see how good we've been and that'll make him happy, eh?" Rosie's lips began to tremble, she turned herself over, face down in her pillow and shook with grief. "Well," Gill patted Rosie's sorry head, "try not to suffocate yourself, Sweetie, and try to let Adam get some sleep, he's got school tomorrow, no matter what he believes to the contrary." She stood on tiptoe to kiss Adam goodnight; he was already sleeping, his face relaxed, his frown, temporarily, erased.

Although she wasn't ready for sleep, Gill took Tilly's first piece of writing into her bed where she could be reasonably warm and comfortable. Let's see, Gill thought, it was the day of Agnes's conception… never a moment's peace for our Tilly… blushing as she writes...

'It is early in the century, I am no longer good with dates... Let's say that I was seven, Jethro twelve, Flora would have been ten. Evangelina was an infuriating, exquisite five year old. So long ago. Consider the changes I have seen... The news these days is of nuclear war, of spaceships, for goodness sake. When I was a child, if an aeroplane flew over Staunley the entire population would run to their doors, necks craned, squinting at what seemed a flying ladder in an otherwise clear sky. I remember the first few motor cars to reach us here, cheerful, noisy machines, like boats on wheels, piled high with rugs, picnic baskets, the trimmings required for a jolly good day out. We girls were not permitted outside, in the street, to gawp (as Mother put it) or to caress the hot metal as other children did. We pressed ourselves against the windows of our house, gasping in envy, leaving a row of open-mouthed clouds on the glass. The village was smaller, quieter and prettier, of course, but not without its trouble spots: the pub over the way, the river in flood, the Ups and Downs, still quarried until the start of the Great War, exhaling a layer of dust across our hedgerows and our gardens.

'I remember a sense of being set apart, an early realisation of the divide between us, the Durrys, and the remainder of the village, the rest of the world. I never considered myself special, only somehow separate. We didn't mix. Apart from Jethro who went away to school, we had our lessons at home, courtesy of a steady flow of teachers who battled with Mother, lost, and moved on. On Sundays and feast days, of course, we attended church, trooping down the village street in our best boots, our smartest coats. Pretending to grandeur we had only half a right to claim. Throughout the service, Mother kept one hand outstretched on the wooden pew, ensuring none of us sat too close. Keeping a place for her absent husband.

'Beyond Ramsons, there existed a universe in which people were busy, wicked, ill-fated, entertained. A place both depressed by heavy fogs and lit by a million lamps. We read of it in The London Illustrated News, a periodical that combined tragic tales, usually set in poorhouses or on the banks of the Thames, with stories of romance and daring. We glimpsed this other universe on posters brought home by Father. It seemed peopled by scantily clad women and moustached men in singlets, their biceps bulging as they lifted lions above their heads. In the village shop, which has always been known as Mrs. Monk's, we saw images of children whose skin, black as boot polish, no soap could lighten. Along with arctic scenes, diagrams of human anatomy and blood-curdling illustrations of battlefields, our set of encyclopaedia introduced us to tribes of decorated, mutilated savages, their lips and necks stretched beyond endurance. We children frequently turned to these pages, fascinated and shamed by the private parts of natives, seen dangling indelicately in supernatural sunshine. What a world! I longed for it even as I dreaded it.

'Our real world centred around Father. He was our keystone, keeping us united as a family, although he was absent for weeks, sometimes months at a time. Without him, we lived slow, dull lives, or so it seemed: lives always on hold, as it were. The fact that I remember Ramsons as a brighter, warmer home when he resided in it may well be due to the lighting of extra fires, the burning of more lamps but we children attributed the increase in comfort to Father himself. He was that warm, that genial. Suspended between the cheerful or the humdrum days, were the hours in which we waited, knowing Father was on his way home...

'I am seven years old and I am aware that Father is expected at any minute. My stomach is alive with things that crawl. During breakfast, because I felt the tablecloth lift and fall like the sheet on a snorer's bed, I knew Flora was also infested to the point where she couldn't keep her legs still. Father: the house is a sponge, heavy with his name. Everybody is busy, except for me. My pleas for the usual beaker of milk are swept aside by Lizzy. The maid's flat, salmon coloured face is creased with effort as she pummels dough. The tip of her tongue sticks out between clenched teeth. She has hair that seems always to have been recently dipped in oil, but her hands are white as a lady's, due, she tells us, to her habit of rubbing lard into them several times a day.

'Dry mouthed, I climb the back stairs to my bedroom and the jug of water on my washstand. I have 'borrowed' a folding tin cup from Mother's picnic set. Since I keep this hidden under my vests, alongside saved remnants of soaps, drinks from this rust-spotted treasure are mildly flavoured with violet or gardenia. Drinking, and the more deadly sister sin of eating, in the bedrooms is not allowed. A hint of soap is nothing compared to the punishment I would suffer if the door were to open now, just as the water touches my lips. I drink quickly. I fold the cup, delighting in its concertina action. I return it to its leather case, a holder that reminds me of Father's collar stud boxes; but then, today all objects lead me back to Father. And I honestly do not know how this makes me feel, apart from the sensation of having a hive of bees inside my insides.

'Is there an air of secrecy to this day, or a space formed by something not understood? Something missing. After all, it has happened before, Father's coming home. This bubbling of expectations. And then his arrival: his bulk in the passageway, blocking the light. All his children lined up to greet him, waiting to be held against his camel's-hair overcoat or his light summer suit. To be squeezed against his stomach, which is round enough to require me to bend if I'm to comply with his shape. But, after the welcome... what happens next?

'Why, when I can remember Christmas and the slide towards the carol service in church, why can't I think what follows Father's greetings? And further back; I'll never forget last summer, when a bat flew inside the house, getting tangled in my bedroom curtains. Eva teething! There, I can even remember that. Cries, dribbling, bright spots of red on her baby cheeks. Eva is five now and has twin rows of razor sharp, white teeth with which she will bite anything, especially the arms of her sisters. It was long ago, the getting of those teeth, but I can still recall the slurping of her sore gums. Yet the last time Father came home is a blur in my memory, details erased into grey grubs, as if his homecoming was a sketch on which I have used an indiarubber.

'I contemplate the mysteries of being away from home, an experience I have yet to enjoy. Jethro attends a boarding school, for example, what must that be like? I believe I should prefer to receive my education at a distance from Mother. There would be a trunk, then, for me, similar to Jethro's. (His school trunk fills me with dread or delight, depending on the occasion of my stumbling over it.) My trunk would be packed with nightclothes, with stationary tucked into satin pockets. My boarding school is called Saint Catherine's Of The Wheel, my dormitory Magnolia. When I unpack for the start of a term, I find kindnesses from home, a cake, black as treacle, which Lizzie has baked, a notebook for Nature Observations, from Flora. Jethro has carved me a zoo, a collection of misfits, for the most part, with stunted legs and disproportionately thick necks. I hide these under my pillow.

'I am, you see, a romantically inclined child. A dreamer. There's a name for what I'm up to, not aversion – displacement, perhaps? On the Market Carney road, a carriage will be bringing travellers from the train station to the village. Meanwhile, I cling to my daydream, inventing rules, timetables, uniforms of blue serge trimmed with golden piping. In the highly polished atmosphere of Saint Catherine's, I make friends easily, becoming part of a clan of girls with names like Bunny and Reptile. We have a password, a secret code. We are a gang of pals.

'There I stand, where the lawns meet the woods, with Vixen and Oily, waving a school jumper over a small bonfire, as dull weather turns to drizzle. Worrying that Bunny and Retile may not evade old Smithers and manage to join us in this feast. In my mouth, the dried, warmed bread – one couldn't honestly call it toast – has stuck to my teeth. It has absorbed ashes that taste not sinister but of adventures yet to come. "Let us drink," I suggest, raising a tin cup filled with water from a stream, flavoured with crushed clover, "to our days here, amongst the chosen few." Vixen holds a marbled tooth-mug, Oily has a tiny teacup from Japan. We clink our assorted cups together and drink deeply. To think that bread and water can be so delicious. If my mother guessed at this, she would need to discover a fresh means of deprivation for her children.

'Despite the imminent homecoming, I remain with my gang by the dying fire. I allow a mist to roll over the school playing field, letting it creep in our direction until it engulfs us from our ankles upwards. We are not so much lost as invisible.

'So what if I do miss the instant of Father's arrival? It cannot make a vast difference, my absence in the hall, my failing to hug his paunch. Nothing connected with his return seems to matter, because the event is somehow shellow, or its heart has been scooped out. I struggle to believe in the school woods, to see, through my invented fog, the faces of my companions. Vixen has buck teeth. Oily suffers from problem skin. With every bit of my will, I try to remain in their company. But it's no use. A recent action has reminded me of a secret I was trying to unearth, a puzzle I wanted to solve. I feel I am within a breath of knowing more than I ought about my family: a knowledge that will obliterate the most substantial of daydreams.

'There it is, the first cry, from Jethro this time. Father is home. Every bannister springs to attention. Every floorboard tenses. Mother calls out, a sound keen enough to be an expression of pain. In the kitchen, Lizzie drops something metal and round. It rolls on the flagstones like a giant coin. Chiming clocks that mistook the hour would raise no eyebrows. Unmanned bells could ring without causing surprise. Right now, a trumpet fanfare would seem only fitting. Feet clatter on the back stairs, hurry down the front stairs, run through the house. Heading for the earliest peep at Father as he strides under the arch formed by the box hedging.

'I stand in my room, clutching the tin cup. Missing out. I will go down, soon enough. By then, they may be seated, ready for luncheon. The Durry family, smiling, excited, around the long table, with a parent at each end. Sun will shine through the French windows, warming a row of backs, lighting an opposite set of faces. There is a glow to this scene, in any case. It may be that Mother, usually a pale woman, will be rosy-cheeked and bright-eyed, as I have seen her on previous occasions when Father is home and the air itself enjoys good health. Somebody must say grace: Jethro, possibly, to show he's well on his way to manhood. Lizzie will bring the meat, Father will carve it. For a short time, the Durrys will talk, laugh, behave exactly as their neighbours do, here in the village and beyond, in a million other homes. But only for a while, I realize. Soon, with the clinking of glasses and the drinking of drinks, with the cheerful toast to Father, the well-being must end. A veil, more debilitating than any fog I have previously conjured, will fall over the Durrys, shadowing their sunshine. Robbing them of their memories.

'You may think yourself very modern, my great-niece, with your pop music and your discotheques. With your free love and your drugs. But we were well ahead of you; we started young, not through choice but on account of a parent gripped by a passion that drove her to misbehave. No matter if the day was sunny, the sky too blue to miss. We saw little of it, once lunch was cleared away.

'Have you grasped my meaning and can you see the connection with music? Were you listening when Flora and I spoke of Mother's sessions at the piano? How she played! In the evenings, when we woke and she and Father rose from their bed, she hustled us into the drawing room, threw open the piano's lid, and produced songs the Devil himself would've danced to. No soul could resist. Feet would tap, legs would itch to be up and on the move. As Mother's hair fell from its pins, as she swayed over the thrumming keys, we found ourselves almost airborne, so light on our toes, pliable, dainty, so darling were we.

'Flora once told me that the only time she felt herself to be loved by Mother was during those soirées around the piano, when she, like the rest of us, really danced to Mother's tune.'

The letter ended abruptly, causing Gill to frown. She'd been there, with her ancestors in the drawing room, held captive by Elizabeth's manic playing. When she registered her true position, propped against pillows on the bed, her neck felt stiff. Her eyes stung with tiredness, her head was heavy. She reached for the bedside light, a pink-fringed antiquity with a twisted brown cord and a Bakelite switch. Had Tilly's fingers curled over Gill's, or gently patted her hand as she flicked the switch, Gill wouldn't have been alarmed or even, she realized, surprised.

6.

But things have their own lives here.

It was the middle of the night; so deep in night's centre. But Gill, who had slept for an hour or two, was wide-awake. The dark was thick as felt in Ramsons; it made Gill think of the war. She imagined Tilly and Flora going about their business behind blocked windows. Peeling fruit, stitching tablecloths, doing decoupage while bombs were transported above their heads. Gill's mother, June, had told of a dog that went mad here in Ramsons, driven to distraction by planes and distant gunfire. Again, Gill thought of Tricksey, the last of Tilly's dogs. What had become of her? Or should that be of him? She wasn't sure.

When the family had arrived in Staunley for Tilly's funeral, there had been no sign of the dog. June had asked after him, or her. She'd inquired of Babs, who'd looked more of a film star than a daily help. An ageing but still glamorous film star, in high heels, fine stockings and a suit Dior wouldn't have disclaimed.

Gill considered what she knew of Babs, information she had gleaned through hints, nudges, half finished sentences, not unlike some misdemeanour in a television comedy show. Finally, at Tilly's funeral, last March, June had delighted in clarifying the situation for two of her daughters - only Gill and Sarah had been present, Kate being abroad, as she often was.

"She wants the house," June informed them, "so much so that she bullied Aunty into agreeing to change her will. Then Babs called our solicitor to Ramsons, and hovered nearby while Aunty discussed the changes. Babs was ostensibly bringing fresh tea and so on, while actually she was ensuring Tilly said the right things."

How appalling. How dare she? And, by the way, how did June know this?

"Aunty phoned me up me, that same evening," June explained. "The poor dear was quite upset - well, upset and elated. 'I tricked her,' Aunty whispered down the phone, 'I telephoned the solicitor as soon as Babs was out of the house and explained to him that it was a plot of hers. I told him to ignore all that had been decided over tea.' Apparently the solicitor wasn't surprised, he'd had his suspicions, knowing Aunty always intended Ramsons should stay in the family. He advised Tilly to keep up the pretence by hinting to Babs, from time to time, that the place was settled on her. He recommended this because he believed Babs might be a dangerous enemy. Suggesting ways in which Babs could improve the value of Ramsons, or means by which she might acquire an income from the house, became an enjoyable game, so Tilly said, over the remaining years." June had smiled at her children as she added, "Babs is about to be most unpleasantly surprised. She has no idea Aunty was capable of being so devious."

Gill searched her memory for a tear: one tear, on June's mildly wrinkled cheek. She saw a handkerchief, plain white cotton, held to the nose throughout the church service. She recalled her mother's head, lowered towards the grave, during the burial. At the sorry wake, a gathering in the village hall, an event devoid of music or comfort, June had sighed, "My last relation gone," much as if her daughters and her grandchildren were not the genuine article. But she had not cried. Not in public at any rate. Gill thought she'd only once seen her mother in distress. When their father had left, taking his golf clubs and a framed set of racing prints, June had run out of the house after him. In stockinged feet. In tears. Crying for him to come back. But on reflection this plea seemed to stem from anger rather than heartbreak. And what *had* saddened June, while coming to terms with the absence of her husband, was that as a single woman she no longer received invitations to dinners and events; she did mourn this, the death of her social life. She'd also been vexed by the fact that she had no idea how to handle bills, or anything electric.

What had Babs replied, when asked the whereabouts of Tricksey? Something evasive, no doubt. Gill pictured the dismissive swing of Babs' hair as she turned away from June. She recalled her mother, clutching a paper plate so hard that it bent almost in two, watching those insufficient hips with hatred. "Beware of that woman," June had muttered to her daughters "she may turn nastier than ever once she realizes she isn't about to rob us of our inheritance." At that time, the will had yet to be read. Gill had never been wholly convinced by the story of the solicitor invited to tea. But as she'd studied Babs, circulating gracefully from villager to villager, she had to admit the woman was dressed as somebody on the brink of becoming an heiress. Final proof of her expectations was evident by the way Babs returned to Ramsons once the funeral was over; in fact she walked up the street and in the front door alongside June and the solicitor. Gill and Sarah took themselves off to the graveyard, to study the messages on Tilly's floral tributes. The flowers presented a jolt of colour in the bleak afternoon. Hot-house tulips that seemed dyed in freshly spilled blood, creamy lilies, early purple irises. Although these blooms accentuated the mound over the coffin, there was perfusion enough, thankfully, to obscure the offending scar of freshly turned earth. Gill had found the soil upsetting in itself. It was heavy clay, cloyed by recent rain, not merely unwelcoming but unforgiving.

Back at Ramsons, June and Babs had been facing it out, apparently, at both ends of Edward Durry's great oak desk. Behind this oppressive, and impressive, item of furniture, sat Tilly's solicitor, a man used to dealing with death but saddened by the occasion none the less. He had rested one hand on his sheaf of papers while the other nervously traced a fading gold leaf pattern on the leather of the desktop.

"Babs and I were like a couple knights," June had later stated, dramatically, "preparing to joist. Lances raised, visors slammed shut." The word visor had conjured motorcyclists, rather then armoured knights, for Gill, and she had trouble banishing a pair of Hell's Angels from her imagination. But biker or knight, Babs had crumpled, bent for once from her angular shape to a rounded droop, when the will was read, when the blow was struck.

The last time Gill had seen Babs was as she stumbled from Ramsons, disappointed and furious, just as Gill and Sarah returned from the grave. There had been moments of extreme awkwardness as the three women sidestepped each other in a dreaded dance under the arch of hedging. It was imperative not to touch, not to engage in eye contact. By then, Babs had regained her sharp shape and held her chained handbag before her like a weapon. The heels of her shoes had also threatened, as did those elbows and even that hair, whipped by sheer fury to lethal, gleaming points.

And here Gill was, the occupant who had ousted Babs. If she should come across Babs, how would Gill behave towards a woman who wanted to take her place? By offering it on a plate, quite honestly. Anybody

fool enough to covet Ramsons now was welcome to it. But, anyway...
no Tricksey and no Babs, so far. Not that Gill had explored the locality
much, yet. She'd been to Mrs. Monk's shop once or twice, to be met
by hostile faces, both behind and in front of the counter. Disapproving
women, mostly, scowling at Gill's hair and at her booted feet. But Babs
hadn't been amongst them. Perhaps, dispirited by failing to secure the
house, Babs had grasped the dog, as a means of compensation, and
run off with him. They would now be residing in a small costal town,
taking bracing walks, twice daily, whilst plotting revenge.

Gill pulled up the covers and closed her eyes, hoping for another
spell of sleep. Behind her eyelids, her ancestors danced maniacally:
or they would have, had Gill allowed them free range. As it was, they
shot momentary images into the darkness, glimpses of throats flung
back, of smiles that were out of control. Elizabeth was most persistent.
Newly impregnated with baby Agnes, she appeared twice as large as life.
Trampling the piano's keys, her fingers were a chorus line of goblins.
Her body swayed, not keeping time with her music but rocking itself
to the rhythm of earlier lovemaking.

My God! Gill sat upright in the vast, sagging bed. She had just
realized that, in order to have things her own way, Elizabeth Durry had
drugged her entire family.

This truth had been less than half understood by Gill before, when
she read Tilly's words. Now she flicked on the light and looked again at
Tilly's closing paragraph. This time the meaning was clear: 'You may
think yourself very modern... with your free love and your drugs. But
we were well ahead of you.' The reason Tilly couldn't remember her
father's homecomings was because Elizabeth rendered her children
insensible each time. Then she must have enlivened Edward – and
possibly herself – so that she could whisk him off to bed for the
afternoon.

What a woman; Gill felt a thrill of genuine shock, as if she'd been
goosed by a passing stranger. To go to that extreme, for the sake of
an hour or two alone with her husband, would take courage and an
overwhelming passion. Not to mention foolhardiness. How could
Elizabeth have known whether or not she would cause permanent
damage to her children? Not only their bodies but also their developing
minds could easily have been scarred. Well, possibly Tilly would go on
to state this was the case; there was evidently much more for Gill to

discover. Drugs, no matter how well dissolved in glasses of cordial, or how carefully blended in celebration foods, have a way of becoming addictive, don't they? Gill remembered wanting to make another Herby Bake for herself and Seb in order that they might enjoy a second night of what could only be described as lust. Again she experienced a tingle of shock: was it possible that she had followed, by mere coincidence, a recipe of Elizabeth's? Might she have added the exact same pinch of this and sprinkling of that as used by her great-grandmother on the occasions of Edward's homecomings? In the depth of night, as she lay staring at the mottled ceiling, it seemed to Gill she had followed a trail when making the bake; she'd held a thread which Elizabeth had left for her to grasp and she had fingered this as a blind person fingers Braille, all the while obeying instructions. How could it have been otherwise? The effect of the bake had been precisely what Elizabeth seemed to desire. It had sent the children straight to sleep and energized the adults just long enough for them to make wild, uninhibited love. For the second time, Gill thought what a woman Elizabeth had been; only this time she admitted, along with the horror, to a sneaking admiration for the old witch.

If the drugs given to the Durry children had been habit-forming, Gill's great aunts might, in fact, have been addicts. Too tired to make sense of this, or to seriously consider its implications, Gill pictured Flora and Tilly gliding through the passageways of Ramsons, as if on castors. The skirts of their Liberty print frocks stuck out like open umbrellas. To disguise the castors, they wore built-up, black patent leather shoes, polished to glinting intensity. Pretending to be serene and affectionate, these drug-crazed women had - on closer inspection - the bland faces of porcelain dolls. Their smiles were slithers of pink paint, their nostrils specks of red, their eyes unseeing chips of semi-precious stones.

Gill turned out the bedside light. The darkness was as uncompromising as before, although this time Gill saw no images behind her eyelids. But there were sounds, rising and falling like blood in the ears. Notes, snatches of tunes from the old piano, travelling through Ramsons, along corridors, up both flights of stairs. The sounds grew clearer as she strained to catch them: music both tuneful and discordant. Ghost music, Gill told herself with a shiver. Songs for the recently stupefied, played by an obsessive. Heavy chords, then the lightest of trills, as if a

bird was fluttering over the keys. Now there was a bass accompaniment
- the stamping of feet, followed by whoops of delight. Then a voice was
added, a baritone, singing with gusto, with great good cheer: the song
of Edward Durry. Gill thought she would rather go deaf than lie in
that bed, listening to a fool sing, eavesdropping on the delight of a man
who'd been repeatedly duped by his wife. She freed one feather pillow
from the flock behind her head and covered her ears with it. How could
a talented, intelligent man like Edward Durry have failed to notice
that his family were given to strange behaviour? Instead of singing,
why didn't the idiot sit in silence, as the others played and danced,
and work out what in the name of devilry was going on? It was just
occurring to Gill that Edward may have known, might have been party
to his wife's mischief and have happily complied, when the music was
enriched by the cry of a baby. Agnes is born, Gill told herself from her
pillow tent. Another little mouth for Mother to manipulate.

It wasn't long lost Agnes, howling from the distant past, of
course: it was Rosie, crying for some comfort. When Gill reached her
daughter's bedside, she found herself as tired and grumpy as a person
who'd been suddenly woken. "Can't you ever let a soul sleep through a
night?" she asked Rosie, which was unfair because, in Bristol the child
had often slept well. Adam stirred on the top bunk, making the whole
contraption shudder. "See," Gill lowered her voice, "now you've woken
your brother and he's got to be a big boy tomorrow and get up to go to
school." The thought of a day without Adam made Rosie cry all the
more. Gill put a cold hand over her daughter's mouth, "Shut up, right
now, you hear me?" she warned. Then, guilty and ashamed, she began
to hum. She hummed 'Rock-a-bye-baby' and she hummed an old hymn,
'The Day Thou Gavest...' which had been sung at Tilly's funeral. Her
hand shifted from Rosie's mouth to her brow, where it smoothed away
troubles in a motherly fashion. But Rosie cried on, and relentlessly
on. "Sleep my little one sleep..." or else, Gill added silently, I shall
carry you away, down the back stairs towards the supply of 'herbs' on
the kitchen mantelpiece. Five minutes later, Gill was hissing at her
stubborn, restless child and feeling the need either to bang her own
head against a wall in frustration, or worse, to bang Rosie's. "I have
to go now, Rosie," she explained with enforced jocularity, "before I
hospitalise one or the other of us." She anticipated the pitch, higher,
and the volume, louder, of howls Rosie would release as she departed

- but she was wrong. It seemed Rosie wanted only peace, the end of humming, the cessation of brow soothing, in order to quieten and doze off again. "All I have to do, to placate you," Gill whispered from the doorway, "is to vanish, eh?" Well, vanishing was a trick Gill thought she might like to perfect, over the coming days and nights.

In the morning, Gill remembered how she'd felt, how her eyes had hurt and her mouth had been dried and sour, when Rosie woke. That memory turned the music and the dancers to mere dreams. Surely she had been asleep, then woken by her daughter's crying? Before she climbed out of bed, she considered the difference between imaginings and dreams; the more she tried to distinguish one from the other, the less of a distinction there seemed to be.

Once Gill was dressed, she shook Rosie gently. The little girl curled deeper into her bed covers. Gill left her for a few more minutes, turning her attention to Adam. He was floppy with exhaustion while his mother dressed him in his new clothes. "You're a bundle of rags, Adam," she told him. "Wake up and be my soldier, hey? Off you march now, to the bathroom." He obeyed, leaving Gill alone with Rosie. She studied the sleeping child and felt a disturbance, like a mild electric current, across her fingertips, over her forehead. It was nothing, she assured herself. Nothing to do with the possibility of pain, or even the vague promise of discomfort. She wasn't cross with Rosie; she would wake her, cautiously, and find little ways to cheer her. Cherishing words came to Gill, like drops of steadying medicine on her tongue: snug, solace, cosy. Mother and daughter would be snug together while Adam was at school. They would be cosy; chums. But she found herself incapable of touching Rosie until Adam returned, a skinny chaperone in a vest and new, navy trousers.

Holding hands with both her children, Gill was as nervous as an infant herself when she entered the school. Staunley Infants was an amalgamation of comely Victorian buildings and modern Portakabins. The First Years used a classroom in the original structure. To Gill, as she led him through groups of chattering pupils, Adam seemed smaller than any other child. Although his expression remained calm to the point of making him appear simple-minded, his grip on her hand was ferocious. In his classroom, Gill struggled to explain why Adam was a day late in attending and how he had got the wrong idea about school. The teacher, a man in his thirties, who would have been good-looking but for a skin complaint that reddened most of his face, nodded and smiled but was frequently distracted by the tugging of small hands, the pleas of piping voices. "Adam," he said, catching the new boy around the waist and turning him to face a corner full of toys, "come and see the Play Area with me, eh? Say Goodbye Mummy, see you later." Dismissed, Gill retreated. It seemed Adam was more interested in the Play Area than in keeping hold of her hand. Perhaps, when he understood that he was there for the whole day, he'd run, crying, down the passage, yelling for his Mum. Gill almost hoped to hear her son's desperate call hard on her heels. But Adam was obviously content: seduced by a hoard of Brio and Lego. She thought, not without a tinge of pathos, how fickle love could be, especially the love of the men in her family.

Ramsons seemed twice as chill and only half as full of life, without Adam. There was a new echo along the hall, the definition of loneliness. Gill helped Rosie to take off her sweet, miniature duffle coat, which was bright red and lined with rainbow-striped fabric: it made the child look like Paddington Bear. With her neck stretched, Rosie stared up at the assortment of jams and pickles in the glass cupboards. Gill opened a door and pulled out one dark jar. 'Pickled Walnuts' the label told her, 'Ramsons: November 1968'. The writing was the finest Italic, in dark green ink. Written with care - with love, almost. Holding the walnuts, bending to show them to Rosie, Gill had a sure understanding of what Ramsons had meant to her great aunts. She saw how it was that a house and a garden had been their entire world, how the building and its surrounding land had epitomised the universe, for them. Each day, with its various weather, must have held the same, not unwelcome, certainty. The women would rise, wash, dress, drink tea, eat toast. There would be post arriving on the doormat, milk bottles waiting on the step. Through the windows they'd watch birds in the back garden, they'd observe the progress of plants. Engrossed in their chores, the sisters must occasionally have smiled, buoyed up by the surety each offered to the other.

Staring into the jar of walnuts, Gill felt the extent of Tilly's loss. When Flora died, her younger sister must have heard this echo in the hall, felt the fresh layer of cold in the air. Seen yet another ghost.

Rosie put out a hand, reaching for the jar Gill held. "The brains of mice," Gill found herself telling the fascinated child, "kept for eternity in the juice that comes from boiling their little, furry bodies." Instantly, she regretted her words, remembering how Sarah had once told her that a single bowl of rice was the grubs of a thousand dung beetles, a lie that had caused Oriental dishes and plain English puddings to distress Gill for many years. Rosie didn't seem perturbed, only interested, as she gazed at the pickled walnuts. But Gill knew the concept of mice brains in boiled blood was likely to leap-frog over pink princesses and fairy castles, to invade a young mind in the dead hours of night, bringing Technicoloured nightmares. So why create the horror story? More importantly, why tell it to an impressionable not-quite-three-year-old? Because I can, Gill thought, and that just about puts me on a par with the dog that licks its balls. But it was true, she had this power, the upper hand, and she didn't seem able to resist using it.

Gill had never relished being on her own, except when she used to wander city streets, behind a camera. She stood at the top of the back stairs, which were steep enough for sudden flights to sudden deaths, and she cried "Seb," with all the air in her lungs. Drawing in breath, she added, "You bastard!"

Rosie tottered from the kitchen and stared up at her mother. Her legs were crossed, which meant she needed, or had just had, a wee. Gill tried to think where the potty was, where it had last been used. She should see to Rosie. There was washing to sort, there were beds to make. And somewhere history was waiting to be mulled over. What a number of chores needed to be completed, in order to survive, to stay dry, to remain safe. Might as well juggle plates on sticks, Gill told herself. The difference between coping and falling into utter chaos seemed little more than a thin, red bloodstain.

Not able to find the potty, she sat Rosie on the toilet and went to get Tilly's second communication from behind the photograph of the Durry family seated amongst the palms and pyramids of Egypt.

'Dear Great Niece,' Tilly began, 'I wonder are you still standing before the photograph? If so, please take a look at the smallest child, the little girl who balances, unsteadily, almost on the feet of her father. That is Agnes as she was approximately eighteen months after the episode I am about to relate. Few images of Agnes remain, which is why Flora and I knew this one so well that in our later years, we scarcely viewed the photograph at all.'

Studying the youngest child, Gill encountered a sweet-faced toddler with long ringlets of hair but who otherwise resembled Adam more than Rosie. There was nothing but fun in the child's eyes as they looked directly towards the camera. No trace of fear or foreboding. Gill caught the excitement of a day out: the trip to Spalding, the likelihood of treats to come. Edward was the only one not staring at the apparatus or the man behind it. Of course, being a celebrated man he would have been accustomed to having his photograph taken, Gill supposed, whereas it was a novelty to the others. Rather than appearing nonchalant, though, Edward was simply intent on the top of Agnes's head, Gill noticed. Tilly had said how fond her father was of his youngest daughter. His lowered gaze substantiated this and moved Gill, generations later, to think of her own father and of Seb.

'I will tell you this tale, on the whole, from Flora's point of view. I shall use the third person, for each part, from now on, anyway.' Tilly continued.

'It is the month of May, the month Flora loves best in all the year. This May is better than ever because she has a new sister. An innocent whose forget-me-not eyes see, as yet, only a blurred but cheery face when they look back on Flora. A baby who has no idea of judging or condemning. Hope wells in Flora like a carbonated drink; no stopper can contain it.

'"You're a regular little mother figure," Lizzie tells Flora as she nurses her sister Agnes. Agnes; Flora loves the weight of her, the sudden drop of her eyelids, the creases she has yet to grow into. She likes to watch Agnes asleep, podgy arms thrown backwards, mouth slightly open.

'"This is the day your mother shows her baby off," Lizzie explains. Lately Lizzie's face has grown patchy, dry and flaky in parts, glowing and threatening to erupt elsewhere. The result of having had her heart tampered with by the baker's boy, she says. Two nights ago, a may-bug tapped at the children's bedroom window. "That will be one of Lizzie's boils broken free," Matilda told her sisters, "streaked with lard and angry as a hornet." Evangelina, usually a brave soul, disappeared under her sheet, leaving not a tuft of hair exposed. The worst of it was that in the morning the may-bug was found to have left a deposit, very like something Lizzie's face might expel, smudged against the window.

'Today, you could file a fingernail on the rough area around poor Lizzie's nose. Flora, meanwhile, is looking her best. Pinched into a white cotton dress, with a collar of Belgian lace, she has clasped her frizzy hair back from a scrubbed forehead. For once, as she slides her gaze over her eldest child, Elizabeth nods approval.

'Now Flora hurries down the road, her mother's purse sweating in her hand. The ladies have arrived for their teas. Before being sent on her errand, Flora heard them coo over the darling Agnes, as they once did over her, she supposes... although she knows she was not a pretty baby. Nor was Tilly, come to that. "My little mouse," that's how Father speaks of Tilly, how he addresses her. He says it fondly, though.

'For once, Flora feels the advantage of being the eldest girl. It was to her Mother called when needing somebody trustworthy. "Flora, angel," she said, "would you run and find us more sugar for our tea, please." The visiting ladies had lifted their heads from the extravagance of lace in which baby Agnes lay, and their faces fused into a single appreciative smile for Flora.

'"If there is no sugar in the canister, you must go to the shop. You know where I keep my purse, don't you dear?" Mother had imitated the other ladies, stretching her mouth into a smile, for a moment. Then her eyebrows had met, like warning thunderclouds. Flora had no idea where Mother's purse might be but she knew when to retreat, when to look willing.

'Lizzie ought to have been dismayed, the supply of sugar should never dwindle to the last grain, as it had done. But she merely reached, absent-mindedly, for the purse on a high shelf, and flicked it down. Puffed with her own importance, Flora failed to grasp the significance of a cream horn, from which Lizzie was pulling out, and sucking, fingers full of cream.

'There is, Tilly decides, no use in climbing the walnut tree. In fact, she ought not to climb anything today. Over her dress, she wears a pinafore but twigs might still snare her hem or sleeves. The walnut is not thick with leaves yet, anyway, it always blooms late; but the fruit trees would give good cover. The Durry children have closed their minds to a certain part of the garden, where entry is forbidden. They know the consequences for disobedience. But the orchard is safe territory and it is worth risking a fall, as Eve did when she plucked her apple, since the temptations from the far side of the garden wall are strong today. Tilly can hear the boys' voices, the splashing of water in the stream. An occasional whoop of joy. She knows who they are, stripped to their waists, trousers rolled up so mud can ooze over their feet. William Stamp, with his shadowing dog. Paul Bettersely and his little brother, Eric. The bigger boys, Kenneth, Jack and their leader, Joseph Miller. So, knowing, why must she see for herself? What if they should catch her spying? At any moment, Eva may come running down the garden, calling Tilly, drawing attention. It is too risky, the dangers to her dress and to her dignity. The boys chatter, almost whisper, then call to each other across the stream. Tilly needs to see them, to eavesdrop on their conversation, to share the coolness of the water on their skins.

'Steadily she eases her body up, through the highest of the plum trees, to sit like an owl on a branch, overlooking the stream. She hardly dares to breathe but she can do nothing to quieten her heart. Below, the boys are on both sides of the water, running through it opposition, attempting to fell each other midstream. Their soaked bodies shiver, their trousers cling. Paul Bettersely has blood on an ankle, a flow he pretends, proudly, to ignore. As he runs, each boy yelps, sounds of war to scare the enemy, to encourage themselves. Nearby, a pair of blackbirds protest. It is little Eric's turn; while his opponent roars he gives the squeak of a captured shrew and the game ends with this, the smallest child, being lifted on his brother's shoulders. Tilly is jealous of the boys' bared chests, of their freedom to paddle, of this chance they have to yell with all their lungs.

'"I need a pee," Eric cries. He is dumped in the stream and is pushed back when he begins to wade ashore. A couple of the bigger boys tell him to do it there, for God's sake. The blasphemy strikes Tilly an invigorating slap. Simultaneously inspired, all the boys are now unbuttoning their flies. Egging each other on, all-together-now-one-two-three pee! Tilly cannot look; but she is compelled to watch a scene divided by her fingers as she half covers her eyes. Crude, shocking, breathtaking and unexpectedly beautiful. A cat's-cradle of sprays, from both sides of the stream, criss-crossing in the air. Six arcs of waters, rainbowing in the sun, rising to patter on the leaves of willow and hazel trees, falling to the ground, or on the heads of friends, or in the fur of Will Stamp's madly yapping dog.

'Flora keeps a tight grip of the sugar with one hand, a firm hold of her mother's purse with the other. She is returning to Ramsons and all is well. It's true, she isn't composed, not a cool-headed child running with pale grace towards the drawing room full of ladies; but she has done her errand, as required. Her face may burn but her courage did not fail.

'In Mrs. Munro's shop, Flora encountered a pair of women who seemed to think they ought to have been invited to greet the baby. They bent over Mrs. Durry's oldest girl, extracting information as if Flora was one of Lizzie's blemishes, to be squeezed until she burst. In Flora's dry mouth the request for sugar sounded almost bitter; and when she spoke her sister's name, Agnes seemed half-formed, damp clay waiting to be fully baked.

'"Agnes, is it? Nothing fancy this time, then?" remarked one excluded woman. "No more Evangelinas for the mistress of Ramsons." This made her companion rock on her heels and smirk. "What does this make?" wondered the first woman, "the fourth girl, is it not?" In Flora's world, adults were rarely rude; although she understood the insult, she was ill equipped to counter it. Yet she did manage to stress the word 'she' when confirming that Agnes was indeed daughter number four.

'Now, recalling those moments, Flora struggles home on cotton-wool legs. She is comforted by thinking herself a heroine, as she steps carefully around a puddle, as she jumps out of the way of Meg Finch who comes trotting by on that great grey horse of hers. Then she loses her balance, wobbles, needs to put out a steadying hand. Sugar or purse, which shall she sacrifice? Both her charges fly as she reaches forwards. She is heading for the edge of the road, where rough stones have collected. Flora's hands reach for their punishment, her body falls at an angle, sideways and backwards, into the puddle. There will he guesses where they are headed and he shudders for his sister.

'Tilly hears whimpering. Within feet of where she squats, a door slams. The wash-house.

'Tilly understands, although she has not had first-hand experience, as Jethro has. When Jethro took his punishment, Tilly was very small and must have been indoors at the time; but later she saw the expression on his face – fear, of course, but also disgust. Now she cannot help but picture Flora, cowering, shaking, anticipating pain.

'It is a rhythmic beating, slaps meet flesh in time to a tirade of complaints: "Your lovely frock. Your best shoes. Showing me up. I will teach you, so I will."

'Flora cries loudly, from pain and because this is unfair. Purse and sugar were unharmed; only Flora was damaged. Why damage her more? Another slap, bringing its smarting pain, and another, especially vicious... until Mother's energy appears to wane. The smacks grow weaker, further apart. They end. Flora snivels and wipes her sore hands on her front. Blood smears tramlines down her frock.

'"Good afternoon ladies," Jethro says. The guests are glad of the distraction. They feel uncomfortable in this house at the best of times; and then to be left with the baby and the best china... Here is young Jethro, all of twelve years old, being the gentleman, asking after their welfare. He throws open the French windows, making the wisteria bounce where it frames an inviting, green garden. "Why not take the air," he suggests, "since it is such a fine day?" He declines to join them, saying he has work to do. His plan is to get them outside, then to disappear. Mother must not associate Jethro with their escape.

'At the door of the wash-house, Elizabeth is rolling down her sleeves. The palms of her hands sing with guilt. Well, she supposes she is sorry. "Stay here until I say otherwise," she orders Flora. Unfortunately, she turns at this and sees the fresh stains of blood on Flora's dress.

'Elizabeth makes an animal's noise, grumble and roar, as she returns to Flora. Her fingers are talons with which to shred the hapless child. But just beyond the door Evangelina, who has seen and heard dreadful things this afternoon, things to provide ammunition in many future battles, hears the chatter of visiting ladies, understands that they are approaching the wash-house and emits a cry to echo her mother's. Stumbling from her hiding place amongst the hebes, she shrieks as if stung by a whole hive of bees. Tilly comes running. From the side lawn, the guests appear, bemused and anxious. Lizzie swallows the last sweet crumbs from her beloved and charges out of doors. Finally, silently, Elizabeth steps from the wash-house, spies the escaped guests, is quickly composed, suddenly concerned. She bends over her Eva and searches for wounded knees; she kisses, in extreme gratitude, the top of that russet head...

'Well, my dear, there you have but one example of the childhood we endured. I shall end with another: Lizzie fell pregnant by her baker's boy. When she finally plucked up courage to tell him he was about to be a father, she discovered he was delivering free cakes and pastries to another girl. He married his new love in unseemly haste, leaving Lizzie no choice but to inform Mrs. Durry of her plight. Strange to say, Mother appeared to have no objection to keeping a pregnant maid in the house; but the moment the baby was born she laid down the law. The servant could stay but the brat must go elsewhere. Lizzie, flat on her back, filled with a mother's milk and an equal flow of fresh love, pleaded and wept. Mother turned on her heels and left the scene. (Mother was a good customer to the shoe-mender in Market Carney; she had a way of walking with her weight full on her heels and often, as I said, turning on them to make a point.) Lizzie's child, a son called Norman, was brought up by his grandparents who lived, admittedly, in this village – but I doubt the proximity was much recompense to either mother or son, since our servant had precious little free time.

'We used to see Norman kicking his heels in the street outside Ramsons or popping his head over the back garden wall when he hoped for a glimpse of his mother. He was a blunt boy, in mind and body. His nose was not unlike a common field mushroom. Still, it was a shame to watch him fret for Lizzie.

'I shall write more before long; not that it matters to you when I put pen to paper, just so long as I finish these stories before the world has finished with me!

Until soon,
Your loving Great Aunt Tilly.'

When she had finished reading, Gill folded the sheets of paper, smoothing each as if doing so would ease any remaining pain. She was glad that she had no further call to hunt for garden implements, pleased that the bucket was dealt with and the spade put safely away. It would seem that there had once been something nasty in the woodshed, or in this case, something cruel in the wash-house. Gill assumed the incident Tilly described was not a solitary one; a woman with Elizabeth's lack of heart must have been frequently driven to envenomed behaviour. No doubt her children, or at least her female children, had lived in dread of their mother's sharp tongue, of her raised fist. Gill was brave enough to own the possibility that dread might be passed from generation to generation in much the same way as thick eyebrows or elongated chins. She knew June had been simply terrified of her mother, the dazzling Evangelina, a woman who had taken such a dive from grace that she was hurled from the position of favourite to that of being unmentionable. And Gill, in her turn, had known what it was to flinch from June. Like Elizabeth, June found dirt offensive, had been rendered unreasonable by soiled socks or jeans that had rubbed against the chain of a bicycle.

Well, Gill was not about to win any prizes in the motherhood stakes herself... My God! She had quite forgotten Rosie. The child had been sitting on the toilet for hours. She cried "Rosie? Rosie?" as she rushed from the breakfast-room, under the beaming Cedric, up the front stairs. The answering silence was charged with flash-photography images: a limp body, a casualty ward, a woman at whom society wanted to throw stones.

Rosie was still on the toilet, her bottom having slipped down so far that her knees made a table for her chin. She was talking very quietly to Mr. Tibbs, who seemed to be there by magic, like a conjurer's rabbit. The stuffed cat's head was very close to Rosie's mouth, this was clearly a conversation for his ears only.

"Rosie," Gill said, kneeling in front of her, "it's time to get off the loo now. Come on, up you get." She thought of corks in bottles and of the old cup-and-ball games as she eased Rosie from the bowl; but the sound that accompanied Rosie's rise was the small, wet farting noise a spoon makes in a new jelly. Rosie giggled and so, as relief flooded through her, did Gill. There was a deep indentation around Rosie's thighs, a red weal that might well sting and hurt. Gill reached for the tub of cream to soothe the skin, praying that Rosie would remain in otherwise good health, dreading what a doctor or nurse would have to say about this tell-tale circle. Then she saw the pooh Rosie had done, the first ever to land directly in a toilet bowl, and she hugged her little girl, praised her, reassured her.

With her daughter on her knee, Gill sat on the top stair, smelling the child's hair, promising herself she would never behave like her ancestor, Elizabeth. Rosie should not know fear; certainly she mustn't experience anything related to dread of her own mother. Gill may have thought apprehension inherited, but she was far from admitting that cruelty could also be inherent – even if the two emotions were inseparable; and even if a person did have a string of unfeeling predecessors.

Rosie's curls tickled Gill's nostrils; how sweet she was, when relaxed like this, when held firm. Gill had always wanted a girl child, had spoken, as early as her teens, of the daughter she would cherish, planning to make crazy, bright dresses for this poppet. She had envisaged herself and her little girl, hand in hand, window-shopping in contented agreement. (In having a daughter, Gill had somehow surpassed Sarah, who was mother to a pair of boys and who had also yearned for a girl, although she never would admit this.) It was yet to come, of course, that companionship, the adoration of the girl for the woman, the shopping, sharing, being friends. Gill's arms tightened round Rosie, who had sagged sleepily on her mother's lap. "Are you Mummy's friend now, Rosie?" Gill asked. "Are we going to get on like a pair of houses on fire?" The little girl's legs gave an involuntary jerk, as if jolted from a set position of hostility to one of amnesty, or so Gill liked to think. Over her daughter's shoulder, Gill studied these short, stocky legs, in their woollen tights, which were a glorious shade of Hollyhock pink. She wondered where these limbs might take Rosie, on their life's journey. The tights were beginning to bobble and, across both knees, they had grown thin and wrinkled. Gill pushed her body forwards, crushing Rosie's torso so that she might caress the legs better, easing away the very idea of hurt. Rosie stood, cross and bothered at having her peace disturbed; Gill was warmed by her belligerence. For once, as Rosie clomped down the stairs, the stamping of small feet was nothing less than a comfort.

It was time to fetch Adam from school, before Gill had even considered what to have for lunch. Having dressed herself and Rosie in thick coats and woollen scarves, Gill was stupefied by bright sun when she tugged the front door open. It was a lovely day. Fresh air rushed to her lungs, giving her an inkling of what sailors might experience, emerging from submarines.

As she pulled the door shut, Gill thought how serious Ramsons had become, when it had been a place of fun for her on previous occasions. Perhaps only an effort was required; putting a cloth to the windows and paint work might rectify much, dispelling the dust that was coating the prettiest of weathers. She toyed with the possibility of replacing each heavy velvet drape with a floral print, something by Laura Ashley whose sprigged designs seemed made for Ramsons. June couldn't object to that change, could she? Surely if an alteration was an unequivocal improvement... Rosie gave a sudden shriek and Gill looked down to find her sprawled across the pavement. She had unravelled her scarf and tripped over the damn thing. Gill turned her daughter right side up, to find real tears on her cheeks and a graze, which was just beginning to bleed, embroidered across her nose. Rosie's left knee now peeped through the pink tights, displaying a gash; it was the shape of smile but it was angry and red.

They were shouting distance from the school gates. Rosie's cries brought a mob of mothers to the scene. The attention was the last thing Gill wanted but Rosie was thirsty for those cow-eyes, that mummer of concern. "Whaaaa..." she went, playing to her audience. "Whaa, whaaa, whaaaa..." A call that was answered, mother by mother;

"Oh the poor mite, she's really hurt herself, hasn't she?"

"Let me see that knee, Darling, oh what a shame!"

"I've got a sweetie for a brave little girl. Here you go..."

Gill stood over her injured daughter, a mute giant. No Fee, Fi, Fo, Fum for her today. She tried an odd umm, and she managed to tell one woman Rosie's name, when asked, but conversation was lost in the ruddy throat of Rosie's upset.

As Adam appeared with his arms full of drawings, Gill was reminded how much was expected of her, now that she had given birth twice. Not only was she supposed to nurture her children, bodies and souls, she seemed also obliged to join the club of motherhood and practise its language. She knew the women surrounding her expected a flourish of exclamations, the odd hello-my-clever-darling for Adam, then a few whoops-a-daisies, a couple of deary-me's, rounded off with an up-you-pop for Rosie's performance. To truly belong, she should kneel on the ground, her troubled eyes level with Rosie's injury, and demonstrate genuine, but mildly amused concern. Gill actually appreciated the precise extent of the permitted amusement; she wasn't incapable of shining, she simply chose to inhabit her own fog. Besides, she hadn't so much as a hankie about her person, with which to wipe Rosie's sneer of a gash. When Rosie let out a monster wail on seeing her brother, frightened, presumably, of losing the ground she had so painfully gained, Gill could happily have accompanied her. She missed something she had never known, an animal's freedom to make an exhibition of itself. Wolves were better off, Gill decided. Having thrown her head to the sky and howled until she hurt, a mother wolf could simply pluck the injured cub by the scruff of its neck and trot away from the pack. Gill did, in fact, yank Rosie rather roughly by the back of her coat, until the child was standing, a bit bloodied and not a little snotty, on her shaken legs. "There," she said, purposely omitting the repeat, "it's not so bad, is it?" Rosie was silent, although she managed what seemed a most accomplished sniffle.

The commotion had flushed Babs from her lair. She was waiting under the box hedge, almost bent in anticipation of succeeding at motherliness where Gill had failed.

Before the blasted woman could so much as call a greeting, Gill swung her children around as if they were bags of shopping at the ends of her arms. Rosie stumbled but Gill hauled her upright and more or less dragged her down the road, away from Ramsons and Babs. Where could they go? The shop was both tiny and unfriendly; they hadn't met anybody on whom they might call; there was no café to visit for warming drinks. The three of them hurried on, Adam asking why, why, why, Rosie maintaining an injured bleat, Gill hissing through her teeth.

"You never looked at my pictures," Adam pointed out, "I did three, but now they're getting bent." He stopped, in spite of the tug at his hand from Gill, to rearrange the pile of coloured papers lodged under his arm.

"I'll see them as soon as we get home," Gill promised, her throat contracting on the word home, since she felt, thanks to Babs, more homeless than ever.

"But we're going away from home," Adam moaned.

"Yes but look," Gill offered, inspired by a watery glimmer in the distance, "we're nearly at the river. Did you know Staunley had a river? We might see boats on it, eh? Or swans." Adam cheered at these prospects; boats were his first love – with swans a close second.

The trio lined the river's edge, studying their rippled reflections. There were no swans gliding on the thin, grey flow, but there was a single rowing boat, moored to the far bank. The red with which it had formally been painted was now a chipped and well-washed pink, through which the letters P, E and W were still legible. "It might once have been called Peewit," Gill suggested. Whatever its name, Adam could happily have thrown himself into the water to reach this prize, had Gill not held him back. "How *do* we get across, then?" he wanted to know. Gill shook her head, having no idea. The river had been out of bounds to her when she was a child. The mention of it used to send a chill through Ramsons, much as if the water itself was threatening to seep over the flagstones. Well, there are always stories, where rivers run through villages. Gill clutched the hands of her children tighter than ever, pulling them back until only her reflected head was visible in the water.

Adam wasn't ready to leave. He sat on the grass and spread out his artwork, under a clear sky. Gill sat too, taking Rosie on her lap. "This one is our new house," Adam explained, his grubby finger on a square of yellow broken by smaller squares. Our new house! Gill thought, smiling at the top of her son's head, where his hair grew in many directions, like clumps of wild oats. Gill thought of Tilly, then, of how she'd known every grass and moss; of how delighted she'd have been, to see Adam's picture of Ramsons. "This one is our car," Adam continued, his hand moving to a fairly recognizable portrait of the Morris, complete with moon faces in every window. "And this is the dog," he finished, pointing to a series of triangles on sticks. "What dog?" Gill asked, automatically. "The one that should be there," Adam answered. He traced the angular outline of this beast. "The dog that goes with our new house."

No cloud passed over the sun. There was no sudden drop in the temperature; and Gill didn't so much as shiver. But she thought she felt the finest layer of ice steal over her bones, settle there, begin a slow process of numbing and freezing her from within. Had she and Seb spoken of Tricksey in Adam's hearing? Gill genuinely could not remember. Could Adam possibly have sensed the presence, or ex-presence of Tilly's last dog? No, that was unthinkable. Worse yet was the chance that he'd found doggy remains, somewhere in the be mud on her now and there will be blood.

'The jump Tilly makes in order to descend, lands her in a clump of the ramsons for which her home is named. The air fills with the scent of crushed garlic. How could the boys fail to notice this? She squats in the white flowers and their stalks flavour her feet. Adjusting her clothing, she considers being discovered; six pairs of eyes will watch. Having clambered up the wall, twelve sets of grubby fingers will cling on, their owners not wanting to miss such a sight. She shifts herself until she is facing the wall, defiantly. Then she urinates.

'In truth, Tilly assumes nobody sees her. Her action makes little noise. It's impact seeps, almost instantly, away.

'Mother opens the drawing room door just as Flora is sneaking by. Unfortunately, a visitor is making an early exit, standing behind Mrs. Durry. This lady sees Flora and notes the state of her. There is nothing else for it: Mrs. Durry pulls the child towards her body. Flora, naturally, stiffens. As the hug does not have the desired effect, Elizabeth bends at the knees and faces Flora eye to eye. "You fell?" she asks in a voice as unfamiliar to her daughter as the hug had been. Flora nods. Tears prick her eyelids. She holds out the purse and the twist of sugar, both relatively unscathed. "Poor soldier," says Elizabeth, handing the sugar up to the watching guest, as if the woman was a servant. "Your dress is ripped and soaked, I see," says this transformed mother, "and your shoes will never be the same again." Oh well, her tone implies, as long as you are safe... For a second, Flora is stupefied enough to be taken in; her mother is converted to an angel of mercy, kneeling before her, smiling, wiping away the first tear.

'Elizabeth stands, excuses herself saying she must ensure Flora is unhurt. Will her guests please help themselves? She is holding Flora's hand but once they are out of sight her grip shifts upwards, tightening about the child's arm. Flora begins to panic, tries to stick her feet to the spot. Elizabeth drags her daughter along the passage to the door at the garden end, a door that is seldom used. Cobwebs brush them as they trail under the balustrade. They pass a furtive Lizzie, chewing in her kitchen. They travel paths, between shrubs and flowers. Jethro, home from school on a weekend exeat, spies them from a bedroom window;

overgrown garden. Gill didn't believe her son was the sort of boy to go digging about like a stunted archaeologist and not share any finds with his parents.

What harm might already have been done to the mind of this child? And how much more was he expected to take, before moving out of shadow into a better, brighter place?

"There is no dog that goes with our house," she said, her voice not achieving the lightness she aimed for. "Maybe you mean you'd like Ramsons to have a dog in it, is that it?" And Adam, looking his mother straight in the eye, with intuition beyond his years, nodded. It was the most altruistic movement of his young life; both mother and son appreciated that.

When they stood, to make their way back, Gill knew her body had adopted the coating of ice; she would never again be entirely free from it, never again feel, essentially, warm.

7.

tracking
prints of their heels across our blurred carpets.

Gill was turning day into night. Because she lay awake for most of the dark hours, she found it impossible to get through a day, while Adam was at school and Rosie played or dozed, without sleeping for some of the time. She fell asleep all over the place, at the kitchen table, on any reasonably comfortable chair, on the bottom bunk bed. Once she curled up on top of a collection of dresses and dreamt she was running through French meadows, fleeing the advancing German army. Too many floral prints, she realized, on waking.

The danger to Rosie, being abandoned while Gill slept, seemed balanced, in Gill's mind, by the child having, consequently, a more humane mother. When tired, Gill struggled to keep her temper at bay, snarling and retreating, like a chained dog. Her anger was an old enemy, one both she and Seb dreaded - it had driven faults, like canyons, between them on occasions in Bristol. When visited by fits of temper, Gill was beyond help, beyond reason. In Ramsons she believed she saw glimpses of this terror, her own anger, lurking, waiting, playing a cruel hide-and-seek with her. If she closed her eyes at night, the temper took shape, appeared almost tangible, a presence entirely red, a demon with a mouth by Munch, in a setting of pure Bosch. So she snatched rest at every daylight opportunity, parachuting into psychedelic landscapes inhabited by people known, unknown, beloved and abhorred. Often she would wake, chilled and stiff in the limbs, to wonder where she was and then, on comprehending, what the hell she was doing there, on a stack of feather pillows in a damp bedroom in Lincolnshire.

When her period came, she hugged an old stone hot water bottle and fell asleep believing she now knew how it felt to be entombed.

Although she never quite missed collecting Adam from school, she had several close calls. School ended at three-fifteen. One afternoon

Gill was woken just after three by a sharp knocking at the window. She thought immediately of Babs, cursed woman, always there, on any horizon; not unlike Gill's propensity towards bad temper. But it couldn't be Babs of course, because the window, on which the tapping persisted, was an upstairs one. Gill pictured Babs attempting to climb a ladder with her talons for nails and her knitting needle heels, catching in every rung. The image cheered her. Maybe it was a window cleaner; perhaps Tilly had booked a regular one and his visits hadn't been cancelled, although this seemed unlikely considering the grime on the panes. Gill rolled off the bed and went to solve the mystery.

It was a bird, its black beak trying, with determination, to crack the glass and gain entry. Gill saw the feathers of this bird, then an eye. A magpie, its blue gleaming officially, like a policeman's helmet – as if it had every right to intrude. "You'd only regret it, mate," Gill muttered, waving the pest away. The bird shot a parting glance at Tilly's dressing table, on which lay the contents of a cigar box Gill had been sorting. Tat, mostly - but bright, shining tat. Hat pins, hair slides and those curls of gold coloured metal used by women of a certain age, a certain class, to keep scarves tight around their necks. Gill had an impulse to heave open the window and toss the rubbish out, into the mouths of passing birds. But turning, seeing the clock, she realized there was time for nothing but her own flight, to school.

Since Rosie's stumble outside the gates, the child had become a favourite with the mothers of other children. They didn't appear to mind how snotty her nose was, how sullen her brow. They smiled radiant, maternal blessings on her and asked, twice daily, whether she was all right, being good, having a lovely time in that big house of hers? It was only when one woman put a similar question to Gill, wondering if she was settling in to Ramsons and not finding it a bit on the oppressive side, that Gill became aware of the extent of her wretchedness. She had invested a deal of energy into being anti-social, priding herself on the sparseness of her responses, the speed of her withdrawals. Now, avoiding the eyes of her current inquisitor, she could have wept for the waste.

If only this were a street in Bristol, with children of many colours and mothers to match. All right, city parents might be besotted with their kids too, but they spoke also of music, exhibitions, marches against injustice, where to buy decent fruit, what the council was up to, what was happening at the local arts' centre - and Gill hungered after those topics, more than she would ever have thought possible.

Yet here was a woman, asking after her in the best way. These were only mums, caring about their little ones. What was so ghastly about that? But Gill noted the feet of this particular woman, in such bloody sensible mustard coloured lace-ups. The woman's legs were confined within appropriately straight, beige trousers to which Gill could never warm.

How would she react, Gill wondered, if I told her the truth? I am wakeful at night, cold, miserable and afraid. Then I let my toddler daughter play with whatever is at hand, kitchen utensils, sewing boxes, garden tools, while I lie, my mind full of weird imaginings, asleep throughout the day. There is no heating in 'that big house of ours', save a terminally temperamental Rayburn and a few blocked fireplaces. I have not cooked one decent meal since my husband left for a poorly paid job hundreds of miles away. The place is stuffed with the rubbish of four generations, interspersed by the occasional priceless treasure. An obsessive ex-charlady is trying to get in and harass me into signing the house over to her, or so my family would have me believe; though why she wants the dump I can't fathom. There must be thousands of insects per inch to Ramsons. There may be mice or even, who knows, rats roaming the corridors alongside the ghosts of Durrys past, not to mention the dog... oh, no let's not mention the damn dog. Grime is thoroughly at home there, while I most certainly am not. What's more, my ancestors, far from being the extemporary pillars of society they convinced the village they were, appear to have behaved very badly indeed, and now they insist on sharing with me each detail of there soiled lives, every misdeed, each crack of the whip and blow of the hand.

Rosie was nestled between Gill's feet, wearing a pair of boots the exact same red as her mother's. Both sets of boots clashed with Rosie's pink tights in a way Gill found excruciating and endearing. "Ramsons is fine," Gill muttered, not to the sensible lace-ups but to her own clumpy footwear.

Adam arrived in time to save his mother from more of this sparkling conversation. He held in his out-stretched arms an item fashioned from the innards of toilet rolls and the tops of milk bottles. "It's a spaceship," he explained, pre-empting his mother's question. What a wise child,

Gill thought; he has the measure of this parent, all right. No doubt he also foresees that the spaceship will join the existing exhibition of cardboard objets d'art on the kitchen windowsill, there to block out the meagre remains of daylight and soak up the rising damp. "It's lovely," she assured him, plonking a kiss on his solemn head.

"We have to go shopping," Gill informed her children. As anticipated, Adam groaned. "We must," Gill said, wondering from whom he had learnt his standard, male reaction. It had always seemed to her that Seb enjoyed buying things; he was certainly better at spending money than making it. The first of his pay had arrived in the post that day - hardly a fortune. They might shop but they would not be feasting. "Or maybe we shouldn't bother, eh?" While speaking, Gill was persuading Rosie to sit on the back seat of the Morris. "No, let's not bother to shop, boring old shopping, who needs it? We can live on the fruits of the garden, squashy apples and rotten plums, and we can catch bugs and fry them for our main course, how about that?" Adam was shuffling his bottom close to his sister's, but he paused to give a dutiful grimace. "Right," his mother grinned. "Mind you," she muttered, mostly to herself, "first we have to get this rust bucket going."

When started, the Morris gave a fair impression of a patient in a TB ward, then it was ominously silent. Gill slammed the driver's door with extra emphasis before pulling her petulant children from their back seats. "A reprieve," she said to Adam, who understood her not one bit, "we shall shop right here, in this, the village of my own folks, just as generations of Durrys have done before us." All the way down the street she continued to twitter in this way. Twitter was one of June's words, of which there were many, employed specifically for Gillian. Sarah was incapable of twittering. Kate's life ran too smoothly to require it. But Gillian, messy, disorganized girl that she was, created her own flock of starlings, noisy and argumentative, squabbling around her on occasions like this. "Not for us the bright, warm aisles of a brand new Tesco," Gill moaned as they approached the village shop, "so undeserving are we that this, the humble Mrs. Monk's, shall be our lot, not that we can afford a lot, come to that..." And even as she held the door open with a red boot, she was mumbling to the fresh air that swept in and the stale air, tainted with tired cheese, aniseed and human sweat, that staggered passed her nostrils.

It was possible that the woman slumped over the counter was the same, once upright, figure who had served Gill and her sisters when they'd wanted gob-stoppers and sherbet dips; but if so, her good humour had gone the way of her posture. Where was the cheery smile that had greeted little girls with pennies to spend? Cremated in a dental incinerator perhaps, leaving those thin lips no choice but to remain clamped over the dentures they hid. By comparison with the shop-keeper, Gill felt positively exuberant. And highly superior in the art of being polite... Her requests for bags of flour and tubs of margarine were met with sneers, as if the server found it most unlikely that Gill would ever actually bake anything. The woman's shoulders tensed when Gill asked for ground, rather than instant, coffee. Her eyes widened in mock disbelief when Gill said she wanted uncut, wholemeal bread, although there was one such loaf among the sliced whites, lonely as a grizzly in a sloth of polar bears. Not an item was handed over with good grace; the shop-keeper managed, in a manner Gill had grudgingly to admire, to show condemnation of, disbelief in or aversion to her customer's entire shopping list, without once opening her malevolent mouth. Finally, the bill let her down; with a sigh, she did open her mouth to ask for the required amount of money. "And does your little girl want that?" she added, indicating, with a jerk of her head, Rosie and a naked, plastic doll. The toy swung from Rosie's chubby fingers by the top of the see-through bag in which it had been incarcerated. As dolls go, and Gill had never been fond of them, this was the ugliest she'd encountered. Its orange body was bloated, blown up to some deluded Third World designer's concept of cute. Its arms were moulded to its torso, while the legs were tightly together, with a superfluous flap of flesh coloured plastic hanging from the feet. Under a slick of painted hair, between balloon cheeks, lurked two pinpoint eyes and a nose that would have been more at home on a toy pig.

"No," Gill twisted the bag from her daughter, "she has plenty of perfectly lovely dollies already, don't you, sweetie?" Desperate to leave before the storm broke, she held Rosie firmly with one hand while counting out money with the other. It seemed she was winning; they were making their speedy exit, when Rosie began to cry. Well, so be it, Gill thought, children do this, it's nothing out of the ordinary; although she felt blood rise to her face at the idea of giving the shop-keeper yet one more reason to gloat. Rosie went limp, her body aiming for the ground. Why, Gill wondered, couldn't she be upset on her feet, like other children? Why does she always have to lie, a giant woodlouse, waving her arms and legs in fury and making a one-toddler show of herself? "Get up," Gill warned her, "and shut-up." The shop-keeper came to the door, tutting and shaking her head. Gill knelt on the pavement beside her puce-faced daughter and whispered for her to hush, or else. Rosie screamed on until Gill hauled her up, over a shoulder, and began to carry her home. The shopping was heavy enough to strain Gill on one side while the child kicked and hit out at the other. More than a few painful steps had been taken before she realized Adam wasn't keeping up with them. They were a safe distance from the shop, so Gill set Rosie down and waited for Adam to catch up. When he drew near, he stopped walking, his head on his chest, his space-ship decomposing in his arms. Gill nodded at him, understanding how he felt. He wanted none of it. He couldn't be seen to be with them, execrable as they were.

She boiled him two eggs for his tea, taking care to ensure that his platoon of Marmite soldiers edged his plate in a well-drilled circle.

When Gill returned from taking Adam to school the next morning, she found a plethora of post on the doormat. Not having slept during the night, Gill's head was sore and her eyes stung as she peered at the communications in her hands. There was a letter from Kate, who was in Japan and who seemed, consequently, as alien to Gill as any science fiction character. The airmail envelope was the colour of the skies that divided them. Had its designer intended to imitate that precise blue, Gill wondered. Amongst other things, Kate said she was due back in Britain soon and she would have to 'pop up to Staunley to claim what is rightfully mine!!!' The exclamation marks annoyed Gill even more than implication that she, the greedy sister, was coveting the clutter in Ramsons: Kate's punctuation showed her for a coward. Why did she say something, and pretend not to mean it?

June had also written, on blank typing paper, to ask what Gill intended to do for Christmas this year. Christmas!! Gill thought, making exclamation marks of her own; how the hell was she supposed to plan that far ahead? She didn't yet know if Seb would be here, his contract might be extended, he certainly seemed to be popular up there, in the land of castles and kilts. June suggested that *(a)* Gillian and the children might like to spend Christmas with her, although her flat was tiny, really, and her oven not quite up to tackling a decent sized turkey. Or *(b)* They could all congregate at Ramsons, getting together for a jolly good family Christmas, just as the Durrys used to do, under that one, special roof.

For a while, Gill paced the downstairs rooms, June's letter in her hand, filling the place with her living relatives. Hosting this great gathering, the old house buzzed as folk laughed and chattered, as presents were given and fairy lights prettified damp patches and turned cobwebs into decorations. Gill pictured herself, wearing a festive pinny, making mince pies, revealing a masterpiece of a cake, pouring egg-nogs. For once, her father was included, having been persuaded to leave his second wife elsewhere; Dad would be on good form, clowning and telling his weak jokes to anyone who'd listen. And Seb was home after all. He was entertaining all the children, a troupe that included his nephews and nieces, Sarah's two, Rosie and Adam and a couple of extra cherubs Gill's imagination threw in for effect. Fires blazed in newly swept fireplaces, seasonal music played from the ancient wind-up gramophone, children giggled, adults kissed under mistletoe, old folk nodded with satisfaction, seeing things done the way they had been done in their young day.

If only, she thought... Of course, her parents were separated, so she would need to put them in separate rooms. Since they didn't communicate, really, in anything resembling a civil manner; they might have to be kept apart at all times. The logistics of this consideration were tangled as the plot of a farce. What about meals? Were they to have trays sent in to bedrooms, as if Ramsons was a hotel? And there was the question of washing, of toileting. There would have to be a system of shifts. But they might collide unexpectedly... An atmosphere built up, behind the tinsel, beyond the sparkling tree of Gill's imagination. A familiar heaviness fell upon the paper chains, causing them to droop. Childhood had been spent with this intruder spoiling each celebration; Gill wasn't allowing her children to feel its presence, to dread its touch. As make-believe lights were extinguished and fires turned to ashes, ghosts seemed to grin at Gill: they'd been there all the time, of course, in hiding. They could have told her that Ramsons had long since seen the last of its great family Christmases. The effort required to transform Ramsons back into that warm, glowing home was more than a mountain to climb, it was the landscape of epic fiction, wasted, war-torn, frozen, insurmountable. Gill nodded to her ghosts, admitting defeat.

There were a couple of bills, with which Gill fanned her face, not having any idea what else to do with them. Seb's money wouldn't stretch to pay them: besides, why should it? One was for work done on the garden, weeks before Gill had moved in. So presumably Man had retired and Tilly had employed a firm to clear the worst areas. The other was the cost of Tilly's funeral – a staggering amount, or so Gill thought. She'd have to reply to June, saying no to both the Christmas options and forwarding these bills; not a pleasant prospect.

There was also a third letter from Tilly, which was not only morbid but ironic, under the circumstances. Gill tucked this into a pocket, to be read when she was feeling more cheerful - although, she owned, that might not be for many a day.

But the very next item of post did cheer her. Inside a pink envelope was a pink card showing a cradle in a treetop. Jon and Bella were now the proud parents of a baby girl. 'We are thinking of calling her either Tamsin or Jasmine,' Bella had written, 'ring to say which you prefer. Perhaps she will be named democratically, by majority vote, then again, perhaps not. I am sore but violently happy, exhausted but wild with joy. When does the depression set in? Jon is like a man on stilts, he's grown several feet with the sheer delight of it. Mind you, the birth was all you warned me it might be... Phone! Lots of love, Bella, Jon and Baby Girl.' Gill smiled, holding the card to her chest. Well, she would telephone, after six in the evening, when calls were less expensive.

She and Rosie dozed, fought and struggled through their day before retrieving Adam from school. The three of them ate Smash and fish fingers for their supper; the Smash, at least, was hot, being made with boiling water. The fish fingers were barely defrosted. "Poor chilly fingers," Gill joked, "they could use some gloves." Neither child responded. "Oh come on, you two," pleaded Gill, "humour me just this once. Not a million miles from here grown-ups will be sipping wine, savouring the first of many courses. People may be bending towards their neighbours at the dinner table, eager to catch every morsel of witty repartee. Underneath linen tablecloths, hands will be straying to warm, unfamiliar knees as adults realize how much they fancy other adults. Relationships are being formed, ideas formulated, controversies debated all over the world except in this one soggy swamp of a kitchen at this one tedious table." Worn down by the thought of what she was missing, Gill leant back until her chair rocked on two legs. "The mashed potato is really nice," Adam offered.

Bedtime was not so bad. Existing in Ramsons was tiring in itself and Adam was finding school exciting and still a bit scary. The children were asleep before seven. An evening of peace stretched before Gill, like freshly fallen snow, hers to shape, to impress herself upon, to enjoy. First, she made herself a pot of tea, next she dug a packet of notelets from a drawer and decided to write to her mother. The front of the top notelet showed a golden retriever lying decorously on a lawn with a ball between its paws. The next one in the packet sported a picture of a poodle, done up with red ribbons. Gill had given this set of stationary not to Tilly but to Flora, for a Christmas or birthday years ago. She remembered buying it, counting out her pocket money, feeling almost smug at having chosen well – Flora had loved dogs. Had this packet of notelets survived because Flora had been friendless, or because she treasured the present? Gill spread all the pictures over the table, greyhounds and boxers, terriers and Great Danes. There was a pair of each. June disliked dogs; besides, sending one would spoil the set.

Gill tried phoning Seb, he was rehearsing during the days but ought to have been at his digs, pining for her, in the evenings. The woman who answered the phone sounded young and almost comically Scottish; his landlady, Gill supposed - Gill hoped. She said they were all out, the actors, and she had no idea when to expect them back. They were a company, then, Gill realized with a sigh, united for the duration of the production. In her first years with Seb, before she had babies, Gill had sometimes been invited to join these companies in cheap restaurants, on trips to see art films or to visit other theatre companies. No matter how attentive Seb had been and he was, to be fair, happy to demonstrate his affection openly, Gill had remained on the periphery, always feeling too dull, too heavy for them with their witty innuendos. Actors are like wolves, Gill thought, whereas photographers are owls, preferring to hunt alone.

In order to stop herself imagining Seb singling out one actress from the pack and making a fuss of her – Gill actually saw him licking this creature about the face and neck – she dialled Bella and Jon's number. But instead of the cosy conversation she'd anticipated, Gill was obliged to whisper her congratulations to Jon's mother, who informed her that

Bella, baby, and Jon were, finally, asleep. The ringing telephone was the last thing they needed, the new grandmother implied, although she did promise to pass on Gill's love, when they woke.

May as well carry on clearing up, Gill told herself. She began opening large tins that had been stacked one on another, in the drawing room. Biscuit tins, each now full of buttons, hooks and eyes, poppers and buckles. She would sort the buttons into clumps on the floor. The majority were mother-of-pearl, some so tiny she had to wet her fingers and stick them to her flesh in order to move them. Some were shaped like flowers, or shells. There were enamel buttons too, hand-painted, exquisite. The clump of bright, plastic buttons grew to a small hill, while the black ones formed a slag heap of their own. Gill couldn't believe each of these had once held together articles of clothing. Even a large family could never have worn such a variety. The brass buttons gleamed at her, suggestively. She turned them over, thinking of blazers and of uniforms. Now she was encircled by buttons, they held her in an enchanted place, inside memories. She saw women dressing up, in frocks with leg-of-mutton sleeves, in gloves that were buttoned to the elbow. She watched her great-aunts and her grandmother as they dressed for church, dressed for dinner, dressed for a walk in the cold. And she wondered if any of them had ever undone their buttons with the speed unharnessed by lust. Perhaps only Evangelina had ripped her clothing from her body, tearing buttons from their place, in a rush to be naked and taken by another. As for the other sisters... it was possible that many of these pretty fastenings had been purchased in the vain hope of having occasions to wear them, and to rip them undone. What harm was there, in buying a few buttons, in having just that measure of optimism?

Rather than enchanted, Gill now felt imprisoned. Suffocated. Recklessly, she gathered handfuls of buttons from all around her body and threw them high so that they fell in a shower of textures and colours on and about her. She flung them up again, until it was raining heavily over her. She hurled the buttons higher: and again she threw them up. The result was more than rain, it was hailstones, clattering on her head, down the back of her neck, spilling over her open palms. Eventually, the storm lessened, fading to a patter before dying out. Once all was calm, Gill realized the torrent had been essential, to clear the build up of stifled air, to purge.

Staying in her place on the floor, surrounded by the mess she had made, Gill took Tilly's letter from her pocket and unfolded it. The lighting was dim but Tilly had used a black pen and Gill could read her words if she held the letter out of the shadows.

'Dearest Girl,' Tilly wrote, 'Do I know which of my great-nieces to address? I think not. Ah well, as is to be expected in a woman of my years, I grow forgetful but only where recent events are concerned. I believe my long-term memory to be accurate, with details in sharp focus and conversations so acute they might be taking place as I record them now.

'It is time to tell you of Agnes, to set you right about her, the child who must have remained a half-grown ghost, whose name you may have caught as one or another of your relations spoke it through a sigh of loss.

'Agnes, the last of her children, was barely tolerated by Mother, although she was a quiet, presentable child of whom any woman might be proud. Any woman but Elizabeth Durry, who lived only for herself and her husband. Do you know, at Elizabeth's funeral we, her surviving children, encountered, for the first time, a sister of hers! Dorothy, she was called. Our mother hadn't so much as mentioned any sister. We thought ourselves without aunts and uncles, on Mother's side. Indeed, we were persuaded to conceive of Mother as a being free from the mundane ties of ancestry, a paragon who had once upon an auspicious time arrived, complete, unattached, perfected, in Father's life. Our newly discovered Aunt Dorothy had tales to tell, which threw some light on Mother's previously dim personal history: but these illuminations came too late. Nothing could affect Elizabeth Durry once she was the standard six feet under.

'I must not jump about or we shall never be straight. I admit, Dear, I do delay writing of Agnes, knowing the ache that surrounds her will sharpen when I recall my youngest sister's life.

' Since Mother wanted virtually no part in Agnes's upbringing, Flora took on the task of mothering her baby sister. It was an enterprise fraught with danger, as they say. Mother would disapprove of some dress Flora had chosen for Agnes, or see the baby enjoying a forbidden treat and chastisement would follow, inevitably. But Flora was constantly in trouble, well acquainted with both verbal and physical stings: it was only for Agnes she fretted. On the whole, for Flora, pleasures far outweighed pains in Agnes's infancy, so she told me many years on, when we two were finally, peacefully, alone with our old age, with our boxes, desks, cupboards and bureaus full of memories.

'You will find Ramsons messy, I imagine; perhaps you are irritated by our hoarding, by our inability to dispose of belongings? I know it drives Babs to distraction, not that her annoyance troubles me. I enjoy watching my cleaning woman shake her china-doll hair in anticipation of having to engage a firm of house clearers when she (as she supposes) inherits the furniture I have stuffed with useless possessions. Sometimes I believe I see, through her glazed eyes, the very auction at which she intends selling the pieces she has already decided not to keep.

'Well, let us not waste time on her. I only wish to excuse my tangle of things, for they are all the things that crept into our lives, over the years, each article attached to a moment in time we felt we could not, should not forget. Amongst them you will discover the wrapping paper of a hundred surprises. The tissue that lay over the warmest of scarves, the sweetest toy bears, the gentlest of soaps. Jethro's first pair of trousers, his last set of knickerbockers, the piping from his sailor suit, the Psalter he carried to church, the laces with which he tied the boots that took him away to war. Can any soul expect us to part with these? Some of my mess consists of sentimental rubbish, such as cake decorations for all seasons and occasions, plastic robins, bright Easter eggs, white sugar babies, birthday ballerinas or the tiniest of trains. But we also kept brown paper, string, every card the postman brought, purses with holes through which coins slipped, tins emptied of biscuits, cough drops, antacid tablets, liver salts and oil for the sewing machines with which all our garments, save one good winter coat apiece, were stitched. Stitched by us girls as we hummed our favourite songs, gossiped over villagers, healed the wounds of sorrow and grief by keeping busy. We created delight, in the form of coverlets and skirts, dresses and cushions - joyful, colourful items in satins, cottons, felts and silks, fashioned as we sat together, side by side.

'Work was our solace, the workroom, which later became the school room, our sanctuary. During our childhood, Mother would leave us to ourselves, so long as she believed us to be gainfully employed. As we grew, we became addicted to a routine of tasks. The more one needs to forget, the harder one is inclined to labour, or so it was with Flora and me. Evangelina went her own, not entirely sweet, way. I cannot say she was a law unto herself, for she was perilously lawless, even under Mother's direct gaze. What it must have meant, to be Elizabeth's favourite! Extra helpings of food invariably found their way on to Eva's plate. Strands of Mother's finest ribbon would appear, gracing Eva's waist, her sleeves, her Sunday hat. Her boldest statements often remained unchallenged, never so much as criticized, while humble suggestions from the rest of us would meet with derision, if not with a flick of Mother's fingers. If

'Elizabeth was selfish, not prepared to accommodate others, to tolerate her children, Evangelina was given to downright self-aggrandizement. We siblings were less than other players on her stage, less than puppets in her show. Shadow puppets, maybe, two dimensional, only worth bothering with when all other entertainment was cancelled.

'I apologise, dear, for condemning your grandmother in this way; but the objective of these letters is truth. Besides, no doubt June has at least implied the kind of woman Evangelina turned out to be. Poor, neglected, June: it is such a shame that Eva, of all people, should have been the only one of Elizabeth's children to become a parent. What a wonderful mother Flora might have made or, I like to think, I could have done a fairly good job myself. How lucky the child blessed with Jethro as his or her father. Instead of which…

'Well, it seems I have strayed, yet again from Agnes. You will need to appreciate the importance of Agnes to Flora, if you are to realize the depth of loss suffered. Flora told me of a single day, in Agnes's infancy, when an entire, rich future had seemed possible, due to the simple fact that one sister loved the other…

'The pair of them are playing in the garden, giving a picnic to a selection of toys. A woollen dog leans over a pie dish, in the lapping position. Sailor Sam, made from scraps of felt, spreads his loose limbs before a tasty array of stones. Two wooden Russian dolls stand, robust and rigid, over a jug of cordial. The larger of these has just given birth to the smaller. Russian stacking dolls breed by splitting at the waist, which might be the method all women employ, as far as Flora knows. Now the recently born daughter is about to produce a child herself. "Look," Flora coaxes Agnes, "here comes another baby. Ohhh, aahhh."

(She has heard birth, at a distance. She does her best to capture the moment.) "Ouch!" The second Russian doll is pulled apart, both halves roll across the grass as the latest daughter emerges. Instantly, Agnes pops most of this new baby in her mouth. On a dull day, last winter, Flora named these Russians dolls, choosing what she hoped were exotic names, such as Natasha and Petra, writing these on the undersides of the dolls in dramatic, purple ink. The newborn is called Tatyana; Flora watches in dismay as the writing dissolves in Agnes's dribble. Tatyana is poisoning the child who sucks her, staining her lips and tongue a frightful shade of violet.

"'No!" Flora shrieks, striking the doll from her sister's mouth, reaching for those tainted lips with the hem of her frock. Tatyana flies away, with seeming indignation, to land in a clump of Sweet Williams. "Ugh," says Flora, as Agnes contemplates the lost toy. Agnes can stand, for seconds at a time, and she does so now. Next, she moves forwards, over the grass. She takes one wobbly step – then another; she sits, defeated. Flora's mouth becomes a cave, filled with surprise. Agnes gets back on her feet, takes yet another step, bends to reclaim Tatyana and is plucked up by Flora, who swings her high above the ground. "You walked," the big sister exclaims, "clever, clever Agnes." Her nose is in the child's soft hair, her head full of baby scents: she inhales summer and the garden, soap and water, peace, pleasure, innocent sleep on fresh cotton sheets. She is proud as any parent. Agnes walked! Hugging the moment, Flora appreciates that there will be other landmarks to cherish. The day Agnes first speaks Flora's name. The time when she plays an entire tune on the piano. Birthdays. Exams passed. Days of celebration. The announcement of Agnes's engagement. Confetti and wedding cake...

'And so it should have been, of course. Well, so it was, for a while, with Flora loving Agnes well enough to be moderately strict with the child, not wanting to be responsible for a spoilt brat, hoping to be party to the emergence of a fine young adult when the time came.

'Agnes was also a favourite with Father. She saw little of him, mind you, as she grew up; but when home, Father could spare any amount of time for his youngest daughter. He called her Nessy, a nickname inspired, he teased, not by the last three letters of her name, but by a resemblance she bore to a certain monster deep within in a Scottish loch. We older Durry children had Agnes to thank for the decline in soporific meals dished up by Mother whenever Father was at home.

' I seem to remember my father as a man in a rush but I may have mistaken exuberance, which was not much in evidence at other times, for hurry. We played rather frantic card games with him, that is certain - Snap and Racing Demon being firm favourites. When there was music, it too was often fast and loud, in Father's presence. If we recited poetry or prose, the words were given at a pace that obscured both sense and sentiment. I suppose excitement gripped us, nothing more, although it felt as if we flew under a stronger spell. He was powerful man, my father. He built plush-seated theatres: shopping arcades in which colourful shop windows were further brightened by shared, central chandeliers: and he designed a multitude of (so called) palaces to which the masses flocked for entertainment. I sometimes think the enthusiasm of the entire population of Great Britain spilled over on to him, travelling with him from city to city, not diminishing one bit, even along the last few lanes to Staunley, where it found a place in which to burn itself out.

'Flora was the least uplifted by those nights around a piano or a table spread with games. She found herself elbowed from prime position in Agnes's world, when Father took Nessy on his lap. Mind you, I'm sure my father never noticed if Flora smiled less than she should. I believe he was busy playing cat and mouse with Mother, daring her, as he called Agnes his pet, to envy such a scrap of a girl. No doubt my mother did indeed fill her bleak heart with jealousy at the sight of Edward's arms enclosing somebody other than herself: a previously rare sight. He never held his son, not even as they said goodbye at the station, when Jethro went to do his all too fleeting bit for his country: he only hugged Flora, Eva and me on the occasions of his home-comings, in the entrance hall – we knew no contact with Father in any other part of the building or at other moments in our lives. But Agnes could climb on Father's lap and snuggle there, her head against his waistcoat, her fingers playing with his fingers, for as long as she pleased...

'...It is Christmas Night. We are as stuffed as the goose we have devoured! (Did we really eat goose? Or is that only in nursery rhymes? I seem to know the taste, to recall a richness not found in turkey meat, so goose it must have been.) There had been a pudding too, baked with silver threepenny bits, hidden treasure, amongst the currents and the nuts. For once, we are each allowed a glass of wine - our cheeks grow rosy from this and from the fire around which we sit, sipping. Father is louder, larger than ever, with a golden, cardboard crown on his balding head. "Tilly," he booms, "play us something seasonal." I oblige with carols that conjure Bethlehem, angels, holly, ivy and Christina Rossetti's bleak mid winter. "Fine, fine," Father admits, "but now play something jolly."

'I frown, trying to think what tune to begin, and find my place taken by Mother. She doesn't speak; she turns up the cuffs of her dress and flexes her fingers over the keys. She strikes a chord, skims a scale. We are poised on a brink, one further shove and we will fall.

'Mother plays for us; she plays with us. We are teased, excited, compelled to jig our toes in time, to rise to this beat, to dance up and down the room. 'Oh shall we dance the Polka?' Oh shall we skip and prance? Mother's nose almost touches the keys, so close is she to this, music of her own devising. With those same fingers, that bring about such misery at times, she brings us to a frenzy of delight.

'Jethro takes my hands in his and we strip some willow, we show sailors how to do the hornpipe, we perform dances we have not previously known, mixing steps from many countries, crossing national borders with an ease that is amazing: and we two are always in time with each other, our harmony is a given, not only do our feet move to the same rhythm, our bloods pump to a shared beat.

'Eva is obliged to dance with Flora. When they pass Jethro and me, they are no more than a blur of velvet skirts, with a flick or two of tumbling hair. I smell their warm, animal scents as they roll on by.

'For a while, Father tries to partner Agnes but he has grown plump, his breathing strains. He sits, taking his little girl astride his knees, and jigs his legs up and down until Agnes, holding imaginary reins, is galloping so fast her cheeks wobble like a milk pudding. Father's head is thrown back but perspiration still slides into his eyes and since he must hold Agnes around the waist, he has no free hand with which to banish it. Faster they ride, a runaway horse and its mad, wild, child rider, spurred by the music Mother creates, thundering over a landscape they would never, usually, dare to dream of.

'At some point, while Jethro and I are tripping our own light fantastic, Mother lifts her head to look about. Father's eyes are closed now, perhaps merely to keep them dry. Agnes is lost, her long, wavy brown hair, loosened from its ribbons, curtains her face. Her head is down, her body limp. Were it not for Father's hands, on which the knuckles show white from gripping, she would fall at his feet.

'Mother raises her arms high over the keyboard: she hits eight notes, discordant and foreboding, repeatedly. We skid to a halt. Father's eyes open wearily, as Agnes lifts her tousled head. Mother stills her hands, leaving them spread over the keys like a threat.

'"Elizabeth," Father remonstrates. He looks suddenly old. His cardboard crown is all awry. "Elizabeth," he sighs again, "whatever it is now?"…'

Out in the passage, the telephone rang. Gill waded through buttons as she left Edward and Agnes and went to answer the call. A man she didn't think she knew was speaking to her, having got her number from Jon in Bristol. He was called Rick and he had met her once or twice, did she remember? At the Arnolfini, for the opening of some exhibition, at her home, once, during a party. He'd seen her work, liked it, wondered if…

It was more than Gill could absorb, the mention of Jon coming so soon after the news of the baby: the idea that she had once given parties to which men called Rick were invited: the Arnolfini, with its smart coffee shop, its clear, white walls that had cried to her for photographs. The conversation was too incongruous to credit, being thrown by the caller into the dank passage at Ramsons.

"…putting together a collection, later to be a book if my backers allow," the man was saying, "of the four corners, as it were, of England, you see." He was silent, presumably expecting a response.

"Uh," Gill offered, "you might have lost me there a bit, Rick. Could you begin again?" He did, with good grace, explain once more that he had a project in mind for a collection of photographs from the geographical extremities of England. Cornwall, Northumberland, Herefordshire and Lincolnshire. Possibly a quartet of projects, in fact, money permitting, of the four landscapes in all four seasons, but hey, he was jumping a whole artillery of guns. One thing at a time. "Take any and everything you see," he suggested, "pretty, downright ugly, barren, unusual. But hey, here I am telling you your job. I know I can trust you, I've seen your work, at the Dockside, once, and at your old home of course, when I came to that amazing party. How is old Ted, by the way?"

Gill struggled to think which of her photos had hung at the Dockside and what had decorated her walls at home. She still had no recollection of anybody called Rick; it must have been some party. And who the hell was Ted?

"The project sounds good," she enthused, "more than good, great. It's so," she tried to drag up an uncommon adjective but failed, "different here from Cornwall, say. So flat." She thought of Noel Coward; hadn't he written something similar? - but funnier, coming from his pen. They made arrangements, with Gill taking down Rick's phone number and address, promising a first batch of pictures within three weeks. Gill was to meet the other photographers at a get-together or two, before the launch. Rick was sure she would like them and they would adore her. She foresaw herself warmed by the companionship of fellow artists, appreciated by an admiring public. Before they said goodbye, she and Rick were united by their confidence in the success of the exhibition and the probable book to follow.

Leaving the puddles of buttons, the plates still gritty and orange from those inedible fish fingers, the litter of a day not wisely spent, Gill fairly danced her way to bed. She placed Rick's phone number and address on the pillow next to her, in the spot where Seb's head ought to have been. As she was drifting off to sleep, a smile came to her lips. Ted, indeed! How Seb would have winced, to be only half remembered, to have his name forgotten by a man called Rick.

9.

*(because I always think the children drowned, no matter what
you say.)*

Gill woke with the same smile on her lips. Happiness lifted her out of
bed, floated her to the bathroom, dared the cold water to irritate her.

She merely tutted when Rosie threw a portion of her breakfast at
Adam, saying "Kids," conspiratorially to him as she wiped a pebble-
dashing of oats from his face. He put on his disgusted look, which
simply made her smile some more. There was much to be done. The
moment Adam was in school, Gill and Rosie visited the only mechanic
in the village. She knew where to find him, having previously noticed
his hand-painted sign over the door of what had been, in Gill's own
time, a stable. When summoned, the mechanic emerged, oil streaked
and good humoured, from beneath a car. He agreed to take a look
at Gill's Morris Minor that afternoon. He seemed so wholesome he
might have been created by H. E. Bates. Indeed, every aspect of this
man enhanced the glow of contentment Gill enjoyed – his strong local
accent, his blunt, filthy fingers, the halo of thinning, auburn hair that
framed his pink face. The rag spilling from his pocket had clearly been
a pair of Y-fronts in a former incarnation.

Gill's smile grew to a grin when she considered her change of luck.
Perhaps, now that she had a purpose, a goal to achieve, other people
would fall reliably into place, willing to help, keen to make her life
less difficult. Passing him her car keys, she had to stop herself from
patting the mechanic's hand.

Back in Ramsons, she unpacked her camera. It needed a good clean,
although, until now, it had remained in its case, in a tea chest. She
worked carefully, lost to the task. Occasionally she would catch sight
of herself in a lens, one distorted, over-eager eye, or an entire face,

bulging with zeal.

Rosie was entertaining herself nearby, singing snatches of songs, talking rubbish to her precious Mr. Tibbs. Gill heard her vaguely, as one hears a muffled radio. Once the camera was free from dust and loaded with film, Gill put it back in its case and hung it around her neck. It was impossible to wait for the car to be mended, she had to take some shots now, while the light was good. After all, here was the village, literally on her doorstep, with its curved main street and its stretch of river. She thought of the abandoned boat on the river bank - its flaky pink paint in harmony with the grey water and the silver weeds. Then it occurred to her: her film was black and white. She had no other film, to hand. Had Rick specified? She remembered little of their conversation. Being asked to participate had overwhelmed her, now she wished she'd thought to put appropriate questions. Colour or black and white? It was too basic a consideration for her to query now, in retrospect. Rick must assume she knew – but she didn't. Her flesh grew hot, her fingers slippery. The camera in its case, which ought to have felt beloved in an old, familiar way, was a millstone, dragging at her neck, obliging her to hang her head.

While making a snack in the kitchen, Gill assured herself that it was understandable she should suffer a bout of insecurity. Of course it didn't matter, immediately, what type of film she used. Once the car was fixed and she was able to shop, she could shoot with both colour and black and white, discarding whatever wasn't required when she knew more about the project. If she was honest, her concern was her ability, rather than what bloody film to use. It had been a while since she'd taken any pictures other than snap-shots of babies or toddlers. What if she'd lost her feel for photography, her perception of shape and light, her flair for composition? She thought these talents were innate: she pictured the infant Gillian, on her back in a pram, observing faces or overhanging branches or passing clouds, with an artist's eye. But even inborn talents may die, if they lie dormant too long.

No point in fretting: she would rather know the truth than suppose the worst. When Rosie had finished playing with her lunch, Gill strapped her into the pushchair and reinstated the camera in its place about her neck. The oversized iron key to Ramsons also hung on a string around Gill's throat, being too large for most pockets, but in spite of the weight, Gill kept her head up as she walked, appraising the depth of sunshine and the length of shadows. Without planning to do so, she headed for the Ups and Downs, instead of the river.

This quarried landscape hardly conformed to the public's concept of Lincolnshire. It wasn't flat or criss-crossed with dykes. It felt as distant from fenland as a mountain range – in fact, it was a younger brother to mountain ranges, with summits that might be achieved after mere minutes of climbing. Released from her pushchair, Rosie stumbled up the hills and tumbled down into the valleys. Gill followed closely at first, anxious for her safety. The ground was chalk, as Tilly had pointed out, mostly covered with a layer of soft grass, kept short and springy by rabbits whose burrows were the bane of dog-walkers. If Rosie should fall, the grass would cushion her. Gill stopped trying to keep up with the staggering child, turning her attention to her camera, making it ready.

She took shots of the sky, across which light clouds ambled, with the hills at the edge of the frame, tufted with grasses along their tops. Shrubs grew where they had depth enough to root but even the gorse had become scruffy as it began to lose its summer lustre. Gill put the lens of her camera inside a couple of these bushes, taking butterfly-eye views of the distinct little landscape. In the distance she discerned miles of stone walling, built to protect a country house and its estate. The stone used for the wall had come from the Ups and Downs, of course; presumably the owners of the hidden mansion had worked the quarry. Their wall was backed, on the estate's side, by high firs and sweet chestnut trees that dripped with their burdens of nearly ripened nuts.

"Come to me," she called to Rosie. Having left the Ups and Downs behind her, to reach the wall she must cross a small road, which she did while holding Rosie's hand. Then she got a great shot, beginning with stones so near the lens she could capture their grainy texture before the structure stretched away in what seemed an endless frontier. She had lined the picture up so the wall was precisely in the centre, emphasising the divide so clearly intended.

She and Rosie retraced their steps, with the child running ahead, falling but not fussing, doing jumping-jacks on the top of one especially sharp hill. Gill got some photos of Rosie, to send to Seb.

The best shot of the day would probably turn out to be the last one. As Gill clambered to the top of one hill, she spied the abandoned pushchair, perched on the summit of the next. It was alone against the sky. Gill knelt, holding Rosie back so she shouldn't get in the way. She pulled her lens until the chair was in focus, until she could see daylight through its wheels, then she took the picture. There was no doubt it would be a winner. There was also no question of Gill having lost her way as a photographer. Her heart beat faster than usual but she felt wonderfully calm. She felt right.

That evening she did speak to Bella. Their conversation was filled with hope. Gill couldn't help but reflect how one-sided this optimism might have been, had they spoken just twenty-four hours earlier.

Seb also phoned. They talked of how extraordinary it would be if they should both manage to make their livings doing what they loved to do. For once, Gill felt equal in all things, better than equal since she had shone artistically *and* cared for the children, that day. Seb was glad to hear the car would soon be mended; he was pleased Adam seemed to be settling in at school, happy to catch the joy in Gill's voice. For a moment, Gill suspected Seb of being altogether too cheerful; was his good mood founded in relief? She pushed this suspicion from her mind because this had, after all, been a cheerful day, with merry mechanics and perfect photography. There was no call to spoil it.

"Not long to go now," Seb reminded her. "I'll be home in just over a month... unless..."

"Unless what?"

"No, unless nothing. Oops, only two-*p* left. Kiss the kids for me. Love you. Bye."

Unless they ask you to stay and do some bloody awful Christmas show, Gill thought. Noddy Goes Crackers In Toyland. The Jungle Book On Ice, or some such nonsense. Where was the artistic integrity in that? In the size of the pay packet, she supposed.

Luckily, her overriding sense of well-being couldn't be suppressed; she concocted a meal out of bits and pieces, bathed the children together, peacefully, read them stories and tucked them up, with their soft toys and clean, sleepy faces, before eight o'clock.

She would fetch the books she wanted and take them to the big, kitchen table since it was too cold to stay long in any part of the house save the kitchen where the Rayburn devoured shovel after shovel of coal. She was beginning to think of this stove as something of a monster with a roaring hunger and a propensity to sulk and spit if not constantly mollycoddled. The coal was kept in a lean-to by the back door; it was getting low but she had done nothing about reordering. She wondered did she mean to teach the Rayburn a lesson? But who would suffer most, when fuel was down to little more than dust?

It would be an evening of making lists. She pulled appropriate books from shelves in the drawing-room and the school room, then she found pen and paper and sat in the kitchen.

Order coal, she wrote first:

Buy card for Bella.

Get more film - colour??

Sports kit for Adam (Charity shop?)

Write to Mum about Christmas.

Lists. They were infinitely more satisfying than other chores, Gill decided. They epitomized order; they implied that an amount of things had already been achieved while intimating a busy, purposeful life to come. Once the car was repaired, Gill was certain her life would be back on the track of a woman who needs lists. She smiled, remembering how Seb had peered over her shoulder one morning in Bristol and muttered appreciatively in her ear, "You write a mean list, Gillian, do you know that?" It had been a comment charged with sexual energy.

Milk and Bread, she wrote now, for good measure.

The books she'd chosen to study were about Lincolnshire's flora, fauna and landscape. After a while, she began a second list:

Ely.

Distant church spires.

Herons, corncrakes etc.

Skegness! Fun fair, closed down? Under cover for winter?

Barren, flat fields, ploughed, waiting for bulbs. Bursts of colour.

Rusting tractors (Take Adam along for these!)

Eleanor Crosses and other stone structures.

Gill envisaged her quarter of the collection, carefully mounted, tastefully hung, in an exhibition at which family, old friends, prestigious acquaintances and admiring critics mingled whilst clutching programmes in one hand, glasses of Champagne in the other.

"I had no idea an uneventful landscape could be so noteworthy," said a man with a spotted handkerchief in the pocket of his white suit. "Ah," Gillian replied, in a tactful voice, "is any landscape truly uneventful? Lincolnshire is perverse, if nothing else." Da-de-da, on she went, talking intelligently to this person and that; sometimes remaining silent as she seemed to study the other three bodies of work – she was too self-obsessed, she must admit, to take a genuine interest in their crags and cliffs; picking up snatches of conversations, most of them concerning a preference (although who would have thought it?) for the section on Lincolnshire, my dear.

In order to continue the dream in comfort, she went early to her bed, with her camera around her neck. She also carried her lists up the stairs, and a hot water bottle she had filled. Consequently, the papers were warm against her cheek when she lay with them.

Contentment was the cure for insomnia. Gill woke to the satisfaction of the well rested. For once, snuggled under Tilly's old paisley eiderdown, she wasn't cold. And the children were already up, which saved her the unpleasantness of waking them. She could hear them at play. Come to think of it, they were at play in her room, rather than in theirs. With an effort, she hauled herself out of her cocoon, up on to her elbows. Only the tops of their sleep-tousled heads were visible, at the foot of her bed. Adam was speaking softly, but also urgently. Rosie made small sounds, not words, only whimpers. Gill turned to the bedside table and picked up her watch. My God, it was after nine in the morning. Adam would be horribly late for school. She threw back the mass of bed covers and fell out of bed.

The children heard her get to her feet. They hushed. "Hey, you two," she said, " we are a lot of sleepy heads, we must hurry…"

Adam and Rosie were sitting, in their pyjamas, on a rug, one on either side of Gill's camera. Between them, like dark vomit, swirled and twisted a reel of film. The camera lay on its front, the lens hiding in the rug as if in shame. The exposed part, the back of the camera, had been violated. The cover to the film compartment lay an inch or two away, separated. Pulled clean off.

"Who did this?" Gill asked. Adam shrugged; he was shivering - only the bed was warm, in Tilly's room. Rosie looked up at her mother, eyes wide and, it seemed, careless. But for that look, Gill told herself, she might have knelt and said never mind, these things happen. Or so she preferred to believe. As it was, her mouth spewed such anger that her throat soon hurt, her lungs ached, her tongue thickened with emotion. One minute the children were hunched on the floor of Tilly's room, the next they were back in their bedroom. There was pain, oh yes, blows had to be struck, a lesson must be learnt. There would be no getting off lightly. Hurt was essential, the sting of a smack, the burn of a pinch. Crying too, was horribly helpful. Piercing screams, her own and those of her terrified children, came some way to appeasing Gill. Upset has to breed more upset, loud, painful, exhausting; or else how was Gill to recover? "You had to do it, didn't you?" she bellowed in Rosie's ear. "Couldn't have Mummy enjoying herself, oh no, not for one sodding day, could you? Well, hate me all you like, I hate you too, you infant witch." As she ranted, Gill kicked toys and books around the lilac room. She was a hurricane ripping through Adam's Lego town, sending cars spinning, demolishing buildings, crushing people. Dolls cried out as her feet tore the limbs from them, soft toys squeaked in protest as they flew against a wall. And Rosie screamed in terror, which was all Gill had left to hope for. "What? You broke my best ever thing," she explained, "now it's my turn to break some of your junk, Rosie."

There was only red remaining then, red eyes, brilliant, burning cheeks, the throat, the jaw, the heart and soul of the demon Gill. Had her liver disgorged itself and appeared at her feet, Gill would merely have thought, there, that's the extent of my fury.

She slammed their door on her children, saying they should tidy up, threatening to return with a rubbish bag before long. For a while, she sat on the top of the back stairs, waiting for her heartbeat to steady, listening to the snivelling from behind the children's door. There was an imbalance, she felt, between the harm done to her and the harm she'd inflicted. But where the lack lay, she couldn't have said. As she grew calmer, so her sense of shame increased; but it was unfounded, surely? Her life had been ruined; was she supposed to take destruction lying down? Hadn't she a right to strike out on behalf of the hopes that had been dashed to death at the foot of her bed?

"How dare they? How dare they?" she cried all the way down the stairs, and while she hurled plates against the kitchen wall. Included now, in her tirade, were Seb, June, Sarah, Kate and a line of Durrys going back to doomsday. She smashed their teacups and their gravy boats, splintered their sugar bowls. Ha! Let them come for these possessions now, the living and the dead. She would not keep them safe; she was nobody's guardian. Nor was she anybody's mother, any more.

That evening, Gill read the second half of Tilly's letter. Her attitude to the plight of her deceased ancestors had hardened with her own distress; she didn't expect to be moved, she read only for occupation, having been bored all day once the broken china was cleared away. She found the place, remembering the previous description of Christmas and the music Elizabeth played at her piano.

'Well, my Dear,' Tilly continued, 'Agnes grew, as children must. She was never a beauty, but being so loved, she had an open, untroubled face, with the clearest, wide, green eyes. She favoured the colour lilac, in her dress, setting off skirts and blouses with a purple sash or buttons of violet. She used to make posies of velvet pansies, to give as small presents or to wear herself, as brooches. You may have found some of these, when looking through things here. We never threw a single bloom away but we could hardly bear to see them, either; they will be hidden under blankets, or between sheets of paper.

'Now, I shall tell you Agnes's story, I must delay no more.

'…The winter of 1913 fell very hard on our village, turning the earth to white steel that would not thaw even in the middle of a day. We knitted for our lives, I remember. Delicate leather gloves simply wouldn't do, we must have wool or we should suffer chilblains. Ramsons has never been an easy house to heat; we children huddled together, forgetting animosities in order to keep warm. Flora and Agnes shared one of the large, front bedrooms, with no heat but an inadequate fire that was lit only in the evenings. Their windows, looking out over the main street, were frequently patterned with frost, which they would scratch clear so as to see what went on outside.

'There was little traffic to watch. Some horses steamed about their business, of course, bringing ale to the public house opposite or delivering coal. Their breath hung about them like cotton wool. To begin with, there was no snow, only ice. Children slid to school; mothers collapsed in their efforts to keep pace, cursing as their legs shot from under them. The river had frozen. Provided we wrapped up sensibly, we girls were allowed a daily walk but only as far as the river to the north or the Ups and Downs to the south. The frozen expanse of water was most alluring, decorated as it was with trapped leaves and branches. We wandered in that direction most days, gasping at the foolishness of boys who ran from bank to bank, waiting for the crack that would herald their demise. But the weather worsened and the ice thickened. Soon the river was a big attraction. Flora and Agnes saw droves of people, whole families, courting couples, groups of friends, slipping down the street with skates slung over their shoulders.

'We were forbidden to go there, by Mother, once she knew how popular it had become. She decided that skating was an occupation fit only for common people, although those she admired and imitated were amongst the cheerful stream of folks heading for the river each day. I believe she didn't care to think of us flushed with the pleasure of speed.

'Many years later a villager told me that Evangelina went regularly to the river, where she begged or borrowed skates and skated until she was quite worn out. Flora and I never witnessed this, of course, because we were too afraid of Mother to disobey her instructions. We may have harboured our suspicions, though, I really cannot remember now. I do think Agnes either knew or guessed. She might even have seen Eva sneak down the street, just as Eva, spying from the landing window, was to watch Agnes when she dared to go against Mother's orders...

'...It is a Saturday morning and Agnes sits on an old ottoman at the bedroom window. Staunley is entirely white, because today there is snow to top the ice and deceive walkers into believing the streets less dangerous. The public house has an air of innocence, with its roof bathed in white and its windows highlighted by the weather. The church mimics those on our Christmas cards. At the dawn of the day, all had been silent, much as if snow had fallen inside people's ears, deafening them; but it is mid-morning now and folk are appearing in the street, each greeting they make echoing from wall to wall. A small dog is playing, rolling on its back, wriggling about until snow sticks to its coat. Children laugh at the dog's antics, their magnified amusement easily reaches Agnes on her window seat. Flora comes and stands behind her sister, resting a hand on her shoulder. Agnes is fourteen and a little too slender, her bones can be felt through the wool of her dress. Flora's attention is drawn to the dog, might it not catch a chill, being covered in clumps of snow?

'"I am going skating," Agnes almost whispers, "this very morning." In response, the hand on her shoulder tightens its grip. "Maisie Trantor has spare skates. She will bring them after lunch," Agnes explains. "Only think, Flo, what it must be like, to be part of the fun. Such an adventure, taking place, in our own, dreary village. In years to come, we shall hang our heads if we cannot say we were there during the big freeze, skating on our piece of river."

'Flora bends her mouth to Agnes's ear in order to remind her of the dangers in going against Mother's wishes. The wash-house is still used for punishments and not long ago Jethro spent an afternoon in the cellar, with no company but fermenting fruit, because he had, apparently, cheeked his mother. "I dread to think what she would do," Flora stresses, "if she discovered you had been down to the river."

'For a while, retribution threatens both sisters: they hear it climbing the stairs, they see it scowl, feel it tapping a cane on the palm of a hand. But Agnes possesses a young person's willingness to believe herself exempt. Mother is bound to be occupied with the newspaper or with her correspondence; Agnes will have no trouble in slipping from the house unnoticed. Enlivened by the prospect, she jumps to her feet and pulls at Flora's hand. Small items of furniture are pushed aside, the rug that covers the floor is rolled up.

'"Imagine skating," Agnes insists, taking a deep breath, raising her chin as if to enjoy fresh, frozen air. She makes light music, something between humming and singing, as she begins to move across the floor. However cumbersome she may feel, Flora is compelled to join her young sister.

'"And turn and turn and now link arms," Agnes instructs as they cover the floor together. Flora has never tied a pair of skates on to her feet, never known what it is to balance on thin metal in order to flow over ice: it is instinct that informs her now. Her eyes close, since she is safely joined to Agnes's side, and she feels a rush of still, cold air against her face. She is out of doors, on the solid river, between the pollarded willow trees on either bank. Other people smile as they pass, delighted with this restricted pastime. Flora and Agnes gain confidence. They become competent, performing figures of eight, letting go of each other's hands and reuniting with ease. They gather speed and glide downstream, out towards the Fens and sheer white, open countryside.

Herons flap away from the bank as the two sisters approach, crows look up, puzzled by this low flying phenomenon. Out here, the snow is deeper, the fields have the look of a pure, white eiderdown. There is no longer any sign of human habitation, even sheep pens and cowsheds are buried. Onwards go the skaters, through a landscape pacified, cleansed, healed. Flora imagines reaching the sea; will that be frozen too? Agnes squeezes her sister's arm, smiles up at her.

'Flora throws back her head and laughs aloud; in skating on a frozen river within the front bedroom of Ramsons, she has discovered how it feels to be utterly happy.

'Less than an hour later, Flora wraps Agnes in warm clothing, warns her to take great care, fusses. They embrace; then Agnes slides from Flora's arms, tiptoes down the stairs. When Agnes appears in the street, to be greeted by Maisie who has, as promised, a spare pair of skates to lend, Flora is not alone in watching. From the window on the front landing, through panes of blue glass and of red, Evangelina also spies. She sees her younger sister as a figure bathed in crimson, wanton, disobedient and wilful. No matter that she, Eva, has made this escape several times during the current freeze; Agnes is defying Mother, and for this she must surely pay.

'As Maisie and Agnes hurry down the street, they shed their crimson aura: Eva sees them turn to blue, two figures kissed by cold – transformed, as if by Jack Frost himself, into a pair of ice princesses from a melancholy fairy tale…

'My dear great-niece, I wonder what you have implied, from hints and half heard conversations? The surviving story is that Agnes, beloved youngest daughter of Edward and Elizabeth Durry, drowned in the River Hern as it began, having been frozen, to flow once again. But that was not so. The truth has lain hidden, as if under a drift of snow. The collective memory of an entire village seems to have been obliterated. When the thaw came, it created a fresh, temporary river: this gushed down the main street of Staunely; and with the snows, verity also melted and was washed away.'

Gill put down the letter and listened to the house. There was more creaking than usual; it was a noisy evening for the floors; doors had decided to open, then to softly close themselves. Water travelled through pipes, dripped from gutters, gurgled in the roof space. And Gill felt herself alone with the dead. She believed, should she draw back the curtain, she would see Agnes and her friend Maisie, escaping down an icy street. If Gill was to make a bid for freedom, and she relished this copy-cat idea, imagining herself fleeing all the way back to Bristol, she was sure that her grandmother, Evangelina, would be watching from the front landing. She fully expected Tilly to tap her on the shoulder, to nod at the letter, encouraging her to read on. Obediently, she did so.

'Even I,' Tilly continued, 'have come close to believing the tale of the poor girl, drowned when she crashed through the ice. Mothers warn their children with this lie. As far as I know, your mother, June, grew up trusting it to be true. My father was duped into thinking that Agnes died on the river bank and was carried home, wet through, stiffening both with death and with cold. But Agnes came home on her feet, just.

'She and Maisie did skate. I have no idea how they might have enjoyed themselves; there was no talk of pleasure from the moment they disappeared around the corner, past the church. Eva, of course, was first to spy them returning, the one friend supporting the other. Agnes was drenched, stooped with cold, shuddering. Eva alerted Flora, who flew down the stairs to the rescue.

'For safety's sake, the skaters ought to have entered Ramsons by the back door. Mother seldom used the rear of the house. (The kitchen, scullery and workroom, overlooking the back garden and orchards, were Lizzie's domain.) But by the time she reached the front of the house, Agnes could go no further, she was ready to collapse. A tell-tale trail of water dripped from her clothes to lie in shellow puddles where the flagstones of the hall were worn down by thousands of previous footsteps. The carpet on the wide main stairway was treacherously dampened by the dragging of a soaking body, as Flora took over from Maisie and helped her sister to a hideaway.

'You will have heard, no doubt, of a secret, lost room here at Ramsons? Childhood is blessed and cursed with such places, fairy glens, hidden caves, rooms without keys. Perhaps it will surprise you to discover that our secret place actually does exist. It was once an ordinary box-room, packed with trunks and cases, amongst which a space was cleared for Agnes. There she sat, in order to dry out before Mother perceived her wet outfit and guessed at her misdemeanour. The box-room has become a secret room, blocked off, unmentioned, but prior to that, it was a room with a secret. A secret Flora struggled desperately to keep.

'Agnes was a popular girl. Our servant, Lizzie, herself the mother of a growing child, was easily coerced into helping Flora to undress Agnes, to dry her clothes and sneak her ruined boots into the low oven (where they cooked slowly, their leather cracking until it resembled the hide of a crocodile, forgotten, not reclaimed until the next batch of bread was baked, several days later.) Lizzie and Flora plied the freezing child with warm drinks, with soups and blankets and heavy shawls. They kneaded her icy fingers, massaged her limbs, rubbed her soaking hair until it stood from her head, electric, amazed.

'Agnes could not be warmed. The world did not possess towels and blankets enough. There was no broth with the strength to reach the centre of the child, where ice seemed to have taken hold. Most importantly, the box-room had no fire. Perhaps if Agnes had been led to the kitchen and placed close to the stove, her body might have thawed, her strength could have been regained. This simply was not possible: all routes to the kitchen included a risk of encountering Mother. When Flora told Jethro and me what had occurred, where Agnes had been hidden, we did not remonstrate with her. We would have chosen a similar course of action. Avoiding Mother was the prime concern. The downstairs rooms, including the drawing room in which Mother sat before a well-built fire, were out of the question. In the bedrooms, fires were only lit during the evening, this being seen by Mother as the one time a person not sick or idle could possibly require heat upstairs. Besides, Mother sometimes patrolled the bedrooms, inspecting them like the workhouse governess to whom, in daring but whispered conversations, we used to compare her. There was nothing for it but to hide Agnes in the box-room, to keep her there until she could slip safely into her bed.

'At luncheon, Mother demanded to know where Agnes was. Missing a meal counted as little less than a sin. Flora stuttered apologies on Agnes's behalf, telling of a blinding headache and a churning stomach. Mother grumbled throughout the soup and the meat course, blaming Flora for making her sister into a weakling. "Headaches," she smirked, "ought only to be suffered by exhausted, mature women or by malcontent brides." She had a taste for innuendo, I remember.

'What a pitiful collection of souls we made that luncheon time. Mother, cantankerous, joyless, positioned ready to strike out. Jethro with a war hanging over him, coming to the realization that he must abandon any hope of following in Father's footsteps. Flora, perched as if on a nest of vipers, eating with unhealthy speed, her usually pink cheeks ashen with anxiety. Eva, infested by her store of secrets, wondering which of them to reveal first, calculating their powers. And myself, full of dread, for Agnes, of course, but also for Jethro, who I loved so dearly and for Flora in her role of liar, which she performed with no talent whatsoever.

'Not long after luncheon, Agnes was helped to her bed, a cumbersome, dangerous journey up and down small flights of steps, across landings that might have been mine fields, so cautiously were they traversed. I believe Agnes knew nothing of this flight to a safer, warmer place. Once settled in her bed, she did not unbend her body, but remained, propped against pillows, in the position she had adopted for the box-room, hunched with fear and with cold. Lizzie and Flora surrounded her with hot bottles, pulled bed covers right up to her chin, broke the rules concerning bedroom fires and lit a blaze before daylight dimmed.

'Nobody thought to alert Mother. Agnes would recover, we assumed, although it became increasingly clear that she had taken more than a chill. She had not stopped shaking since being pulled from the water. I peeked in once and saw Flora lying almost on top of Agnes, attempting not only to convey some body heat into the child but also to still her trembling limbs. For the most part, throughout the afternoon, Flora stroked her sister's head, her rigid hands, those arms that could not be dissuaded from hugging her own, numb torso. All the while, Flora offered sympathy and encouragement. "You will be better soon," she promised, "and we shall watch the thaw, then the arrival of spring, together."

'Darkness fell. The gong was struck for tea. Flora sat, petrified, by Agnes's bed. "I cannot leave her," she told me when I called for her to descend the stairs with me. "Make my excuses, would you, Tilly?" My heart skipped beats at the prospect but fortunately Mother was in one of her dazes at tea, she hardly noticed the subtraction of two of her children. She was in the habit of mixing herself various concoctions, ostensibly for her stomach or her heart. We were aware of the garden where she grew her remedies, tucked behind evergreen hedges, but we had no idea what plants she used or what quantities.

'I suppose, in every life, there are these drastic days, when the world seems to change its direction. Agnes's fall through the ice was to bring a flood of emotion, followed by courses of action which might never have been considered without the shove we felt, between our shoulder blades, from fate. It was at that teatime, when Mother's hands were unsteady and her eyes unfocused, that the concept of using her medication as a weapon for our defence first came to me. Seeds sown during the worst of weather sometimes do take root and flourish, I have found. I apologize for speaking in riddles but I write my thoughts as they enter my head. I make discoveries along with you; and mine are no less disturbing, believe me.

'I went to visit Agnes as soon as tea was finished and immediately I saw that the doctor must be called. Mother was informed that Agnes had taken a severe chill and was most unwell; Jethro was the one who spoke to her, braving her glazed stare. I made her a pot of coffee, hoping this might clear her mind before Doctor Morrab, our family physician, arrived at the door. Lizzie was sent to fetch him. He was a good man, round as a barrel, completely bald; his skin shone as if his equally good wife had polished it. He wore glasses that created half moon shaped ditches on the tops of his cheeks; I saw these marks as signs that he and his wife were blind to his expansion over the years. Having come to appreciate the impossibility of winning most races with death, he no longer hurried unduly, even in dire emergencies: but he was fond of Agnes and he did make haste to visit her. Mother welcomed him but excused herself from the sick bed, saying she did not keep the best of health herself, these days, and would rather not catch Agnes's cold. Her speech was only mildly slurred, no more than that of a person having taken a drink or two. Doctor Morrab nodded his understanding. He knew my mother thought herself a herbalist, with a resistance to 'proper' medicine. It is interesting, in retrospect, to note that Mother did not put a stop to this visit from Doctor Morrab, for she frequently attempted to heal our ills with her own brews before calling him out. Thankfully she was already under the spell she had cast earlier that day, not that the doctor was able to offer much comfort.

'He told Flora that Agnes had a high fever; she must be kept warm, given quantities of water to drink. He produced a phial of medicine, which he tipped down her throat, gently wiping the dribble it left on her chin. He stooped over the child and tut-tutted, asking how she had come to this state.

'"Oh, she has been out in the snow too long," Flora fibbed, "her feet were absolutely frozen after her walk. She shakes as if still feeling the cold," Flora added, "but we have warmed her through and through."

'"No," the doctor explained, "it is from fever she trembles, fever and shock." He said he would call again, in the morning. Flora must not worry unduly, these things pass.

'Well, I shan't drag the story out, although it took what seemed the longest time for Agnes's fever to reach its climax...

'...Agnes is conscious of being observed, she knows eyes are studying her intently. She will give them a show worth the watching. On the ice, she is weightless, a creature of air and light with blades for feet and a stream of thistledown hair trailing in the breeze she creates. Other skaters, wobbling and clutching each other, stare at this beauty; they laugh with delight as Agnes glides by. She is grace itself, upright but pliable, utterly charming. Maisie straggles behind, churning the ice where Agnes has left it clear and clean. Now Agnes dances, she turns, she leaps and lands perfectly, she balances on one leg, the other high and straight in the air behind her. Now she spins, still only on one leg, round and round, arms outstretched, her blade making a single, tidy mark, a pure circle. Everybody gasps, they cheer, they sigh with amazement. Clever Agnes. Pretty Agnes. What skill, what dexterity. From nowhere, Father appears, beaming his admiration.

'But Agnes cannot stop the spin, nor can she slow it down. Faster she turns, her arms lifting and falling like a bird in a panic. Out of control. Nobody notices, not Maisie, not Father, not even Flora who is also amongst her audience. They simply clap their gloved hands and praise her. "No," she cries as her blade behaves like a corkscrew, drilling its way through the ice; but the others cannot hear her, they are wearing ear muffs and besides, the snow has muted sound; even her screams are inaudible as she feels the first lash of icy water.

'When she is completely submerged, Agnes ceases to scream: silence reigns here, where cold is a cudgel, beating her to a numb death. Colour no longer exists; under the ice there is nothing green, or grey, or even white. But she sees her hair, spread out about her, and this is still brown; and it makes her weep and kick and fight for air. Miraculously, she rises to the river's surface.

'Agnes continues to rise, beyond the broken ice, away from hands that had been held out to lift her, above heads that gawp at her departure. Upwards she travels, growing warmer by the minute as she breaks through cloud and finds herself in a clear, azure sky. There is no ground visible under her feet, only a distant layer of cloud, heavy with its burden of snow. Over her head, she feels the sun, bright as summer, drying her body and her hair, dispersing heat to the depths of her being. She feels no fear, only a pleasure that approaches ecstasy. Surely she will meet an angel soon? Or a shining saint. The sky is golden here, blue is beneath her, tinged with pinks and purples. Agnes rises still, smiling all the while. She spreads her arms, trusting that there will be wings attached to her shoulder blades, and she is lifted at a greater speed.

'Flora takes one of Agnes's hands, and I hold the other. The offering of her arms is the first indication she has given, for many hours, of consciousness. We speak her name, cheered by the flickering of her eyelids. Agnes smiles, she sighs contentedly.

'Agnes is too close to the sun. It will melt her to particles of moisture, or she will burn to cinders. She must reverse her journey, must fall away from this intense heat. Her legs flay helplessly about: her arms seem gripped by some force she cannot overcome. With a final effort she conjures up skates for her feet, iron weights tied on to help drag her down. It works; she falls, thank God, she falls.

'But her descent is too swift, she will not be able to land without breaking. Already she is through the clouds and can see the white world below. The hole in the ice waits for her. She speeds towards it. Hands try to grab her as she enters it: this time they fail. Her eyes, ears and nose fill with freezing water; weeds lasso her ankles. For a moment she floats under the ice, seeing Flora's face as if through layer upon layer of glass. Flora's mouth moves, silent as a fish, desperate as a mother.

Agnes sinks and dies...

'We may not have cried aloud, but the grief we felt caused a wail in our hearts that could not be silenced. Agnes's death marked the beginning of a period of tragedies and troubles, which affected our lives for their durations. I believe, had Mother not been the tyrant she was, that the greatest of those disasters, the saddest of those tragedies, might have been avoided.

'I need you to know my mother, in every one of her guises, before I dare reveal any further family secrets, my dear. I picture you in Ramsons, as I am at this moment, snug by the stove, reading my words. I hope there is a man by your side and that he will comfort and distract you. Whatever your situation, please don't let this history distress you unduly, for it is only that now, a history.

'Your loving Great Aunt, Tilly.'

Gill wasn't snug by the stove, she was sitting on the bare floorboards of Tilly's old bedroom, her back against an oak chest, an eiderdown around her shoulders. She was without a man to comfort or distract; and the family history did upset her. It struck a warning in her head.

As if sleepwalking, she got to her feet and went to the window. She knew Babs would be out there, waiting her turn; and sure enough, Gill thought she saw the slim figure, elegant and evil, half hidden in the arch of a doorway opposite. If Ramsons should be sold or given away, if Babs was to take possession and refurbish it, wouldn't the cursed history of the Durrys be vanquished? Lost under coats of paint and new kitchen units? Gill couldn't conceive of a day when she might hand over the heavy key and step contentedly into a rosy future.

She made her way to the children's room. Their door was open a fraction but no light came through the crack. A faint smell of urine hit Gill when she gently pushed the door further. It took some time for her eyes to adjust to the darkness of the little bedroom but once she could see, she discovered Rosie on the bottom bunk, curled in sleep, hugging Mr. Tibbs close to her face. Adam wasn't in his bed. He was squatting in the furthest corner, under the window. Gill saw his eyes, tiny points of light, lift and lower. He had not eaten or drunk anything for at least twenty-four hours, Gill realized. Neither had she, or Rosie.

"Why are you out of bed?" she asked Adam, not unkindly. He didn't so much as shrug. She crossed the room to him, crushing already broken toys underfoot. He shrank from her and she felt tears arrive in her eyes. She squatted too, directly in front of him. "I'm not cross any more, Adam," she whispered. "I'm only sad."

8.

Last night a voice called me from outside my bedroom door.

From time to time, the phone would ring. Sometimes Gill answered it but when she did pick up the receiver, she invariably wished she hadn't.

First, June wanted to know her plans for Christmas. "I have none," Gill answered, tersely. "I suppose I might go to Edinburgh if Seb's still there." June said she didn't see how Gill could drag herself and two small children all the way to Scotland, in the depths of winter. With June's use of the word 'depths', severe weather fell on Gill's already clouded hopes of a cheery, sociable holiday. And had she, as June assumed, intended to take, let alone to drag, her children with her? She convinced herself she had.

Bella called in order to announce that she had reached the tearful stage of early motherhood. Gill suggested she eat large amounts of chocolate. Bella moaned about being the size of a terrace of houses already. Gill closed the conversation, pretending she had something more pressing to do than comforting her best friend.

She could barely bring herself to speak to Seb when he rang. He was having a fantastic time: working, playing, feasting, celebrating, and no doubt screwing some nubile actress or worse, a teenage theatrical groupie. If he needed Gill's blessing, he could whistle for it.

The final time Gill answered the telephone, the caller introduced herself as the secretary from Adam's school. "We wondered why he's been absent for the last few days?"

"Ill," Gill mumbled, "we are all ill. Contagious," she added bleakly, cutting the woman off. After that, she disconnected the phone.

The doorbell also irritated Gill, with its insistent clanging so close to the kitchen, in the cupboard under the back stairs. As far as she was concerned, nobody of any importance would come visiting her. Without her camera, Gill could see no good, find no purpose. She'd have avoided herself, if this were an option.

Along with one morning's post that included another of Tilly's letters, there was a card from one of those do-good organizations. Offering help to parents who were suffering from stress, these noble minds had come up with no better name for themselves than *Parents In Need*. Gill thought this inapt; as far as she could see, parenthood and need were synonymous. It was like having a club full of clerics and calling it *Vicars Who Pray*.

There was also a scribbled note from the mechanic to say he'd mended her car: Gill supposed he must have been one of the people to ring her bell. Had she told the man where she lived? Or had her fame spread throughout the village..?

"Have you seen her, the hermit great-niece of the last Miss Durry, living alone in the big house, going slowly mad?"

"Not so slowly, as it happens, my dear, the signs are that she spends her time tossing buttons."

"Tossing buttons?"

"Don't ask!"

Gillian believed, should she open the front door a fraction, she would hear this kind of gossip buzzing in the foggy air.

At least there was now the possibility of escape. Along with his note, the genial mechanic had posted the car keys. Gill and her children would shop properly, as did the masses, in a supermarket. She thought she might stock up, in case of snow or other impediments. If she never needed to visit Mrs. Monk's shop again that would be fine by her.

Not only was Gill taken aback by the amount of energy and organization required to dress the children, then to load them into the waiting car but she was also disturbed to find she'd lost the ability to drive. She knew how to start the engine, how to change gear and so on; it was avoiding the other vehicles on the road that threw her. Cars and lorries came at her from all angles, entering her vision on both sides, appearing in front of her without warning. Had the motoring world doubled in volume and speed during the last couple of months? This was one explanation, Gill told herself as a delivery van missed her by inches. The other possibility was that she had become an alien, slow-witted, flabby creature that didn't belong on this tarmac planet.

One who should be lolling on a distant star, its useless fingers waving at the cosmos, its dim but untroubled brain full of nothing but synthetic songs. She liked that idea: any other civilization must be easier to cope with than this whizzing, horn-honking, fist-raising culture of metal and wheels.

Gill had little idea which way to head. She turned south on the A1, towards Peterborough and, so the sign said, London. It was tempting; she could be there by evening. Sarah lived in London. As Gill drove, flinching each time a vehicle sped past her, she pictured her sister's house in Clapham, tucked in a long row of similar, compact, comfortable homes. They would be warm there. They'd be safe. Then she saw the bright lights of commerce, including the Tesco sign, and the Morris almost steered itself down the slip road towards this enticement.

Having parked, Gill took an enormous trolley from the rack; the idea of filling it swamped her. She sat Rosie in the front and insisted Adam should hold on to her. If the roads had been alarming, the aisles of the supermarket were pandemonium. Shoppers pushed aggressively at one another. Somebody trod on Adam's toes, causing him to cry out and then to hop about under Gill's feet. From hidden speakers banal music was insistently audible above the hum of voices. Rosie's eyes and mouth were round with awe as, seated in her lethal weapon, she leaned towards the shelves, grabbing tins and packets. "Stop that," Gill warned, replacing a box of instant whips. Having her face on a level with Rosie's made her uncomfortable. She rarely looked her daughter in the eye.

Rosie seemed to share Gill's discomfort, or perhaps she merely grew bored with the word 'no'. She started to snivel, then to cry with her usual energy. "Out," she pleaded as snot bubbles circled her nostrils, "Get out." Gill found a tissue, wiped Rosie's nose with a touch too much force, promising as she leaned into the moist, troubled face, "You can go back to the car if you don't shut up, understand?" Rosie turned her whole body from side to side, as far as the confines of her seat allowed, also kicking her legs against the metal until the shopping shuddered. Adam let go of Gill's coat, which he'd been holding by the pocket. "You see?" Gill cried at Rosie, "Adam is ashamed to be with you, you're such a pain in the arse." A middle-aged man looked up from the tin he was examining. A pubescent boy sniggered. Gill pushed her trolley faster, away from a gathering audience. To think, only minutes ago she'd been relishing the idea of shopping, of being swept along in the scurry of people occupying these aisles, of possibly sharing a light-hearted moment at the check-out. It occurred to Gill, as Rosie's screams drowned the awful music and caused eyebrows to rise, what a dearth of adult company she suffered from, these days. But when a woman did approach, to advise her to lift Rosie from the trolley before the poor little mite injured herself, Gill was reminded that humanity itself was alien, opposed, ganging up against her in a scowling mass of disapproval.

Of course, once Rosie was out of the trolley, she wanted to be back in it. She also desired everything within her reach, each bright object being a magnet for those chubby fingers. Plastic and rubber were especially appealing. At one point, Gill found herself wrestling with Rosie over a squeaky bone. "It is a toy," she owned, "but it was made for a dog, not for a naughty, noisy girl. Put it back."

Inevitably, Rosie ended up on the floor, legs flaying in a way that had become familiar, face contorted as if in extreme pain. By this time, the trio had reached the long queue to pay. "What?" Gill shouted at the women who frowned on her. "What would you do, then? Buy her every damn thing she wants, including doggy chews and toys? Tie her to the trolley? Kneel by her side while the queue moves slowly on and over you?" Nobody responded. In fact, as the music of the tills accompanied the crowd's hubbub, Gill was unsure whether or not she had spoken aloud. Her head hurt and her throat was dry. Clearly she now inhabited a desolate landscape where thinking and speaking to oneself are indistinguishable. Where the chance of engaging in easy conversations with others, let alone of encountering any soul mates, was as unlikely as a troop of kangaroos in Trafalgar Square.

The man in front of Gill was wearing trousers that were too short for his lanky legs. His ankles were extraordinarily tanned. But his hands, neck and face were white, pasty even. Yes, he seemed to be a pale person with exceptionally tanned ankles and feet. Gill stared down, trying to guess why only his legs had been exposed to sunlight. Had he perhaps sat for many an hour, head and arms beneath a parasol but legs stretched out until his naked feet toasted to this rich gold? No, she realized on making a surreptitious bend towards the floor, there had been no sun whatsoever. The man was wearing tight, golden brown socks, the exact shade that skin turns in ideal, holiday conditions. Mesmerised by this optical illusion, Gill had to be tapped on the shoulder by the person behind her when the queue moved on.

The shopping tobogganed into piles while Gill struggled to open carrier bags, calm Rosie, find her purse. Adam had abandoned her, going on ahead to sit, legs swinging in affected nonchalance, on one of a series of chairs provided for the elderly or, in his case, the frail. In order to pay, Gill had to lift Rosie, whose knickers and tights were more than a little damp, and stuff her back into the child's seat. At this, Rosie opened her mouth for a final howl and Gill grabbed a tube of Smarties from the nearest display. The skill with which she put this in Rosie's hand and also, instantly, into her mouth, should have won her an award. With any luck, the child would swallow the plastic top, necessitating a trip to hospital: Gill experienced a moment of peace just contemplating the possibility of Rosie's being cared for by professionals.

In the car park, under cover of a darkness that had fallen while she'd been bathed in neon lighting, Gill forced Rosie's fingers from the Smarties's tube. It wasn't an easy wrestle but no matter what the protests, it was essential the sweets be shared between brother and sister; although, since the plastic top had disappeared, down Rosie's throat or not, most of the bright sweets ended up sprinkled like magic beans over the bags of shopping.

After the race back in the glare of headlights that was the A1 by night, Gill found the grey flagstones of the hallway almost welcoming. By the light of a single, overhead bulb, jars of jams and pickles winked at her from behind the smeared glass of their cupboards. Deeper in the house, a barometer lied about the weather while the Grandfather clock remained confused as to the hour. Gill no longer bothered about them; she preferred muddled instruments to harsh precision. She'd rather not know the proper time or how cold it really was. From now on she'd do as she pleased, eat when hungry, drink whenever, sleep as tiredness dictated.

By her calculations the shopping from Tesco, if consumed wisely, could last until Seb returned. It was 1980, the year of the tin and the packet; storing food no longer meant growing, steaming, pickling or laying out your own produce. A family might live for months, maybe years, on the contents of a supermarket trolley. As she unpacked her carrier bags, she felt an unusual but not unwelcome smugness. But within minutes she was remembering a summer afternoon she'd spent, alongside her Aunty Flora, preparing runner beans for their Kilner jars. Topping and tailing, the work was called. Hours later, lying in a bed full of teddy bears, Gill had sucked and sniffed her fingers. They had tasted of earth; they had smelt of a green that was perpetual and, somehow, maidenly.

Well, she had beans enough for a siege now, mostly the bright orange variety, swimming in sugar and tomato sauce. There was spaghetti to match, which both children would eat morning, noon and night if allowed. Shame there was no freezer in the house. Gill would have found a hoard of fish fingers and minced meat as consoling as a barricade.

Apart from the likelihood of an encounter with Babs, Gill couldn't have explained quite why she cherished being shut up inside Ramsons. It was only the cold, she told herself, making her shun the village. Once this winter was over, she'd emerge with a smile, she'd join playgroups and who knows, maybe even make occasional appearances at the W.I. On second thoughts… she winced at the thought of flower arranging or weaving. There would be no need, anyway. As soon as Seb returned, she'd have her camera mended and begin work on the project she'd been assigned to do. Only, wasn't the assignment for shots of Lincolnshire in the autumn? A season that was already over? She couldn't quite remember; didn't want to think about it. She hurled a tin of peas across the horrid, vast, ice-cold kitchen.

The tin only missed Rosie's head by inches. Good God, Gill thought bitterly as her daughter voiced her upset, now I'll have to live with her howling for another eternity.

It was evening, evidently. Beyond the windows the garden was a dense, dark jungle. Perhaps it was night, actually, Gill thought: hadn't she driven home in darkness, some hours ago? She could see if there was life in the pub across the road; that would give an indication of the lateness of the hour. It didn't much matter. It was dark and they were hungry. Dinner first, then bed. Life could be that simple if you just let it.

Except, here everything was so damned difficult. The Rayburn couldn't be bothered to give off any heat so cooking was not an option and they ate their tinned ravioli cold, with slices of bread and butter. The children were grubby, Gill had to admit. It had been several days since they'd been bathed. Both enjoyed a bath, so letting them splash about would be something positive and enjoyable, on this day which had so far not been remotely merry or bright.

Ah, but of course, there was no hot water. While Adam and Rosie stood on the bathroom's floral lino, shivering in the nude, Gill ran up and down the back stairs, like a demented mother on a school sport's day, carrying kettles full of boiling water. The children then sat one on each side of a bucket of hot water, in the old iron bath. The bath itself was so cold Gill had visions of backsides frozen to the metal. She found two flannels for the children to perch on. Floating on its tragically tiny circle of water was a single duck who had been fashioned in the days when care was given to detail. Painted in red, green and yellow, it possessed sculpted feathers and a pleasingly pert tail. As she watched the toy being flicked from child to child, it occurred to Gill that the bucket containing all her little ones' delight might be the same item Tilly had used on her final night at Ramsons. She had to get them away from it: they would be stained for life. Distraught, she hurried for towels from the airing cupboard, on the back landing. In her mind, she was already lifting Adam, dropping him on the lino and reaching for Rosie; saving them. Behind the doors of the airing cupboard were not only towels but also piles of clothing, including nightgowns. Touching one of these, Gill saw herself in a long, white nightgown and a pair of wellingtons, burying a bucket under an apple tree. So long ago, it seemed, that the incident might have been one of Tilly's tales... but it had been her, Gill, wearing that gown; and she *had* put the bucket in the ground, purposefully, in order to avoid moments such as this. How could she have forgotten?

Her hand shifted from the nightgown to the towels and she pulled out two of these. Something moved across the newly exposed towel. Something *moved*. Gill's instinct was to step back, shut the door, pretend to have seen nothing. But she was curious. She lifted a third towel. Several red-brown creatures scurried from sight. Gill shut the door and shook out the towels in her hands, not once glancing at the floor of the landing.

The children fell easily into sleep. Gill hummed to herself as she cleared up the bathroom and then the kitchen. A track from Cat Stevens' L.P. 'Teaser and the Firecat' drifted into her head, the words so appropriate she found herself smiling as she mumbled them: *If I laugh just a little bit maybe I can recall the way that I used to be…*

At one point she saw herself as Snow White, sweeping a stone floor with a broom made of twigs. Keeping house until her luck changed, while the Wicked Witch paced outside devising her downfall. The Wicked Witch had a familiar look. How hard Gill concentrated on Babs, as every last hint of warmth seeped from the Rayburn. It was a triumph, the way her mind dwelt on that woman, conjuring a face whitened by creams and powders, offset by ruby red lips. While she was on her feet, Gill might fetter her thoughts: but it was no use, she couldn't remain upright forever.

The moment she collapsed on a chair, the second she thought the word 'cockroach', the entire house crawled with the things. Floors turned chestnut as the insects covered them. Tea towels came alive. Rows of tiny antennae were visible at the edges of drawers, weapons of an army in waiting. Gill's feet began to itch, her hands to tremble. She tore at her clothing, unbuttoning her jeans and flicking the elastic of her knickers as if to release trapped roaches. Tilly's latest letter fell from her pocket to the floor; surely it would be devoured by insects if Gill let it lie? Her spine curled reluctantly as she bent, her fingers froze half an inch from the paper, expecting cause to recoil.

Gill put the letter back in her pocket. She stood on a chair and pulled down all of the tins from the shelf over the Rayburn. With shaking hands she tipped some herbs and spices from each tin into a mug and then added hot water. As she carried this potion to her bed, she felt the crush of creatures with every tread of her feet. Somewhere, in an old film or on television, Gill had watched a man catching bugs on a bar of damp soap - not cockroaches but bedbugs, not that the species mattered so long as the solution worked. She chose a bar of Camay, still wrapped in its pink, waxy paper. *'You'll look a little lovelier each day…'* she was promised, *'with fabulous pink Camay.'* Fabulous indeed if it could banish this infestation. The bar slid from its wrapping, leaving flakes like dandruff on Gill's fingers. The scent of roses filled her throat a moment later when she gulped a couple of dreadful mouthfuls from the mug of herbs.

The fact that the used Camay was covered in nothing more than a smattering of eyelashes and pubic hairs didn't convince Gill that her bed was without unwelcome visitors. The roaches had seen the light, literally, and fled, as roaches do; but they wouldn't have scuttered far.

125

Her body heat would draw them back, she was afraid. Yet she had to sleep, the weight was increasing on her eyelids and around the back of her skull. Each limb ached to be stretched out and then relaxed. It was too cold to lie on top of the covers. She got into bed fully clothed and lay rigid as an effigy, the bar of soap in one hand, Tilly's letter in the other.

Propped high on pillows that undoubtedly housed swarms of insects, she unfolded her letter. Here I am, she thought, surrounded by more life than a person should have occasion to encounter, reading post from dead people. The plural was intentional: Tilly's may have been the hand holding the pen but Gill knew these stories were recounted by the lot of them - the Durrys, damn them all. She took another, hefty swig of the herbal drink.

Gill skipped Tilly's opening words, the 'dear-great-niece-I-hope-this finds-you-warm-and-quick-unlike-me' bit and let her eyes, which were increasingly heavy with impending sleep, fall on the latest instalment in the family saga.

'As I implied,' Tilly had written in her precise yet curly handwriting, 'all our lives were deeply affected by the death of Agnes. Mother was especially stricken, to a degree she couldn't have anticipated. To begin with, we saw less of Father. He explained his absences by insisting he was busier than ever before. The growing number of newspaper articles praising his architectural successes did give credibility to his excuse - but he was engaged in designing a series of Playhouses along England's East Coast, work close enough to home for him to have spent weekends with us, had he chosen to do so.

'His remaining children missed him dreadfully; we could have used an ally as Mother grew ever more ill-humoured. None of us blamed him, though, for keeping his distance from a house so cast down in sorrow. Had the chance to escape Ramsons, under almost any condition, presented itself to us, we would have fled without a backwards glance. Jethro seemed suddenly keen to go and fight, for example. One afternoon, I caught him crossing days off a calendar and, although I gave him only the smallest shake of my head, my blood froze at the prospect of another bereavement.

'From the moment of Agnes's death, Flora, as you may imagine, was inconsolable. Her grief subsided from fierce fits of weeping to a nightmarish state of vacancy; it was as if she inhabited her loss. We were none of us able to approach her: hers was an impenetrable abode through which she wandered aimlessly, swollen-eyed, maudlin, her fingers bitten until they marked all her clothes, and each piece of linen she touched, with mournful spots of red.

'As for Evangelina, well, she too was altered. She grew straighter, taller, nourished by fresh supplies of power to wield whenever she chose. I believe she thought to benefit from Agnes's demise: but it was Eva, second only to Flora, who ultimately suffered the greatest blow. It began with a quarrel over a comb, of all things. Your grandmother had hair to match her fiery temperament, as no doubt June has told you. It's a shame colour photography didn't exist when Eva was a young woman. Mind you, I find it hard to conceive of a camera being able to capture the many reds, the multitude of tones, within a strand of Eva's locks. No woman was ever more proud of her hair. To torture Eva, one need only threaten her with scissors or a razor. (Which I am ashamed to admit, we did, when she was especially irksome).

'Have you ever studied the screen that was employed as a divide for the largest bedroom? It is one of the few items crafted by all five of us Durry children. A carpenter constructed its frame, of course, but every image on the stretched canvas was pasted there by us children. A labour of love, it was one of the most satisfying occupations we were to undertake. First we had to find interesting or pretty pictures, a search that included post and greeting cards, Pictorials and posters from our father's theatres. Because Jethro took part, there are less of the hearts and roses you tend to see on such screens and more wild animals, more acrobats, fire-eaters and flying machines. We would lie in a circle, on our stomachs, with the day's collection of pictures in a heap at our fingertips. A strange creature we must have seemed, with our legs bent backwards, our weight up on our elbows: a starfish, perhaps, or a spider deep in concentration, creating something even more durable than a web.

'Our task lasted for many months and so there were, obviously, occasions when one or the other of us would be absent. One spring day, Eva was chosen to accompany Mother on a shopping trip. Mother deemed Eva to be the sole person in the house, besides herself, who possessed a modicum of good taste. The rest of us regrouped around the pile of pictures on the bedroom floor and decided, unanimously, to include an image Eva had already shunned.

'It is a rural, domestic picture, not a work of great talent but engaging enough. It implies a mischief we children found alarming and arousing, a combination that enforced the decision to include it against Eva's wishes. It is there still, although badly scratched, not by Eva as you might suppose, but by a naughty Jack Russell who liked to jump up on furnishings. The poor old screen has ripped in places. It has been kicked, both accidentally and on purpose. Dress fastenings have caught on it as women swish by. Sunlight has drained colour from it. Yet it survives: a record of times gone by and, with the exception of this one domestic painting, a catalogue of mutual, childhood preferences.

'Had Eva been a lovable sister, we would no doubt have kept the offensive print to ourselves, locking it in a bureau rather than displaying it. It was an act of pique, if not of revenge, to paste that image on the canvas, to then surround it with other, smaller pictures, so that the thing could not be removed without ruining a large area. We intended to wound Mother's favourite.

'In the picture Eva so disliked, the artist has shown us a kitchen that seems to belong to a run-down farmhouse. The furniture is plain but solid, a large oak table, which has not been cleared of the day's meals, various chairs, an ugly, dark dresser housing a selection of pewter ware. The floor is merely compacted earth, reddish-brown, mottled by litter. About this floor and across the table, chickens roam freely. In a huge fireplace mere cinders glow because, like the table, the fire is untended. There is a small dog, asleep on a pile of what might be clothes awaiting a wash. Also asleep, in a chair, arms folded over a more than adequate bosom, is a young woman whose dress is faded and torn, whose bare feet are decidedly grubby. Her head droops but we can see that she has rosy cheeks and a pleasing, though slightly slack, mouth. Behind her stands a man...'

Gill is on her feet, no longer cold or tired, no longer disturbed by thoughts of insects. She walks through the bathroom, across a small landing, up two steps, along a short corridor. There are more rooms to this part of the house than she had realized. It is a warren in which a single bedroom might easily be lost. But the object of her exploration is not a missing room; she is hunting for the largest bedroom, which was once shared by Evangelina and Matilda and for which, the girls not being close companions, a screen was fashioned. Gill opens doors, sometimes having to apologise to those she surprises. In one room a round, plain woman sits, slumped on a narrow bed, rubbing what looks like lard into the soles of her feet. In another Gill spies Great Uncle Jethro, hooking his thumbs through a pair of red braces, turning before a long mirror to admire the cut of his newly issued, military trousers. When she mutters, "Sorry," he gives his descendant a neat bow. Gill grows cautious, not daring to imagine how it will be if she should disturb Elizabeth and Edward. She hears laughter and understands that she can't be far from Agnes. When she opens the right door, she is transformed, promoted, into the leading player. Eva stands before the unfinished screen, frozen with horrid fascination, glaring at a picture she has seen before, and had rejected. In fact she expressly asked for it not to be included because, displayed in this way, it is bound to haunt her. Her hateful siblings have stuck it right in the screen's centre. A pronounced taunt.

Like her, the woman in the painting has copper coloured hair. In natural waves it falls, down beyond her shoulders. The subject sleeps; she is slovenly, lazy perhaps, but for the time being sleep renders her innocent — she is about to be assaulted.

Soon there will be such anger; Eva feels it, like coals, firing her guts. For the moment, though, there is stillness, the stare of a rabbit hypnotized by a snake. She cannot take her eyes from the picture; and it is not the idle woman she studies, it is the stocky, cheeky faced young man who has crept up behind her. The gleam in his eyes highlights his intent. The tip of his tongue peeps through his lips, a sign of concentration. He holds a lock of the sleeping woman's hair in one hand, a pair of scissors in the other.

Eva feels his breath on her neck, she can smell his meat and ale sourness. She feigns sleep now, and her scalp tightens as he runs the lock of her hair between his coarse fingers. He is entirely male, a strutting cockerel, a creature of the farmyard, good only for labouring with other animals and, Eva shudders to own it, the act of copulation.

He sneaks a glance over his shoulder, to make sure he will not be caught. One beam of sunlight has stolen, like the young man, through the open door. It rests on his head, accusing him.

Eva knows his fingers have begun their task. She can feel a calloused fingertip against her flesh, in that most sensitive spot, directly behind her ear. She could not move if she wished to; but what disturbs her is the willingness with which she stays, caught by a strand, held by a single thread that she experiences for the first time but which she nevertheless recognizes as lust.

Perhaps the man intends to snip himself a keepsake, merely. It is possible that he will cut only a token piece of hair, tuck this in the pocket of his breeches and creep back into the yard. The lock of hair will remain, perhaps, curled against one of his buttocks, a neighbour to feathers, strands of tobacco, seeds and straws, until he is drunk one night and remembers it. Then, having dug about in his back pocket, he'll hold it up before his cronies, a trophy to support an unsound boast.

This supposition is enough to prickle Eva's feelings; but it is far from the worst possibility. Whatever the artist meant to imply, Eva sees malice in the chubby young man's eyes. He is too foul, even for the lazy serving girl; surely she has spurned him in the past. Eva thinks he means to crop her entire head. In order to teach her a lesson, he will leave her with nothing but unsightly tufts of hair.

Her hands fly to her scalp, cradling it. She gathers all her locks under her protection but she still sees them at her feet, rusted springs, lifeless, woodland creatures, fallen leaves. Her best, most precious blessings, hacked from her by a brute.

Eva stamps her feet, she screams, throws back her head until it aches. Her eyes bulge with fury. She will not have it. How dare they? Oh yes, they have heard her now. Here they come, Meek, Mild and Stupid, with the dull child Agnes in tow. "You, you, you," Eva yells. Then words fail and there are only sounds of hate, cries of revenge and, finally, dreams of escape.

Eva turns her back on the screen, swearing never to so much as glance at the cursed thing again. On this day, she promises, her emotions shall detach themselves from her family, like leeches that have been salted.

When the screen is finished and unfolded across the room she shares with Tilly, Eva throws shawls, dresses, even underwear, over her side of it; although Tilly has thoughtfully ensured the 'hair painting' – as the thing is now known – faces away from Eva. Then Elizabeth's favoured daughter waits.

Gill is pacing the big room, her back straight, her head high. She is content to accept that she is Eva now. How better to understand herself than to become her most troubled ancestor? What talents there are, what energy there is, going to waste in this sterile house, in this tedious village. Eva is a cat, on the prowl. She preens herself in readiness, because she sees that Life is also waiting. Innocent as yet of Eva's forthcoming impact, Life stalks the potted palms of a Mayfair club, tipping his cigarette ash on an Italian marble floor. Life takes a cab to the most fashionable restaurant, dines with the famous and the infamous. He is the man, the one man, and Eva is the woman who will perfect him. It is unthinkable that he should not bide his time until she, Evangelina Durry, makes her entrance; but she does think it. She dreads him meeting some other woman, some false blonde, perhaps, or a dark beauty. Most untenable is the possibility that Life might mistake another redhead for his chosen companion, because he must have a preference for this colouring, after all. Ooohhh! Eva moves to the window, leans against it, both hands high on the cold glass, fingers spread, body pressed close to the pane as if she might melt through her prison, into freedom.

An argument over a comb, Tilly wrote. Gill sees how it is. Agnes has died and everybody is moping about, duller even than usual in blacks and greys. None of them seem prepared to move on, except Jethro who has finally ceased parading his uniform at home in order to parade it in the war. His send off at the station, although muted, was the one bright moment in an age of tedium; and that only because there were other, more jovial families on the platform, waving flags and whistling at their young men.

With this morning's post, Tilly received confirmation of her acceptance by the College for Gentlewomen in Golders Green, North London. She is to train to become a teacher, or possibly a governess. Father has decreed that Flora must remain at home, to help Mother and keep her company. However, being a modern man, he will allow his second daughter to take a profession. She cannot, of course, begin her studies until the war is over, both Tilly and the college in question agree on this; but she is destined for London, once she has done with folding bandages, knitting socks, or whatever. Eva could have eaten the letter, she so hated to see it in her sister's hands. "What about me?" she asked, petulant as a three year old. Her mother had smiled, a sly movement of her dry, old lips, and replied, "I would not dream of losing you, Evangelina. I need to see you day by day, if I am to stay sane." It is just possible she was teasing, a rare act for Mother: but Eva felt the ill wind of a cage door closing in her face.

Now she grasps an opportunity, provided by Flora's taking an afternoon walk, to sort through the few possessions Agnes left behind. Why ever not? They'll only sit here, year after year, fading, disintegrating. Maybe there is something Eva can sell. She has decided to save enough money for a fare to... to anywhere other than here. The beads are mostly cheap glass, not even semi-precious gems, they have no value but the sentiment Eva deplores. The books being childish, Eva discards all of these. Flora has placed Agnes's clothes in a trunk, lining each layer with tissue paper. Eva disturbs the dresses; she shakes out the skirts; she creases the blouses, which are of no use to her, having no bust darts whatsoever. It is a waste of time, this search for something worth having. She moves from the trunk to the dressing table and toys with the idea of taking Agnes's hairbrush, which is decorated, on the back, by a peacock in silver. But the brush still holds many of the child's long, mouse-brown hairs; Eva cannot touch it. However, there is a comb that seems unsullied, in fact it looks unused. Besides, a comb will wash. A grown-up object for the child to have possessed; it was a present from Father, who loved to spoil Agnes. The teeth of the comb are concealed by a hand that rests over them, the fingers gently curving to a point. Carved from malachite, this hand is the green of a wet leaf, a water lily, Eva thinks, trying it in her hair. Green and red complement each other as she hoped they would. It sits prettily above her left ear, easing a curl from her face. She simply loves it.

The front door opens and Eva quickly returns Agnes's clothes to the trunk. She slips from the room and is hurrying down the back stairs before Flora has finished clumping up the front ones.

During tea, Flora's face slackens with astonishment; she has spotted the comb, which Eva has left in her hair. Too late now, Eva thinks, tracing the malachite fingers with her own: no point in removing it. The idea of apologizing to Flora flits across her mind, irritating as a gnat. Good God, she thinks, how like a basset hound Flora seems! And Mother looks a hawk today: her talons, protruding from her black, fingerless gloves, shred slices of bread and butter, scratch the roses on the porcelain plates. In fact, what a miserable quartet they make, fit only for performing the bleakest of dirges. Not a dash of joy, nor a speck of colour between them; except for the comb in its nest of burnished hair.

After tea, Flora stops Eva on the front stairs. She has bulk on her side, Eva cannot pass. The sun is low in the sky outside, spreading a pink light through the stained glass so that Eva's face is puce as Flora looks down on it. But the fury is all Flora's and her colour rises too. "Give me back that comb," she demands, holding out an unsteady hand.

"Why?" Eva counters. "What makes you think you have a right to every single thing that once belonged to Agnes? Has it never occurred to you that the rest of us might like a memento, that we miss her too?" For a second, Flora is trounced by this attack. She reaches for the bannister as she considers what she may have to part with. Imagine bequeathing the peacock hairbrush to Tilly, or the coral necklace to Eva – no, Flora simply can't. As for this comb, which Agnes adored, well, Flora must have it back, on the dressing table, at all costs. "I will take it from you if you don't return it this instant," she warns Eva, borrowing Mother's turn of phrase if not her tone of voice.

"Try!" Eva sneers, "I dare you to."

The sisters collide as Eva turns to run back down the stairs. Flora grips one of Eva's arms, pulls at the seat of her skirt. Eva spins around, smashes both fists into that vile, fleshy stomach. Flora cries, Eva screams. Cloth rips and skin stings. Tilly and Mother appear at the bottom of the stairs, the one fraught the other furious. They add their voices until the house seems a zoo of creatures bleating, growling, shrieking. Their blood is up, at last. No more pretence of a life in any kind of order. Frustration swells to outright hatred; grief finally implodes. Mother strikes at daughter. Sisters claw each other's eyes. And Flora knots her fingers in Evangelina's hair and tugs until she has in her hand a bloodied auburn tress, complete with those other fingers of green and the comb they conceal.

Gill would collapse now, if only she could. She'd like to sit on the stairs, feeling for the patch of scalp that has been so fiercely assaulted, trembling when her fingertips come from the wound sticky and stained. But her ear is gripped by yet another hateful hand and Elizabeth Durry pulls her to her feet. She is dragged back up the stairs, into the largest bedroom, where she is thrown against the screen so that it falls before her as she hits the floor. "You can stay there," Elizabeth yells, "until I decide on a fitting way to deal with you." In the doorway, Flora and Tilly have become one snivelling body, two headed but without a brain or a single ounce of courage.

Eva gets to her feet. Shock has cursed her voice with a tremor but that is the only sign of weakness as she calls her mother back. "I will not stay," she says "and you cannot make me." Elizabeth opens her mouth but Eva lunges forwards and stops it with her hand. "I am not afraid of you," she explains. "I could beat you in any fight, if need be, and I won't cower to you any more." She removes her hand and while her mother splutters ineffectually she releases an eloquent fountain of truths and secrets, until there is an end to interruptions. She tells her mother how all her children have defied her, in their way, in their time. Jethro used to help himself to Mother's herbs, did she really not notice how his eyes would glaze over? How he would look like a bush-baby one minute and be dead asleep the next? As for the meek, obedient Tilly, well, she has been seeing a young man, right here in Staunley. "Under your nose," Eva taunts, much as if she has enjoyed the flirtation herself. "Oh yes! Matilda has been sneaking off for long, intense walks, hiding with *him* in church on weekdays, leaving her lover before they reach the bend in the street so that those inside Ramsons might not see them together."

As Mother turns to glare at Matilda, Eva spits out the next revelation: "Flora steals food, of course. Nobody could grow that fat on the portions you serve at table. Not only does she raid the larder but she has a contract with Lizzie: I've yet to discover what her side of the bargain might be. Lizzie makes biscuits and cakes when you are out, Mother, then she disguises the smell of baking with boiled cabbage or a pan of offal. Perhaps, in return, Flora has been supplying Liz with trinkets from Agnes's jewellery case, there certainly seems little enough left…" At this, Flora disentangles herself from Tilly and flies once more in her sister's face. As they fight, Eva cries, "Don't play the righteous with me, you're more to blame for Agnes's death than anyone, you let her go skating, you encouraged her."

"Skating?" Mother bellows, prising her daughters apart. "When did she go skating? Who encouraged that? What is this?"

Eva inhales deeply. This is the moment for which she has waited and planned. Here is an end to her misery; she need only spread out her remaining secrets in one grand, liberating gesture. And so she tells. Flora knew Agnes was going to the frozen river. Tilly and Jethro knew she had fallen through the ice. Lizzie helped to hide the freezing child. They all conspired, therefore they are all to blame.

It is clear Mother means to box each and every ear, to leave no shoulder unshaken, to sting all her daughters' cheeks with slaps. And then to continue retribution in whatever way she sees fit. She is ripping at her cuffs, trying to roll up her sleeves in readiness. Her flesh has turned a violent colour. Her eyes are slits of yellow. She takes one step towards Eva and is halted by a cry.

"Murderess!" Eva accuses, holding her mother off at arms' length. "But for you, Agnes would be here today, wearing the damn comb in her boring, brown hair, being annoying, being childish, just *being*. You killed her, so don't get holy with us. But for you, she would have gone straight to the kitchen and stripped off, sat by the stove, warmed her blood. All right, so she went skating, against your will. What a crime! But not one to die for, in most families, would you say? What kind of mother are you, to make yourself so fearful a child would rather freeze to death than admit she had disobeyed you? I call you murderess and I mean it, with all my heart. We feel no love for you, nor any loyalty. The only emotion you have nurtured in us is dread. And hate. We hate you." Eva is done, her knees are failing her, she is sinking. "We simply hate you."

Elizabeth need not have bothered with her words of banishment. Eva has no intention of returning, no idea of taking anything other than a few essentials, which Tilly hastily packs in a carpet bag and carries after Eva's departing figure.

"Where will you go?" Tilly asks, catching up. Both sisters shake as if standing at the centre of an earthquake. "To London, I suppose," Eva answers. They are conscious of Ramsons behind them, the windows only dimly lit, the doors closed. Only recently there could have been a person in every window facing the street, now the house is as good as empty. Eva will not hug Tilly, although she experiences genuine regret at the prospect of not seeing her again. "I will be in London before long," Tilly reminds her. "Good for you," Eva turns her back and leaves. Tilly watches her go, thinking how like the lion her sister is, with her tussled mane. Still proud, even after losing the struggle. Although... On reflection, Tilly finds it impossible to decide whether Eva is defeated or, in fact, victorious.

When Eva has rounded the bend in the village street, she stops to remove a shoe, because there is grit or something trapped there, irritating her. To her horror, as she shakes the shoe, a colony of insects falls to the ground and scuttles towards the gutter. Shuddering, Eva inspects the shoe. One creature remains, she catches sight of it burrowing under the inner sole. It has tiny pinchers and a fat, bronze body. As she sits on the side of the road, Eva finally succumbs to tears. She pulls the shoe from her other foot and hits this against the ground. Then she stands, in her stockings, and shakes her skirt, imagining it must also be infested.

A man called Roland Perring, whose weak chest has kept him from the war, is on his way to Ramsons, hoping for a glimpse of Matilda Durry, when he sees Evangelina holding her skirt as if it might burn her fingers - dancing, in fact, in her stockings, like one possessed. What a turnabout, he thinks with a smile, for him to be spying, unnoticed, on her when she has frequently been the one to sneak up on him. She is not as good at spying as she likes to think: Roland has spotted her, darting behind a tree or a column, a light-footed enough nymph but not, as she seemed to assume, an invisible one. Now he sees her mad dance through to its end, watches her rout around in her bag, pull out a purse and, abandoning everything else, step gingerly into her shoes and turn away, heading south.

Minutes later, Roland is still considering the gaping carpet-bag. He decides to leave it be. He always did think Evangelina an odd fish.

*

Gill wandered through Ramsons, thinking of the lost room and of how she had previously considered this romantically, as a cave in which treasures were hidden, whereas now, should she come across it, she expected nothing more than troubles and ghosts. It occurred to her that there had to be a missing room in their old home, in Bristol, and that if they could discover this all would be well. Yes! She should telephone Seb to insist they buy back their home and hunt for the room that would make everything fine again. She saw this untapped space as a solution to problems of storage, entertaining and work. Adam and Rosie played there, on smooth, pale floorboards, while she developed her photographs and Seb learnt lines. Visitors slept there, in four-poster beds. Parties were held; people relaxed on vast floor cushions, praising Gill's exquisite taste for colour and texture. "Thanks," she said, "and to think we never knew this room was here, until we'd left the house!".

She was surprised to find herself in her usual bed the next day. A bar of Camay soap was dissolving in one clammy hand, while Tilly's letter was scrunched in the other. Instead of the ramble she thought she had taken and the fights she believed she'd engaged in, it seemed Gill had lain here, in the same position throughout the night; but she was exhausted, rather than refreshed, all the same.

The children were already up; they were, in fact, locked in their bedroom. Gill had no recollection of having turned the key, which was on the outside of the door, but she thought it only sensible to contain them, against dangers, and decided she would lock them in each night. There could be no falling down stairs, that way, and no chance of them helping themselves to any of Elizabeth's herbs or Tilly's left over medication. Their bedroom stank, Rosie had clearly peed somewhere: her sheets were dry but her pyjama bottoms weren't. The idea of Flora's pretty rugs becoming tainted by urine upset Gill and she smacked Rosie more than once as she dressed the child in the oldest clothes she could find. "If you can't use a toilet, you can't dress nicely," she explained. Not that Rosie cared what she wore, or how smelly she grew.

Gill dished up porridge for breakfast, although it was quite possibly nearer to lunchtime. The winter sun had climbed high enough to look down on them through the smeared windows. Adam ate as if the meal, be it breakfast or lunch, could well be his last. But Rosie played with her food, until Gill was obliged to inhale deeply and take a good look at things. It was something-o'clock on a freezing November morning, or early afternoon, and here they were. Adam had practically eaten his dish. Gill was too tired to eat all at. And Rosie thought food was either a weapon or a toy. Consequently, there was porridge all over Rosie, the floor and the surrounding walls. Gill took a step towards her daughter and shouted, "Use your spoon. This is your spoon. This is your hand. Put the spoon in your hand and use the fucking thing."

The use of the word fucking, aloud, in front of her children, was both shameful and cathartic.

Not consciously thinking of cockroaches but perhaps having an infestation on her mind, Gill then copied her grandmother and stamped her feet, slapped her own body, danced, shook, twisted about on the cold kitchen floor until some of her audience laughed and laughed, while others howled, and howled.

10.

It was no one's voice, perhaps it came from the umbrella stand.

It was growing even colder. Gill insisted that, along with their pyjamas, the children wore gloves, socks and jumpers to bed. She took to putting on woollen tights herself, under Tilly's old nightgown, and wrapping shawls around her shoulders. Her reflection in the long mirror of the wardrobe showed her balancing on one foot, being half way into the tights, trying to shake the unoccupied woollen leg in case any creatures were nesting there. Attempting to keep a pair of knitted shawls from slipping off her back, her stoop was suggestive of osteoporosis. Still, she was nothing if not colourful: the roots of her hair were dark brown below the henna she had last used months ago. Her skin was grey as grit, with mauve shadows highlighting pink eyes. The tights were pillar-box red, the gown was still a crisp white, and the shawls were a riot of pastels.

Post was now her only means of communication. She was still writing letters to Seb, although it had been a while since any were actually sent. There was also a card, which Adam had made and Rosie had scribbled on, waiting to go to Bella and Jon, congratulating them on the birth of whatever-her-name-was. In a Cuban cigar box, Gill found a stash of unused stamps and although many of these were in old currency, some were modern enough to use. But she wouldn't contemplate leaving Ramsons, not even to go the hundred or so yards to the post box.

Most incoming post was of little interest. Free newspapers and advertisements were fuel for the Rayburn. Postcards from Seb told her too little and nagged her too much. Why was the phone not working? Why didn't she get in touch? Never mind him deciding whether or not he was coming back for Christmas, oh no, and where was the money he should be sending to her? Postcards! If she saw one more shot of Edinburgh by night she'd eat the damn thing. June was also in postcard mode: she kept sending views of the Clifton suspension bridge, with similar nagging messages on the back. Then there were notes from

Adam's school and bills from people she'd never heard of.

"Oh lookee here," she told the children over the first meal of one chilly day, "it would seem I have won five thousand pounds, just so long as I buy the abridged version of the complete works of Robert Louis Stephenson, bound in mock plastic, but then again I owe almost as much to some funeral directors and car mechanics. And here's a lovely picture of The Downs, from your granny who implores us to open our doors to all and sundry for the festive season." Hours later, she caught Adam holding the postcard from June before a pair of eyes that had glazed with longing.

As far as Gill was concerned, Tilly's letters were the only ones worth waiting for. At least they imparted information and concerned themselves with Ramsons. Why bother with the rest of the world when it couldn't be bothered with her? Days dragged by, damp and bleak, while Gill anticipated the next instalment from her great aunt.

The nights were no better. Gill was defeated by cold, finding it impossible to keep warm in bed, no matter how many blankets and eiderdowns she piled on. Lack of sleep and a poor diet gave her a feeling of being bloated by frustration, constipated with angst. She was also ever conscious of the infestation that crept through the house. In the corners of her vision, roaches taunted her, scurrying from sight when she turned her head their way. Her flesh itched and was made sore, her feet often tingled from the amount of stamping she did on real or imaginary creatures.

The children became distant and difficult, in their individual ways. Like characters from one of their picture books, Rosie grew more monstrous each day, while Adam turned as pale and gaunt as a ghost child. But then, Gill also seemed to be following a fairy story trail, a walk in the footsteps of wolves.

It was no longer possible to be even-tempered. She came to realize she'd given up the struggle to control her temper when she found herself, one afternoon, with a screaming, kicking Rosie in her arms, heading for the wash-house. "You don't deserve to live in a decent home," she shrieked, as Rosie cried in terror, "if you can't stop pissing everywhere and you won't learn to eat like a human being, and you refuse to allow me some sleep from time to time, then you'll have to live outside, in this shed, until you can behave." This and other bubbling, poisonous sewage spilt from her mouth, unstoppable as any flood.

By the time they reached the wash-house, a fog was lifting, Gill was once more aware of her behaviour, of its total unreasonableness; not that she could stop the rising bubbles, she still craved the release as each one burst from her innards. "This is the place for wicked girls like you," she spat, hurling the child through the door onto the filthy floor. "It's no use your crying now, it's too late. Mummy's had it with you. Mummy needs a time without your screaming in her ear, do you understand?" Rosie cried for her life, taking great, tragic gasps between sobs. Gill leant against the closed door feeling, right through the back of her body, each of Rosie's desperate kicks. She considered leaving Rosie to stew, walking away, not returning until the child had learnt her lesson. Undoubtedly, as she ominously rattled the door's padlock, Gill was enjoying her daughter's distress.

Once she owned up to her enjoyment, guilt took over. Gill sank to her backside on the sodden earth, so that the wash-house door now attacked the small of her back. Through the bare branches of the walnut tree, she spotted Adam's troubled face, on a level with the windowsill of his bedroom, where he was squatting, in semi hiding. The worst of it was Gill couldn't remember precisely what had triggered her outburst. The recent past had taken place in, and been swept away by, an orange tidal wave. Beached, dry as tinder, only shame and sorrow remained. She opened the wash-house door and Rosie fell against her legs, a small, damp bundle of unappealing clothes.

The next day, another letter from Tilly arrived on the mat. Gill, who had taken to wearing a coat indoors except when she was in bed, put this latest episode in her pocket. She had looked forward to receiving it and she was glad to have it there, waiting, tempting; but she realized it might contain more shocks, more news of serious flaws in the personalities who had bred her. It might highlight her own faults, she supposed.

I will try harder, Gill promised herself. I will wrap my children in love and warm clothing and let them play, get mucky, stumble, giggle, as children ought to do. While making this decision, she was watching what had been constant rain turn to light, gentle snow. She knew that to a child even the thinnest layer of snow meant delight. "Look," she told her two, turning towards the kitchen table at which they sat drawing on the backs of used envelopes, "it's snowing." They raised their heads, the curly hair and the dead straight, and blinked like amphibians emerging from under stones. Admittedly, it was dim in the kitchen, but Gill appreciated that they squinted because other, internal, lights had grown dull. Enthusiasm was listless, from lack of exercise. Her children had to be beckoned, encouraged, before they would leave their seats and join her at the window. When she bent to lift Rosie, the little girl collapsed, much as if she was made from fluffy snow. Gill was left holding the shoulders of the cardigan Rosie wore, an ancient hand-knitted item that had once belonged to Tilly. When pulled up, Rosie's body hung from this Fair Isle relic, straining the buttons. "Don't be silly," Gill snapped, "let me show you the snow, for God's sake. You like the snow and you are going to have fun in it, all right?"

Dressed as if for an expedition to the North Pole, the children duly went in the garden to have fun. Gill heard them giving the occasional whoop and, for once, she smiled, remembering how it felt to be small in the snow. Her favourite part of preparing to go out in what June always referred to as 'bad weather' had been rediscovering and donning her woollen hat. This had been red, with a multi-coloured bobble; she missed it as she saw it bounce in her mind's eye. She had shared a sturdy, German toboggan with her sisters. Their united strength had been required to pull this up any hill, so it seemed only fair they should sit together, three torsos straining forwards, six legs scraping the ground, to make their exhilarating, often hair-raising descent. Gill recalled the warmth of that sister sandwich, of having her arms tight around Sarah's waist, while Kate clung to her. Usually, they ended in a heap, thrown from the toboggan, wriggling and giggling and trying to fill each other's mouths with snow. Her hat would be pulled off then and it would fly into the white distance - an exotic, wingless bird.

Now that she could relax knowing Adam and Rosie were out there, enjoying themselves, Gill reached into the pocket of her coat and retrieved Tilly's letter. She sat at the table, on the chair Adam had vacated, and gave only a passing glance at his pictures, most of which involved what passed for people standing on boxes of various sizes.

Today's letter told a tragic love story; it explained why a woman, as pleasant on the eye as Matilda had undoubtedly been, remained unmarried.

'I don't ask for your pity,' Tilly had written, 'only for the time it takes to read a story that might, otherwise, go untold with me to my grave. Oh, I confess, I should have liked a husband – well, not any husband but I'd have liked to have Roland Perring by my side. Still, who knows? Maybe I was better off unwed. I never knew the stigma of being jilted, never suffered the pain of widowhood. Over the years I met so many women betrayed, bullied or robbed of their independence by husbands; I have seen how marriage can be a bit of a roulette wheel...'

As Gill read, Tilly came alive: she was young, clever, in love with that man called Roland Perring, who chose Tilly from a plethora of maidens, most of whom had been left behind by soldiers. Roland had a weak chest but, according to Tilly, he also had strength of character. He was educated, well read, concerned for humanity. Tilly first noticed him in church: he might have stood out under any circumstances, with his sharp bone structure and his nut brown eyes, but bearing in mind the dearth of young men kneeling in Staunley church at that time, he was truly exceptional.

'When I say his eyes were nut brown,' Tilly wrote, 'I mean they were that shade of chestnut, which you find when days are neither sunny nor dull, if you cover your eyes but allow some light to seep through your fingers. A colour not yellow, orange or even quite brown but a secret, luminous combination of all three. Over the years, I have often been able to recapture Roland's eyes, simply by closing my own.

'At first,' she added, 'I thought I must be imagining his gaze on the back of my neck (as you know, our family pew is close to the pulpit, so almost the entire congregation sits behind us). I had never received attention before, from any man. My scalp tightened when I considered what might be going through his mind. I was more than naïve, I was ignorant in the ways of the world. I knew no model for relationships but my own parents who were as secretive as they were passionate. Sitting in church, hearing but not listening to the sermon, I wondered how it had begun, between Mother and Father. Neither mentioned an initial meeting. There was no talk of a time before their wedding. This didn't surprise me, on reflection, since Mother implied that life had not been worth a flea until she was married to Father. But there must have been a moment when they first saw each other, when the choice was made. They would have courted, I supposed, like any couple. Yet I comprehended how strongly Mother would disapprove of my having a suitor, somehow.

'He slipped me a note; it was as simple as that. He offered to take the hymnals as the congregation left. This was Roland's third week in Staunley, where he was staying with an uncle who needed help and company in order to avoid being hospitalised. Three Sundays of sensing him, perhaps, picking me out as worthy of special regard, wondering if it could be so - and then the note, pressed into my hand with the agility of a conjuror producing a coin. I met his eyes, as I gave him my hymnal, and I saw another place, more colourful than a church window, bright with possibilities.

'The note, which was folded to a tiny size, told me his name, his medical condition and his present address. It begged me to meet him, by the river, that afternoon if I could. I thought him astute to have realized my family might not approve and then to have chosen a Sunday afternoon, when young women do often walk out alone. It is a shame we weren't introduced to each other at a village event or in the home of a mutual friend; but Roland was new to the area and his uncle was a recluse. By first meeting in secret we did rather set a seal of dissemblance on our friendship; especially since Eva took it upon herself to spy and report on us. Mind you, our friendship was innocent enough, believe me. I barely let him touch me: but when he did brush my hand with his, or take my elbow to steer me to safety, I felt a shock, a current speeding to my heart, making me giddy. Then, finally, I understood why Mother wanted Father to herself.'

Although Gill knew there had been no happy ending to this tale, she found herself craving one. It didn't *seem* impossible: in spite of Elizabeth's prohibition, the relationship flourished throughout the war. Roland's was the shoulder on which Tilly cried when Jethro was killed in action. He was a willing listener when Tilly needed to talk of Agnes and of Eva, when she wanted someone to appreciate how she missed her father. He spoke little of his disability but did offer vague hints about how he was doing his bit for his country, as best he could, saying his uncle's house was good cover, whatever that might mean. Tilly merely smiled discretely. She would take his arm and let him lead her off for brisk walks over the Fens, then find herself setting a slower, safer pace as he tired. Their situation was the opposite of most in that they felt secure whilst the war lasted but knew they might be separated when peace was finally declared. Roland had left London once, finding it hard to breathe in the city; he would have to stay in Lincolnshire when Tilly went away to study.

'I did go to London,' Tilly confirmed, 'and I can't pretend to have had anything but the best of times there. Parting was a not-so-sweet sorrow for me, though. I don't know how I brought myself to walk away from poor Flora who stood waving at the door of Ramsons before turning back to a life alone with Mother. Then leaving Roland at the station, our situation as always the reverse of many, with me being the one to depart while he remained on the platform. It was indeed heart-wrenching: but I was never less than happy at college, I must admit. I'd dreamt of such an escape, into the company of women like myself, keen to learn, eager to form friendships, more than ready to taste a little freedom. The things we used to get up to, well, we thought ourselves very risqué - but no doubt we were tame compared to students nowadays. Having a secret beau, whose letters arrived with endearing regularity, gave me an edge I felt I hardly deserved. I became the oracle to whom all manner of questions were put: should I keep my gloves on when we walk together? Ought I to let him kiss me? Do gentlemen prefer rouged cheeks to plain? As if I knew! But I did rather revel in my new-found, if somewhat unfounded, glory; I did my best to provide answers that were entertaining if not necessarily ideal. Have you ever been popular, my dear? Isn't it a treat? Popularity was as unexpected a rapture to me as sudden beauty to a formerly blighted woman.'

Gill remembered a photograph she'd seen not long ago. Bella had been with her when it was found: yes, it was during her first day in Ramsons. The entire concept of friendship bewildered Gill at that moment, sitting alone with her back to the snow. But that photograph had been suffused with the joys of companionship, she thought. It had been taken during a picnic, an outing, on a heath or common somewhere in London. It showed a group of women leaning one against the other, relaxed, secure. Content. Tilly had been smoking, which was a bit of a shock to Gill. And there was a message on the back of the picture, something about a gang. 'For Flora's eyes only' it had said; but of course Tilly would have intended Roland to see it as well.

Gill closed her eyes and found herself in sunshine, with Bella and three other young women, on The Downs, high above Bristol. A late spring day…

They are reclining on an old, pink counterpane, with jumpers and cardigans rolled up under their heads. They share a joint and, apart from Gill who really can't stomach alcohol, a couple of bottles of wine. Somebody even thought to bring a heap of chocolate bars. Gill is midway through her first pregnancy. Jude, who has left her toddler and her baby with their father for the day, is advising Gill to drink gin and take boiling baths; she's only joking, of course. Everybody teases Gill because she often moans over her lost figure, the threat to her freedom, the likelihood of never finding time to take photographs again. The talk grows both deeper and less logical as the sun slides towards the distant woods. Bella puts a hand on Gill's bump and sighs with envy. "Have it," Gill offers, "swap me that chiffonier you got at the auction. Allow me occasional visiting rights if you like - just to placate Seb - and you can keep one ornament on my chiffonier. How about it?" Bella is obviously about to tell her not to be daft when the baby moves, as if in protest. Both women jump; they laugh. "Oh my God," Gill cries, "I'm going to give birth." Her friends appreciate that she doesn't mean right now - but that she's been hit, perhaps for the first time, by the reality of the near future. For a while, everything and everybody is still, silent.

Then a hot air balloon climbs over their heads, gasping like an old asthmatic. The women share this too, squinting into its billowing skirts; voyeurs; imagining.

The moment on Tilly's bed, when Gill had felt Bella's baby move, when they had spied the photo of Tilly and her friends, smoking all in a heap, that mirror image of her own experience seemed to Gill to have been orchestrated by whatever these forces were – the ones controlling her life. She was more than uneasy with this consideration; but at least she could remember friendship, or what friendship had been. She read on.

'Roland and I communicated almost daily,' Tilly explained, 'burdening the postal system with tomes of thoughts and feelings. He told me the village was nothing more than a backdrop without me, a setting over which curtains were drawn, lights extinguished. Silly man! Of course, I drank such nonsense down like the honeyed water it seemed. But my state of bliss was periodically ruffled by thoughts of family.

'Once I actually saw Eva. I was out with Father; we enjoyed several evenings together, seeing shows at his theatres, dining in the best hotels. It was the only time I have needed an evening gown: I possessed just the one, a silken triumph in peacock green with a cluster of tiny beads across the bodice. How I longed to dance with Roland while wearing that dress. The skirts were gently weighted, to ensure they swung around the ankles... Anyway, there I was, on Father's arm, in the foyer of some grand hotel, when I caught a glimpse of Eva and almost fell to the floor. She looked so well. I realized I had been imagining her homeless, poor to the point of rags, starved: but she stood, tall and haughty, wearing furs and a hat that must have cost a pretty penny. Her air was that of a woman quite capable of holding her own against all comers. She was in a group but also noticeably with a young man who clung covetously to her waist. He was too shiny for my taste, her escort, even his shirt appeared to have been polished. But Eva was downright handsome. If she saw me and Father, who hadn't noticed her, she gave no sign. Her party turned towards the rotating doors and the street beyond. As she passed, I observed how she wore one of Mother's brooches, a large emerald set with diamonds that winked defiantly in the whole world's eye.

'I never mentioned Eva to Father but I did write of her to Flora. There was not much in the way of a response, I remember. In fact it was because of the stark letters I received, none too regularly, from Flora that I begged Roland to make her acquaintance, to become, if possible, like a brother to her: as we both hoped he would indeed be, one day. He managed an introduction, through the church society to which he then belonged. Thus he was able to meet Flora in acceptable situations, to offer her his arm for a stroll around the village without causing tongues to wag.

'I'm unsure as to what Roland actually did during the war years but I always suspected him of being involved in code-breaking or some such work. He was careful not to elaborate. Once he began to see Flora, he became my expert informer, leading me to believe he would have made a more than adequate spy, if that occupation was possible from the comfort of a neatly proportion house in a small, Lincolnshire village. He not only repeated the snippets of information he gleaned from an extremely hesitant Flora, he told me what was being implied in the public house, by the church's congregation, over the counter of Mrs. Monk's shop. He mentioned his doubts, adding that gossip is hardly ever reliable: consequently, he met with Lizzie, our serving girl, who put him absolutely straight about the goings on inside Ramsons.

'It was as I suspected. Flora was being, well these days I think one might employ the word abused. Put down at every opportunity. Made to look and feel small whilst growing very large with the eating she did for comfort. As if carbohydrates would cushion her from a sharp tongue and the odd blow. As if she hoped to hide her true self, her strongest feelings, beneath armour of flesh and fat.

'Being fond of Flora (in fact actually in league with her, in a way I shall explain later) Lizzie was distressed on her behalf, while also finding her own situation untenable: Elizabeth tormented both servant and daughter by blurring the distinction between the two. Thus Flora would sometimes be told to fetch and carry, while Lizzie was ordered to sit and eat at the table with her mistress. Elizabeth would share her fire with Lizzie of an evening, leaving Flora to freeze in an unheated bedroom. And so on.

'Perhaps you are a mother yourself, by now? If so, you must have trouble comprehending Elizabeth's attitude to Flora. I suppose Flora's birth had marked the beginning of the end of Mother having Father entirely to herself. Most difficult to grasp is the force of emotion that drove our mother, possessing her. For her, there was no light but that in Father's eyes, no pleasure but the joy of his company. His absence more than depressed, it oppressed her, rendering her limp as crushed flowers. As some people have hobbies that absorb them, so Mother had Father. Some give themselves to religion, to contemplating their God; Father was my mother's religion and she carried him with her at all times, an imaginary rosary whose beads she worried, muttered to, caressed with such constancy that her fingertips shone. This does not excuse her but it may go some way towards explaining her.

'I only made the journey home from London during the longest of the holidays, for the summer break. On my first return visit, I was concerned for Flora in terms of her treatment by Mother, of course, and possibly this blinded me to a development I ought to have noted and dealt with. Then again, Roland was also guilty of not having read the situation well. And I was so happy to see him, when I could sneak away to spend time in his company. Nothing further mattered as we ambled over the fields discussing our future, a time we believed would be as cheery as the sunsets that turned the crops to roses and the streams to ribbons of gold.

'It was the following summer before I saw, too late, what was really causing the greater portion of Flora's anxiety. Of course, being the dear man he was, Roland had made himself indispensable to Flora. And since he kept the depth of *our* relationship close to his heart, a secret too precious to hint at, Flora thought him interested in winning her. When I discovered that she had, consequently, fallen in love with him, I felt I could blame nobody but myself. Oh she asked me, in her stumbling, almost stuttering way, if, like her, I loved him above life itself, a phrase that must have tasted of Mother on her lips. "Because, Tilly dear, if you do," she assured me, "I shall step back, as it were, instantly, and not so much as glance in his direction again."

'If, *like her*, I loved him... How fateful a pair of words can be. They sealed my future that much is certain. How could I marry a man my sister loved? To do so would be to inflict a lifetime of misery on Flora, who had suffered enough already. I could never have been with Roland in her company without feeling I was flaunting him, the trophy of a winner, making her the loser. No: I gave him up.

'I behaved as if I had lost interest in him. I was cold towards the dear man, unresponsive to his puzzled questions, unsmiling in his company. My heart lurched in his direction whenever he looked hurt but I dragged it back, like a dog on a leash, while his heart was surely breaking a little more each day. I attempted to force him to leave us alone, hinting that he had displeased both Flora and myself: but he was steadfast; he loved me and he sensed that all was not as I said. Eventually, I told Roland the truth. He was astonished Flora could have thought him keen on her, assuring me he had never given her cause to believe this. No matter, I told him, the damage was done.

'He left the village, a gentleman to the last.'

Gill felt the weight of more snow on her back. A thicker fall, which muffled the world beyond the kitchen. The light was heavy too, sulphurous but beautiful as a blessing. Her feet were tingling; not from the cold, she understood, but from a desire to run down the village street and call Roland back. She saw him as he passed Ramsons for the last time, bent from carrying his luggage, his chest caved in with sorrow. She heard herself as if at a distance, crying to him not to go, telling him she didn't mean it, pleading with him to turn around. "Never mind about Flora, we are the ones who matter," she shouted. But Roland stumbled on, until Gill's voice grew weak, her heart thumped with pain.

Coming to the realization that the voice didn't belong to her was like struggling to wake from an anaesthetic. It was Adam who called, from outside. The beating wasn't an aching heart, either, but the sound of his fists on the back door, trying to attract her attention. Adam was quite capable of opening the door for himself... unless. Gill must have locked the children out. With a sigh, she went to the door. "What?" she demanded to know, turning the key.

"Mummy, the sky is falling," Adam said, using an expression he remembered from a book about a hen. Gill told him not to be ridiculous. Rosie was behind her brother, a shadow clinging to his waist just as Gill used to hold Sarah on the big toboggan. "It *is* falling," Adam assured her, "it's rocking anyway, getting ready to fall on us, let us *in*."

Gill saw that she was blocking the door. During the last few minutes, or was it hours, she'd forgotten that she had children. Like Tilly, she'd been a student, a lover, a sister – but not a mother. When she gave Adam a shove, back into the slippery garden, she felt she was in fact dismissing Roland Perring once and for all.

It wasn't that easy, Adam had hold of her coat, he pulled her through the doorframe. Rosie, whose feet were trodden on in this tug of war, squealed. Gill just wasn't ready for them; they could come back in when she was. Not yet, though. "Skies don't fall, you stupid boy," she shouted at Adam, "now go and play some more until I say you can come in, do you hear me?" And she pushed the pair of them back a bit further, down the path towards the nearest lawn. They collapsed in a messy, wet, complaining heap.

And then, as they lay in snow that was rapidly turning to slush, as Gill turned her back on them to head indoors, then the sky really did fall.

11.

We are very humane here.

When Gill heard the front door open, she thought it merely another ghost, coming to tell her of some pickle they once got themselves into, or some sorrow they'd endured. The dead were positively chatty these days. They popped up everywhere, at any time. Jethro might appear, for instance, as a boy in velvet breeches, riding through the house on a broomstick that clearly represented a horse, breezing past Gill as she was dishing up the porridge. Or he was just as likely to be seen in the night, a young man in a doorway, enjoying a cheroot, blowing smoke rings round the moon. In fact, almost all the Durrys flitted from child to adult before Gill's eyes. Only Elizabeth never aged or grew younger. She was forever fifty, turning stout around the waist, with wisps of grey hair amongst the brown, a matriarch who hadn't even wanted to be a mother. Although she stalked the entire property, including the outbuildings, Elizabeth was most often discovered at a front window, watching and hoping. Unlike Elizabeth's daughters, Gill wasn't afraid of her. It did occur to Gill that this was because nobody, not even her infamous great-grandmother, was as frightening as she was herself. But she shrugged off this consideration when she thought of Babs and how her name alone could bring about a sweat.

So when she heard the front door open, Gill expected nothing more sinister than a late Durry; but a voice called "Hi there!" in a way no dead person would and Gill became fearful, anticipating the appearance of a face that might be deathly pale but would in fact be chillingly alive. She plucked up her courage and responded, crying "Babs?"

It wasn't Babs, it was Sarah, followed by Kate. Her eyes might have been adjusting to the lack of light but Sarah's mind was focused. "Hello you," she said, giving Gill a fleeting hug, "why on earth did you think I was Babs? Has that woman been pestering you? Has she been hassling you about the way Auntie tricked her out of the house?"

Gill muttered a single no, which would have to do. Something, other than this intrusion itself, was niggling her, but she couldn't quite capture it and pin it down. She remembered previous greetings, when she was only an aunt to Sarah's little boys, before she was a mother herself. Seeing Sarah had been exciting as finding an ice cream on an otherwise barren beach. Gill used to yearn for her big sister, for those snippets of guidance Sarah tossed frequently and nonchalantly in Gill's direction, for the rare and therefore treasured hints of approval the elder sister bestowed on the younger. Well, Gill assumed there would be little enough approbation for her today; and she was in no mood to be guided anywhere but to a riotous party amongst scores of fashionable artists who were famous for being permissive with their bodies and generous with their drugs.

"Just as well..." Sarah noted, yanking Gill from the clamorous studio flat of her mind to the concept of Babs who was distinctly more silent than many a ghost.

"Isn't it odd," Sarah mused, "not being greeted by a yapping dog? Have you seen or heard anything of Tricksey yet?" Gill offered yet another no; she was in the process of being hugged, more enthusiastically, by Kate who then stepped back and took in Gill's dishevelled appearance. "I know," Kate sympathized, "I feel as low as you do. I loved him too. We all did, I suppose. I just can't believe it."

"No," Sarah agreed, shaking her head, "nobody can credit it. So sudden... such a waste..."

Gill stared at them: was their father dead, or what? She pictured her dad, his skin grey from lack of oxygen, laid out on a mortician's slab, his heart having failed. His second wife was nearby, weeping.

"Bastard!" said Kate. "Not him, of course, I mean the sod who shot him." Even in her under-nourished, insomniac state Gill knew then that they weren't talking about Dad. "I've no idea what you're on about," she told her sisters, pushing past them into the kitchen.

"John Lennon's been shot," Kate cried, following her. "He's dead. How can you not know?"

"How would I know?" Gill countered. "There is no TV here and the radio is spasmodic at best, snapping and crackling like a bowl of electrocuted Rice Crispies... in fact, I believe it did finally go pop. So, I don't get news. John Lennon is dead, you say? Well... I'm sorry." All three sisters were silenced for a while, thinking of the vacuum left by a man who had led their generation. Taking note, rather gloomily, of the rift his demise was already causing between them. Before long, Sarah and then Kate also took in the state of the kitchen: this too filled them with gloom. Kate actually burst into tears.

"Oh, come on," Gill advised her, "it's not as if you knew him personally." A vision of Kate and John Lennon in bed together, in a public place, flashed before Gill's eyes. Their sheets were extraordinarily white. She tried to think of a lyric and came up with 'tangerine taxis', which did little to help her share Kate's grief.

"No, no," Kate said with a sniff, "I am sad about John Lennon but that's not why I'm crying. I keep crying, don't I Sarah? I can't seem to stop. I have some good news, you see, to balance the bad. I'm pregnant!"

Gill was sorry not to be able to respond with the dramatic whoop or gasp, which she knew was expected of her. It was as if she could hear herself making these sounds, see herself jumping across the lino to Kate's arms, being joyful; but she had no way of mustering the energy or enthusiasm required. She did smile, she sat down, shook her head, muttered "Well I never..."

Sarah gave her the glare that had been employed throughout their childhood; it said 'Get it right for once, Gillian, or suffer the consequences.'

"Congratulations," Gill offered, a child in classroom, guessing an answer.

"Thanks," replied Kate. No longer tearful, she was now bordering on joyful. Gill decided there was no hope of keeping pace with her younger sister's mood swings if Kate insisted on leaping from the national news to the state of her womb without so much as a moment's respite.

Interestingly, Gill thought, Sarah seemed to have put on more weight than Kate, as if enjoying a sisterly phantom pregnancy. Her hair was less glamorous too; what had been a wavy perm was growing out and Sarah had swept the remains into a clump that resembled a small, distressed mammal clinging to her scalp. Also, she'd let her hair fade back to the natural brown, the colour of school sandals, which was the unenhanced norm for all three of them. Whereas Gill still boasted blood red tips to her former spikes, while the blonde highlights in Kate's long, layered cut hinted at sex and a husband's adequate income.

Kate. Oh how Gill had loved Kate. Little sister, pretty little one. Where was the delight she always enjoyed in Kate's presence? Here was the estranged, beloved sister, home from foreign shores, warm, alive and in the same room as Gill. They should be sitting, heads together, chatting until their throats ached, giggling, exchanging secrets. Of course, three was, in their case, a crowd; never more so than today - the house seemed to Gill to bulge with bodies. There was no chance of relaxing with either sister when the other was hanging about. This had always been the way of it, a friction rubbed up between them when they were all together.

Now little sister Kate was going to have a baby; or so she said. Gill couldn't see Kate as a mother, quite frankly. Too much luggage to cart from airport to airport for one thing. If only the supposed mother-to-be was supporting a rounder protrusion, as Bella had been when last seen, Gill might have been able to suspend her disbelief.

"Aren't you going to ask Kate when the baby is due?" Sarah bossed. Gill moved her head slowly in Kate's direction, her skull was insupportably heavy, her eyes the same. It was going to be a long, cumbersome day. She glanced at the clock on the mantelpiece. It said five to eleven, as ever. With a supreme effort, she raised one eyebrow in question.

"July!" Kate announced, proud as if she'd just invented summer. "So I can have it here, in England, without worrying about it becoming acclimatized to the heat and by Christmas next year, we'll be back in Singapore, putting up Chinese lanterns in place of tinsel."

"Talking of which," Sarah said, sweeping crumbs from a chair and sitting at the big table, "where are your decs, Gill? We thought Ramsons would be awash with paper chains and those German glass baubles the aunts used year after year." Gill gazed at her sister without a glint of comprehension; in fact, she told herself today would more than likely be the day during which she perfected the art of looking blank.

"Christmas is coming," Sarah explained, "it's the ninth already, you'll have to get a move on. My lads have turned our house into the usual glittering chaos. I insisted they waited until the first but after that there was no stopping them."

"You do it," Gill suggested, "I'm not in the mood." When her sisters exchanged frowns, the similarity between their features and movements struck Gill as comical.

"But Ramsons was built for times of celebration, don't you think?" Kate asked, clearly envisaging a future in which she and her not yet developed family would play, sing and wish each other happy some-time-or-another. Gill watched as the eyes of both her sisters dimmed, and she knew they were considering Christmases past. She understood how rosy were the cheeks they recalled, how sweet the marzipan icing their unreliable memories.

"I'm going to get dressed," she informed them, heading for the back stairs. As she began to climb, she distinctly heard Kate say, "Oh... I thought she *was* dressed." To which Sarah replied, "Yes, but for what?" The word droll came into Gill's mind and was instantly turned to the word troll because that precisely suited her lumbering steps and matched the lack of lightness in her heart.

In truth there wasn't a great disparity between Gill's day and nightwear. She'd simply needed to escape the chatter. Christmas; for goodness sake, how had they got to Christmas so soon? She peeled back the bedroom curtains, which hadn't been opened for some time, and saw that the pub was bedecked with coloured lights, left on although it was probably the middle of the day now. Through one of the pub's windows she could just make out a tree, also lit. This distant, fairy pyramid blurred as her eyes filled with tears. She was certain she would miss Christmas this year - it would pass her by entirely, because she had been bad. Very bad. The pathos was really quite enjoyable; the tears seemed to illustrate some point Gill had been hoping to make for a while.

It occurred to her that the bedroom smelt. Not wanting to encounter bugs on the landing, she'd taken to using a potty at night. This was now full of thick, rather orange pee. She pushed it out of sight then pulled an old counterpane over the bed, covering, with a swish of fabric, soiled sheets, used tissues, books with their spines broken and every one of Tilly's letters. The counterpane settled into a lumpy landscape that wasn't remotely inviting, but Gill infinitely preferred it to a kitchen full of sisters.

In fact, she found Sarah and Kate in the drawing room, surrounded by cardboard boxes. They were going to relieve her of a few bits and pieces, make life less cluttered for her.

"Mum has given us a list, too," Sarah explained, "so we can take a few small items for her and lay claim to others, sort of thing. All right?" Gill nodded, planting her hands deep in the pockets of her long cardigan as if to demonstrate having no wish to prevent anybody from taking what they wanted. Apart from the worm-riddled piano, Gill hadn't considered a single piece of furniture, any wooden box or pretty glass, more her own than another. As her sisters began to wrap up ornaments and silverware, she thought she should be suffering from pangs of possessiveness, since she had, in a way, possessed everything for a while. But her great-aunts' belongings didn't behave as if they wanted to belong to her. Mind you, they would sit uneasily in any place but Ramsons, of that Gill was certain; still, if there were cries of distress at them being removed, these would come from the silenced mouths of the departed rather than from one exhausted caretaker who merely stood by and watched at what felt a vast remove. Who needed carriage clocks or Toby jugs these days? Unless you constantly drank champagne, went into mourning and had the gentry round to dinner, what use were crystal glasses, strings of jet beads or silver candlesticks? Did Sarah seriously contemplate using the best china? Only when her boys were safely out of reach, Gill hoped. Could Kate actually anticipate a time when she would sit down to a meal spread over the embroidered linen she was hugging to her chest? And had she no idea how infested everything was? Gill prayed that many roaches and many mites would leave in the boxes that were being rapidly filled.

Kate reached up and took a picture from the wall. A small watercolour of a beach in Norfolk, it had been painted for Gill by a boyfriend who preceded Seb. At last Gill felt a stab of covetousness, a lurch somewhere between her stomach and her knees. But she kept quiet. She turned away, leaving them to it. There was nothing she could be bothered to fight for any more.

The visiting sisters moved from room to room, packing small items, marking furniture as theirs, with coloured dots. Gill considered asking whether she might continue to use those pieces chosen, but not removed, by Sarah or Kate - or should she shun them, plonking her behind only on unmarked chairs, not soiling selected tables, eating standing up, perhaps, with a tray attached to her neck, like a cinema usherette.

Gill followed them, an unwanted servant, her fingers kneading balls of fluff in her pockets, her mouth set in a slight pout. As they sorted through the waste and the wonders, Sarah and Kate exclaimed at this and that and said "I remember..." to each other until it became a chant in Gill's head.

I remember sewing,
I remember eating,
I remember giving,
I remember loving…

"Where are the children," Kate asked suddenly. "Not both at school, surely? Rosie's far too young, isn't she?"

"I'll get them," Gill replied. She made a wall of her back as she climbed the stairs, so that Kate must understand she wasn't to be followed.

The appearance of the children created a natural break. Kate instantly plucked Rosie into her arms - but as good as dropped her when she inhaled the scent of the child's hair, which had rubbed against a variety of secretions. Sarah, kneeling on a damp rug, gazing into the pink eyes of her nephew, suggested coffee. Gill slumped off to the kitchen, muttering. She had dressed both children in clothing with long sleeves and high necks but still, if glimpsed, the marks on their bodies could well be misinterpreted; and, although she had briefed Adam how to answer, she worried over the questions Sarah would inevitably be putting to him.

Once she was in the kitchen, a mood of defiance hit Gill; what had she to worry about, after all? Her sisters had no right to judge. Let them try spending a winter here, with the eternal damp and the everlasting insects, in freezing weather that bit into a body twenty-four hours a day. See how Sarah liked it when the sky fell on her children, or how Kate enjoyed coping without hot water. They had no idea: a pair of summer visitors… turning up out of the blue, like swallows flying against nature. It was in her power to make them suffer, to hold them prisoner in Ramsons. A pinch of this and a spoonful of that, stirred into their coffee, and there would be no driving back to their gas central heating and cockroach-free fluffy towels. But for the discomfort of having to keep them company, Gill might have been tempted. Then again, much as the idea of Sarah slumped and useless did appeal, the prospect of her being gone was a damn sight more attractive. Gill picked up an axe and set about creating kindling for the Rayburn. She was currently splintering what had been one of her great-grandfather's tool boxes. Last week she had chopped up a garden bench. Just as well Sarah and Kate were taking what they wanted; quite honestly, it was a bit of a race against the axe for anything made of wood.

Gill only had powdered coffee and powered milk. Combined with not very hot water, they formed a buff liquid polka-dotted with greasy white blobs. This the sisters drank from a set of Dutch mugs that were mapped with the stains of age. A question and answer session took place: it put Gill in mind of some quiz game she and Kate had watched as children, when their television viewing had been restricted by June. Either 'Double Your Money' or 'Take Your Pick', or perhaps the one was a portion of the other... Gill struggled to remember. Anyway, responding to Sarah's probing, Gill seemed to be playing the 'Yes/ No Interlude' from an old programme, avoiding positive answers.

It was unlikely that she had got any biscuits. ("Bikit?" echoed Rosie, "bikit, bikit.") She thought she did appreciate how cold the house was.

Adam hadn't been well enough to go to school, much.

So far she had not discovered any lost rooms.

It was true, the phone was out of order.

Possibly the children were more than usually unkempt.

And Christmas would not be celebrated by June, or anybody else, in a cheerfully decorated, warm and cosy Ramsons: not over Gill's inert, lifeless body it wouldn't.

Throughout this sparring match, Kate studied her mug. A blue boy, wearing clogs and baggy trousers, was depicted there, before a row of windmills. He was apparently capable of reducing Kate to tears.

"Have you actually run out of coal?" Sarah asked. Gill had a sudden understanding of how different things would have been, if only Sarah had stepped in to occupy Ramsons instead of her... Careful housekeeping ensured the house was kept warm, clean, glossy as a magazine. By virtue of being the eldest, Sarah had persuaded June to permit minor changes, fresh coats of paint for example, the installation of a new sink, a decent cooker. Having money and influence, Sarah had transformed the place into a home again. Gill smelt freshly-baked bread, narrowed her eyes against the glow of perfect white walls.

"Yes," she replied, losing the game: she had run out of coal, actually.

"Maybe there's some left in the cellar," said Sarah, "I remember Auntie kept a heap down there, for emergencies. Have you looked?"

"No."

They both glanced at Kate, who had never ventured down the stone steps to the cellar. Even when adults offered a guiding hand, she had shied from making that descent. Afraid of a few shrunken apples. Troubled by the odd cobweb. "Shall we see?" Gill suggested. "Eh, Kate? Shall we all go down to the cellar, together, like coalminers in search of a rich seam?" Kate enveloped the blue boy within her hands, as if protecting him was a task she shouldn't be asked to abandon.

"Adam would love to see the cellar, wouldn't you?" Gill prompted. Adam hid his face. "We can pretend it's a cabin, deep inside an old ship," Gill tempted, more animated than she had been in months. It wasn't only the prospect of mischief, of hearing Kate squeal or seeing her squirm; it was an opportunity to overcome at least one hurdle, by sharing risk with other people. Because Gill was also frightened of the cellar, just as she feared the lost room, the various out-houses, the undersides of shrubs, holes in crumbling walls, built-in cupboards and every hollow between here and where ever home might prove to be.

"If you're going to be a mother soon," she pointed out to Kate, "you'll have to deal with cellars... and whatever lies within." Although Sarah agreed that Kate should accompany them to the cellar, she glared at Gill for employing gothic language. "I think we should all get a bit of fresh air first," she decided, "before we go down to any cellars or upstairs, where we run a risk of coming across the lost room and the like."

"Oh, I'm not frightened of the lost room," Kate assured them, "are you?" Neither Gill nor Sarah committed themselves on this. "I always picture the lost room as a benefit," Kate continued, "a place one might find when every other room has become too messy or overcrowded, when the house is somehow not enough. I dream of discovering that special room, having stumbled down some stairs and clambered up others, having trailed along endless passages and landings. I open a door and I'm inside a perfect, comfortable place that is entirely mine. The furnishings are red or pink, soft, deep. I sink into the room, I am instantly at home."

"The dream of a woman who has no home, who has yet to put **down** roots," Sarah suggested. "Whereas I, who have trouble keeping my house, and my life, in the order I would prefer, think of the lost room as the final straw. I approach it by a similar route of stairs and passages, peeking through doors on every side, armed with mops, buckets, bottles of bleach. I know I've found the right room the moment I open its door, because it is worse than anywhere I've ever been. It stinks. It's dim with dirt. It is an absolutely filthily hole into which I also sink, but to my knees, exhausted, defeated."

Kate shook her head, no doubt hoping to dispel this image in order to preserve her own. Both she and Sarah looked at Gill, inviting her to reveal what she thought or dreamt concerning the lost room.

"It isn't cosy or filthily," Gill mumbled, "it is simply a place where innocents are left to die."

"Right," said Sarah, who had worried over her own disclosure, in terms of its impact on the children, "no more of this. We must go out, eh Adam? We need a walk. What's your favourite place? The Ups and Downs or the river?"

"The river," Gill answered for him. A walk to the Ups and Downs meant passing the school gates. On the other hand, going to the river involved traipsing through the centre of the village where they risked encountering all kinds of people.

"Oh goody," piped Kate, still supposing the way to communicate with children was to adopt what she considered their language. Neither Adam nor Rosie had said 'goody' for aeons, but never mind.

"We'll have to pass Mrs. Monk's shop if we go down to the river, won't we? I reckon we'll have no choice but to pop in there and buy a bag or two of sweeties, don't you think?" Her question was directed at Rosie who actually jerked to life - an automaton whose start up button was marked 'sweeties'. Adam, on the other hand, was reluctant to leave the house no matter what treats were on offer. Sarah noticed this as she helped him into his coat. "What's up, little man?" she asked. He was close to trembling, holding his knees rigid against possible signs of weakness. In response to his aunt's enquiry, he rolled his eyes upwards whilst keeping his head down, a gesture that contained a hint of brain damage. Sarah wrapped him tightly against the weather and other menaces, constricting his throat with a brown scarf she recognized as

Flora's, a tubular, hand-knitted affair, disturbingly akin to a string of skinned weasels.

As they pulled the front door closed behind them, Gill realized what had been bothering her ever since Sarah arrived. Big sister had let herself in. She had a key. Was this *the* key? Had she crept in, at night, through an open window, and stolen Gill's key? Gill asked her outright. Sarah blushed, just a touch. "Mum had a copy made," she admitted, "before handing the original over to you. It took some doing, I believe, but you know Mum, she likes to keep her hand on the helm, so to speak." Gill felt a sulk settle over her, like a pelt of grey fur, matted, old and smelly. June didn't trust her – well, what a surprise.

While the visitors took the children into the shop, Gill waited outside, stamping her feet to ward off the cold and the likelihood of seeing somebody she would rather avoid. Of course, this list was unending, since she had no desire to speak with anybody, but it was topped by Babs who Gill imagined she could glimpse darting from hiding place to hiding place, a speeding chameleon, criss-crossing the corners of her vision. On reflection though, Babs was not one to speed or to hide. She was brisk, not hurried. She was brazen, never furtive. Gill rearranged Babs into a straight-backed, sharp-edged phantom, one whose high-heeled shoes and pencil skirts rendered her incapable of sneaking or scurrying about.

"Was that Mrs. Monk who served us?" Kate asked as they continued down the village street.

"I suppose she must be her, or a descendant. I honestly don't know," admitted Sarah, who had a couple of carrier bags full of shopping, "what do you think, Gill?"

"I think she's like Mrs. Monk," Gill offered, "or she *is* Mrs. Monk but she's lost the ability to be pleasant. I expect she sold it, by mistake, getting flustered one day when the shop was terribly busy. She wouldn't have discovered her loss until she was reckoning the takings at night. By then it was too late; she realized she must have handed it over the counter, along with several other items, in a white paper bag, just like those sweets Rosie is about to choke on." Gill's final phrase saved her from comments on the oddness of the story. Seeing how fast Rosie was devouring her jelly babies, both Sarah and Kate dived to save the little girl from making herself ill. Their efforts were rewarded by one of

Rosie's best ever screams of fury.

"Dear me!" said the young aunts, unwittingly echoing Matilda and Flora, experts in the field of mock horror.

Having been away at the time of the funeral, Kate wanted to visit Tilly's grave. She was berating herself for forgetting to bring flowers as they arrived at the spot to find the grave already brightened by a bouquet of Michaelmas daisies.

"Nothing to do with me," Gill told them. Then she wandered off on her own, unexpectedly delighted by icy air on her cheeks, by just being out of doors on what was, after all, a dull, chill day. She knew her sisters would be sorrowing, as if Tilly was actually under that lump of earth. Maybe she should tell them about the letters, or more drastically, let them read the letters. Otherwise she would not only be housekeeper at Ramsons but a life-long keeper of secrets. Her first night at the house came back as a daydream, with herself in the leading role, costumed in that long white nightdress and Wellington boots. Some secrets must remain untold, not matter what. Hadn't she made a promise, under the moon?

She sat on a bench by the dry-stone wall that enclosed the graveyard and was taken aback when, of all the companions she might encounter there, it was Evangelina who perched beside her. Eva was younger than Gill remembered her, seeming to be between middle and old age, a woman aware of her flesh and the narrow margin of time for which it will remain firm. Perhaps it was due to this consideration that Eva kept her chin high, stretching her neck. Or maybe she was attempting to see into the distance.

"Tomas died before me," Eva announced. "I did try not to emulate my mother, not to display excessive grief; but I felt as she had felt, burying the one person on this earth who meant a thing to me." She turned her head and smiled at Gill. The first smile Gill ever saw, or so she believed, from her grandmother. Eva's teeth were not good, far from straight, even further from being white. The smile was sweet, though, being an indication not only of her feelings for Tomas but also of her willingness, after all these years, to share these with another human being. Gill returned the smile. She also stretched her neck, looked into the distance.

"We had such times," Eva whispered, confidentially. "Nobody knew! I doubt anyone so much as suspected. We were crazy for each other, do you know? Below us, the bottles in the pharmacy used to sing along with our antics. A person would look at Tomas and think him round, plain, perhaps a trifle too wholesome. So he was, at work, during the day… but upstairs, by night, he was a ferocious lover, with the appetites of a devil. He was a naughty man, Gillian, can you believe that? We used to roll about, from bed to floor, from floor to wall, bouncing, well… I shouldn't say more… You will be shocked." This last was a demand, not a question. Dutifully, Gill sucked in her breath, lowered her head until she was staring at Eva's shoes, which were navy blue pumps, suede with leather trim, designed for lightness of tread.

"Of course," Eva sighed, "Tomas was also moody, given to smoking and drinking in excess. Fond of his own concoctions, which did little to enhance his temperament, I'm afraid. He could turn from laughter to anger at the wink of an eye, at the mention of a certain customer. His fury was a quiet beast, it did not bark, it barely growled. It sat in waiting, breathing heat. If it did pounce, one had better beware, one had better move fast. I was often keyed up for flight, ready to descend the stairs, more carefully but not less quickly, than the first Mrs. Knibbe. I danced on eggshells, during my years with Tomas. I danced on glass; but at least I did dance, not like those dried-up old souls, eh? Those two old maids, teaching ABC and making their mountains of cakes." She indicated Flora and Tilly, who were watching Gill's sisters and the children. "Still," Evangelina stood, brushed down the front of her coat, patted the French pleat in which she wore her hair, "at least they had a living soul to mourn them when they died, which is more than I could boast." Gill opened her mouth to protest, she'd gone to her grandmother's funeral, alongside June; but she hadn't been sorry, hadn't known her grandmother well enough to miss her.

"You are very much as I was," Evangelina warned, "very much the issue of Elizabeth, rather than resembling Edward. Driven by passions. By the way," she nodded at Sarah and Kate this time, "they are plotting against you, do you see? Even as we sit here, talking of love and death, your sisters are fretting over the state of your children, planning moves to return soon and rescue them from you." Gill observed her sisters and saw that what Eva said was true. Sarah looked decidedly devious, Kate had adopted a conspiratorial frown.

"I won't let them," she said, her words sounding small, mean. Eva pulled a face, bit her bottom lip. "Is that a good thing, or a bad?" she asked - and disappeared before Gill could answer.

"Oh my God," Kate gasped, as she and the others arrived by Gill's side, "look who it isn't." Less than a hundred feet away, Babs stood, smiling and waving as if she saw each of them on a daily basis and was a firm friend to all. She was not a phantom then, as Gill had lately begun to believe: Kate and Sarah saw her too. Perhaps this made her less frightening, Gill wasn't sure. Babs was holding onto a wheelbarrow in which, Gill noticed with amazement, Tilly and Flora's old gardener, Man, was reclining, his knees covered in a jolly tartan rug, his right arm raised in a weak imitation of Babs's wave.

"What's she doing with Man?" Kate whispered.

"He's her father," Sarah pointed out, "don't you remember? It was because she was the daughter of their gardener that Tilly and Flora let her help them out in the first place. Hello Babs," she called crisply across the graves, "hello Man." As Babs and her father responded, coming a bit closer but keeping a respectful distance, Gill saw that she'd been wrong about the wheelbarrow. Her mind had played a trick, making wheelchair into wheelbarrow because the old chap had once been a gardener. It was a shame to think he couldn't walk any more, when he had been such an active man, a hard worker in all weathers. Gill remembered how often she'd encountered him, on the paths at Ramsons, pushing a barrow of dead leaves or uprooted weeds. He and Babs made an unlikely pair: the daughter was tall and slim, whereas the father, slumped in his chair, was bordering on obese. Babs wore high boots with pointed toes, a severely cut black coat and tight, black gloves. Man was dressed in what seemed a flock of old sweaters, one on top of the other, then his rug and, best of all, a pair of slippers that had a single, matted, pom-pom between them.

"Which of you is living in the house, then?" Babs asked. As if she didn't know! The nerve of the woman, after months of nosing about, spying, lurking under windows, to come up with this. While Sarah answered the question, Gill held Babs's gaze. She found more amusement than malice in her opponent's eyes but the one was no less disturbing than the other. 'Cleaner,' Gill thought, to give herself courage, 'charlady.' Babs shifted her eyes from Gill to Rosie, was about to bend, to greet the toddler. Gill grabbed her child's hand and moved away. She walked quickly, then she ran, not staying on the paths but straying carelessly, mulching floral tributes, hurrying home, tramping over the dead.

Nobody mentioned Gill's flight once they were assembled back at Ramsons. Sarah made fresh tea with proper milk and she produced a couple of packets of biscuits and some cakes. These inevitably drew the conversation back to those visits the three sisters had made as children, to the high teas Flora had dished up with a modest but triumphant air.

"Did we actually eat tongue and all those other cold meats?" Sarah asked. Her sisters nodded, their taste buds remembering also the sharpness of home-made pickles, the warmth of freshly hard-boiled eggs.

"There was one time," Kate recalled, "when things were already turning sour between Mum and Dad, and we didn't see Dad very often, there was one summer's day when he turned up here. We had the French windows open and he appeared in them, framed by wisteria, grinning just because he'd arrived."

"Bang on tea-time," Sarah remembered, with a smile. "And Tilly was convinced he'd smelt Flora's baking from miles away..."

"And Flora went as red as a tomato," Gill added. "She flustered about, fetching another plate, peeling grease-proof paper from a second cake..."

"Coffee and walnut," Sarah suggested.

"Lemon drizzle," said Kate.

"Ginger loaf," said Gill.

"Then Mum and Dad sat down with us, and the aunts, and we all tucked in together," Kate told everybody. This may not have been quite the case. At the time, her parents were hardly on speaking terms: but in memory they sat, joking with Tilly, praising Flora's cooking, listening to the tales their girls had to tell of frogs in the brook and slow-worms under garden stones.

"I'd forgotten how the aunts loved Mum," Sarah muttered as she began to gather the plates that had been cleared of their unsatisfactory, stiff, shop-bought offerings.

"She was more daughter to them than niece," Kate said. "Mum must be grieving still, for Tilly, I suppose. We ought to get her here, to have a session of going through stuff, to settle her memories." She shot Sarah a glance, which Gill interpreted, thanks to Eva's warning, as meaning here was an opportunity to return soon, to check on or rescue

Gill's children. But then Sarah disarmed Gill by looking her straight in the eye and saying, "Thank you Gill. Nobody's said it, as such, but we are grateful to you for preventing us having to consider selling Ramsons. It's obviously not easy, living here, but we appreciate your effort. This house is our sanctuary, really, isn't it? The place where we were, perhaps where we still are, most likely to experience happiness. Especially Mum, who had such an odd set of parents, such a weird home above the pharmacy. She'd hate to see Ramsons sold."

'Where there is happiness there is also the ultimate sorrow,' thought Gill; and she wondered if there was a way to stop her thoughts from taking these melodramatic plunges. "Time to explore the cellar," she said aloud, "no more dalliance."

It was agreed, the time had come to see inside the cellar. They stood in the passage, before the entrance to the cellar. Behind them was a door to the garden, a door no longer in use but through which Sarah, Gillian and Kate had run, skipped or shuffled as children. The top half was glass, green now with lichen and mould. Beyond it hung the vine that climbed the balustrade, a vine still beaded with a few withered grapes. With the exception of the almost imperceptible expansion of Kate's waistline, everything seemed to harp back to better times. Sarah pulled the bolt from the cellar door and the five of them held hands, an uneasy train going into a tunnel fraught with dangers.

"I remember the smell of apples, pungent even in the middle of winter," Sarah almost whispered, taking the first downwards step. But today, the apples and the other fruits had been overwhelmed by a stench that filled the entire cellar like a fog, a stink that rose now to assault those who dared disturb what ought to have remained secret, what should have been permitted to rot in peace.

That evening, when she had Ramsons to herself again, Gill considered each individual's reaction to the discovery in the cellar and was encouraged by the fact that she, rather than Sarah, had taken control and resolved the situation. It was true that Adam, in his distress, had clung to Sarah; and Kate had cried out "Sarah, I'm going, I'm going now, all right?" as she charged back up the stone staircase. Then Rosie, who hadn't understood the cause but was conscious of the fuss, had also gravitated towards her Auntie Sarah for comfort. Ah, but what had the blessed Sarah actually done, faced with such a crisis? Gasped! Shuddered! Practically retched! It was smelling salts and hankies all round for Sarah, so to speak: while Gill had rolled up her sleeves, found a sack, grabbed a spade, and *done* something about it. She had even thought to fill a bucket with coal, from Tilly's emergency supply, before emerging with her grisly burden.

"Don't bring the children out into the garden," she'd advised, setting off for yet another burial under a fruit tree. "They're terrified of falling skies and the like. Stay with them, will you? I won't be long." She'd felt aligned with the house and the garden at that moment, a capable woman. She rather thought she might have whistled as she dug; certainly, the exercise had been bracing in the icy air. A robin had watched her from a frosty perch and she'd winked at him because they would both benefit from this episode; he'd have freshly turned soil to hunt through, she had the solution to a puzzle. Or so it had seemed...

Except that now, alone in the dark, she was still questioning what had happened. The discovery of the corpse did not, in this case, provide all the answers. And the fact that there was a corpse pointed to foul play, which of course was more than a little disturbing bearing in mind Gill was on her own, in the same village as the woman to whom the finger pointed. In retrospect, she wished she hadn't been so eager to send her sisters packing. Not that the entire equine population of Dartmoor could have persuaded Kate to remain after the trip to the cellar.

The final straw for Sarah had been the state of the garden. She'd been standing in the frame of the back door when Gill returned from her grim task. "I asked Adam what you meant, about him being terrified of falling skies," Sarah had said as Gill approached cautiously over the rubble, "and he began to tremble, Gill, to actually tremble for God's sake. Presumably this is the explanation?"

Gill had nodded.

"How much of the roof has come down?" Sarah asked, sounding more than a little as if she held Gill responsible.

"It's a chimney," Gill explained, kicking a rounded piece of clay to prove her point. "A chimney and some surrounding masonry. When Adam looked up, during the snow, it was crumbling before his eyes, then it fell, with a loud crash, quite close to him and Rosie. Now, I dare say, you can see why he's afraid. He believes, possibly correctly, that more of the sky will come smashing down around him if he ventures out again. Come to think of it, I probably have a five year old agoraphobic on my hands." She had distinctly not felt as flippant as she sounded but the lightness of her tone coupled with her efficiency in the cellar appeared to convince Sarah that Gill was managing remarkably well, under the horrific circumstances.

There had been promises of help in the near future, of course, as Sarah and Kate threw themselves and their acquisitions into the estate car that so rarely came into its own in London. "I'll call the phone company and get you reconnected," Sarah assured Gill, not having discovered that her sister had merely unplugged the telephone, "and I'll tell Mum she has to release some of Auntie's funds for you to begin renovations. At least you have coal now, but you must order more straight away." Kate was crying openly by his time, such a luxurious monsoon of tears that Gill had almost been able to taste their salt.

Why hadn't Gill said 'take me with you'? What madness prevented her from pleading to be squeezed between boxes in the back of the car and carried to Clapham? Perhaps she'd remained silent because she didn't believe in Clapham, with its avenues of tastefully decorated homes, its Common, its busy roads. With its Christmas decorations and news stands proclaiming the death of John Lennon. It was a district of the mind only. Real life was here, under this counterpane, amongst the clutter. Or it was an endless walk across a fen in weather that clung like Miss Havisham's veil - grubby, grey, rough on the cheeks, sticky on the tongue. Gill saw Tilly take that walk, alone. A wind from the North flayed Tilly's eyes, inflicting tears. Roland had gone; Flora was at a loss to understand why. Inside Ramsons, Elizabeth imitated the weather, moaning through her days, troubling papers, pulling at curtains, banging doors. And Tilly tramped across the Fens, following the lines of ditches, disturbing water voles and snipe, making mud. Heading nowhere.

The ghost of Tricksey scampered to catch up with her mistress. Gill found herself smiling at the speed with which a body in a cellar became a cheerful, running ghost. There was a discrepancy time wise, of course. Tricksey hadn't been around when Tilly was recovering from her doomed affair with Roland. A clump of tissues was obliging Gill to arch her back as she lay and considered the expression 'doomed affair' and the way certain phrases are only reasonable in the written telling of stories, when events turned to fiction. Imagine saying aloud,

"It was a doomed affair."

These efforts to side-step recent memory failed, leaving Gill no choice but to recapture the smell of Tilly's dead dog, the weight of it in the sack, the possibility that it had been kicked down the stone steps and left to die. No wonder she was eager for it to trot along at Tilly's heels again, reincarnated to a tolerable guise.

The falling chimney had interrupted Gill's reading of Tilly's letter, leaving her with a head full of unfinished stories and a garden full of debris. Like Adam, Gill also feared what might befall them next now that one part of the house had gone beyond mere threats. How was she to convince herself that drainpipes wouldn't curve, strain, burst from their clasps and swipe her or the children across their backs? It seemed more than likely that the Rayburn would combust... hardly spontaneously, but after months of wheezing. There wasn't a pane of glass in the house without a crack or fault; Gill now assumed each was on the verge of shattering, awaiting its cue, its gust of wind, the weight of a certain raindrop, one flick of frost.

Gill failed to see how any information Tilly had yet to impart could trouble her more than the present did. From a head sized dip under her pillow, she dug out the letter she had yet to finish reading and found the phrase 'a gentleman to the last', which transported her back to what she felt a safe distance.

'With Roland gone,' Tilly wrote, 'life in Staunley settled into a bearable routine for Mother, Flora and me. I took the post of governess to four boys, the sons of a local magistrate. I was able to do this and reside at home, since the boys lived less than a mile from Ramsons. Flora and Lizzie treated me as the man of the house, as it were, cooking up treats for my supper, taking the shoes from my feet for polishing. I provided a buffer between them and Mother, I suppose, for which they were grateful. Thankfully, the real man of the house, Father, began to make more regular appearances as he started to feel his age and work a little less. We joined forces in spoiling him, filling his home with flowers, popping out to buy him an ounce of his favourite baccy, ensuring the port was decanted in good time. With Mother thus placated, knowing Father would not keep long from home, and without Eva stamping on the floorboards, Ramsons was able to settle into peace. Folk rarely mention these spells of quiet, I have found, when they recount a lifetime's events; but now, sitting here in what may well be my final summer, with the evening sun stealing through the French windows - why it should steal in, I can't say, when it's such a flushed, bright caller, and so welcome! - I see us then, a quartet of women, fussing as if for a royal visit. (Like many men of that period, Father did rather resemble the king, with receding hairline and full beard; although, of course, Father was a foot or so taller than his monarch.) We also enjoyed the aftermath, once Father left. We would arrange canvas chairs on a lawn, cover an outdoor table with a cotton cloth and relax, drinking fruit cordials, waving insects away with our summer hats.

'Do I sound as if I hardly missed Roland at all? I believe I more than half expected him to return, pink-cheeked from having made haste, demanding I change my mind. It was quite some time before I realized that he was truly gone, (possibly dead, considering his ill health) certainly not likely to enter my life again. By then I had partly erased him in any case. The feel of his hand in mine was lost, as was his individual scent, a combination of good soap, tobacco and liniment. I did recall his form, the height of him beside me, the shape of his bones, too exposed really since he was underweight. His voice only echoed in snatches, not necessarily saying the dearest things but teasing or gently reprimanding... "Oh Matilda, how *could* you?" My name was especially clear, all three syllables stressed as never before, and never since. And, as I said, I could always conjure his chestnut brown eyes.

'Life has a way of overtaking, devouring, loss and grief for most of us, by throwing something else in our path: often enough, what blocks our way is simply more loss, greater grief. Less than two years after Roland walked from Staunley, Father died. A slip of the hand, that's how Mother used to describe the cause of his death. In a way, she was right, although we rarely concurred because the need to steer her from the subject was urgent. Hers was the sorrow of legend, of epics even, infinite, without edges or limitations. A selfish grief that left no corner free for others to occupy, should they also wish to mourn.

'Initially, Father was brought home to us alive, if not wholly well, in a motor car, an imposing, chauffeur driven beauty, the like of which the village had not previously seen. I remember it purring in the square while we stroked its claret coloured body, its creamy leather seats. Father was propped up in the back, looking regal with his left foot raised on a pair of cushions. He thought it all a deal of fuss, his naked, swollen toe, the journey in a friend's motor car, what seemed the entire village turning out to greet him, ogling the vehicle.

'"Get me out of this contraption Matilda," he pleaded, "and on to dry land." At this, those who watched made appreciative noises; folk were fond of Mr. Durry and proud too. He had grown portly, I struggled to help him walk up the front garden as he leant half his weight on me and half on a silver topped cane. He was a bear of a man, chubby, fearsome, playful and cuddly. So solid that when he died I had the greatest trouble believing him gone; how could that bulk have vanished from our lives? There was also the question of his mind. If his stomach had been vast, so too was Father's knowledge and comprehension. He was the most able man I ever knew: coming to terms with the sudden end of those abilities, the turning off, as it were, of a brain as full, as active, well... it took me years. More than before, with Agnes or with Jethro, Father's absence became in itself a presence: an object around which we shuffled, a barrier into which we occasionally bumped, a framework through which we felt obliged to tiptoe.

'He died of blood poisoning having cut his toenails, not long before his stately journey home, with a pair of rusted scissors. Had he not nicked the skin of his big toe, he might well have lived to enjoy a quiet old age. As it was, he left this world just a few days before his sixty-sixth birthday.

'As I have indicated, Mother was thrown into grief so great that she swayed as if at sea, a bleak figure alone on deck in the worst of storms. Some who love deeply are reduced to silence and numbed to stillness when they mourn; my mother wailed and howled, she rocked, she stumbled, she lashed out at objects both animate and inanimate. In addition to being a danger, she was, in fact, an embarrassment, behaving in a manner better suited to those with swarthier complexions who inhabit hotter, steamier countries. (This latter comment is not my own but one of many I overheard in the village at the time: yet I admit, I also found her behaviour un-English, alien in its intensity.) The one person who might have persuaded her not to make an exhibition of herself was our poor, dead father; for the remainder of us, reasoning with her was a lost cause.

'Most terrible of all, being most public, was Father's funeral. Mother insisted on a glass hearse, severely draped in black, horse-drawn through the village to the church. Behind this trudged Flora and I, two daughters holding up a weeping, broken mother, a woman who acted as though paralysed from the waist downwards, so little did her legs want to carry her to that graveside.

'In church her cries echoed as if a Greek chorus was dispersed throughout the building, hidden behind pillars or pews. The rector was marvellous in his restraint, by comparison, pausing frequently for each wave of sound to pass. I caught many of the congregation, which included professional colleagues of Father's, wincing at the sight of Mother's rocking body and at the knell of her keening.

'Worse was to come. Having supported Mother on the brief journey from church to graveyard, Flora and I kept a grip on her arms as the coffin was laid on slats across the open grave. It is always a shock, seeing the steep banks of clay, noting the depth of a final resting place. Our soil is the colour of sunburnt flesh, here, as you may by now have realized: a freshly dug grave is a wound, sliced in the clipped green grass. Mother almost fainted when she looked down into the oblong made ready for Father.

'(I thought I had trained my memory to obliterate that day but still, in this elderly mind, I find some ghastly details all too clear.)

'The coffin was lowered as the rector recited the Interment. Was it during the passage concerned with changing our vile bodies to be like Jesus Christ's glorious one? That I do not remember; what I know is that before the rector finished there came a shriek so unearthly it might have issued from the skies, or from below the ground.

'"In there," Mother screamed, "that's where I ought to be."

'The rector stepped forward, caught her by the shoulders, tottering perilously close to the edge of the grave himself, in order to assure her that she could, indeed, share the grave of her husband, when the time came. Mother shook him off, weaving her entire body back forth until there was no holding her. "Now, you blubbering fool," she told him, her face a terrible palette of colours that had run together with tears and mucus, "I ought to be there now. With him! With Edward! Cover me over with your soil, it's all I ask of you." With that, she threw herself into Father's grave.

'This is where fantasy confounds memory, I'm afraid. Over the years my mind has conjured an image of my mother sprawled, face down, on top of Father's coffin. There she lies, still as the stone angels that guard surrounding graves, having achieved her desire. Apart from her wrists, where the flesh shows above lace gloves, she is entirely black, looking not unlike a rook shot down in mid flight.

'The reality was even less tidy. I believe those of us who were close by did catch Mother as she threw herself forwards. I remember only managing to grab part of her clothing, a tenuous hold that left me suffering a horror of being propelled into the grave myself. I'm almost certain the rector stood, at one point, with a leg on either side of Father's grave, straddling it, stretched beyond endurance. By this time the pall bearers and others had rushed to help, producing nothing short of chaos. My mother hung, half in, half out of the grave, an unsightly wreck clasped by a dozen arms. She struggled all the while to make a final downwards leap but we did eventually haul her back to land and 'contain' her; which is to say we sat on her until Father was covered with soil, packed in tightly by the grave diggers, who were called from their dinners to complete this task with uncommon haste.'

Gill wished she had her camera to hand; for the first time in weeks, she felt compelled to gather images that might express loss, grief, loneliness. The contents of Tilly's chest of drawers, perhaps, turned out in a heap on the bedroom floor, like this. From the larger drawers, Gill created a rag merchant's heap on the rug at the foot of her bed. This she topped with gloves, handkerchiefs and scent bottles from the two small drawers. Sitting on the bed, she considered this not insignificant collection, which was somewhere between mountain and molehill. Along with strings of beads, small mirrors, the type that slip easily into the pockets of handbags, glinted throughout this pile, giving a festive, Indian air to the moment. It was, somehow, a happy heap, colourful, perfumed, not in any way the keepings of a depressed person.

Gill sighed and fell back on the bed where, within seconds she was creating another heap of belongings, inverted on top of Tilly's possessions so that entity resembled an egg timer. The top pile consisted of Gill's own things, clothes, old soft toys, the watch she had from her father for her nineteenth birthday, her camera. With extreme care, she balanced herself, horizontally, across this precious collection, realizing as she drifted into place that this was exactly where she had always aimed to be. Lighter than the finest silk handkerchief she lay, smiling to discover how it felt to be actually on top of it all.

In being woken, Gill tasted the sweetness of the sleep she had enjoyed: long denied sleep, rich as drinking chocolate laced with rum.

And then she could not cope; how could she? Her eyes stung from having had the lids pulled apart, her back ached because she'd been lying bent back over the foot of the bed. She was cold, hungry, cross at being dragged from her haven of rest.

Rosie had wet herself - soaked her bedding through: but it wasn't the sopping sheets that had woken Rosie and caused her to cry on and on in that head-splitting way, it was the disappearance of her toy cat, Mr. Tibbs. "Never mind the blasted cat," Gill hissed, "look at the state of your bed, smell it too, go on, smell the wee you make me clean away in the dead of night when I haven't even an up-to-date washing machine or a reasonable amount of hot water." Having ripped the sheets from the bed she thrust them in Rosie's face. With determination that was nothing short of admirable, Rosie pushed the offending bedding out of her way and leaned towards the place where Mr. Tibbs lay, squashed between the damp, stained mattress and the wall.

"Oh no you don't," Gill cried, fighting her daughter to be first to reach the toy, feeling squirms of pleasure, power, victory as she grabbed and held him high in the air, out of Rosie's grasp. The squirms merged, becoming a snake that forced its way up through Gill's body, hissing threats, lashing out, swallowing kindness whole. It propelled her to the bathroom, wriggling her free of the child who clung to her ankles, deafening her ears to cries for mercy.

"He's already soaked in piss," she told Rosie when they reached the bathroom, "so we might as well finish what you've begun and send him on his way to the sewers." She held Mr. Tibbs by an ear, one that had been chewed almost to shreds, and dangled him over the lavatory pan.

For a moment, Gill saw herself; she was separated from her own flesh and bones - as if she was the ghost, this time, spying on a Fury, a maniac bent over a toilet in order to torture an already distressed, frantic, child. How could that demon be her? See the veins swollen with malice, in the hand that clenched Rosie's toy. As true a villain as ever struck a blow or thrust a blade. Or, possibly, not a true fiend but a Gillian who was beside herself, exhausted, frustrated, hanging like a dead game bird from the lavatory chain.

"Give me one good reason not to flush him away," she challenged her desperate daughter. Rosie's face was contorted with emotion, awash with snot and tears. The sound she made was neither cry nor shout but an almost biblical gabble that rose and fell with her gasps for breath. She took fierce but ineffectual plunges at Gill's arm.

The tang of triumph grew bitter in Gill's mouth. Her grasp on the chain was weakening.

Gill let go of the cat's ear and Rosie almost threw herself in the toilet pan, hauling Mr. Tibbs out a second before Gill appeared to be going to pull the flush. Far from running back to bed with her rescued treasure, Rosie stood facing Gill, clutching the dripping Mr. Tibbs to her chest until the yoke of her Strawberry Shortcake nightie was wringing wet. Slumped, defeated, Gill held Rosie's gaze for as long as she dared then whispered, "I'm sorry."

The little girl padded back to an unmade bed.

In Tilly's bedroom, Gill found a heap of rubbish on the floor. Kicking her way through this, turning Liberty print blouses and paisley scarves into momentary kites, she made for the bed and crawled up and then down to her usual dip in the middle. She was shaking. One sleeve of the cardigan she had on was wet through; her whole body stank of urine. I am a sewer rat, she told herself. The word vermin came to inhabit her chest, heavy yet restless, scurrying round to catch its own tail, which whipped her across the chin. She knew that any person, living or dead, who might peep at her, would see a woman whose hands sometimes lashed out in her sleep. A woman who had wanted a life in the city, with parties, music gigs, sex, fun, friends, a variety of restaurants, a career to be proud of – and who had landed here, on an over-used, under stuffed feather mattress, in a room filled with the junk of a of a pair of maiden aunts, deceased.

12.

And then the empty glasses...

'As you may imagine,' Tilly continued in her letter, 'The Twenties' tended to creep, rather than to roar, past us at Ramsons! Young women in butterfly dresses did brush our duller sleeves from time to time as they flitted across a road in town, but by and large fashion hardly touched us. The world beyond was changing with such speed, cars taking to the roads, industry developing, music 'swinging'; and yet we seemed to have ground to a stand-still. Well, we had no gramophone, no radio to keep us up-to-date and even had we possessed these items, Flora and I would have been hard pressed to gain the freedom to employ them.

'We suffered, and I do not use that word lightly, a decade of coping with a grieving mother. For months after Father died, she insisted on using only half the house and covering most of the furniture with drapes, so that Ramsons had an abandoned air and certain places in certain lighting were haunted by elephantine ghosts. We asked, tentatively, should we perhaps move to a smaller property, since we were depleted so in numbers. "Leave behind your father's home?" Mother cried, commencing a tirade that shook the foundations of the house she would not forsake. The very suggestion triggered a period of obsessive constancy, in fact, until we dearly wished we'd held our tongues. At first, there was to be no moving objects about in any room that had been used by Father. Then she decreed that everything must remain exactly as it had been, throughout the entire house, down to mops and buckets Father could not have known existed. This drove poor Lizzie to distraction; I once caught her darning a duster! You can imagine how we sidled about, I expect, afraid to speak above a whisper, frightened to open a fresh bar of soap when need be; tolerating the intolerable.

'It could not endure, this regime of restrictions: but it took the arrival of the unexpected to prompt Flora and myself into action. And believe me, your mother, June, was as unexpected as summer snow, to us.

'On an August evening, without any warning, Eva reappeared! She came to the front door of Ramsons, bold as the brass that adorned it, pushed past Lizzie, and strode directly into the drawing room, which was still partly under wraps, so to speak. We found her there, dressed à la mode in cream organza, holding a baby. Needless to say we assumed the child was illegitimate and that Eva was about to demand we rear it for her while she went on with her adventurous, if sinful, life in London: but Evangelina, guessing our thoughts, wiggled her left hand under our noses, displaying both engagement and wedding rings.

'"You must call me Mrs. Bradshaw now," she bossed, handing the baby over to Flora who had been standing with her arms and her mouth wide open. While Flora went "Ahh," and "Ohhh," over the child, I asked where Mr. Bradshaw might be. Were we to meet him any moment? I imagined Eva would reply that he was just parking his motor car. Apparently not. He was occupied on business, in town, I was informed.

'Neither Flora nor I ever did meet Dennis Bradshaw. Had I not seen Eva's wedding photographs, in which a man slightly shorter than the bride stood, wearing the dazed expression one associates with press-ganged sailors, I might have been tempted to wonder if he actually existed. I also never quite ascertained what business Dennis Bradshaw undertook; whatever it may have been, it was clearly not lucrative enough to keep Evangelina in the manner to which she hoped to become accustomed. As you know, the marriage did not last.

'"I am testing the ground, sort of thing," Eva told us without preamble. "I read of Father's death in the papers, and was sorrier than you can suppose. Now that I have my own family I appreciate Mother more, or would if she might be persuaded to accept me back. What do you think, Tilly? Will she give me the prodigal's welcome or will she shoo me away again?"

'"Mother is changed," I ventured, "less aggressive but more agitated, since Father's death. You must dare to find her out for yourself." At this, Eva nodded her head. Had we bet money on Evangelina's hair remaining uncut, we would have won. She was every inch the modern woman, made-up, beaded, wearing buttoned shoes, but her hair was not bobbed. She wore it pinned loosely back and a strand broke free when she nodded in agreement with me. I wondered if that single golden thread might be sufficient to soften Mother's heart.

'Between the three of us it was decided to leave the infant June out of harm's way. Flora bounced the child on her lap while I led Eva to the part of the garden where Mother sat.

'There was such a look of love on Mother's face when she saw Evangelina. I have never forgotten it. The change in Mother's features was instant, a reflex; her narrow face grew wider with joy, her eyes seemed filled with sun. Then she remembered herself and clamped these signs of weakness.

'My main concern, as Mother flew at Eva for having the audacity to 'crawl back here when it pleases…' was that the baby should remain undiscovered. I called Lizzie, asking her to bring Mrs. Durry a cooling drink and then to stay with her while I saw Miss Eva, or rather Mrs. Bradshaw, to the door. I knew, you see, that Eva was not a natural mother, that she would have need of Flora and me as the years went by. I wanted nothing more than to be in a position to fill that need: if Flora and I were not to be wives, we might at least be surrogate mothers. Otherwise I foresaw the pair of us proceeding from tainted youth to bitter middle age, with nothing to cherish but memories.

'What a wise move it was, in retrospect, to keep all knowledge of June from Mother. I was absolutely right, as you know, in my surmising of Evangelina's maternal inclinations. Your grandmother, dear, was born to flirt and dance and dine out. Changing soiled nappies, pulping up food, staying in with Baby while the wider world bustled by her window, these were never on her agenda. Domestic bliss was a contradiction in terms to Eva, especially when sharing domesticity with a man she did not love.

'Personally, I doubt if Dennis Bradshaw was June's father. I always thought him a dupe captivated by Eva, inveigled to the alter just in time for her to avoid disgrace. We shall never know. What did become clear was Eva's preference for another man, the pharmacist you later knew as Grandfather Tom. Poor Dennis would not have stood a chance once Tomas Knibbe appeared on the scene… or was Tomas there before Dennis? It is possible; Tom was a married man, at any rate, and not free to wed Eva, no matter if she was carrying his child.

'Rumours abound, don't they, concerning Tomas and his first wife? No doubt some of these have filtered down to you over the years. That the first Mrs. Knibbe was 'difficult', I can confirm, having visited your

Grandfather Tom's pharmacy, in Market Carney... What a cavern of mystery that pharmacy was with its high counter and deep shelves. Tomas sat in a booth at the back, grinding powders, smoking the Lord knows what, sipping brandy at all hours. Sunlight would filter through high windows, scattering the colours of glass bottles like confetti around the pitch-pine surfaces. It was tempting to stand a while, before pinging the brass bell on the counter, and inhale the gallimaufry of aromas that, along with alcohol and Tom's suspect tobacco, included lavender, eucalyptus, camphor and sandalwood. At times a curious burnt smell overpowered all others, very much as if Tomas had actually been experimenting with fire and brimstone.

'Where was I? Oh yes, with the first, somewhat alarming Mrs. Knibbe, who was not Dutch, as Tomas was, but came, I believe from further East. I heard her scream at Tomas once in a language that may well have been Russian. To say she was highly strung is an understatement that would, in her time, have turned the town of Market Carney delirious with mirth. She was a renowned manic whose cries travelled the length of the High Street, even when the windows of the apartment above the pharmacy were shut tight. It was said that our local town was the third or fourth venue to which Tomas had removed himself and his strident wife. For one whose existence consisted of packing up, moving on, rebuilding a business every few years, Tomas had the countenance of a mild, untroubled man. Do you remember him? His head was uncommonly round, wasn't it? And his skin had the tone and texture of flesh not used to facing the light of day. In fact, as his hair receded, he reminded me in many ways of a pink grapefruit, somewhat yellow around the edges, easy enough to sweeten but yet, essentially, pithy. Not the type of man, one would have thought, to inspire great passion: but his two women, the first Mrs. Knibbe and your grandmother, loved him with the distraction usually dedicated to stars of screen and stage.

'I cannot say when Tomas and Evangelina first met, that is another detail around which rumours collided in the slippery way they have. One story claimed that Eva met Tomas when she was 'in trouble'. This may well have been the case. Tomas was not adverse to helping women through all manner of difficulties. As a pharmacist he would, I believe, have made an excellent gynaecologist, for he understood the female of the species both inside and out. However, Eva obviously requisitioned him too late.

'Clearly, by the time June was two months old, Eva was weary of life in London and wanted nothing more than to settle in Market Carney, only a few doors down the street from Knibbe's Pharmacy. Dennis Bradshaw must either have been a most understanding man or a person without a glimmer of comprehension. He did as his new wife wished, establishing her in the town of her choice, in spite of the inconvenience this caused him... I believe he began by travelling to London for work and ended taking lodgings there and returning 'home' for less and less frequent weekend visits.

'Do you start to see how things were with Flora, Mother and myself? Our hard-earned equilibrium was doomed once Eva reappeared. The seat of turmoil was a mere seven miles down the road, threatening scandal, offering the delight of child rearing, rekindling emotions we assumed were long since extinguished. (I overheard one woman tell another that it seemed a shame, the youngest surviving Miss Durry having captivated two men while the elder sisters had not an admirer between them.)

'Is it possible, do you think, that evil actually does beget further evil? I make no excuses, within these letters, which may well be confessions but which ask for understanding rather than forgiveness. It is just that it now occurs to me how Flora and I had the worst of examples to follow: we watched somebody else getting away with murder - oh yes, I never for a moment thought it anything but a murder, cold- blooded, planned, executed and disguised. And he got away with it! And where one person succeeds, surely others may also triumph.

'You must be asking yourself whether your Aunt Tilly has succumbed to the dementia, which claims the minds of an unfortunately large percentage of elderly persons. If not, to what can I possibly be referring?

'Talking of dementia, poor Maisie, who was, you may remember, the one to lend Agnes a pair of ice-skates on that fateful day, went slipping back to her childhood before she died. Flora and I kept in touch over the years, although Maisie married a coal merchant and moved to Hartlepool. Before she left the village, Maisie was troubled by guilt and remorse, to the extent where she never could sleep more than two or three hours a night and might be seen, no matter what the weather, pacing the lane outside her home. We corresponded regularly when she left, rejoicing in the births of her children, commiserating over the grime her husband brought from his yard to her otherwise perfect house, telling her about Eva and June and our little school here at Ramsons. For half a century, she seemed settled and at peace; then we received a letter from one of her daughters, enclosing a scrap of babble Maisie had written to us but forgotten to post. The daughter wrote of her mother's disturbed state of mind, of nightmares and daytime hallucinations during which Maisie appeared to see 'small, round objects, fluffy and white like cotton-wool balls, moving about her room, bouncing on every surface'. Flora and I studied the scribbled mess that was our letter from Maisie and found, amongst other rubbish and a few clear, sensible phrases, two recipes for apple and tomato chutney, a lucid description of her local church, and a heartbreaking request for us to give her very best wishes to her dear friend, Agnes.

'Maisie's daughter wrote only once more, saying her mother spoke very occasionally but that when she did, it was always of Staunely, of her parents, the rector, Sunday School and, of course, of old friends with whom she played in the eternal childhood of her mind.

'No, I have not 'lost my marbles' (as I heard somebody on the radio say recently). I admit, murder sounds too dramatic an accusation to throw at a mild-mannered pharmacist who lived in Market Carney some sixty odd years ago; but there is no other name for what your step-grandfather committed. Of course, if ever a crime was justifiable, here was such a case. The man's patience was stretched until he seemed a trampoline on which his furious wife stamped and tossed herself about. He had not a moment's respite, according to close neighbours who heard the woman carry on at fever pitch each day and right through the nights. I saw her only rarely. The first time, she was on Tomas's arm in the High Street, a tall, slender wife enjoying a stroll, stopping to gaze in the shop windows, behaving perfectly normally. The last time was not long before her death. She was half hidden behind the glass of her husband's booth, hunched over a cup of something hot. I remember the steam giving a shine to a face that would otherwise have been dull and listless; but even at that juncture, she was a strikingly good-looking woman who might have put the rest of the local ladies to shame in happier circumstances. She caught sight of me and glared with deep distrust, with outright dislike; I was shocked by it in spite of all I had heard about her. Do you know, I have no idea whether or not

Tomas spoke her language; there's a thought! When she railed against him, he responded in either English or Dutch, never in the same tongue she used. Clearly, she was a tortured soul, an immigrant cast away from her family, childless, without purpose. One could almost begin to sympathize with her... I hope her death was instant... We shall never know.

'If I can do so without trivialising Mrs. Knibbe's demise, I might call hers a classic case of 'did she fall or was she pushed?' She died at the foot of the stairs on which she had spent much of her time. She used to balance there, on the top tread, declining her body towards Tomas in his booth, wailing or crying. One morning she stamped her feet in fury, took flight and dived to her end. Supposedly. Like Chinese whispers, word of her death spread, grew, changed shape until Market Carney was jittering with tales... Her tongue, so used to ranting, had been bitten clean off... She died with her feet turned backwards, as if trying to return to her own country... There was not an unbroken bone in her body... While she lay dying on the cold floor, she spoke to Tomas in perfect, clear English, which she had known how to use all along.

'Images of a twisted, mangled body invaded every head in town, waking little ones in the night, chilling adult flesh. Tomas laid low, closing the pharmacy to emergencies and regular customers alike. He saw officials only, the doctor, the policeman, the funeral director. The coroner. In death, Mrs. Knibbe finally attracted the attention she had craved.

'One of many points raised, behind garden walls, or through half-drawn curtains, was that in the town of Market Carney, the doctor, the coroner and the pharmacist were firm friends rather than mere colleagues. They could be seen together of an evening, in the snug of The Traveller's Rest, smoking cigars Tomas ordered directly from Amsterdam, drinking small beers and large whiskeys. On a daily basis, these three men were accustomed to helping each other out. Small wonder that the cause of Mrs. Knibbe's death was quickly confirmed as accidental, permitting her funeral to take place sooner rather than later.

'Even those who believed the tale of a fit of temper, who thought Mrs. Knibbe might well have been furious enough to lose her footing and tumble to her end, were converted to the more terrible conclusion with sleep-inducing additives, they were the weapons of our rebellion. Having been well taught in the art of blending and mixing, we simply took an eye for an eye.

'Flora and I cared for June whenever Eva asked. We spoilt the child as only doting aunties may, cooking her treats, making her 'princess' frocks, playing at her level, on our hands and knees, for hours at a time... but only once Mother was asleep and behind a locked door. Oh yes, we had to lock her in; and we had to calculate down to the last minute when she would wake, when to turn the key. The sweetest joy is often tinged with a sharp edge of danger...'

Without finishing it, Gill screwed the letter up before pushing it back under her pillow. Why, she asked herself, while a moth dance around the light she didn't dare extinguish, why couldn't I belong to a common-or-garden, back-to-back, working-class family from Wolverhampton? She lined up an alternative set of ancestors, grubby but cheerful folk with hardly a possession to their names... Their names were short and sharp, like the teeth she put in their grinning mouths. Bill, Joe, Meg, Dot, Jim. They had bad habits but they were good people... Gill was in a bleak bedroom, assisting at the birth of Dot's fifth infant, when Adam cried out as if shot through the heart with an arrow.

Rosie had bitten him. Not a soft, sisterly nibble but a lunge of the jaws. She had left marks in Adam's white flesh, just above his elbow. The victim stood, wearing only pyjama bottoms, in deep shock. Genuine tears flowed down his cheeks, leaving clean lines in the grime. Gill considered him for a moment, so thin and so upset, before turning to Rosie.

"Did you bite him? How could you bite him? You're not human. We don't bite our friends, let alone our brothers, in this world, on this planet. But then you're not a little girl, you're a devil child, The Devil's child, you horrid creature, you little bitch." On Gill went, wading into the wasteland, striding to the point of no return. "You must understand," she told those who watched from inside the bedroom walls, "that I have to hit her, otherwise she'll grow up thinking it's quite all right to be a vicious beast, won't she?" Still, as blows fell and the child screamed, the walls voiced their disapproval in both Gill's ears, and over her shoulder, and full in her face. "What?" Gill cried, spying Tilly's frown amongst the rest. "What was it you said, you old, dead, hypocrite? An eye for an eye? How about a tooth for a tooth, then?" She looked down on Rosie, who she had thrown across the bottom bunk. "Fine," Gill agreed, pulling herself away from the snotty, trembling face.

"This is what you did. This is how it felt for Adam." And she opened her jaws wide as a shark before bending her head towards Rosie's plump left arm.

She didn't bite her daughter. She only just didn't.

Frantically, Gill tipped the entire contents of her handbag out on the kitchen floor. It had to be here, somewhere. There was no way she'd be fool enough to throw it away. What was she thinking? She never threw any bloody thing away; she was a Durry, after all. Boiled sweets, used tissues, sticky loose coins, three combs and a leaking tube of Savlon. Her bag was full of rubbish. Shells, odd beads, bus tickets. Where was the fucking phone number? Nail clippers, for Christ's sake. A tampon in a ripped wrapper. Endless bits of paper, receipts, shopping lists, but no sign of… Ah, thank the Lord. Her palms were so slippery she had trouble picking up the precious flyer.

With trembling fingers, Gill reconnected the phone and dialled the number. A perfectly ordinary, female voice said "Hello?" and Gill sank to her knees on the flagstones. One word and she was crying. A simple greeting, nothing more, and she had turned to wet jelly.

"It's all right," said the woman who was there to save her life, "you take your time. Don't speak until you feel ready, O.K.?"

Stupidly, Gill nodded her response.

"I expect you're having an especially awful day, are you?" the helper asked.

Gill sniffed, with feeling. There was a very long pause during which Gill moved from her knees to her backside and, looking up into Cedric's baby-angel face, wept some more.

"It isn't always possible to speak to a stranger, the first time you call," the woman pointed out, with no reduction of sympathy in her voice. "Now you've dialled us once, you can always call again, eh?"

Gill mumbled an umm.

"Could you at least tell me your name, do you think? Just your first name? Mine is Pamela, by the way and I have three, often very difficult children. How about you?"

"Gill," she said as she put the phone down and cut Pamela off. But it was enough. To have called up, instead of hurting Rosie more, it was enough, for the time being.

She sat gazing at the flyer, which had come sailing through the door of Ramsons in what seemed a different age. 'Problem Kids?' it asked, rather jauntily. 'Need Help?' Gill cried and cried. She soaked her sleeves in misery. 'Just ring' said the piece of paper that had been enough. Gill hung her head and wept her way towards another dimension of sorrow. 'A friendly voice…' promised the flyer that was a narrow but buoyant plank to cling to during a storm that took on the colour of blood.

13.

seeking the unborn
in a worn out photograph,

"After all this time," Gill gasped, "we've found a television!"

Having determined to make an effort to care for her children in a more consistent, responsible manner, Gill had been searching for Christmas decorations. The television, which had been hiding in a cupboard, was an exciting find, of course, but it did rather clash with the cosy, positively Victorian picture of Christmas that had come to inhabit Gill's head. Dickens himself would have approved of the welcome she planned for Seb, when the actor returned, laden with presents.

It didn't occur to her to shop for anything. Although Seb's gifts were envisaged as modern and expensive, the presents she intended to bestow would be homemade, fashioned from scraps, recycled from the mountain of tat on which she was camped. The fact that most people descend on supermarkets and buy quantities of extra, often unnecessary food for the holidays also escaped Gill. She was hardly conscious of food at all, these days; it was unusual for her to remember to feed herself or the children until her own stomach rumbled. Then she'd open a couple of tins or make a pan of porridge. While the children ate like starved fledglings, Gill spooned up her helping absent-mindedly, her thoughts always elsewhere.

The television worked, surprisingly, but it looked peculiar. It took a moment for Gill to understand exactly what was wrong. It was supposed to be a colour television, not black and white like the one they'd rented in Bristol. She thumped the thing and adjusted knobs while enthusing to Adam, "Colour television, what a treat." Adam had previously encountered this luxury, at the houses of friends, and had come home begging Seb to get colour for them. "Just wait while I sort the picture out," Gill said. But there was no improvement, no matter what she did. The picture was discernable, just, but the screen showed only shades of green. Bright emeralds or deep mosses against murky, watery backgrounds. Green animals roamed through wildlife programmes, stalked by green birds, spoken of, in a hushed, reverent voice by a very poorly looking presenter. In dramas, all streets resembled grass tracks buzzing with green vehicles, no matter if the traffic was police cars, ambulances or post vans. Everything people held, or sat on, or ate was green and nobody gave the impression they would live much longer. Watching made Gill feel queasy but Adam and Rosie planted themselves in front of the TV as if their quest for the meaning of life was finally over.

"God knows how you two can sit there, hour after hour," Gill commented on one journey through the school room, where the telly was installed, "it's a bit like living on Mars, I should think. And I don't mean existing on chocolate bars, I mean being on another, not very colourful planet." At this, Adam glanced up and smiled. It was a hazy smile from a face glazed with too much watching, a face slightly tinged with reflected green from the screen, since he sat far too close to the picture; but Gill mirrored him instantly and happily. She had missed that smile.

Everything would be all right. Gill was about to restore order, to kick chaos out of doors. In the pocket of a now almost knee-length cardigan, which Gill wore day and night, she carried a toilet roll. To some this might have seemed a symbol of upset, a sign that her body was not to be trusted; but it was, in fact, the prop of one concerned for the well-being of her children. Why Gill had previously failed to keep toilet tissue on her person, she couldn't have said. It seemed an obvious essential to her, as she swiped at Rosie's nose each time she passed the toddler or had any contact with her. In the bathroom, of course, it reverted to its original use whilst also becoming both flannel and towel. It was invaluable at mealtimes when it served as cloth, bib and even plate or dish. Gill wrote a letter, in her head, to a jolly little women's magazine, lauding the toilet roll and its myriad uses. She failed to attribute the sore patch around Rosie's nose to the humble, serviceable toilet roll; nor did she blame it for the blocked sinks or the way surfaces were littered in white or grey clumps that ranged in size from cuckoo-spit to ostrich egg.

Armed with her loo roll and a genuine desire to make amends, Gill intended to muster the energy required to hack down the bramble forest of the past and plant in its place a homely, aromatic present. She couldn't understand why she hadn't done so the day she moved in. What lethargy had kept her from this task? She looked back on the months of October and November as one who has been ill, under the weather or under some spell. In vain, Gill tried to remember whether or not she had been using the leaves and herbs from the canisters above the stove. It was possible she had drunk too deeply of a poisoned cup, dulling not only her capabilities but her memory too. Well, for the moment, she would swallow only water, to cleanse her system, to purify her mind - until Seb arrived home with a case full of booze.

He had called to say he was coming, hadn't he? Gill was sure she had spoken to Seb recently, before she disconnected the telephone, again. The reason she had to pull the wires from the phone was that he had been angry, or upset, or both. Words of accusation had been fired through the earpiece. Question followed question, their tips wounding her until she cried out. Why didn't she... how could she... what was she...? "Goodbye," she had shrieked, only then seeing Adam, waiting for a word with his dad. But before that, surely she had put one question of her own. Was Seb coming home, to Ramsons, for Christmas? And he had answered, "Yes, of course." Yes. Of course. Of course he had.

A hundred times a day, she ran down the stone passage to greet him, much as Tilly described the Durry children rushing to welcome Edward. He grew more handsome with each arrival. His arms carried an increasingly large amount of treats. His affection became more apparent, his voice a rasp closer to breaking with emotion. His beard tickled her cheek as she stood on tiptoe to receive a kiss. As his bear hug squeezed the breath from her, she teased him gently about his rounded stomach. It didn't matter that he had left her alone once too often; she was all forgiveness, all indulgence. The man with the plethora of gifts was actor and architect, he was doctor and pharmacist, father, grandfather, husband and saviour. Gill loved him beyond anything.

So, she must prepare. Spaces ought to be cleared, for bottles of wine, for rich food, for piles of presents. The drawing room was the obvious choice for a Christmas such as this. In here they could gather, around a roaring fire, to eat chocolates and pass gifts to one another. The chimney needed sweeping but Gill would see to that in time. First she had to find a temporary home for the objects on the mahogany sideboard. These included stained silver goblets, a tarnished candle-

190

snuffer and a disabled shepherdess. "You would almost certainly be residing on a dresser in Clapham by now," Gill told the porcelain figurine (clearly modelled on a woman who'd never seen a field or done a day's work in her life) "if you were still in possession of both your hands." The shepherdess, whose surviving hand was raised to her brow as she searched for lost sheep, or more realistically for a miniscule lace handkerchief she expected somebody else to pick up for her, looked remarkably unaffected by her plight. "Only the soiled and the injured were left behind," Gill sighed. "No matter. Where shall I home you, eh, while we celebrate the festive season?"

Tucking ornaments away inside the sideboard seemed the best plan but the cupboards and drawers were already stuffed to the point where, once opened, they refused to close again. Gill fetched an assortment of carrier bags, most of which boasted the name of Huttons, the small, exclusive department store in Market Carney. Flora and Tilly had always stopped, rather than shopped there, rarely purchasing more than token articles; Hutton's had been, quite literally, their window on the world of fashion. Flora, Gill remembered, did actually buy the odd item that was, frankly, ludicrous; a handbag coated with pink beads, a cigarette lighter shaped like a woman's finger, even a brush for grooming a pony – although she was famously petrified of horses. Gill had also loved the store, with its pale, oak fittings and soft carpeting. However busy, the shop remained blessed by the hush of good taste. The air throughout was expensive, perfumed; the pink lighting as discreet as a lady's boudoir. A child on holiday, while Sarah and Kate went to Woolworths with Tilly, Gill had sometimes been singled out to accompany Flora to Huttons. Hand in hand, the two escapees would pause, before entering the art nouveau doorway, to gaze at the dummies who posed in patterned silks, plaster hands reaching for bright cocktails, or who were seen frozen in the middle of a brisk walk towards the courts, sporting brilliant tennis whites, swinging absolutely pristine rackets. To Flora, whose knowledge of life was restricted to Ramsons and the surrounding countryside, the windows of Huttons represented the entire, other life she had forfeited. Often she would need to head directly for the ladies' powder room, having found a certain scene too enticing, too disturbing. It was those limbs, Gill supposed as the carrier bags brought Flora and her weak bladder back to mind. Those tidy arms the colour and texture of rich tea biscuits, the unblemished legs, when, only weeks after his wife was buried, Tomas employed Evangelina as a live-in housekeeper. Once reopened, Tomas's business underwent a telling change for a while. The sales of cures and potions dropped dramatically but, folk being unable to resist the scene of a crime, Tomas found it hard to keep up with the demand for soaps, tins of talcum, combs and so forth. Some intrepid shoppers were even rewarded with a glimpse of the auburn witch who had prompted their pharmacist to commit his black act.

'I might protest Flora and I were motivated by a moral need to free baby June from a murderer and a temptress; but really we wanted a child to cosset, under any circumstances. A plan was devised whereby Eva sent messages to Lizzie's home and her son Norman brought these to us. To attract our attention, the lad would whistle hopelessly amateur bird calls, the owl being favourite no matter whether it was night or day. Of course, Norman never entered the house or gardens, he handed us our notes from Eva through gaps in the hedging or he made missiles of them and launched them over a wall. Even so, it was brave of him. If her daughters were frightened of Elizabeth Durry, the young folk of the village were terrified, especially since her display at Edward's funeral. I used to imagine another hedge, beyond the box that graces our front garden. A circle of deepest, darkest yew, like a large ripple from the yew within which Mother grew her herbs, marking an area around Ramsons. Any soul might safely circumnavigate this hedge, keeping low, remaining on its outer side; but only the brave, the exceptionally stupid or those cursed with no choice were bold, foolish or unfortunate enough to be caught inside.

'So it was that, when a note from Eva landed in our lives, we set about turning the tables on Mother. What sweet irony there is in the fact that our reasons were both the same as, and the opposite of, Mother's. In order to be relieved from the burden of motherhood, to spend time with the man she loved, Evangelina was content to comply with us in altering Mother's state of mind; while Flora and I added this or that to Mother's beverages simply so that we might enjoy looking after a child. Were we doing wrong? I think we had no choice. Without the warm scent of an infant to look forward to, the grasp of tiny fingers, a baby's chuckle, what lives would Flora and I have lived? We'd become no more than servants to a woman mad with grief. It wasn't to be borne. Those doctored teas in winter, or the summer cordials treated taut below a pair of shorts or a pretty skirt. Slim wrists that could turn in unlikely directions but still appear delicate. Hands that tapered to perfect tips. A world peopled by ideal couples. Male and female, prised from the same moulds time after time, dressed up, playing their parts, with nothing but a pane of glass between them and the impressionable likes of Miss Flora Durry.

On her knees on the drawing room floor in December 1980, Gill suddenly understood the reason for Flora's haphazard purchases. She wondered if Hutton's was still open for business; she could have used a few props herself, to enhance fantasies of life beyond these four walls.

"Now look," Gill told Tilly, who was somewhere close to her right shoulder, "some of this has got to go. I mean stamps, tins and envelopes full of them, not even foreign, half of them, just red or blue with a monarch's head. What value can they possibly have?" Tilly argued on behalf of the children of Africa for whom the stamps were kept: en masse, the commonest of stamps were worth a few pennies.

"Only if you sell them," Gill pointed out. "Kept in a drawer, like this, they are nothing but useless bits of paper, if I may say so without sounding too like Alice and her pack of cards. Talking of cards, did you know that there are six or seven different packs, or part-packs, in this shoebox alone? Did you honestly believe that you or anybody else would find time to sort through the lot and ascertain if, by some miracle, there might be one complete pack here?"

Looking up, Gill saw Tilly had moved to the long table. By the yellow light of an oil lamp, she sat playing a game of double-pack rummy with three of her four siblings. It was Tilly's turn to deal, which she did with care, counting under her breath. Her light brown hair fell to her shoulders in the kind of waves that take all night and many twists of paper to achieve, and which respond to the pull of gravity throughout each day to become no more than faint ripples by evening. Flora had her back to Gill. Her hair, which tended to frizz free of any pins or grips, formed a fluffy halo against the light. She was seated next to Agnes, who had pulled a chair up to the corner of the table. Flora bent to help Agnes sort her hand of cards into suits and Jethro gave a sharp cough, to stop what he considered cheating.

"She needs some help," Flora pleaded.

"I do not," Agnes insisted, kicking her legs in a circle so that all three other players complained.

"You might be more generous, Jethro," Tilly muttered, losing count. "Oh botheration. You always win anyway."

Jethro smiled at this truth.

Gill, and the card players, heard the front door open and close. Instantly, Jethro extinguished the lamp. A gale of whispers swept around the table.

"Why did you do that?"

"Sorry, I wasn't thinking."

"Where shall we put them?"

"Sit on them, quick."

"Have we got them all?"

"Umm."

"Sure?"

"Yes. Do alphabet shopping, now, begin! Your turn, Flo."

Gill also heard and also felt, the swish of fabric as a figure hurried by, behind her back. Her scalp grew tight, her heart was pounding. The departing figure had to be Eva, the spy who knew what was in everybody's hands. The approaching figure had to be Elizabeth, made ghastly by the candle in a brass holder she carried in front of her face.

"I went to market and I bought an aardvark, a bluebottle, a cowslip, a dynamo, an eggcup..." Flora struggled.

"No, it was an egg-timer," Jethro interrupted with consideration. "You're out. My turn. I went to market," and he began to run through the list with admirable speed.

Mother arrived at the far end of the table. She had been to a meeting at the rector's home to discuss the possibility of having several of the rounded yew trees, those closest to the church door, removed from the pathway they lined, and a light installed above the arch of the porch. It had been noted that entering the church during the winter months was a gloomy, often forbidding experience. Yews being sacred, the assembled guests had decided against felling even one or two. (Although the rector had pointed out that he believed the yew was as much a pagan symbol as a Christian.) On the other hand, a lamp to make God's doorway visible and more welcoming seemed entirely sensible and Christian. Elizabeth had found the proceedings tiresome, the company dull, the refreshments stale, but she was pleased to have been invited. Her inclusion in village affairs was, she felt, usually limited to supplying money when requested.

"Why are you sitting here in the dark, you little ghouls?" she demanded as her candle threw them into pale silhouettes. "We are not poor, we may not be squanderers but we have lamps, we have oil, we do not need to huddle in darkness." She pushed her candle further from her, sliding it along the table until she could see who was who and what was what. Now she was lit from under her chin, her nostrils glowed red like coals, her eyes were nothing but lids and lashes. "At what letter of the alphabet have you arrived, Jethro?" she asked, to the children's surprise.

"At *H*, Mother," said her son.

"In that case I should think 'humbug' would be most appropriate," Mother told him. Leaving the candle she walked down the room. Her shadow climbed the wall, it slipped across the ceiling. When she bent to the floor, her shadow was a bull, ready to charge. She picked something from under Matilda's chair and returned to the full light of her candle in order to examine her find.

"The three of clubs," she muttered, placing the card on the table. "A common, unexciting little chap." The children waited, their heads down, their hands in their laps. Mother slid the card along the polished surface. It stopped only inches from Flora's nose. As Elizabeth picked up her candle and left, she was chanting, "I went to market and I bought an accursed bunch of cheating defrauders."

The four young Durrys remained silent and, Gill knew this in spite of the lack of light, motionless. When Tilly did rise to her feet to light the oil lamp, it was some time before Gill understood that the three still seated were frozen, a tableau, while Tilly's back was bent and her hair white, clipped short and worn dead straight, as it had been in her old age.

"You see, Dear," Tilly said to Gill, "the main problem we faced with Mother was her unpredictability. A game of cards could result in ineffectual name-calling or a thorough beating all round, one simply never knew." The tableau at the table dissolved.

Tilly took a gentle hold of Gill's shoulders and turned her to face a corner of the room. Gill saw an older Flora now, seated in a high-backed chair, holding a baby, muttering endearments. The fact that this babe in arms was her own mother, June, made Gill's head spin, as if she was peering down a well that had no floor.

"No mother could have loved an infant better," Tilly whispered. "I was incapable of depriving my sister of these stolen hours. A lifetime of wariness may have taught me to take care but an eternity of savagery could not have prevented me from attempting to make this possible. Some might accuse Flora and me of sinning, like the Macbeths, against nature; but was it natural of Elizabeth to turn her favourite daughter from the house, merely because Evangelina once told the truth? Was it normal for a mother to render herself so terrifying that a child would freeze to death rather than admit to having disobeyed? One might almost argue that we were redressing the balance of nature when we dosed Elizabeth with her own medicine, when we shut the door of her room and turned the key, setting Lizzie to keep guard on the landing in order to warn us of Mother's having woken. Have you nothing to say?" Tilly asked suddenly, her grip on Gill's shoulders tightening to the point of discomfort.

"I believe I may have 'rendered myself terrifying' lately," Gill confessed. "I don't know how to stop or how to make amends. Evangelina said I was like Elizabeth. Perhaps, in a different way, I ought to be drugged and locked up. I should be taken off for treatment. Am I ill? Sick in the head? Am I, Tilly? Sometimes a padded cell doesn't sound unappealing. No, seriously: a white room in which I can do no harm to myself, or to anybody else. A room from which responsibilities have been hosed clean away."

Tilly said nothing. Gill understood that they were both thinking of the lost room and of locked doors, of frightened children, errant mothers – and of misdoings both long past and recent.

Yet again, Gill was sitting in piles of rubbish. Her lap was full of old postage stamps while the floor around her was a sea of playing cards, rubber bands, pencil stubs and boxes of soggy, useless matches. 'I can't do this,' she thought, 'can't shove this much junk aside and make way for a jolly future.' She saw Christmas as a series of carrier bags, with her family taking pot luck, diving in to discover if they'd got something new or something very old. Ancient clutter or modern. Stuff. Things. Her world consisted of only this. Nothing active or creative. Nothing spiritual. Only a seemingly endless accumulation of belongings, many of which were labelled as not being hers. Some of which were broken. There were damp items that ought to have been kept dry and things that required moisture but were withered for the lack of it. Many treasures had been sacrificed to spiders or other greedy creatures. It seemed mites were hungry for knowledge, judging by the number of books they inhabited. Nothing was in good health. Nothing shone alluringly or smelt enticing. And worst of all, a person couldn't eat any of it.

Only the dried leaves and seeds in their canisters over the stove remained useful, in their way. Of course Gill had previously concocted an assortment of beverages; she couldn't think why she'd denied this to herself. She had drunk deeply, having a great need to escape. And she would do so again, in order to drum up the energy required to cope with the slag-heap in the drawing room. Then she'd be of good cheer in this season of comfort and joy, comfort and joy... Ah, better already, as the first few gulps hit her stomach. Warmed, uplifted. How could she have fooled herself into believing she was stronger without this? It was a bit of a magical mystery tour, as the men from Liverpool would have put it, because no two mixtures were ever quite the same - today's tasted of aniseed, mostly – but what harm had any of the combinations done her, she'd like to know as she let nothing her dismay, her dismay. Oh yes, there would be men, in green coats with gold epaulettes and vast red buttons, to sing on Christmas day. Merry gentlemen, God rest them. Come in a troupe to save us all from Satin's sin when we are gone astray. Gone astray. Gill stood amongst them, was dwarfed by them. She sniffed, wrinkling her nose to smell their potpourri of aromas; pipe smoke, strong ales, sugared candies. They were in good voice, one and all. The room throbbed with the resonance of them. Gill was not dismayed, only enthralled by the round they created as they sang over and under each other until her stomach prickled with pleasure. She had to strain her neck to see who flanked her, these gents being not only merry but quite exceptionally tall. On one side was Grandfather Tom, who inhabited a medicinal air laced with rum and tobacco. A naughty man, all sex and sandalwood. Pills and potency. Bouncing naked around his bedroom like a pink rubber ball. On her other side was Edward Durry, who was certainly cheating by hiding a pair of stilts down his elongated trousers, so thin and straight did he seem.

"Mind the worms," Gill advised him, as the merry men raised their voices for a final chorus. "If those stilts are made of wood, bearing in mind the colonies of woodworms in Ramsons, they'll be on their last legs by now! Lord," Gill beamed, "but that was a good one, God rest us if it wasn't."

All around her, the singers blew themselves out until their girths were as great as their heights. Gill was positively crushed between these balloon men. It seemed more than likely they would explode before long, covering her in yet more debris.

"Oh tidings of comfort and joy," they boomed, voices swelling until every particle of air was sucked from the room.

"Come...fort and joy..." now they were dragging their words, winding down. The air slipped slowly from them, their size diminished. Gill was relieved, really, to feel spaces on either side again.

"Oooohh tie-ii-dings," the merry gentlemen concluded, "of comfort and everlasting, death-defying, grave-robbing, imagine all the people, all you need is love, love, I can't get no satisfaction.... joy."

14.

What sort of a life
is it?

Tilly was becoming a bit of a nuisance, persistently following Gill around.

"I hear what you're saying," Gill promised her. "You and Flora had no choice, I see that. What do you want from me? Forgiveness? A blessing? Just because I'm living, doesn't mean I'm in any position to absolve the sins of the dead. Not that I think you sinned so terribly, after all. You locked your mother in her room now and then, in order to have a life. I'd do the same, if June prevented me... which, come to think of it, she has done, in a different way, by transporting me to this distant colony, stranding me in Ramsons, surrounded by a sea of garbage. Why couldn't she just leave me alone to enjoy the life I was living?"

Gill shouldn't have ended with a question, inviting Tilly to respond, when really she was too busy for these conversations. She had work to do. Today she was hanging paper-chains across the kitchen. Sadly, Gill never did find those boxes of bright decorations that she knew to be hidden somewhere about the house. It was a case of making do, in the solid tradition of women in Ramsons. Newspaper, torn into strips, had to suffice. Of course Gill had coloured the paper first. How dull untreated newspaper would have been! No, she'd filled one dish with strong tea and another with the pink vinegar in which red cabbage had once been pickled. The strands of cabbage had been put aside, in a colander, in case they might come in useful later. Cunningly, Gill dipped alternate strips of paper in each dish, so that the chains were brown and pink. They were stuck together by glue made from flour and water. Ingenious invention, she congratulated herself. It was a pity the pink bits smelt and the glue was unreliable; but already, as Gill wobbled on a chair with a length of chain in one hand and sellotape in the other, she could see how improved the room was going be.

In order to wrap the chain around the light fitting in the middle of the kitchen, she had to climb on the table, which was now stained with pinkish oblongs where the vinegar strips had been put out to dry. Was that a roach, hurrying across the ceiling? The dust here was thick and tacky, the cobwebs hung like black lace. That Babs woman ought to be sued for laziness, for not having cleaned an inch of the house in all the years she was supposed to have looked after old Auntie. "Why did you put up with her?" Gill asked Tilly. Another question, oh dear, there'd be no peace now.

"Do you really not know?" Tilly asked back. Gill shrugged; perhaps she did know, in that dim way she had of understanding many things through a web of intuition and surmise. Hadn't she once heard a mumble on this subject, from the far side of a closed door, from behind the cover of a clump of hollyhocks?

The chain came unstuck at the far corner of the room and fell in a tangle around her heels. She cursed.

"Mother was given to using bad language, you know," Tilly announced, "in her later years. The fact that she was no lady became all too apparent, once she was deprived of her refined husband. Fine garments and fancy accessories did little to improve her then. I'm afraid to say, she was basically common. The daughter of a farmhand, a girl no amount of love or coaching could refine. 'Bugger off,' she'd shout at me when I appeared with her tray of supper, 'bugger off and take that muck with you.' Nothing was to her taste, not the food, nor the drinks, and certainly not her remaining children."

Draped in her paper chain, Gill climbed down from the table to begin fixing it in the corner again. Now… What could she do? Sellotape was useless on this greasy ceiling.

"Aren't you just a bit curious as to how we managed the timing?" Tilly queried. "Where is your natural propensity to require answers? For example, how can you not be bursting to know precisely what plants Mother grew behind her hedge of yew?"

In an old sweet tin, whose lid depicted a red bus navigating its way around Piccadilly Circus, Gill found a collection of drawing pins. London, coloured green, red and yellow like the wine gums that had once been in the tin, winked as if to encourage her as, with the heel of her shoe for a hammer, she banged a pin through the paper chain, into the plaster above her head. A shower of grey dust fell in her eyes, leaving a hole and a crack in the ceiling. Never mind; the chain was in place. She would have decorations, come what may. The ceilings might crumble, the furniture collapse, but there would be paper chains hanging in Ramsons this Christmas.

"How do you think we coped when little June began to run about?" Tilly persisted. "Once the child became noisy and active, as healthy children should, we were faced with an entirely fresh set of problems. Shall we discuss these now? Gillian?"

Gill got back on the table and wound the chain around the light once more. The place was about to be festive, if the effort killed her. She was struck by a vision of herself, electrocuted by the sticky light fitting, hung up by the wrists, dressed in shreds of newspaper and smelling like a barrel of fetid, pickled cabbages.

"It is an art, the balancing of drugs." Tilly sighed. "Your step-grandfather knew this well. He was a man practised in the science of the scales. He had a feel for powders. I've seen him dip a finger on top of the amount he had weighed out, and lick off the tiniest excess until he was satisfied with the precision of his measurement. Precision is essential in medicine, Gillian." She was shadowing Gill again, standing by the table, looking up. Her old, tortoise neck was stretched as far as it would go. Her eyes were small spills of liquid in her horizontal face. "You shouldn't simply tip out a spoonful of this, a handful of the other, as you do. You might end up in any kind of a state. As I keep trying to warn you, there are potent drugs in those canisters. Mother had good reason to hide her plants behind that deep, dark yew." Tilly waited for a response. Finally, she lowered her head before shaking it in the manner of one who acknowledges the overtures of defeat.

When her work was done, Gill rested her arms on the kitchen table and contemplated her achievement. The chains were slung rather low, and there were perhaps more strands than was necessary or desirable. The kitchen seemed ensnared rather than bedecked. An adult might become imprisoned, crossing the room. But, Gill was quick to remind herself, there was only one adult here, so far, and she was prepared to lift the chains carefully over her head, like a lonesome country dancer threading her way through ghost comrades. One plus, other than the evidence of her determination to make merry, was that the aroma of vinegar had given Gill an appetite. She smacked her lips; her craving seemed to be for gherkins and, less predictably, tinned fruit cocktail. She found there was a tin left over from the Tesco shopping spree, thank goodness. And pickles such as gherkins were not beyond the realms of possibility in this house replete with things that floated in jars.

Stumbling over her prone children, who now lay on their stomachs for most of the day and a great part of the night, alternatively watching the green TV and dozing, Gill crossed the school room and headed for the cupboards in the passage. There were no gherkins to be found but the pickled walnuts seemed to press forwards, offering themselves to her yearning. "Dinner," she declared as she re-crossed the school room with a jar in each hand.

Gill counted out the walnuts, dividing them into three portions, which she put in blue and white bowls. Presented this way, they looked more than ever like the brains of small mammals. Quite a large colony would have been slaughtered to produce this offering, Gill decided. The kitchen now smelt twice as strongly of ancient, used vinegar, as Gill had tipped the liquid from the walnuts into an already clogged sink. She chewed her first course with resolution, if not with the relish she'd anticipated. Adam scowled at the contents of his dish. Gill considered telling him they wouldn't bite, but on reflection decided this might not be wise. Rosie, who had been previously informed, if Gill's memory served, that these *were* the brains of mice, picked up one walnut at a time and ate her way through them. She did pull a face with each swallow of her throat, but at least she was eating, for once.

"What do you think of the decorations, Adam?" Gill asked, hoping to prise his gaze from his dish. Her son lifted his head and squinted at the ceiling, much as if even the dim lighting of Ramsons pained his eyes. Then he looked at Gill, not smiling exactly but nodding his approval in his own, quiet way.

"Not quite up to shop standards," his mother admitted, "but at least they're not green, eh? Oh," she had a sudden inspiration, "I forgot the red cabbage." She got up, fetched this treat, topped Adam's walnuts with a helping. Spread over the nuts, the cabbage had the appearance of bright, eccentric hair; another fact Gill chose not to point out to Adam.

The fruit cocktail was more successful. Adam had always liked this pudding, preferring it to the healthy, real fruit salads Gill used to chop up for everybody in Bristol. What a shame there was only the one tin to share between the three of them, Gill thought, as she rolled a waxen cherry inside her mouth, around her palate. It seemed a long while since she'd tasted anything sweet. She rather thought she'd run out of sugar for their porridge and all the drinks she made these days were bitter. The cherry disintegrated on her tongue. She must have another one. It seemed suddenly vital to her existence that she should repeat the process of rolling and sucking a syrupy cherry. Adam had finished his helping, but there was some left in Rosie's dish. Amongst the yellow slices of peach and the green grapes, Gill spotted a final, remaining cherry. Red and round as a mouth waiting to be kissed, or so she fancied. A jewel, a gem to be chased through the juice and captured, so. To be lifted on the spoon, so. To be popped, mmmmm, into her almost dribbling mouth.

A distant, spine-chilling noise issued from deep inside Gill's daughter. A grumble equal to any volcanic tremor, building to the smoky, rumbling stage as the child rocked her chair and waved her furious arms, then erupting, overflowing, harmful, orange as sunburnt clouds, flaming through the wide jaws, hot as molten larva. "Christ almighty!" Gill cried. She wanted to flee but the scream held her around the ankles, biting hard. Adam put his head on the table. His forelock fell in his upturned spoon. He covered his ears and quivered, a seedling, a young ash tree in the stream of volcanic mass. Gill spat out what remained of the cherry; it was no longer round but it was still red and edible, just. "Here," she shouted to the puce face across the table, "have the bloody thing back."

But Rosie was not to be placated by a chewed version of what had been her perfect, saved-until-last prize. She screamed on, beyond all reason, until Gill – and maybe Adam too - considered joining her might be the only way to cope. In fact, it was Adam's tortured face, when he lifted his head to show eyes that were dry, but pink with pressure, that prompted Gill to action. "Enough," she shouted. "I'm sorry, all right? Bad, bad, Mummy, stealing Rosie's pudding, I'm really, really sorry. But for Christ's sake, Rosie, it was only a sodding cherry. One sodding cherry. You can't punish me, and Adam, this hard, this long, for one buggery, buggery cherry out of an entire fruit salad." Her daughter's cry was driving her mad at an alarming rate of knots, sending her hurtling towards the falls, the weir over which she would be tossed into oblivion. When she was either dead or incarcerated, she told herself hysterically, folks would shake their heads and say, never mind, it was bound to happen, Gillian always was one cherry short of a fruit cocktail.

She plucked Rosie from her seat and carried her away. The child kicked, she tried to bite, she shrieked directly in Gill's ear. They climbed a set of stairs. They crossed a couple of landings. They went down some steps, up some more. Both were oblivious of their environment, ignorant of direction; the struggle against the other was all that mattered. Everything got in their way, and all of it was kicked aside. Boxes flew, tubs rolled, books flapped their pages like disgruntled seagulls. Gill didn't care, she saw red; the inside of her daughter's throat, the colour of the scream and of the throbbing in her own head. Something broke: a delicate object, splintering to rubbish, creating a momentary distraction as the pair of furies swept by.

*

There was a party going on. The drawing room was bursting with friends and relations who had, Gill realized, all come by instinct rather than by invitation. A crowd of gatecrashers, really, but she was enchanted to see them. In their honour, she put on a velvet frock, a low-waisted treasure that swung alluringly when she moved but also tended to rip its old seams if she bent or turned too fast. "Whoops," she cried as she leant to replenish Edward Durry's glass. He, like her, was more than a touch tipsy. He swayed on his shiny-shoed feet, until his glass and Gill's decanter clashed. "Mustn't break this one," he told her, holding his long-stemmed glass to the light, "belonged to my mother, this set, as did much of what you see about you. She threatened to cut me off without so much as a cup and saucer, of course, once I wed my Elizabeth, but I was her only child. I like to think she forgave me for marrying for love, but possibly she simply never bothered to change her will." He studied Gill with bloodshot eyes, his cheeks growing pinker by the moment. He had a neat, light brown beard, above which was an appealing fuzz of softer hairs, which extended, past his sideburns, to the very top of his head. "I'm told you also wed the object of your affection," he said.

"Is that so?" Gill nodded; she anticipated her great-grandfather's next question, which was: "So where is this most fortunate young man?"

"He is here," she answered, "somewhere. Showing off, no doubt. He's an actor, you see." Her first four words might well have been untrue. Seb was the one person she hadn't definitely seen, yet.

"I hope to meet him," Edward told her, "I have spent much time in the company of actors, managers, actor-managers and so on. I found them all charming. Often they were scoundrels, but always they were charming with it."

"I shall find him," Gill promised, suppressing a hiccup, "and bring him to you. I should circulate, anyway."

As she searched for Seb, it became clear to Gill that this party, like many others, was getting out of hand. The most unlikely folk struck her as being decidedly worse for wear; Jethro, for example, was examining the ankles of a woman he couldn't possibly have previously known, a friend of Gill's who hadn't been born when Jethro went to war. Flora was flirting with a man of the cloth, a gentleman whose cheeks appeared to have been sculptured with an ice-cream scoop. Bella, surprisingly either still pregnant or very pregnant once again, was chatting loudly to Lizzie the maid about the joys of motherhood, and all the while she was circling the index finger of her left hand round and round the inside of a cream horn. Oh my! Gill turned her head from Grandfather Tomas and Eva, but not before she had a pretty good idea of what they were up to behind the drawing room drapes. Tilly, flushed and girlish, had cornered Bella's Jon and was carrying on a babbled, one-sided conversation with him about certain poppies that used to grow and to be harvested not very far, in fact no distance whatsoever, from the spot on which this party was taking place. "Not the symbolic, red poppies you find along the wayside," Gill overheard Tilly explain, "something much darker in tone, if you know what I mean."

Then there was Sarah, holding young Agnes by the hand, teaching her to jive. And, standing just outside the back door, a girl Gill assumed to be Maisie Trantor was peeking in, but not daring to enter. Behind her Gill saw the shadow of Man, the gardener, who also hadn't the courage, or the audacity, to actually step into the house. While Gill considered tugging these two through the door, Kate hurried by, gabbling in fluent Russian to a thin, furious woman who could only have been the first Mrs. Knibbe. It was confusing, this mix of generations. Gill's head began to sizzle as if caught in a neon, fly-trapping device. She took a long swig of whatever was in her glass, and instantly regretted it. Now her stomach was also heading for the fizz of death. Nausea overcame her, a surfer's wave under which she fully expected to drown. Her head was in the kitchen sink, her nostrils full of her own vomit mingled with the stench of vinegar and blocked drains, when Elizabeth Durry made a regal appearance, clapped her hands and demanded that everybody must gather around the piano. As she lifted her head, Gill knew she was fully recovered; her great-grandmother was clearly either healer or witch.

Elizabeth played with the energy of an orchestra. There had never been dancing like it before, there never would be again. The party-goers whooped and cheered, they swung each other about. They did the Hokey-Cokey and the Tennessee Waltz. They Polka'd and they Cha-cha-cha'd. Gill danced with her great-grandfather and her step-grandfather and, for all she knew, her real grandfather too. She was a top, spinning on a single point. Her kicks were high as the lark flies; her leaps would have crossed ravines. She was ballerina and Bluebell girl and she loved everybody, especially the other women who whizzed by, cheeks bright, eyes half shut, mouths open in surprise at their own agility. The ripping of seams was commonplace then and shoes sometimes took flight across the room. Tresses of hair fell from pins and clasps and whipped about as if blown by storms. Everybody was in accord, each dancer moved in time with the others. Nobody was without a sense of rhythm; even Flora puffed in perfect time.

Elizabeth struck a chord and the room erupted in applause as a favourite tune began. The dancers linked arms, they threaded through each other, offering themselves from person to person, growing lighter on their feet with every step. Elizabeth Durry smiled satanically; but the music was the sound of angels who, as Gill happily told herself, had no fear of treading anywhere. Gill smiled at Jethro, she grinned at Agnes, she laughed with June, with Sarah and with Kate. Like the little dog in the nursery rhyme, she laughed, to see such fun. It was clear she could also have jumped over the moon - for this was joy; she recognized it, acknowledged it, melted into its arms and lay there, floating. She had always known it was to be found here, in Ramsons. June had hinted as much to her three girls, Tilly had written of it in her letters. There had been bites into it, Gill rather thought, on occasions when sponge cakes were somehow especially light. There had been sniffs of it, when a sachet of herbs under a child's pillow prompted the sweetest of dreams, the deepest of sleeps. Gill sank to her knees eventually, tired out. Now that she had stumbled across this fully blown joy, she understood her life would be a search from this moment on, a continual quest for a second taste, for something to come close to this bliss.

Her collapse was against the piano, which still played, although Elizabeth's hands had come to rest in her lap. Gill began to wonder if the machine was secretly a mechanism that played by itself, a pianola - if perhaps Elizabeth had tricked them all, all along. The music was gentle now, tunes to send a soul to sleep. Its vibrations caressed Gill's back.

"What has Matilda told you, eh?" Elizabeth suddenly demanded, giving Gill a wakening kick, sending her lolling towards the floor. "Said they had to keep me and Eva's brat apart, I dare say. Did she?" Gill nodded, too sick to complain on her mother's behalf. "That's as maybe," Elizabeth carried on. Her vowels, Gill thought, were flat as the Fens, her consonants dredged from the slurry of a farm. "I do not profess to any fondness for children, I would have sent the child packing, back to her slut of a mother," Elizabeth admitted. How Gill wished she'd stop, and make the piano cease too. Gill's head was throbbing, it seemed her brain was crying for release from its skull cage. "But they went too far, my daughters, much too far, if you take my meaning." Elizabeth bent over Gill, who was almost prone by this time, having slipped closer to the floor. "You stay awake now," the old woman warned, "I deserve some of your attention. I have been made to sound the miscreant, maligned on paper and in every speech my children made. I don't deny my faults; I had my reasons, which only the passionate amongst us will comprehend. But I was a victim as well as a wrong-doer and nobody dares acknowledge that." Another kick from Elizabeth brought Gill's head up with a jolt, and she saw that Edward had joined them, had pulled up a chair besides the piano stool on which his wife was seated. Although it was Elizabeth's legs that needed restraining, his hand rested on her hands, which lay still in her lap. When he applied a slight pressure, the piano music came to an end. The quiet was the cue for all the Durry children, and Tomas, to sidle over to the threesome and form a semicircle in which to enclose them. Gill pushed herself up, using the side of the piano, until she was sitting straight.

"Jethro," Edward said; and the proceedings began.

"You never loved us," Jethro told his mother, "at times, I thought, you could not bear to have us near you. You banished us, to our rooms, to the garden, day after day. In my case, it was a pleasure to arrive for a term at school, to leave this house and go to war. A pleasure not to be within the compass of your distaste."

"… the compass of your distaste," Edward repeated. "Harsh words indeed, Jethro, and enough from you, I think. Flora, you may speak now."

Flora lowered her head, not wanting to look her mother in the eye. "I was frightened," she whispered, "simply frightened of you. I used to try so hard to do what was right – not in order to please you, I knew I could never manage that, but just to keep you from turning on me."

"Am I to have an opportunity to respond?" Elizabeth butted in. Flora's head dropped another inch; she was obviously not about to say more.

"Certainly you shall," Edward reassured her. "Let the children have their say first, my dear, and we will try and set things straight afterwards. Now then, Tilly, what about you?"

"I'm glad you include yourself, Father," Tilly said. Her colour rose but she kept her head high, looked from one parent to another without flinching. "I believe you must shoulder part of the blame. How often did you stay away a night or two, a week or so, longer than was absolutely necessary? Can you honestly claim that work was always a genuine excuse? We were desperate to see more of you than we did," she almost snorted at this, "good Lord, if ever a family had need of a father to lay down the law…! But there is more, worse; I think you knew how Mother treated us, and you did nothing. You saw behind the hedge of yew, you understood what ingredients were added when Mother made fruit cordials for us children to drink at your home-comings. You complied. Perhaps you never fully grasped how evil your beloved wife could be, how hard her blows fell, how scathing her words: but an inkling is unforgivable and I accuse you of having more than that and of taking no action whatsoever."

Clearly nobody, least of all Edward himself, expected this. All were mute, taking in what Tilly had said. Gill let her head roll back, to ease the ache, and a chord sounded from the keys she hit. She muttered

"Sorry," to the assembly, but the general reaction was one of relief. Grandfather Tomas smiled at her, just as he used to do when she stumbled or spoke out of turn as a child.

"Well," Edward sighed, "I appreciate your honesty, Matilda. Now, Agnes, no doubt you want your say?" But Agnes shook her head, snuggled up to Flora's side, mumbled, "I only wanted to have some fun." And Edward nodded, relieved that his favourite child was abstaining from this painful session. He pressed his wife's hands firmly with his own as he indicated to Evangelina that she might now speak. Eva stepped forward; Elizabeth tensed.

"You banished me from my own home..." Eva began.

"You stole," Elizabeth retaliated, "you threw insane accusations at my head, and I was meant to accept..."

"I was your daughter," Eva spat, "but you never accepted that..."

"Oh," Elizabeth interrupted, "and you were the perfect mother, I suppose, leaving your child with her aunts for days on end, knowing I was reduced to a rag doll while they played Mummy and Daddy on your behalf..."

"Mummy and Daddy!" Tilly retorted, taking her step out of line.

"Besides," Jethro joined in, "you made rag dolls of us, often enough."

Now they were all talking, no shouting, at once, and the semicircle became a tight, angry band of bodies, pressing against the three who had no escape, who could only shrink back into the piano. Tomas stayed a pace behind the Durry children and made futile attempts to placate them, to pull them back to a reasonable distance; but the four girls and Jethro were not to be robbed of this unique chance to speak what had dilated into their collective mind.

As voices climbed and blood grew heated in those around her, Gill struggled to make sense of what she was hearing. Of course, the children of Edward and Elizabeth had much to yell about, but most of this was now known to Gill: what she thought she was learning from Elizabeth, on the other hand, was new information. New and chilling.

"With his help," Elizabeth screamed above the din, pointing a shaky finger at Grandfather Tomas, "with the aid of our admirable pharmacist here, who, of course, had already stained his soul with one black sin..." Grandfather Tomas, who was restraining Eva from actually tearing at her mother, shook his round, hairless head and smiled the inscrutable smile, which had so often been sufficient to fend off troubles. But Elizabeth was not deterred, her voice was the strongest and now, with this denunciation, her grievance most potent. Gradually the others were quiet, although from time to time, Evangelina emitted a low growl, the sound of thunder that may or may not be abating.

"I was unkind," Elizabeth admitted to the drained faces in front of her, "I was unfeeling. From the day I met your father, I knew only one type of love, and this overwhelmed everything else, banishing the love a mother is meant to enjoy; I own up to that. It made me selfish, sometimes even cruel. All this I confess and regret. But I never took another life." Flora lifted both her arms in a gesture of frustration. "No, Flora," Elizabeth noted, "I will not take responsibility for Agnes's fall through the ice. I tried to prevent her from skating in the first place, as a conscientious parent should. I am not guilty of causing, or of desiring, the death of another living soul. And that is more than most of my own children can say."

Like a chain of paper people, the Durry children collapsed. Now they sat in a row before their parents. Gill felt sickeningly sober; a diver whose lungs had filled too fast with a rush of air. Her head no longer throbbed, her mind was clear to deal with the implication of Elizabeth's words. Tilly looked directly at Gill, leaning a little out of line as she spoke; "I have been trying to tell you. This revelation is what I wished to forestall, but you would keep moving away, avoiding the issue."

"They did me in!" Elizabeth declared. "I use the vernacular of a common-or-garden victim because I know you find me common and I was undoubtedly a victim. I gave them life and yet they stole the life from me. Matricidal viragos, plotting with their three heads together, rendering me a fraction less capable every day. And you," she pointed at Grandfather Tomas, "abetting them along the way, when home-grown medication was no longer strong enough. How I cursed the lot of you, as I lay bedridden, my legs heavy as logs, my head like a tombstone that has no choice but to study an inert body. You thought I did not know, you fools. I knew, believe me. It's wonderful the way one's senses perk up when the limbs are robbed of movement. I heard every word, each cry the child made, each 'shush' you told her. I smelt earth on your fingers, when you had been digging for fungi. I inhaled the scents of my own herbs on those hands that had picked them. I saw through the tiny cracks you made when you checked at my bedroom door. I watched your shadows move about at night, when you thought me dead asleep. Your hands told me tales of chill expeditions, of thorny accidents when you'd been out gathering. And yours, Flora, practically tapped out your guilt in code, so much did they twitch and tremble. Finally, I tasted even the most heavily disguised flavours. Do you imagine I could not discern those bitter drops you blended in my beverages? I was the expert, don't forget. I taught you all you knew. If there had been any point in my continuing to live, I should have declared your crimes to the authorities and had you imprisoned, just as you imprisoned me. But, when I said I cursed the lot of you, I swore only because you took your time. You were so painstakingly slow about your work. How many times I almost begged you for a decent draught, to speed me on my way towards the husband I saw constantly, waiting for me in his grave."

Elizabeth's children were staggered. Jethro and Agnes hadn't known how their sisters surreptitiously took their mother's life. Flora, Eva and Tilly hadn't thought their mother conscious of their wickedness, nor had they once stopped to consider the possibility that Elizabeth might be longing for her own demise. Tilly began by muttering, "I felt such guilt, for years on end, but all the time you wanted it..." and then the second round of crying started up, each child wailing to be heard, both parents shouting back. Gill blocked her ears, she swayed her body against the din. It was more than she could take, this caterwauling. She stood, in order to make her voice the loudest, but they gave no sign of having heard her plea for quiet. Finally, she threw her arms across the piano keys, creating the sound of disruption and rage. Again and again, she played her inharmonious refrain, until her head was as battered as those strings inside the piano.

She understood, before she turned her body round, that they had gone. Her music had banished them, the living and the dead. When she did swing around to look, she saw only the mess one might expect in the aftermath of any party. Not a guest remained; and Gill was thankful for this. She knew she wouldn't encounter her ancestors again; she was absolutely alone. Except, of course, for Adam.

Gill's vision blurred with tears as she went in search of her boy. She found him asleep in front of the green screen. He would be with her tonight, she decided, they could cuddle up in the big bed, keep each other warm. As she bent to lift him, Gill glanced at the television screen and saw the face of a man called Max. Not only was this face horror-story green, it was distorted in pain. The man called Max was acting; opposite him a woman appeared, also sad, and an even deeper green. Gill shook her head, wondering in what life she'd known Max. In what world had she, and another man - called Seb - been the friends of this person who was crying acid drop, crocodile tears in front of her while her own eyes streamed with the piteous, salty, snot-inducing, real thing?

15.

...Still it is not enough
to have memories, they
must turn to blood inside you.

A second before she woke, Gill was aware that something was wrong.
By the time her eyes were open, she understood what the trouble was:
Adam had vanished. Hadn't she felt his skinny but warm body next
to hers during the night? He ought still to have been there, beside her.
She remembered what a comfort the child had been, in the coldest
part of the dark... although Adam had not slept well, he'd twitched
and grumbled. Now he had twitched himself away, Gill thought as she
dug clumps of sleep from her eyes. She had slept for hours, unless
the clock was telling lies. It was months since she'd had such a deep,
uninterrupted rest and she was grateful to Adam for breaking the
torturous cycle of insomnia. But still, she couldn't help considering a
life without Adam. This idea played like a film in her head. The setting
was a free, undomesticated space, a vast, green area. Although isolated,
the area, which soon became a meadow laced with flowers, shared with
butterflies, pipits and swallows, was actually in the middle of a city.
Should Gill desire cinema, theatre, shops, concerts, good food, she had
only to skip, in classic 'Sound Of Music' style, through wispy grasses
to the perimeters of her daydream.

In a minute, she would get up and look for Adam, because she *was*
anxious to know he was all right; but for the moment, she lay back
and closed her eyes again, listening to the hush that had replaced the
squabbling of ghosts. Yes, Ramsons was almost silent. No hum of
electricity, not so much as a glug of water on the move. When she
concentrated, the noises that came to her were exterior. The pub was
getting a delivery; she heard barrels rolling over paving stones. A small
bird, most likely a robin, gave insistent chirrups somewhere under the

bedroom window. A jet thrust through the sky, at some distance, at a great height. Far removed from Gill, these activities went on, while she relaxed, exhausted, relieved to be alone, thinking only of herself for once.

The next time Gill woke, it was dark outside, beyond a narrow gap in the curtains: so she turned over and went back to sleep. If she did suffer from a vague sense of disquiet, this was vanquished by an almost instant drop into the welcoming arms of slumber.

The third time Gill woke, she slid out of bed, her legs stiffened from hours of sleep, and went to the window. It was still dark outside; or maybe it was dark again? Perhaps this was a second night, or was it a third? Had she slept for a fairytale length of time, under her feather covers? She stretched like a princess, standing in her window, gazing at the pretty lights in the pub across the road. She felt so refreshed, almost reborn. Hours of rest had warmed her bones, left a soft, woollen cosiness around her head, given the sensation of springy turf under her feet.

It occurred to her that she might have enjoyed her time at Ramsons, even found pleasure in being alone, if only she'd been able to sleep these past months. It was, after all, a remarkable house in an unspoilt village, to use estate agent speak. Had she not been worn out, Gill could have made new friends, invited people round for coffee, maybe followed in Flora's footprints and become an expert in the art of the risen sponge cake. A special friend broke away from the imaginary group who were now enjoying Gill's make-believe hospitality; a woman with a sense of humour akin to Gill's own, with attitudes not home-grown here, in Staunley, but bred in a city where anything went. Veronica, Gill called this woman, not certain where the name had been until that moment. Ronnie; best of all friends. Ronnie and Gill got tipsy together and discussed the backsides of famous men. They spent long evenings huddled around a one-bar electric fire, threading beads, drinking too much tea and eating their way through quantities of chocolate biscuits. Like a pair of kids, they dressed each other up in Eva, Tilly and Flora's old frocks, squeezing their breasts into tight bodices, easing fabric over hips they hadn't previously considered wide. Of course, they smoked roll-ups made from the dried leaves in the old canisters, but the effects were of being lifted, lightened, filled with irrepressible laughter. One day, they went together on a spree, a shopping spree, to Cambridge, where there was a flea-market full of damp but colourful offerings, things to mock, to delight in, to shun or to die for. On the way home, in Ronnie's car, which was only a sparkplug more reliable than the Morris, they planned another outing; an evening trip, they thought, to the theatre or a concert. "We'll have to find somebody to have the children over night," Ronnie mused, "if we want to stay out late."

"Shit," Gill cried, brushing Veronica aside as she hurried from the bedroom window. Her assortment of clothing, topped by a long, tartan dressing gown that might have been Jethro's, hindered her progress, obliging her to perform a mobile striptease as she sped from room to room.

How long was it since she'd seen Adam? Sod this great, rambling house: her son could be anywhere. If Ramsons was unravelled, Gill told herself, and laid in a straight line, it would stretch for bloody miles. But, far from being direct in any way, the place was a maze. "Adam," Gill yelled, "where the hell are you?" Once again, she saw a life without him, a dismal existence this time; one she lived out in shades of grey, under a rancid cloud. In that world, every journey led her to another musty dead end.

She now wore only somebody else's old vest and a pair of her own knickers. Her legs shot into view with comic regularity as she ran along passageways, pale limbs, flashing before her eyes like a drummer's sticks. Her breath came from her intestines, in great gasps, sweat began to stick her skin to her meagre clothing.

Then she saw Adam. He was safe, thank God: he was sitting quietly on a step. Not fretting as she'd predicted, not clutching his empty stomach or throwing a fit or weeping copiously. Just a little boy, too little for his age, perhaps, since he'd grown so thin; just a boy, also only wearing his vest and pants, shivering on some half-landing. She sat beside him, not quite touching his bare arm with her bare arm. He wasn't shivering, he was shaking; trembling all over, almost rattling – as if an underground train ran right through him.

"Adam," she said but he didn't turn his head. "Time for breakfast, eh?"

Adam clenched his jaw, steadying his mouth before making the effort to speak. It was then that Gill remembered, as if punched directly in the heart. She understood that his words might be the last she would hear from him, if this threat of darkness, which hung low as a thundercloud, should engulf them. She pre-empted the two words, the question, by a split second during which a life that was no life at all played itself out in her terrified head.

"Where's Rosie?" Adam asked, his voice so quiet and strained Gill might have been tempted to pretend not to notice it. But pretence was over; make-believe had been rubbed away. The pounding of her heart was her reality; the fact, face it, face up to it, that Rosie was missing, this must be noticed, taken note of, acted upon. Words were no help to Gill; her answer to Adam was a look he had probably been anticipating, dreading, for hour after freezing hour as he sat and worried.

"You must stay here," she told him. "Promise me you won't move, Adam. I can't have you..." she halted before the word 'lost', as a condemned person stops in their tracks when confronted by the firing-line. Adam made no response. Gill kissed him on the top of his troubled head. Then she ran from him, quickly reaching the foot of the stairs, passing under Cedric's berry-and-dirt stained cheeks. In the passageway, Gill felt the cold flagstones beneath her naked feet, smelt the seasons laid to rest in cupboards and in cellars: fruits, pickles, jams, bodies, dust.

Nothing remained in her life then but the frenzied search for Rosie. Looking for Adam had been a ramble, by comparison. There was no method to her hunting, only madness in which panic was the driving force and stumbling the constant form of movement. Her body caught on every jagged edge, tripped over each obstacle, plunged down flights of steps, collided with doors. Gill had no control over this bruised, splintered body. Frustration and fear quelled the pain as she bumped her way about crying "Rosie, Rosie, Rosie," with increasing dread. If she stopped shouting, the house replied with the silence no mother can bear: so Gill called as she staggered, cried out as she pulled furniture aside, wept noisily while crawling under beds. And when her lungs were empty and her throat raw, she sniffed tears back up her nostrils and made a steam engine of her breathing.

"Tilly?" Gill begged, collapsing on a step, perhaps the same step where Adam had sat in the cold. "Come on Tilly. All those visits when I could have done without you... Where are you now that I need you? This isn't just another of your stories, this..." but again she halted suddenly, frightened to name what was happening. "I believe," Gill whispered, "I might have taken Rosie to the lost room. For a while,

I knew it, its precise whereabouts were no mystery. Knowing where the room was seemed an inherited intelligence when I was in extreme, in extreme…" she couldn't say distress – *this* was distress, whereas carrying Rosie away to the lost room had been an act of vexation, performed by a lunatic. "But now, I don't know anything. I can't remember anything. You must help, Tilly. You must. Lead me there, please." She lifted her head and waited until her chin trembled and her neck ached. Nothing happened. Tilly had gone.

Gill searched again, but it was no use. She had run into her personal brick wall; she wouldn't find Rosie on her own, she appreciated that. The pumping of her blood was savage, her brain felt flooded with it, right to the stem. The noise in her ears was the throbbing of a thousand looms, the hum of a hundred washing machines. There was only one solution: she must call the emergency services.

By the time she reached the telephone, her courage was failing. If only *she* could rescue Rosie, how preferable that would be. But then, if the worst was to happen, what could she say in her own defence when asked why she hadn't phoned for help? The call must be made. Gill's hands ached as if recently crushed. They were capable only of fumbling in their attempts to trace the wire to the socket in the damp wall. But it was imperative that she should connect herself with life beyond Ramsons.

The moment she felt the brittle ends of wires, despair shot through her. The wires were torn, the phone had been ripped from the wall the last time Gill had unplugged it. The loss of hope was absolute, leaving no room for any future, turning her body to stone. Gill sat on a high-backed chair, holding the telephone wire. She didn't weep or tear her hair, she didn't even rock herself for comfort. Frozen to the spot, she sat, hardly breathing, trying to ward off all thoughts, to obliterate images as they charged through her consciousness, each one more baneful than the last. Trying not to exist.

The idea that Babs might help came to Gill like a feather drifting through sleet. Of course! Babs was the only living person, the only person living nearby at any rate, who was likely to know the whereabouts of the lost room. Much as Gill loathed the woman, she had no choice but to beg for her to come inside Ramsons and show the way.

The front door had warped, it required a tug, a wriggle, another almighty pull, before it would scrape open. It was a shock to find that there was daylight outside: dimming light but still... the sky was the pale pink little girls see when they dream of ballerinas. Gill tipped her head back and opened her mouth to it, as if the beauty, the energy, of colour at dusk could be digested by, integrated into, her poor, woebegone body. A man came out of the pub, feeling in his trouser pockets for something, for keys, perhaps. He must have seen Gill, she supposed, as a shadowy figure under a hedge of box. She stood and waited for him to move on, not wanting to be truly visible in her layers of sweaters and her unwashed jeans, in this pair of Tilly's slippers that looked as if a dog had once hunted and tormented them. What had she done: allowing herself to become a thing fit only for flitting unnoticed across a road? For slipping by houses with her back towards their doors and windows. To travel like this, sidelong, backwards - a creature not only inhuman but unworthy of the pavement under its feet.

Babs lived in a terraced cottage on the main village street... except... Gill wasn't certain in which of these seven houses she would find Babs. The cottages curved with the bend in the road, their front doors separated from the pavement by one stone step apiece. Gill resigned herself to peeping in each window, like Tom or Wee Willy, like a gossip, a voyeur, an unwelcome guest, a spy. Not this house, which was glowing with life, with children on the floor of the front room, playing in warm, peachy lighting, unaware of the frozen face at their window. Nor this cottage, in which an elderly woman sat by a built-in electric fire, toasting already puce toes, watching a television that boomed at terrific, wall-shattering volume. Through the third window, Gill saw Man, Tilly's gardener, reclining in one of those vast chairs that tip back so far they almost become beds. It hadn't occurred to Gill that Man lived with Babs, although she did remember, after seeing them together in the graveyard, that Babs was his daughter. Perhaps this was his cottage, and Babs lived with him; maybe she'd never left home. Or possibly Babs had moved away from Staunely in the last few days, in the time since Sarah and Kate's visit...

Babs appeared in the arch that divided the front room from the back.

Gill moved from the window to the door, throwing herself against this, banging it with the palms of her hands. Babs opened it straight away, causing Gill to fall into the room, almost into the cleaning woman's arms, in fact. Babs, dressed as if for a cocktail party, took one hasty backwards step: she didn't greet Gill, but waited, in her high heels, with her gleaming-raven's hair, for Gill to explain herself.

"That Miss Durry's girl?" Man asked, bringing his chair with him as he leant forwards for a better look at this creature.

"Tilly," Babs snapped, not taking her eyes off Gill. "We call her Tilly now, Dad, same as everybody else. And yes, this is her great-niece, or rather, this is one of them." Babs looked Gill up and down, her disapproval coming to rest on Tilly's ruined slippers.

Determined not to shed tears, Gill tensed her jaw and managed a "Hello," to both of them. "Babs," she said, her voice already beginning to climb out of control, "I need your help. Need you to come back with me, to Ramsons, if you can… please…" she was preparing an explanation when the other woman threw back her head and gave a laugh so bubbly it seemed she was gargling Champagne. "I knew it!" Babs enthused, "I knew this day would dawn and you'd come running here for help. Didn't I say, Dad, she'd be running to us before the year was out?"

Man nodded, sorrowfully.

"Well, you've got some cheek, I will say," Babs told Gill. "I'm not about to help out now. I've sworn never to set foot in that place again, haven't I Dad? Surprised, are you? I only wanted it to sell. I believed it was my due, you see, our due, eh Dad?"

Man rocked uncomfortably, not committing himself.

"By God we earned a right to that house," Babs reiterated, "Only Dad wouldn't go inside, not even after Tilly died and the place was empty. I did try, pushed his wheel chair right up to the door, but he went peculiar. Had an odd turn, didn't you, Dad? Couldn't go in there, poor old so-and-so."

"I'm trying to find the lost room," Gill blurted out.

"Lost room!" Babs snorted, "No such place. Only a little box room they sealed off after the girl died of hyperthermia."

Gill snatched a handful of silken sleeve, muttered several pleas.

"Don't you go grabbing at me," Babs warned, "you don't own us any more. Oh but, of course, you'll plead ignorance where our humble history is concerned, won't you?"

"If it is a box room, you could still show me that…"

"Why should you worry," said the woman in the little black dress, "if my granny was your granny's serving girl? Your lot called her Lizzie,

218

the name Elizabeth being too good for her type. How she worked. How she shielded those children from trouble, over the years. The danger she was in... Then she had a baby, a boy, called Norman..."

"My boy is waiting," Gill interrupted, rocking her weight from hip to hip in her anxiety.

"Well, my granny had to give up her boy," Babs cried, "if she wanted to keep her job. Give him up. But he lived in the village, with relatives. And when he was a lad he got to be your aunts' errand boy, their go-between. Little soul, longing for a glimpse of his mum, over the garden wall. Terrified of Mrs. Durry, he was, too scared to so much as visit the back door. That's him," she sang, turning Gill around to face Man, who was listening with a slack jaw and a deep frown. "My Dad. This man you lot can't even bother to name properly, he's Lizzie's Norman." Babs paused for effect before ending, "Now do you understand?" She was steering Gill towards the door, pushing her out on to the pavement, digging bright nails into Gill's shoulders. As she left, Gill noticed Tilly's old copper kettle, gleaming rosily in the hearth at Man's feet. It occurred to her to ask for it back, then to demand to know how great a part Babs had played in the demise of Tricksey; but she was in too much of a hurry to return to Ramsons and her searching.

It was dark as Gill crossed the road; a moon was rising. Time keeps passing, Gill thought, and a fresh burst of sweat broke over her entire body.

Gill climbed the stairs, her legs wanting to give way, her feet cased in metal, her hands coming apart at the seams. On the small landing, under the coloured glass, she stopped, feeling a rush of air on the back of her neck. She knew her face would seem a patchwork of pale lights, would be dissected and made more terrible by the moon on the window, but she turned around.

The woman behind Gill on the stairs was hardly a woman at all; she was no more than a girl. Her clothing dripped ice-cold water, leaving tell-tale puddles on the treads. She gave Gill five shards of ice to hold – her fingers, which Gill enclosed in her own, sticky hand.

"Agnes?" Gill whispered, but the girl shushed her, gazing anxiously over her shoulder.

Agnes went ahead of Gill, tip-toeing on tiny feet. Gill felt a giant by comparison, a great rolling statue to be pulled, manoeuvred by this slight child, this figure in her shades of grey, who might have been fashioned from water, she was so soaked and so cold. "Don't distress yourself," Agnes advised Gill. Her wet hair sent a shower of drops over Gill as she turned to speak. "We shall soon be there. It only seems a great journey at times like this, but in fact the room is nearby. It's right at the centre of the house, you see; in Ramsons, one is never any distance from the lost room."

Gill trundled along behind Agnes, not quite a dead weight, but one with a pumping, thundering heart full of dread.

"I died in my bed, you know," Agnes said, and Gill was taken aback to hear mock gloom in the girl's voice. "Not in this room at all, although history will insist I sit here, rigid on a broken down old chair, until my blood freezes and I fall, a Z-shaped ice statue slowly melting to oblivion." She was smiling directly into Gill's eyes as she conjured this scene. Agnes's eyes were indeed, as Gill had always supposed, the colour of river water; but they were lively, they sparkled with mischief, and Gill understood this was because Agnes had suffered just the one experience of distress, illness and death. Most, almost all, of her short life, had been a joy, thanks to Flora and Edward. Even the last day on her feet had been delightful, until her accident. It is the fate of victims of violent ends to be remembered only for their deaths, Gill thought: whereas what survived to shine in Agnes's eyes were those times she'd spent in the garden or playing card games, or climbing the Ups and charging down the Downs.

And Rosie: what would happen to her eyes, in the future?

Agnes had stopped pulling Gill's hand. Hadn't she said 'here', when talking of the lost room? Hadn't she said 'Not in *this* room'? They must have arrived, although there was no door before them, only panels of wood, painted white, lining a landing between two of the bedrooms. Gill watched Agnes attack a join in the panelling with the heel of one of her shoes. "It looks like a part of the wall," she explained, "not having a door knob or handle, but being hinged, it will open, once you get leverage."

Her shoe broke, the heel hung in defeat... like a loose fang. "Bother!" Agnes said, then, "Never mind, there's always this," and she pulled a large silver crucifix from the folds of her dress.

Gill took a step back, knowing the door was about to open: and it did. Agnes flicked a switch and light fell on what was really only a little box room, full of rubbish, cluttered with cases and trunks.

"There," Agnes declared, "not so much as a ghost, let alone a living child."

"Then where is she?" Gill cried.

"In bed," Agnes answered, with conviction, "where all little girls should be at this hour."

As Gill gasped in surprise, Agnes dissolved into less than a puddle, into less even than a patch of damp.

It was true, Rosie was in her bed. In her bed! The sweet thing, sleeping, smelling of baby breath, warmth, pee. Why had Gill not thought to look here, of all the places she'd searched? Because I considered myself a monster, Gill answered herself, because I believed I was capable of insane cruelty. But to believe it and to be so, these were not the same. In reality, all she had done was to put her child to bed, snug and safe. Snug and safe. Tucked up, in her bed.

"I'm sorry, my love," Gill said, bending to kiss Rosie's hot cheek. "I'll make amends now, I promise. I never meant you harm, it's just you have been too much, too much child for me, somehow."

*

She took next to nothing with her. Woollen clothes, for comfort, Mr. Tibbs and Adam's teddy bear. The little money she had left. The photo of her family amongst the pyramids of Spalding: because, after all, nothing was *their* fault.

In the school room the television crackled like a box of green fireworks. The three escapees shuffled past this into the passage, where Cedric beamed down on them for the last time and the jams sent waves of farewell. Gill heard the house inhale, building up pressure.

"Hurry," she told Adam and Rosie, taking their hands in hers, "we're going home."

"Home?" asked Adam.

"Bristol," Gill confirmed, not having been certain of it, until that moment. Through Adam's small, cool fingers, Gill sensed his pleasure, his relief.

The front door was reluctant to open but Gill gave it a great tug and then, once they were through to the other side, an almighty slam. Both Gill and the house shuddered at this exit.

Beyond the tunnel of hedging, the pub windows winked in welcome. She would phone from there, for a taxi, or for Sarah to come and fetch them. It was tempting to turn and look back at Ramsons. A few lights would be burning, a slither of smoke might yet seep from the kitchen chimney; there would still be semblances of life. But Gill was not about to fall for that trap; she was, she realized with an intake of breath, elated at having broken free. The world, ice cold, clear as the frosty sky, invited her into its company. With her back to Ramsons she whispered, "You can't have me and my children." She gripped Adam's hand, and Rosie's, as she added, "No, you shan't have us."

Printed in the United Kingdom by
Lightning Source UK Ltd., Milton Keynes
140788UK00001BA/13/P